ATTACK OF THE GODS

ATTACK OF THE GODS

*High Priestesses of
Lemuria - Book 2*

ANDREAS FARMANN

Chakra-Atelier

Contents

For Lenka.

Prologue

Portal city of Pyrrha, in the desert near the Nile Valley, in March of the year 1869 of Buddha

With utmost care, Gan'olin raised his head to peer over the top of the massive boulder of reddish sandstone, behind which he had taken cover just seconds before. Promptly, a blazing hot ball of witch fire whizzed up, narrowly missing the flap of his right ear and blasting a few glowing shards of stone from the boulder.

Cursing obscenely and emitting indignant trumpet sounds from his trunk, the Omean mage, who outwardly resembled a rather small-sized elephant walking upright, dropped into cover again. Now he had the proof he had been looking for—indeed, the proof he had been fearing for weeks, if not months! The protective spells that had shrouded his adopted home in the North African desert for millennia and kept out both the magically untalented and the malevolent for so long, were weakening.

Soon, the henchmen of the Spanish-Ottoman Inquisition, who had been gathering at the desert city's outer perimeters for months and by now had reached the strength of an mid-sized army, would also be able to physically overcome the magical shields. And then the remnant of Pyrrha's peace-loving population that had chosen to remain in the city would have to fight.

The portal through which, over a period of more than two years, the council had been evacuating a large part of the over three hundred thousand people that had called Pyrrha their home to the inner world had died shortly after the last solstice celebrations without warning, just like the others. Sabotage? A consequence of the permanent energetic bombardment by the Mago-Inquisitors, which had strained the age-old shields to the utmost? Or simply the result of the progressive weakening of the Source, for whose creeping failure Pyrrha's mages still did not even know the reason?

It didn't really matter. Their escape route to the inaccessible world inside the planet's core was barred, as were, strangely enough, their telepathic contacts with their compatriots down there. They were trapped, and they would have to fight their way out physically, even had they been willing to leave the remains of Pyrrha's immense wealth in magical devices and knowledge to the Inquisition—the better to capture and enslave their fellow mages in the rest of Gaia.

Another ball of witch fire hit the rock behind which Gan was hiding. The air hissed, smelled of hot dust, and sharp pieces of broken rock bounced off the elephant being's thick skin.

The Omean, who had made his home on Gaia so long ago that he would have called himself an Earthling without hesitation, shook his head, wondering. These strange inquisitors really had no idea of how to use magical means to fight. Ignorant they were, half-wits! Still, the sheer number of his opponents made them highly dangerous.

And now they also used fairy magic. So, were the rumors that had reached them with the last fugitives to get through the blockade true? The rumors that the Spanish Inquisition had recently found a means to break the will of enemy mages and force them to fight for them? It had to be true, because Gan could not imagine that a fairy would ever voluntarily fight for someone like the Spanish-Ottoman sultan. Humans could be bribed, or intimidated, but freedom was the very essence of fairies.

When the air around him hissed, thundered, and crackled again, and the boulder trembled under Gan's massive front paws, the elephant creature had had enough. Trumpeting angrily, he rose and, with two energetic pulls, climbed onto the block, which, as he only now realized, must be a fragment of one of the monumental statues erected during Pyrrha's founding period, destroyed centuries ago, when the protective fields hiding the city's existence was established. Part of a finger, probably.

Furious with rage, he roared his anger and despair at the troops of attackers stretching along the horizon. There had to be thousands of them, maybe even tens of thousands. And yes, now he could make out the colored glittering dots in the crowd. Fairies, no doubt about it. Witch fire now pelted him from at least ten directions simultaneously, but all the fireballs bounced off his protective spell, already prepared and anchored in the general field, without even grazing his thick-skinned body.

Gan muttered a few quiet words, swung his trunk like a centrifuge, and hurled a barrage of lightning bolts and ramming rolls of condensed air out into the lines of the besiegers. Satisfied, he watched as several hundred of the figures collapsed. Not fatally wounded, he hoped, but at least this would give them something to think about.

Fear-filled screams sounded through the outer shield, which still held despite its weakness, and the crowd of blue-skinned figures in ruby-red robes fell back somewhat. They had probably no longer believed that anyone in the city would ever fight back. Gan personally had been involved in the government's decision to refrain from unnecessary provocations by the Spaniards. Of course, he had voted against it. But now it no longer mattered. The Mahdi would understand. The end was approaching fast.

Now Gan could also see that the blue-skinned ones were pulling the other members of the army along with them on leashes. They were humans and other beings dressed in white linen. Despite the distance, he could make out green-skinned djinns, humans of various skin colors, fairies, and even some desert dragons.

Moved, the Omean shook his head. Indeed, slaves. These beings were not here voluntarily! If the attackers broke through the shield in a few weeks at the latest, there would be a massacre. And the Pyrrhean troops would have to fight against their own friends.

Gan shook with anger as he formulated a confounding spell and put all his anger into it. Curse the Spanish Sultan! What folly had gotten into those idiots in Granada? Live and let live, that had been the principle of the Mediterranean civilizations regarding Pyrrha for thousands of years. And now this!

Just as more and more of the glowing hot balls bounced off his magically enhanced aura field, he raised his trunk and sent his spell across. No compulsion, he wasn't strong enough for that anymore, not with the Source's steadily diminishing energy. And, he had to admit to himself, there were just too many of them anyway. But he could still confuse them a little. Unless they had installed their own protective spells around themselves. But in the ruby-white sea of cowled figures, he saw none of the greenish glow that would have indicated personal shield spells being used in the siege army. Why weren't they protecting themselves? Were they that reckless? Or did they lack the knowledge needed to do so? No matter. Gan watched with grim satisfaction as the first of the inquisitors looked around, puzzled, and no longer seemed to know why they were there at all.

The bombardment of fireballs slowly died down. The last of the ball lightning-like spells now whizzed through the air far away from him, some even hitting the Inquisition's own people, who abruptly burst into flames and had to be hastily extinguished with healing spells by their comrades standing next to them. The elephant creature chuckled maliciously, enjoying the sight of the confused faces.

The Omean brushed the front of the inquisitors several more times with his trunk. Shortly thereafter, the onslaught of witchfire died down completely. Loud shouting rang out as the attackers hurled accusations at each other, trying to figure out what had happened, who they were in the first place, and what they were doing here, in the middle of the desert.

From further behind, more beings in red robes pressed in, probably not caught by his spell. They would quickly resolve the situation, and the attack would begin anew. Gan spat out and turned away. He had to gain distance quickly because he didn't have much energy left to maintain his protective aura. He had put too much of it into the confusion spell. If they shot at him again with their damnable fireballs, it was all over for him.

Puffing heavily, he fell into a loping stride, slowing only when he was nearly half a mile from the front and several hills lay between him and the enemy army. His wide, lipless mouth was twisted into a grimace. He had to inform the Mahdi immediately. This did not look good. He had walked the entire perimeter. The attackers had now brought in enough people that they could almost completely surround the city. The portals were dead, no longer usable for escape. And the slaves, that was a new development.

The presence of the fairies possibly also explained why the shield had just started to fail just now. Fairy magic could not be used to harm other beings, and these strange leashes would probably not change that. But sabotaging an entry barrier was something else. The fairies were bound to be good at that. After all, they themselves got in everywhere.

It was a pity that the last of the winged beings had left Pyrrha slightly more than two hundred years ago. Their advice would have come in handy in their present situation. They had "other tasks" to do, the envoys from the distant planet Sirius Quinta had only said, lifting their perfectly plucked eyebrows enigmatically, before they had moved off in a large, multicolored iridescent air caravan towards the northwest.

Gan's massive knees almost buckled as he fully realized, for the first time, what they would all face if Pyrrha fell. Until now, he had expected death at the stake. For himself, as a member of Pyrrha's leadership, perhaps also torture, and a public execution in one of the main squares of Granada, the Imperial capital where the "Most Holy Sultan-Emperor and King of the Three Worlds," Philip II, reigned supreme. That had already seemed unpleasant enough. But perhaps, he considered, he would more likely end up with one of those strange ribbons around his neck, forced to hunt down and capture his fellow mages still at liberty.

He shuddered. They would not take him alive. He would make sure of that. But what about the other three thousand Pyrrheans who had stayed with him and the Mahdi to help defend the city? Friends, confidants; lovers, some of them. Beings who trusted him. He wanted, he had to at least try to save them. But, how?

When despair threatened to take him, he broke into a run again, and the stony desert floor trembled beneath his massive feet. The effort would distract him. And then he would discuss their last options with the Mahdi and the rest of the council. They would be planning the destruction of their home, the portal city of Pyrrha— the city that had been, for long millennia, known as the center point of Earth, if not of the whole galaxy. *His* home. All the running in the world could not have kept his grief at bay, though. Big tears mixed with the sweat that ran in streams down the face of the elephant creature hurrying through the hot desert air.

MAP OF
EUROPE & ATLANTIS
NORTHERN ATLANTIS
SOUTHERN ATLANTIS
EIRE PENINSULA
KINGDOM OF SCOTLAND
SPAIN-OTTOMAN SULTANATE
GULF OF ATLANTIS
MEDITERRANEAN SEA
Dublin
Cork
London
Oxford
Edinburgh
Inverness
Copenhagen
Gothenburg
Hamburg
Innsbruck
Paris
Venice
Rome
Constantinople
Athens
Rhodes
Alexandria
Cadiz
Granada
Algiers
Aegean
Atlantia
Dublin

I

The Refuge

Algiers, March 19, 1869 A.B.

Three disparate figures moved through the colorful crowd that populated the winding alleys of Algiers, a major North African port. Men and women wore wide, garishly colored scarves or black and white cloaks. Many of the women and girls were veiled, so that only their cheerfully glittering eyes could be seen above the cloth. Others walked with their faces and hair uncovered—probably they came from other countries.

The one of the three who fit best into this picture was named Kaura. Small, dark-skinned and with elegantly flowing steps, she walked through the crowd unveiled, following the almost two heads taller silhouette of her friend Seneca Lumisworth, headmaster of the Scottish Lockwood Society, whose blond dreadlocks interwoven with magical bells shone brightly in the evening sun. All who knew him simply called him Sen.

Kaura and Sen were magicians, as was the third in the group—only five inches tall, blond, with violet dragonfly wings and—as she liked to point out with pride—an enormously large vocabulary of creative profanities. Ariane Tinkerbell was a fairy—and despite her small size, not one that could be easily overlooked.

The three were bound for Egypt, where they hoped to find the ancient portal city of Pyrrha. Now, despite having successfully overcome the blockade of the Spanish-Ottoman rulers by means of a cloaking spell created by Sen and his people, their ship, the *Pride of Edinburgh*, had sustained severe damage in a storm. which, it was hoped, could be quickly repaired in the North African port city.

While the captain was organizing the repairs, Sen had agreed to show the other two around the city, most notably the famous mage quarters of the djinns, Mira'aleitha. Many years ago, the Scottish warlock, who was about two hundred years old, had been to the city before—a visit which had obviously left a lasting impression on him. The enthusiastic expression in his eyes testified to this.

"You'll be amazed!" the tattooed Scotsman enthused, winking confidentially at Kaura, his feelings of attraction to the younger-seeming woman being an open secret to all who knew them. "Mira'aleitha is better than any Oriental fairy tale. And the djinns are such a delightful people! Not to mention their excellent sweets! And Mira'aleitha coffee is in a whole other league altogether! Even you won't find fault with it, Kaura!"

His companion had spent her last years as a young woman with no memory in the Baltic port of Inmarsund, having been taken in by a local merchant family. This trading hub near the western border of the Mongol Empire was known all over Northern Europe for the high quality of tea and coffee that could be enjoyed there. It was not until the previous night, that Kaura had fully recovered her memories—and surprised her fellow travelers with the revelation that she was an ancient Lemurian high mage with a mission of utmost urgency for the fate of Earth, because of which their journey to Pyrrha was found to be even more important than they had previously suspected.

Many among the passers-by carried large, Arabian scimitars, some also Spanish rapiers, and Kaura saw a group of very dark-skinned men, probably from the inner regions of the continent, trotting along with quivers of glittering throwing spears slung around their shoulders. There was a confusion of smells, sounds, colors, and other sensory impressions that made the hustle and bustle of London seem almost staid. No one seemed to pay attention to the fairy, who fluttered confidently beside her friends, although some people gave her shy glances out of the corner of their eyes. Ariane was oblivious to this, however, visibly enjoying the aliveness of the street scene all around her.

Sen tapped Kaura on the shoulder and pointed to the right.

"Here we are in Al-Wata, the lower part of the city. See that fort over there, up in Al-Gabal, the hill quarter? It's called the Kasbah and it's right in the middle of the medina, the city center. That's also where we find the streets of the djinns," he remarked with a sideways glance at Ariane.

The mage pulled Kaura with him into the tightly interlaced maze of white houses with flat roofs, on which multicolored linens on crisscrossed lines blew in the wind. After half an hour's walk up and down stairs, through souks with all kinds of offerings—once they passed through an alley where only gold jewelry was sold and everything shone in the light of the torch baskets like a hundred thousand little suns—and past enormously high, brick and white-washed minaret towers, they reached a large square behind which rose the massive dome of a mosque.

"The Square of the Roaring Lions," Sen said. "Before the Spanish-Ottoman pact of Lepanto and the formation of the current status quo, large slave markets were regularly held here, selling captives from all over Africa and Europe. Since the two empires joined and both are ruled by the Sultan-Imperator in Granada, that is said to have largely ended. At least here."

He screwed up his face. "I assume that the Ottoman pirates are still preying in the Mediterranean. But they are probably now selling their "wares" in less conspicuous places. And their new Spanish fellow citizens, meanwhile, are busy applying the same principle in West Africa, shipping people like animals to the New World."

A gagging sound rang out next to him. Kaura looked like she was about to vomit.

"I'm sorry, Kaura, I didn't mean to upset you," the Scottish mage said with a regretful sideways glance. "I know the subject is weighing on your mind." Slavery was one of the topics about which the usually calm woman could easily get involved in heated discussions.

Sen turned around.

"Come. Over there is the entrance to the Shining Quarter. That's where the magical beings live."

Pigeons fluttered into the air in front of their feet as Kaura and Sen purposefully crossed the square, Ariane riding on Kaura's shoulder, where she seemed to feel more and more at ease lately, often preferring this way of transportation to flying herself.

From the minaret, the call of a muezzin to evening prayer began to resound. A large part of the passers-by stopped. Many unrolled their brightly colored prayer rugs, knelt down and turned towards the east. Another part of the evening life, however, simply continued, and so the three also walked on leisurely through the exotic-looking hustle and bustle.

At the opposite end of the square was an alley entrance marked with a large golden archway, which they now approached from the side. The gilded stone arch was decorated all over with Arabic characters in relief. At the highest point, just below the roof made of shiny ruby-red glazed tiles, was emblazoned a symbol, in the form of a small, outdated oil lamp.

"Djinn Alley," Ariane breathed in awe. "Never thought I'd come here, to the old lamp-hinies!"

But Sen's face had already become very serious—and worried. Ariane noticed his expression and fell silent. She fluttered forward to Sen, who had gone a little ahead, and sat on his shoulder. Now she saw for herself what made her companion suspicious. The alley behind the golden gate was dark and seemed to be deserted. No street torches were burning, the palm trees in the middle of the cobbled street surface seemed withered.

Slowly they walked on, passing under the arch.

Sen lowered his voice.

"There should actually be a lot more going on here. Everything looks completely deserted. And pretty run-down. The last time I was here twenty years ago, Mira'aleitha was the richest, liveliest, most opulent neighborhood in the whole city! I fear bad things may have happened here."

He approached one of the boarded-up stores, examining the planks of wood nailed across its entrance. "This has been shut for a long time. A couple of years at least. Should the Spaniards...?" he broke off as a boy of about twelve years old hastily turned into the deserted main street from a side alley, passing close by them. The boy was well dressed, his white cloak seemed freshly washed.

Sen waved at him.

"Salaam Aleikum, friend! God be with you! Do you know what happened here? Where are the djinns?"

The boy stopped and eyed the three travelers. When he saw the fairy on Sen's shoulder, his expression became hostile.

"Isn't one slave enough for you, European? Do you need more of the same?"

He pointed with his hand to Ariane. His Atlantean was accented, but well understandable. "Tough luck, my friend. There hasn't been a slave market here in years. All gone. People have been scrambling to buy the wares, especially the djinns. The ones the Sultan's men from Granada didn't take away directly, at least."

He spat at Sen's feet and turned away.

Kaura grabbed him by the sleeve and held him back. The boy stopped with an unwilling expression on his face.

"You misunderstand us, friend. Ariane here is not a slave. We are new to the city and were looking for the djinns."

"Just to think of that," grumbled the fairy, ignoring them. "Slave, my face! That would be a disaster. For the buyer, I mean."

She thought hard for a moment, then darted like an arrow in front of the young man's face and stared at him out of her violet eyes. "Are you saying they sold fairies as slaves? Fairies? Why, that's impossible!"

The winged being seemed totally confused. "How could anyone keep a fairy in bondage? She would just wish herself away, after all! Talk, boy! Have you seen this for yourself?"

The hostile glare in the boy's eyes had given way to a sad expression. He nodded.

"Yes, unfortunately. Not a pretty sight. The strangers from Granada came with their own wizards, wearing red cloaks. They put metal collars on the magical creatures they could get hold of, making their abilities accessible only to their holder. Only a few escaped."

He seemed to wrestle with himself for a moment, while Ariane palmed her neck with a sour face, seeming to digest the information. She probably imagined how such a collar would feel.

"I believe you. I didn't see at first that you weren't wearing a leash," the boy said. "That one is with you, Exalted One?" he asked the fairy, pointing to Sen.

Ariane waved her hand magnanimously.

"Yes, we took him on shore leave. He needed some exercise." She tried to giggle, but failed miserably. "No, seriously, that's Sen. I work for him, though not as a slave. This is Kaura, and my name is Ariane," she introduced herself.

"I am Ibrahim, mistress," the boy replied seriously. "Come. I'll take you to the Refuges' envoy." He turned and walked back in the direction from which he had come.

Kaura and Sen exchanged a glance and then started moving as well. Through dark, winding alleys and stairways, Ibrahim led them deeper into the former djinn district. Every few hundred yards there still was a store or a small snack stand open, emitting comforting light in the growing dark, but they only saw humans in any of them. Ibrahim seemed to know them all.

He greeted them in a friendly manner, but did not linger anywhere. The strangers were stared at curiously. Ariane received almost worshipful looks. An old man playing chess with another in front of a shabby-looking coffee shop rose and made a bow when he saw her fly by.

The fairy guard blew him a kiss, hesitated for a moment, and then fluttered along after her hurrying human companions.

A short time later, they reached a small open bazaar that seemed to be literally stuffed with bales of fabric of all kinds and colors. Ibrahim motioned the three to enter. Inside, they were greeted by an old, gray-haired woman, her tanned face marked by thousands of deep smile lines. The boy gave her a hug and then talked to her in Arabic, pointing again and again at the fairy and the two humans. She asked him something, and he answered earnestly. Then she smiled, pulled aside a thick curtain of heavy ocher silk, and made an inviting hand gesture.

Behind the curtain, a medium-sized courtyard opened up before them. They entered a lively, plant-covered oasis, set between roughly hewn walls of reddish shimmering sandstone. Ferns and potted palms produced an atmosphere of being in a small, well-tended garden, and dense climbing plants hung down from pots suspended on the wall, with many small oil lamps in niches in the wall in between, bathing the whole scene in a warm, flickering light.

Inside the courtyard, beneath the glittering stars dotting the North African night sky, about ten tables were set up, at which, among human men and women, sat some human-like beings with greenish skin and large, black topknots. They were drinking peppermint tea or coffee, eating small sticky sweets with their fingers, and conversing in a hushed murmur that gave the scene a soft, cozy atmosphere. Some were playing chess or cards.

A few of those present looked up curiously, but turned back to each other when they recognized Ibrahim.

The boy led Kaura and Sen to a somewhat darker corner of the open area. There sat a white-haired Arab with a friendly, open face, calmly pulling on his pipe as he seemed to observe the scenery. He looked at the newcomers with interest.

When he saw Ariane fluttering out behind Kaura, a friendly smile entered his face.

"This is the Envoy," the boy said over his shoulder, then addressing the old man. "Sir, I met these three outside the gate. They say they were looking for the djinns. I think they are friendly to our cause."

The man rose and put his hand on Ibrahim's shoulder.

"You did right, my boy."

His voice was deep, and his Atlantean completely accent-free, when he addressed the little group of foreigners. "Welcome to Mira'aleitha, the Mages' Quarters."

He indicated a small bow in the direction of Sen and Kaura, then laboriously knelt down on the reddish, irregular sandstone slabs and lowered his forehead toward the ground in front of Ariane.

"Welcome, Sa'aleitha, Exalted One. I am your most humble servant. My name is Abdel Naredhar. Envoy of the Refuge. Are you seeking asylum for yourself and your two servants?"

Ariane looked down at him thoughtfully.

"Thank you, brother. Now sit up again, my dear, or you'll scrape your knees or tear your beautiful white nightgown! And we wouldn't want that, would we? I'm sure you don't have that many of them. And then, if you please, you'll tell us what's going on here."

A few minutes later they were all sitting comfortably on the oriental carpet around Abdel's table. Ibrahim had just returned with a large metal pot of strong mint tea, small glasses, and a plate full of different pastries, all of them looking supremely sweet and sticky.

Abdel leaned forward a little.

"So, you don't know what happened here?" he asked.

Ariane, who had sat herself in the middle of the table for the sake of simplicity and was drinking her tea from a filigree glass cup specially made in fairy size, shook her head. She instinctively felt that she could trust this man.

"We sailed here directly from Britain, and we're on our way to Pyrrha," she said, therefore, without looking at Sen or Kaura.

The envoy nodded, understanding.

"No request for asylum, then. Too bad. The Refuge could desperately use some more fairies."

Interest lit up in Ariane's eyes.

"That means they weren't all caught. Good to hear. Yet, tell us from the beginning!"

The Arab bowed his head in agreement.

"Yes, Exalted One. As you have already seen, all non-human inhabitants of Mira'aleitha had to leave the city. Until six years ago, magical beings in Algiers were left to live largely unmolested, although all of North Africa had already been formally a part of the Spanish-Ottoman Empire and therefore under the jurisdiction of its Inquisition ever since the Pact of Lepanto. However, the Spanish initially had an interest in maintaining the city's status as a free port. Today, many think that this was only so that they could more easily recover their hostages captured by the Algerian pirates, knowing where to find them. Occasionally, a liberation squad from Granada would raid the city, but they always left quickly. In short, the people here felt fairly safe from prosecution, even the djinns, fairies, gnomes and desert dragons. Too safe, as it turned out on that fateful day just over six years ago."

He sighed heavily, and continued. "At that time, several thousand djinns lived in Mira'aleitha. In addition, there were Lebanese forest elves, fairies, trolls, land nymphs, giants, and centaurs who had come here from all regions of the world, as Algiers had become known as a safe haven for persecuted aleitha."

He furrowed his brow. "You must understand, the Siberian witch realms are not particularly attractive to many, even if they still offer almost complete safety from the Inquisition. Too cold. Nine months of winter a year. Or ten."

The old Arab shuddered, and incomprehension of how anyone could endure such climates was written all over his face.

"There were many who were willing to take the risk of being closer to the emperor in Granada, in exchange for being able to live openly in one of the world's great cities, in a warm climate. Anyway, one day they were suddenly here. Hundreds of Inquisitors, accompanied by magical helpers, who had probably been enslaved just as many of my friends here were later."

His hand made a helpless gesture, and the pain of not having been able to help was still clear on his face.

"All entrances to Mira'aleitha were sealed off within the hour, as were the port and the city gates. Anyone caught trying to escape was killed with witch fire if they resisted capture. The invaders were accompanied by fair-skinned, white-haired people with strange machines made of metal, which showed them the way to those of the djinns and fairies who had gone into hiding. There seemed to be no escape. The humans who were living in the quarters—at least those who were not found to have magical abilities—were allowed to move about freely and were not bothered or punished, even if someone was caught harboring a magical being. On that day, thousands of them were locked in cages, brought to the Spanish galleons and taken away. No one knows for sure why powerful sorcerers like you" —he nodded reverently at Ariane—"and the djinns could be captured just like that. Those who escaped reported that from one moment to the next all magical spells or wishes inside the quarters had ceased to work. Such powerful magic none of them had ever seen or heard of before. No one knows what happened to our friends that were taken away in the ships. A few score were not shipped, but leashed by the Inquisitors and put up for public sale at a great slave market lasting several days, presumably to cover the expense of the operation."

Abdel explained that some friends of the djinns had raised enough money to buy at least a few dozen of the slaves, with the aim of giving them back their freedom later. But there had still been plenty of rich buyers eager to pay for the control of other's magical powers. The prices paid rose to astronomical heights, so that not many could be ransomed.

Gloomily, the old man stared into space, then continued.

"However, the spell-blocking energy field that they had laid over the city had produced yet another effect, one that apparently they hadn't foreseen, and that saved at least close to fifty djinns and a few fairies. You see, inside Mira'aleitha, there is a sacred zone that can be accessed only by way of magical portals. At the time of the attack, these entrances closed automatically because the spells upholding them lost their power, and all who were in the sacred area at the time were locked inside. When the Spaniards left a few weeks later, the portals opened again, and the remains of Algiers' magical population set out to save what could be saved. Together with the few ransomed djinns, they began to secretly find the abducted slaves and free them by force. In the meantime, there are again several hundred beings who live in the former Sacred Zone and have built a small village community there. This place is called the Refuge."

"But," he continued, "no one has yet found a way to remove one of the metal bands from the neck of one of the former slaves. This means they can still only use their abilities if someone else holds their leash and explicitly allows them to. Not even our friends who have ransomed djinns quite officially have been able to fully free them."

Sen was on the brink of saying something, but the old Arab raised his hand, stopping him.

"Some even approached the Inquisition's headquarters in Granada with the problem. The answer they received was that the collars were intended as a permanent solution and that their contract of sale did not allow for the purchased items to be given back their freedom. If they were no longer wanted, the material would have to be resold or returned to Granada for further recycling."

Abdel fell silent.

Ariane's face was a mask of restrained anger, and Sen's and Kaura's similar feelings stood clear in their eyes.

"May we talk to the superiors of the Refuge?" asked Sen. "We have an expert on psychomagic with us, on the ship. Maybe my friend can do something here."

The old Arab raised his shoulders hopelessly.

"I am sure that the Council of Elders will receive the Exalted One and her friends with joy." Again, an awed nod toward Ariane. "But what a circle of thirteen powerful djinns can't achieve, I think even your expert will find difficult to solve. I do hope I'm wrong about this," he added.

Sen stood up.

"I still want to try, at least. Can we visit you again tomorrow morning and bring our friend with us?"

Abdel shook his head.

"I need a day to announce you at the Refuge and ask for the consent of its elders. The day after tomorrow you can come. Ibrahim will guide you. What ship are you on?" asked the old Arab.

Kaura told him.

As they said farewell, Abdel asked Ariane for a blessing. With a gentle smile completely uncharacteristic of the guard fairy, she pressed her small hand to his forehead, and a beatific expression entered the Arab's tanned, wrinkled face.

Ibrahim led them back through the darkness, crisscrossing the winding alleys until they were back in the busier part of town.

"Aren't you afraid of being mugged?", Kaura asked him.

The boy shook his head.

"No outsiders venture into the old djinn quarter anymore, ever since there have been a few, shall we say, supernatural occurrences that the freed djinns have taken care of. Now most of the non-Gifted believe that Mira'aleitha is haunted by the spirits of the enslaved mages. All those who still dare to enter are friends. But you should keep a watchful eye out when we're back in the harbor area. Avoid uncrowded alleys, and don't walk too close around corners."

He turned to Ariane. "And if I may suggest, Exalted One, you should try to avoid attracting attention. As long as no one gets close enough to see that you are not wearing a collar, you will probably have no problems. But otherwise, the authorities may take an interest in you. After all, Algiers is part of the Empire, even if few here have much love for the sultan's people. See you the day after tomorrow."

With a quick wave, he disappeared down a side alley.

The small group reached the ship without any problems. On getting aboard, officer of the watch informed them that the repairs would still take several days. The galleon had completely lost her foremast, the rudder was broken, and it appeared that additional damage had also been found in the ship's inner structure that required the attention of the shipwrights.

* * *

Early on Thursday morning, a deckhand came in at breakfast, announcing Ibrahim's arrival. The boy was immediately invited on board and looked with interest at the ship's deck with its gleaming copper guns and its multitudes of lines, blocks, and hatchways.

After having been invited to breakfast and devouring everything set before him voraciously, the boy led Kaura, Sen, Simon and Ariane into the narrow streets of the port district. The fairy still had not fully recovered from discovering that many of her sisters had been taken as slaves, but seemed a little bit less depressed than the day before.

She had refused to hide but fluttered close beside Kaura to at least keep up appearances.

"Actually, these caftan-heads here might as well see that there are still free fairies in the world," she had muttered angrily.

Ibrahim had nodded and added that magical beings still had more friends than enemies in Algiers. However, the fairy immediately understood Abdel's wish for them to remain as inconspicuous as possible so as not to betray the secret of the Refuge.

This time they chose a different route. Ibrahim proved to be an excellent tour guide, stopping again and again in front of this or that building worth seeing. But he used these opportunities mainly to keep a lookout for possible pursuers. As they strolled through another of the whitewashed cubic apartment buildings, the lanky North African cast a quick glance along the alley.

"Nobody around," he whispered. "Quick, in here!"

He pulled Sen by the hand through an archway, and the other companions followed.

They left the courtyard on the other side of the building, and strode briskly around the next corner. After a few more turns, Ibrahim pushed aside the iron grille of a locked shop and slipped through. Carefully, he pulled the grille shut again when everyone had followed him.

Inside the store, it was cool and dim. Shelves covered with white, dusty-looking cloths seemed to have been waiting for a long time for the owner to return and receive customers again. The boy led them through a low wooden door into an adjoining room, which must have been some kind of office. Behind it, a gate led into a backyard overgrown with wild, prickly bushes. A winding, barely visible path led through the thicket.

Without thinking, Kaura put a simple spell around herself that kept the thorns off her clothes.

Noticing Sen's surprised look, she smiled.

"I'll treat you to a little introduction to Lemurian comfort magic sometime," she said softly. "There's quite a bit that should interest a bon vivant like you."

The Scottish headmaster raised his eyebrows.

"I'm sure it should. Well, I guess you'll grace us ignorant laymen with your superior magical knowledge whenever you see fit... I'm certainly very interested in an exchange. Of any kind."

Now it was Kaura's turn to raise her eyebrows. She did not comment any further. While they had been talking, they had come out into a deserted alley through yet another abandoned house with boarded-up windows.

Kaura realized at first glance that they were now in Mira'aleitha. No living being was to be seen. The windows were either boarded up or just empty, yawning caverns. In this area, many of the stores also seemed to have been broken into and vandalized. Debris and broken timbers littered the street. Past rains and the wind had piled up mud and sand in various places, so that the cobblestones were only partially visible.

Quickly, Ibrahim led them on. Two blocks further, they came to a large building that looked like something between a market hall and a mosque. Inside, the hall was full of rubble, and large pieces of plaster had fallen from the ceiling. Ibrahim led them past the main entrance to the side of the building. There was a kind of vendor entrance there—a slightly larger but unadorned gate with rough iron fittings that looked like they were still being maintained, glistening with fresh grease.

Ibrahim leaned casually against the whitewashed wall next to the gate, tapping the wood in a very specific rhythm.

"This is the visitor entrance," he said. "Residents have other ways to get directly from the Refuge into the city or surrounding areas. In the last five years, a lot of work has been put into creating new passages and escape routes."

With a creak, the gate opened a crack. The strangely expressionless, rigidly grinning face of a goateed man appeared. The face spoke in a fine female voice, which, in combination with its rigid expression, felt extremely sinister.

"Who there? Identify yourselves, morons! We were expecting you, but dontcha think you can sneak spies in here or anything!"

Kaura had just noticed with a mixture of shock and amusement that the head had no neck and seemed to float freely in the air, when the voice gasped and then crowed loudly, causing everyone to cringe.

"Ariane, old bagpipe, what are you doing here!!!? Has the Scottish sneezy-weezy weather become too damp for you, too?"

The goateed face deformed like a limp piece of leather and fluttered to the ground. Behind it, a broadly grinning, somewhat chubby fairy with green eyes and wings appeared. She sped toward Ariane like a cannonball and collided with her in mid-air. The hug looked more like an aerial wrestling match than a friendly greeting,

Kaura thought, but she knew enough about the fairies' customs not to be surprised.

"Mirelle," Ariane gasped breathlessly. "Don't push it, you fat bug!"

Her friend seemed to be about as happy about this pet name as if she had been addressed as beloved sweetheart, grinning even wider and slapping Ariane repeatedly on the back.

"Miserable sewer rat, how happy I am to get your misshapen face under my eyes again! It's been a long time since guard fairy school! Have those mage idiots at Lockwood finally realized that you're no good and kicked you out? You only wanted to go there because of that cuddly fairy boy, anyway—and of course because of that head monkey, whose tattoos you found so cool... is that one still around or has he tattooed himself to death by now?"

Ibrahim cleared his throat in a measured way.

"Venerable Guardian of the Gate. I do not wish to disturb your reunion, but humbly suggest that perhaps we had better not stand out here in the street, making noise. May we pass?"

Mirelle casually waved her darkly tanned fairy hand and eyed the white-robed boy from above.

"Don't worry, bedsheet, no one will find us here. And if they do, we'll flatten them, my little Ariane here and me. Come in, friends. I am Mirelle, the venerable guardian of the even more venerable gate to the ultra-venerable refuge of the monkey-cool djinns. Makes you drool with venerability, doesn't it?"

Once everyone was inside, she pushed the gate shut and locked it. Inside, however, was not quite the right way to put it. They were not standing inside the dilapidated market-hall, but in the middle of the hustle and bustle of an open-air souk. Hundreds of creatures of all colors, sizes and shapes scurried happily about. Rarely was there a human figure to be seen.

As the noise level around them rose, Kaura realized that they must be in a different place either physically or dimensionally. The sun hung quite a bit lower in the sky—it was afternoon here, not early morning like in Algiers. The air felt a bit cooler and drier on her skin.

Ariane was introducing the others when the Lemurian turned back to her companions.

"Mirelle, this is Simon, our psychodude from Lockwood. My friend Kaura, lemur super chick, never needs a tanning bed like you"—she cast a skeptical glance at Mirelle's tanned neckline. "And here we have Sen, my beloved superboss..."

"The head monkey," the latter interjected with a grin. "Would you like to see my tattoos?"

Mirelle opened her mouth wide in astonishment.

"Nooooo, the head monkey himself, holy pretzel! I didn't think I'd ever see something like that! Can you survive without the constant rain dripping down on you on your islet at all, jinglehead? You're probably all dried up by now! Soon only a few shriveled tattoos and bells will be left of you. We better get you something to drink. May I touch?"

Without waiting for a reply, she poked her little index finger into Sen's upper arm, where the base of an esoteric symbol tattooed in paint was visible.

The principal of Lockwood College smiled kindly at her.

"I'm pleased to meet you, too, Mirelle. I'm afraid Scottish understatement doesn't allow me to greet you with some juicy curses."

The fairy magnanimously waved it off.

"Other countries, other customs, bellhead. Lunatics can't be helped. How can you be so nice? And even think it's a good thing? I would burst after two days. Come on! The head honchos are waiting for you."

Nimbly she fluttered ahead, right into the middle of the melee.

A little later, they were all sitting cross-legged in a cool, carpeted room. Some sun fell into the room through the small openings in the thick walls, making the gold-leafed murals shine.

Three djinns were sitting across from Sen, Kaura and Simon. They were slightly shorter than average humans, but more massive in build.

Two of them seemed to be male, the third female, although anatomically they differed only slightly from each other—the djinn lady was only recognizable by a slightly more finely cut face and longer eyelashes than her companions. All three were naked except for a loincloth. Their skin gleamed greenish, and their long black hair was curled up into long pointed cones on top of their heads, much like the orderly coils of rope on the *Isadora*'s deck. They seemed completely ageless—at least Kaura lacked any sense of whether she was looking at older or younger beings.

The female sitting at the center put her hands together in front of her chest and tilted her head slightly.

"Welcome to the Refuge," she intoned in a sing-songy but virtually accent-free Atlantean. "I am Aarifa. My companions are the high councilors Ra'id and Jamal. We are pleased to receive a visit from outside mages for the first time in a long time. And from a Sa'aleitha"—she nodded over to Ariane, but the fairy was engaged in conversation with Mirelle and not listening.

The guests returned the gesture, and Kaura took the floor.

"I am Kaura Alenu'ala, envoy of the Fern Temple of Lemuria. My companions here are Seneca Lumisworth, chief of the mages of Lockwood in Scotland, and Simon Beauville, also of Lockwood. Our venerable companion back there is named Ariane. We are traveling to Pyrrha to try to end the threat that the Sultan's Inquisition poses to all mages. We had to call at Algiers to repair our ship. While there, we heard about what happened in Mira'aleitha. My deepest condolences."

The djinn tilted her head and smiled gently.

"We are all here to gain experience. The Spanish and their Sa'aleitha allies will reap the fruits of their deeds. We have already forgiven them."

She leaned forward. Her eyes sparkled mysteriously. "That won't stop us from freeing our brothers and sisters, though. Abdel has let us know that you"—she fixed Simon with her deep black eyes—"want to look at the collars and the holding spell."

The young Scot nodded slowly.

"If I may. I've been studying how to counter compulsion magic for a long time. Maybe I'll find out something that has eluded you until now."

Aarifa tilted her head slightly and stroked the upper arm of the djinn to her right with an affectionate gesture.

"Ra'id, show him!"

This djinn, unlike the others, had a fine dark cloth wrapped around his neck, tightly woven and with a silky sheen.

Serenely, the creature untied the knot behind his neck, and attentively folded the cloth into a small package, which he placed next to him on the seat cushion.

A gleaming silver metal collar appeared, encircling the man's throat so tightly that Kaura wondered how he could even swallow. On the front of the metal was engraved the symbol of the Spanish-Ottoman Inquisition, four squares superimposed with an eye in the center.

"None of us have seen exactly how it is done," said the djinn. "The bands can even be put on by the non-Gifted. Once they slip it over the head of one of their victims, it automatically conforms to the wearer's anatomy and cannot be removed. Or at least, we have not yet discovered an opening mechanism, either magical or manual. The metal is flexible and adapts to every movement of the neck."

He swallowed, and the metal seemed to stretch in order to allow his larynx to move. "In fact, it almost feels like part of the skin and is hardly physically disturbing. Only, as you know, wearers of these things are helpless and their actions may be controlled by anyone holding the leash."

He opened a small leather pouch that he wore attached to his loincloth. Inside was a thin chain made of gleaming silver.

"Each leash is matched to the collar that goes with it. I cannot get more than about a yard from the wearer of the leash unless he attaches the leash to the collar. Nor can I move farther than about a hundred yards from the leash without experiencing severe cramps and collapsing within minutes. I can only move freely now because we've found a way to disrupt the collar's distance spell so that I can carry it around by myself and it 'thinks' I'm being escorted."

Sen had turned pale.

"And you say these infernal things work on human mages as well?"

Aarifa nodded.

"Yes. It seems to work on any magical being that we know of, even including the Great Ones, which you call fairies. They also enslaved human mages."

The Scottish chief magician took a deep breath.

"This is far worse than I feared, Aarifa. Probably the Inquisitors have used these collars not only here. Maybe soon well see armies consisting of thousands of Gifted slaves overrunning the hitherto free lands on behalf of the Sultan."

The djinn nodded again. Her expression was grim.

"Yes. We also believe that they are training their prisoners some-where for combat purposes. Our experience shows that the slaves can be killed in combat. However, the collar also prevents the wearer from laying a hand on himself. Those unfortunate ones can-not even escape into death, even if they wanted to."

Kaura shuddered, and involuntarily touched her neck, where she just wore the Ta'elekai now, its soft cord mended after the violent encounter three nights ago. All too well she remembered the feeling of cool metal when one of those collars had already started to wrap itself around her during her dream meeting with the unknown goddess—when, at the last moment, she had managed to access her power and thus escape, regaining her lost memories in the process.

In the meantime, Simon had sat down at Ra'id's side and was carefully examining the curved metal of the collar.

"No visible seams or hinges," he murmured. "The metal feels deformable much like silk, only more elastic. I feel a small ring that probably serves to attach the leash."

The djinn grumbled in agreement as the Scottish mage continued. "Energetically, I detect several streams of power reaching into Ra'id's brain from the collar. Some of them directly to the center of willpower, but movement, perception and speech centers also seem affected. Really diabolical, that thing. And it seems to tap its energy directly from the wearer's spine."

He turned to Aarifa. "Has anyone ever tried just cutting the power to this thing?" he asked her.

The djinn superior swayed her head.

"When we tried to magically affect these things in any way, there were, well, unfortunate side effects. Much like little lightning strikes, but fortunately they didn't cause any permanent damage on the ones who tried to help. So, no one so far even got close enough inside to even attempt such a thing as cutting the collar's energy supply. Not even a circle of thirteen djinn, which is the maximum number of mages we can channel into a combined spell."

Simon looked at Ra'id thoughtfully.

"May I try it?" he asked him. The djinn nodded. "I would give anything to finally be free of this thing. Do whatever you want!"

Now Kaura approached as well.

"Can I see before you start?"

Simon nodded, and she placed her delicate hands on the warm metal. Attentively, she felt the structure of the cool, silver surface.

"This is the work of sylphs, if I'm not mistaken," she murmured. "Only the Silaphesian cultures can combine such craftsmanship with magical fabrics. But they must have installed an emergency circuit somewhere! Probably well disguised. Hmm."

With a slight groan, she straightened up again and nodded to Simon. "I want to think. Go ahead and try it if you want."

Ariane, meanwhile, had retreated with Mirelle to a quieter corner of the room.

"Boy, is it good to see you, old crow!" she murmured, touched. "How did you end up in this sandblasting bathtub?"

The other fairy, it turned out, had been escorting a larger convoy of steel silk materials from Moraniu to Constantinople. On shore leave in Algiers, she had decided to visit the sanctuary, had accidentally gotten caught inside during the attack, and had remained trapped for several days afterward. No one had known what had happened outside before the portals opened again, and all had lost their magical abilities as well as the djinn outside.

"We were hungry, my ass, I'm telling you, old lady! There were only a few souvenir stalls and small snack bars in here at the time. At least there's a spring in the main sanctuary where we could drink. But when we came back out and realized what happened, we all yodeled our thanks to the Great Mother. Bad thing."

Ariane lowered her voice.

"Doesn't that make you angry, Mirelle?" She pointed over to Ra'id, where Simon continued to probe at the djinn's collar.

The tanned fairy shrugged her fleshy shoulders. "Oh, you know, we could have all stayed on Sirius Quinta. But it's much too boring there, if you ask me. Advanced civilization. Fairies everywhere. Group sex parties. Peace, joy, and pancakes."

Involuntarily, she licked her lips. "Okay, the pancakes on SQ are really good. But other than that? Bah! At least there's something going on here with the big wingless flatfoots. Half the Milky Way is having a rendezvous on Gaia right now. Everybody wants something from them"—she pointed with an affectionate grin at the three humans—"and these stone-age barbarians are far too primitive and ignorant to just give the asses a nice kicking. If the Kai'ala and their so-called "gods" tried to pull something like that on us, they'd fly all the way to Andromeda from the knock, and still bust their blue noses there!"

Mirelle leaned even closer to Ariane, lowering her voice to a whisper. She pointed at Kaura. "What I don't understand is why your little friend there is playing this game along. She said she's a high priestess, didn't she?"

Lost in thought, they both looked at the Lemurian. Suddenly Mirelle started, and her eyes widened in surprise.

"But, by the fucking scarf of the Great Ix, Ariane! Isn't that...?"

"Shh!" Ariane put her finger to her lips. "You're very perceptive, Mirelle, I'm impressed. I didn't recognize her until the second time we met, that's how much she's changed. But whatever game she's playing right now, she doesn't want to be recognized, I'm sure of that by now. Or she has put this multi-layered oblivion spell that she seems to be carrying onto herself. I don't think anyone could do that to a mage of her level against her will, not to her, of all things. Anyway, our chief purpose on this planet is to help her. That's the only thing I'm still sure of. And I'm sticking to it."

Mirelle nodded and winked confidentially at her friend.

"All right. It's not up to me. Nevertheless. Even if she's playing some game, the Lemurians themselves can't have degenerated as much as to only hug trees! They have always been a bit gaga, but, hey, they're the Old Ones, one of the mother civilizations of our galaxy and this plane of reality! They've basically taught our ancestors to read and write, so to speak, not to mention casting spells, and they controlled half the known universe at one time! Even if she doesn't have one herself anymore, a High Priestess should at least be able to turn off the planet's travel inhibitors, call in a starship from the outer rims and bring in someone who has a little more experience with the Kai'ala. Vermin experts, so to speak!"

She giggled maliciously. "And the Atlanteans play their own game anyway. Nobody knows on which side they stand, since the Lemurians checked their lust for expansion a few thousand years ago. They seem to be happy enough caressing their crystals, now, and not to let anyone peek in their tarot cards, the white scoops! That will end up in still another surprise, only for whom? Lovely show here, anyway, I wouldn't want to miss it at any price."

Ariane eyed the corpulent fairy with the green wings thoughtfully.

"I don't know, Mirelle. Kaura should know more than she says, but I don't think she has a starship, nor does she know how to call one, except for the plan with Pyrrha, going through the portal to Aalid to ask them directly. If they saw any easier way, the Lemurians wouldn't bother sending someone like her halfway around the globe in primitive sailing ships, that would just be stupid. No, they have a problem. Either they've forgotten everything because for ten thousand years they actually just hugged trees and everything went just that little bit too easy for them, or it's something else. Some kind of plan."

She sighed. "And of course, I agree with you. This show is long worth the risk of a few years of slavery. As well, those three and their friends have grown dear to me. I really like this version of her quite a bit better than the old one, I'd say."

She gestured vaguely towards Kaura. "She'd grown too hard, too serious. I'd help them open that portal even if it wasn't the Ix's will."

A brief silence ensued. Then, the blonde fairy suddenly smiled.

"Say, Mirelle, you must have picked up some nice hefty Algerian curses and insults over the years, right? So tell me, I'm all ears..."

Meanwhile, Simon continued to try to get inside the energetic compulsion weave from all sides through the protective spell of

Ra'id's collar. So far, he had avoided all traps, but still had not come much closer to the core of the magic amulet. Disappointed, he shook his head.

"I'm sorry, Ra'id, I can't find a way. These spells are of a kind I've never seen before. Completely smooth. No loose ends where you could attach any opening spell. "

The djinn smiled gently.

"No need to be ashamed, mage. For years our best Aleitha have been trying again and again. And sooner or later we will find the solution. We have time."

Kaura, meanwhile, sat on her pillow, rigid like a statue, and stared ahead, seemingly far away, almost asleep.

Then she startled awake with a little jolt.

"I suppose you have also tried to have the collar wished open by fairies. What happened when you did that?"

Aarifa shrugged.

"Simply nothing. The fairies say they felt the same resistance as usual when reality bends to their magic, but the collars remain unchanged. So, the wish seems to come true, except that nothing happens."

Kaura nodded her thanks and turned toward the corner, where Ariane was still talking animatedly with Mirelle. The two seemed to be playing some game involving ugly grimaces. "

Ariane, could you come over here for a spell? I want to try something."

The fairy fluttered over, landing on the carpet next to Ra'id and Kaura.

"I'm listening with all of my elephant ears."

Theatrically, she held her hands behind her pointed ears like little shovels and spread her purple wings.

"Can you wish the collar open, please?" asked Kaura. "I want to see if I can detect a reaction of its protective spells to that."

Ariane nodded, pulled a small, twisted wooden stick seemingly out of thin air and waved it like a miniature conductor.

"Now?" she asked. Kaura brought her face close to Ra'id's neck and concentrated. Then she answered in the affirmative. The tip of the wooden stick began to glow. Everyone leaned forward to see better. Then the fairy tapped it in the middle of the Inquisition's symbol on the front of the collar. The device shimmered bluish, but nothing happened.

Nevertheless, Kaura nodded with satisfaction. She turned to Simon.

"Did you see the thin blue line at the top of the metal that lit up for a moment? That was the defense circuit against magical influence, a kind of inverted weave. A little to the left of the eye symbol, there was something like a little gap or lump. I think that's where I can get in. Can you do that again, please, Ariane?"

Just before the blonde guard fairy waved her staff again, Kaura settled into a state of almost supernatural calm. Her thoughts disappeared in a whirl inside her and gave way to a vastness in which everything seemed possible. The warmly glowing tip of the staff seemed to approach Ra'id's neck in grotesque deceleration. Someone was speaking, but sounds were also slowed, stretching into elongated, vibrating cacophonies without meaning.

She prepared a weave within herself with which she hoped to enlarge and push through the gap as soon as it would open. The finished energetic symbol glowed dimly in a corner of her expanded consciousness, ready to be used in a split second.

With agonizing slowness, the tip of Ariane's wand approached the shiny metallic structure of the collar. When it was about a finger's width away, the blue glow reappeared, surrounding the silvery ruff like a billowing, semi-transparent mist. Now she also saw the blue line at the upper edge of the metal band, which further intensified its glow. And there was the gap! With all the strength of her consciousness, she threw herself into it, pushing the tool-weave, infinitely diminished now, in front of her. Careful, she had to be careful not to touch the blue glowing edges! Then she was through and found herself in a space that felt cramped. Narrow and dark and somehow, evil.

She saw the magical weaves in front of her, densely packed, ensuring the function of the compulsion collar. In the center, large, all the loose threads of energy converged in a kind of pyramidal tangle held by thick strands that disappeared downward out of her field of vision.

"The core circuitry," she muttered, "and that down there must be the tentacles connected to Ra'id's spine."

Without further ado, she used her tool-weave to loosen and un-ravel a loose end of a strand in the lower part of the pyramid. The whole ball seemed to wobble, but nothing else happened. Then she grabbed a second strand and pulled the loose end out of the pile. Now, the effect was immediate. The entire pyramid fell apart, and threads of light whirled through the room like broken rope before glittering and dissolving into nothingness.

All at once, the feeling of confinement was gone, too. Kaura withdrew from the still faintly flickering space and opened her eyes.

In the outside world, no more than a second had passed. Ariane's staff was still touching the collar, just as she was about to withdraw it. But the blue glow was already gone. As the fairy slowly withdrew her hand, the metal around the djinn's neck seemed to deform, going limp and wide.

With a soft clink, the band, now only a thin loop of circular chainlinks, fell down onto his shoulders.

Ra'id sat there for a moment as if frozen. Then the green-skinned being reverently palpated his neck, his chin, and the metal loop resting on his shoulders. Carefully, he grasped the loop with both hands, pulled it over his head, and placed it on the carpet in front of him. His black eyes gleamed moistly as the djinn man bowed deeply to Kaura and Ariane.

"Thank you," he said simply. Kaura realized for herself that she had never seen Ariane embarrassed before. Now she blushed, and lowered her eyes, looking at her bare feet, while she put her staff away.

"It was her doing," the fairy murmured softly, pointing to Kaura. The latter nodded.

"Without Ariane showing me the way, though, that wouldn't have been possible. The collar's cloaking spell was very strong, and well made. It took an exceedingly powerful loosening spell to activate the defense mechanism to a high enough degree so I could detect the gap and get inside it, too. I don't think anyone but a fairy could supply that much power," she added, then casting a sideways glance at Aarifa, considering. "Except maybe the djinn. I know too little about your powers to judge."

The djinn looked at her thoughtfully.

"We will try that out. But even if we can't trigger the mechanism, we have enough fairies here to reproduce the experiment in the same way. The most important thing now is that you two"—she made a motion toward Kaura and Ariane—"Tell us exactly what you did. I need to know if this is repeatable. And if there are any pitfalls we need to watch out for."

Kaura nodded in agreement.

"I suggest that we try it again with another collar wearer afterwards. And that we initiate some of your strongest people beforehand, who will try to emulate it. We also need to see if their way of working with the weaves is sufficiently similar to mine that they can do it the same way."

"And then we celebrate," Ra'id spoke up again, still numbly fingering his neck. "The new hope for thousands of Aleitha around the world!"

Aarifa called in a young djinn girl dressed in white silk and gave her some instructions in a language Kaura could not understand. A little later, the room was swarming with other beings. Three fairies had come, four djinn, and two older human mages had arrived as well. One member of each species wore one of the silver bands around their neck.

Kaura explained to those present—they were those inhabitants of the Refuge with the strongest magical talents—what was at stake, and demonstrated the procedure once again together with Ariane, at the fairy's collar. Then, the two strongest of the djinn tried to take Ariane's part, but did not manage to trigger the defensive spell enough to see the gap. When the Refuge's fairies tried, with Aarifa to find the gap and deactivate the collar, it worked.

Even after hearing Aarifa's account of how she experienced the spellwork inside the collar, it took the other djinn two more attempts each to find the gap in time. But then the silver chain fell from the neck of each of the mages who had worn it down onto her shoulders.

One of the two djinns, a female, beamed proudly.

"Yes, I think I can do it again," she said. "You try it with Suleane, Ra'id!"

Together with the fairy, the djinn sat down in front of his still collared fellow, and the device fell off right on his first try.

It turned out that a total of four of the djinn and mages in the Refuge were strong enough to open the collars, as well as Simon and Sen. However, the spell-gap could only be made visible by the fairies, no matter how hard the other mages tried.

The afternoon passed with returning all former slaves present in the Refuge to their freedom. In total, there were over a hundred collared beings, which meant a great effort for Ariane and the five other fairies, but which they took on with joy. The beaming faces of the freed slaves were more than enough for reward. When the last collar fell in the early evening, word about what had happened had already spread throughout the neighborhood.

Aarifa had had a feast prepared in the great hall of the sanctuary, which the fairy, the two Scots and the Lemurian did not want to miss. Quite apart from the fact that that would have been extremely impolite, as Ariane noted offhandedly.

"I thought rudeness was your highest virtue?" joked Simon.

The fairy laughed out loud.

"You got that all wrong, brainwave juggler! I'm just being honest. Never rude. And to get some properly cooked fairy food, for that I'd put our little sailboat in a time warp and not let it out until I was done eating!"

Almost all of the three hundred inhabitants of the Refuge had gathered in the hall. The members of this colorful hodgepodge of different beings sat along the low tables arranged in a circle on specially brought rugs and brocade cushions, talking and gesturing animatedly.

Some green-skinned djinns had taken it upon themselves to provide for the physical well-being of the guests. Incessantly, new delicacies seemed to appear in mid-air, distributed to the tables by a long line of helpers.

Temptingly fragrant dishes in all colors and shapes presented themselves to the overwhelmed guests.

"We're all vegetarians here, for simplicity's sake," Aarifa noted.

"It's amazing, amazing, great food" Sen mumbled next to her with his mouth full. On the table in front of him, Ariane giggled, having already drained at least two thimblefuls of local honey wine.

"Fortunately you are not also such anti-ank..., auk..., uh alcoholics, like those dear caftan wearers elsewhere in this nice little town. By the bare-breasted Ix, the others will be so jealous when I tell them about this! Is there anything to smoke? I haven't had a joint in a long time!"

Aarika just looked at her in confusion, but then turned back to the other guests when no one else said anything. After two hours filled with physical delights, accompanied by speeches of thanks and praise, some gifts for Kaura and Ariane and performances of colorfully dressed artists, fire artists and storytellers, the guests prepared to leave.

Kaura bowed to the djinn elders.

"We are sorry to have to take our leave so soon. However, our ship is waiting, and our mission cannot be delayed. I am very happy that our stay here was of such great benefit to you! The party was beyond words, thank you very much!"

"We have to give thanks, High Priestess!" replied Aarika, the others just nodding gravely. "Go now with our blessings and our sincere desire for the success of your venture. Visit us again soon, when things have calmed down a bit. And do not worry about loss of time. When you leave us, you will find that less time has passed in Algiers than you may suspect."

Under the star-filled, velvety night sky, they easily found their way back through the now almost deserted souk, guided by Mirelle. Most of the stores, coffee terraces and food stalls were closed. Almost everyone else still seemed to be in the main hall, taking part in the celebration.

Ibrahim slipped through the gate ahead of them, while Ariane took her leave of Mirelle with some ribald abuse, both fairies grinning madly with joy. Then, with a soft clack, the large wooden doorwings fell shut behind them, and they found themselves back in the empty alleys of Mira'aleitha.

Dazzled, everyone closed their eyes for a moment as the twilight of the Refuge abruptly changed to bright afternoon sunlight. The coolness of the desert night gave way to the billowing heat of Algiers. The hot air smelled of dust and withered plants.

Kaura looked up at the sky. Indeed, here it seemed to be only early afternoon. They had left Algiers barely four hours ago, though it seemed they had stayed in the Refuge at least three times as long. She wondered if the different time structure was a constant effect, or if it could be regulated according to the needs of the visitors.

Simon gave her a shy sideways glance.

"I asked Aarifa about this before we left the festival. It seems that the Refuge is located in a magically created time bubble. Whoever is in it can leave this bubble at any time in the outside world they choose. The only condition is that one cannot travel back in time. The earliest time of leaving is a few seconds after entering. So, theoretically, you could bridge several centuries into the future with a short stay in there. The djinn seem to be very good at temporal magic. But Aarifa also said that so far only a few have tried such extreme things. And of course, they never came back. So, it seems that traveling back in time has not been mastered even in the distant future. Or maybe the few long-term travelers liked it there so much that they saw no reason to return."

Kaura nodded.

"Uh-huh, interesting. Thanks. But my friend, do you always read my mind? That's not very polite. A lady needs her privacy, after all."

The young Scot blushed and lowered his gaze.

"I usually shield myself, of course. It would be much too annoying to hear all the thoughts around me all the time. I just happened to pick it up. Sorry."

"It's okay." The Lemurian smiled. "I could shield my thoughts as well, after all. It just didn't occur to me. Can you all do that in Lockwood?"

"I don't think so, since it takes quite a bit of practice and magical potency," Simon replied. "It's not talked about that much. Doug, my boss, is proficient at it, of course. And I suppose Sen is as well. Strong enough for it, anyway. Eagle, most likely." He shrugged.

Kaura grinned wryly.

"Well, then I guess I really have to watch what I think around you guys. Full transparency takes on a whole different meaning like this..."

The mage looked confused.

"Do you want me to teach you the shielding spell? I thought you already knew it."

"Yeah yeah, it's okay, of course I do," Kaura muttered, wondering if she had ever harbored any erotic fantasies about tattoos in Sen's presence. But really, it hardly mattered. In Lemuria, after all, no one bothered to shield their thoughts. There you could be sure that no one would condemn you for complete honesty, whether in words or thoughts. Why should that be different here?

Together they hurried after the others who, under Ibrahim's leadership, had already gone a little further down the alley.

They left the neighborhood through another abandoned store and parted from Ibrahim below the Kasbah with an exceedingly cordial farewell. Sen wanted to give him a gold ducat for his help, but the Algerian refused, seeming offended.

"What you have done for our collared friends is more than enough! Know that you will always find welcome in Algiers and in the Refuge, as well as unconditional support if you ever need help. When you get back here, go see the merchant Uzayr in the port district and ask for Ibrahim. I will find you. Farewell, friends. The Great Mother be with you!"

Waving his white cloak, the boy disappeared into the bustle of afternoon city life.

Ariane looked after him pensively. "Nice kid, but still looks like a bedsheet on legs," she muttered.

2

Templars of Rhodes

Two days after leaving the port of Algiers, the *Pride*, still traveling under the alias *Isadora* in these Spanish-Ottoman dominated climes, had an encounter with some of the Algerian pirates who were still troubling merchants sailing in this part of the Mediterranean, despite the Spanish sultan's repeated efforts to eradicate them.

The Scottish ship continued to stay relatively close off the North African coast to avoid too much scrutiny from the Imperial fleet, whose patrols they expected to be most concentrated near the Iberian Peninsula and around the Balearic Islands.

Sen and Simon had put their cloaking spell back on the four-masted merchantman, but it paid to remain on the safe side, as Captain McGregor often used to say. Indeed, they had not seen any official patrols since Gibraltar. Instead, now this xebec manned by decidedly wild-looking men was sailing up at high speed. Xebecs, slender Mediterranean sailing vessels with triangular sails were the type of ship favored by local pirates because of their maneuverability and speed.

Sharp commands echoed across the deck of the Scottish galleon as the crew cleared for action and raised the gunport lids. The two ship's boys spread sand over the decks and other men installed boarding-nettings and dreadnought screens for the hatchways, while bowls of glowing charcoal were brought from the galley to light the fuses.

"They have the weather-gage, and they are faster than we are by a fair margin," Sir Elias told Aran, who had just arrived back on the quarterdeck after surveying the preparations for battle.

"But their guns are not much to look at," his first officer replied. "If they really want to get at us, they'll have to board, and quick, before we get one of our broadsides in."

"And that's exactly what they're up to, if I'm not mistaken," interjected Joe, who, along with Kaura, Abigail, and the Lockwood mages, had also joined them on the spacious quarterdeck when the lookout had reported the approach of a potentially hostile ship. Joe, heir to a powerful London merchant dynasty, was the nominal owner of the galleon. And he quite openly slept with both Abigail and Kaura, a fact that kept arousing some jealousy in Sen, who otherwise liked the younger man very much and had come to respect him as a good friend and intelligent philosopher.

The figures on the deck of the xebec were now already visible to the naked eye. They approached the galleon from astern, so the *Pride* could not use its great guns while it was still trying to evade the pursuers. The captain had already had two rotary guns installed on the quarterdeck. These small guns had a shorter range than the heavy fourteen-pounder culverins on the main deck—but they could be swivelled and directed downwards onto the much lower deck of the sleek, flat pirate ship, once it got into range.

The pirates intoned a many-voiced roar that went through marrow and bone. The noise was probably intended to intimidate more timid natures from the outset and induce them to give up. Some of the shabby-looking men on board of the pirate drew their cutlasses across their throats in a meaningful gesture, grimacing hatefully.

Sen had put a looking-glass to his eye and was staring intently over at the other ship.

"I see several figures with silver collars on the quarterdeck. Two djinns and a fairy."

With a sideways glance at Eagle and Irene, he continued, "We will have to intervene. But try to spare the slaves. Captain, best leave that to us. Kaura, can you help us, if need be?"

The Lemurian nodded.

"However, due to the nature of my magic, I may only weave to hurt when my life or the lives of my friends are in immediate danger." She pointed at the knife-wielding figures, some of whom were now resting muskets on the bulwark and a few more handling two small swiveling guns in the bow. "Looking at them there, that should be the case pretty soon."

Descending from the top of the mast, Ariane darted in, waving her wand like a prehistoric mace, and grinning madly.

"We're ready for battle, superboss! We'll show those cutthroats! Diana and her fairyhood have already put the protective shield around our sweet little dinghy. Today, the cutthroats are going to cry little tears because they don't get any necks to cut, those lunatics. Really, such a noise. There's really no need for that. It almost sounds as if they seriously believe that they won't sink right away, along with their shitty barge."

One of the xebec's front guns flashed. The shot fell short, however, and produced only a beautiful-looking, rainbow-colored fountain in the *Pride's* wake.

"Ha, they can't aim those little farts either, dirty peppermint-tea-aunties! Yay, here we are! Heere! Heeere!" the fairy chirped loudly and waved both arms in the general directions of the pursuers.

The pirates couldn't hear her, because they had already started roaring again, as if they had scored a direct hit.

The captain meanwhile told the men standing behind the guns to wait.

"Shield, what does that mean?" he asked, turning to Sen. "Can we even shoot through that? Out, I mean?"

Sen nodded.

"If it's set up right. Diana and her fairies are among the best. Still, you should have a little test with a musket first before you use the heavy hummers. Better safe than sorry," he used the old Scotsman's own favorite adage right back at the captain.

Sir Elias gave some instructions, and shortly thereafter a musket shot whipped diagonally down to the pirates sailing up closer and closer from the windward side.

The distance was still far too great for a hit, and again all that could be seen was a small fountain on the surface of a dark green wave, far off the bow of the sleek pursuer.

The pirates seemed to believe that this was meant to intimidate them, and they laughed frenetically, neighing like horses. In the meantime, the three slaves with the silver collars could be seen clearly. They were standing—or rather, fluttering, in the case of the fairy—on the quarterdeck next to a gaunt, hard-faced man with a full black beard. This had to be the xebec's captain.

Behind each of the three stood a bald, black giant who held the filigree, silver leash of the respective slave in their hands and stared at the stern of the departing galleon from sinister eyes. The one holding the fairy leaned forward a little and said a few words. The small creature, recognizable from the *Pride*'s deck only as a small, glittering spot, swung its staff, and from one moment to the next, the sails of the Scottish galleon, full of the breeze just a moment ago, fell limp.

However, the calm lasted only a moment. Eagle slanted her gaze upward and spoke a few words, and the wind immediately returned. The pirates' shrieking howls of joy immediately turned into angry roars. Now the xebec's bowchasers opened fire again as they came within firing range. However, the iron balls they were loaded with bounced ineffectively off an invisible obstacle in midair just behind the galleon's stern instead of hitting its rudder.

"Good work, Diana," Sir Elias muttered, calling to the two men at the aft guns, "Open fire! Aim for the sails. Maybe we can still shake them off without too many casualties."

Sen wanted to say something and point out that the pirates' slaves had to be kept from harm but checked himself. When they had repelled this attack, they could still turn around and free the prisoners.

Both rotating guns barked up almost simultaneously and hit full on. Loads of concentrated shrapnel drove into the foresail of the Mediterranean ship and tore large shreds from the canvas. The speed of the pirate ship suddenly decreased noticeably. It was still slightly faster than the galleon, however, and would soon have caught up completely. The gun teams worked feverishly to reload their charges while the two ships swept through the choppy Tunisian sea with impressive bow waves.

Now the two djinn slaves, prompted by their leash-holders, also intervened in the battle. Large, glowing fireballs left their outstretched hands and burst like burning oil on the outside of the invisible energy bubble that surrounded the Nelson ship.

Suddenly, hard blows also thundered against the massive hull from below.

"They're trying it from below!" shouted Simon to Diana, who was fluttering above the deck. At a hand signal from the fairy guard captain with the glittering pink wings, two of her "girls" swung in beside the side of the galleon with glowing wands and sailed like terns just above the tips of the waves alongside the speeding ship, drawing esoteric symbols in the air.

The protective bubble surrounding the galleon was still enveloped in a hail of burning air, fed by ever new fireballs, lightning bolts and thunderclaps rushing at it from all directions.

Suddenly, Kaura noticed that her lids were dropping. An immense sleepiness came over her. Beside her, Sir Elias swayed, and some of the crew members slowly slid down over the cannons, already asleep.

Fighting the urge to close her eyes completely, the Lemurian saw the weaves of energy trying to enter the minds of the *Pride*'s crew like writhing serpents. Simon ran, shouting something, from the hollow towards the starboard companionway leading up to the quarterdeck, but then began to sway as well and collapsed, unconscious.

In her inner space, Kaura formulated a strong mirroring weave that turned the weaves back to their originators, and at the same time placed a wake-up impulse over her own ship.

Sir Elias next to her straightened up with a jerk.

"What was that? I must have dozed off for a moment. Now, in the middle of the action? This is impossible!"

"They tried to put us to sleep. Those djinns are very, very strong," Kaura told him. "But now their own plan backfired. I guess they didn't expect that!"

She pointed aft towards the pursuers. The slender ship slowly drifted off course and fell back, its sails flapping. Nothing moved on board. The helmsman was slumped over the tiller. The gaunt pirate captain lay across one of his bald slavers and seemed to be sleeping peacefully. It looked the same all over the deck. Several dozen bloodthirsty figures, armed to the teeth, lay there, cuddled together in sleep.

Only one small figure on the quarterdeck fluttered, pulling her chain and waving desperately.

"The fairy is still awake!" shouted Ariane. "Wear, now! Turn around! We have to save the slaves!"

Sir Elias gave the orders, and the big ship turned in a perfect maneuver. Barely five minutes later, they went alongside the Xebec drifting on the waves. Ariane and the six fairies of the watch command had already flown ahead and waved vigorously. Diana was engaged in conversation with the fairy who had remained awake, gently explaining to her that they were friends and that she and the other captives would be freed presently.

Nimbly, some of the *Pride*'s crew members jumped down onto the xebec's much lower, long-stretched deck and dragged the two unconscious djinns to the bulwark, where they were secured in lowered swap slings and hoisted up to the galleon. The fairy was able to fly herself, accompanied by Ariane, who held the leash in her hands like something exceedingly disgusting.

In the meantime, Sen's guard fairies had also searched the rest of the ship. Four of the winged creatures just emerged from inside the ship, with two heavy-looking levitating chests between them.

"Hey ship boss!" called Diana up to Sir Elias, blinking her pink eyes. "We've been through the filthy box. Needs a wash, just like those dirt lovers." She pointed at the pirates spread all over the deck, still asleep and unlikely to wake up anytime soon. "That's why we made some little holes in the hull. Splashes nicely, down there. We should get out of here soon. There's gold in those boxes. So, we brought it right along. Maybe we can use it to ransom a few more slaves."

Sir Elias stared down at them.

"You're sinking the ship? And what about them?"

He pointed at the pirates.

"I guess their disappearance wouldn't be a big loss for the world," crowed the fairy. "Wouldn't like to know how many nice people they've sent to the fishes, themselves. Or to the slave markets. But we're not like that, of course. We'll pile them up nice and neat in their two dinghies. After we have sunk their weapons. Without a ship and their weapons, at least they can't hurt anyone else for a while."

Ten minutes later, two dinghies full of still unconscious Mediterranean pirates bobbed in the swell, while the *Pride* set sail and continued southeast, heading toward the Libyan coast. The nameless xebec was drawing more and more water. It would not be long before she disappeared forever into the depths of the ocean.

The people on the quarterdeck looked back at her, with a troubled look in almost everyone's eyes.

"There is always something tragic about watching a ship sink," Sir Elias remarked. "Even if it has brought misfortune to as many innocent people as this one probably has."

"The pirates are better off having met us than if the Spanish or the Venetians had caught them," Aran replied. "If they had, those guys would probably all be hanging from the yardarm now."

"Hanging is still way too nice a way to treat those lousy buggers," Ariane grumbled, perched on Kaura's shoulder, her blonde hair flapping in the breeze. "One should put them in a slave market themselves. Well, probably no one would want to buy them anyway. Smell bad and are ugly like hell. And all those obscenities they were shouting at us!"

Then suddenly something seemed to occur to her, and she screwed up her face. "Still, it's too bad we didn't take a prisoner or two with us. They probably would have known some dirty words I've never heard before. Well, I guess one can't always have everything..."

On deck, the two djinns had woken up and looked around in amazement. Diana and the other fairies were gently helping the two massive, green-skinned beings up. As it turned out, they were a couple. The collars were quickly removed with the help of Kaura and Ariane. The freed slaves were exceedingly grateful. The fairy's name was Delpha. She asked to be put ashore on Rhodes, where a larger fairy colony was supposed to have settled under the protection of the Knights Templar.

Shedir and Caph, the two djinns, spontaneously decided to accompany the group to Pyrrha.

"I've always wanted to visit Pyrrha," said Shedir, the djinn woman. "And it's probably as safe or unsafe there as most places."

Kaura swayed her head, not sure if she agreed.

"It's hard to say. The Spanish know about Pyrrha and have been trying to conquer the city for years, as we've heard. That will probably make it dangerous to get in. But the very fact that they haven't managed it yet, despite all the sultan's power and resources, shows that this ancient center of magical power shouldn't be completely defenseless."

* * *

The next few days passed with good winds and no further unpleasant encounters. At about the longitude of Tripoli, the galleon turned east, gaining more distance from the African coast. Between Crete and Kithira, she sailed into the warm waters of the Aegean and then veered off to approach Rhodes from behind, the ancient, neutral capital of the Order of the Knights Templar. There, mages were still welcome, as far as anyone knew. Officially adhering to the same religion as the Spanish-Ottoman Inquisitors, the Knights had nevertheless developed a much freer understanding of it and, it was said, based their politics on a belief in the equality and worthiness of all beings, magical and non-magical.

More than an hour before the island came into view, the *Pride* was hailed by a Templar patrol, a well-armed sloop bearing the distinctive Maltese crosses on its main sails. The wizards had already removed the camouflage spell from the galleon a few days earlier, and Sir Elias had had the flag of the Scottish merchant fleet set, the white St. Andrew's cross on a blue background. Only the *Pride's* physically repainted stern still bore the ISADORA lettering below the windows of the aft deck cabins.

In the meantime, the crew had expressed the wish to rename the galleon permanently.

"*Isadora*, that sounds quite different from *Pride of Edinburgh*," the bosun, a heavy-set man with an angular, scarred face, had purred. "Like Spanish red-light districts, full lips and feminine forms." He had made a hand gesture in front of his huge chest, seemingly imagining an even bigger bosom. "That way no storm will be able to hurt us anymore, because the wind gods all want to cuddle with our lady!"

The idea had gone down well with the crew, and now everyone imitated the bosun's gesture when the captain came by on his deck tour. The latter was not averse in principle but referred to Joe Nelson, being a representative of the ship's owners. Finally, however, it had become too much for Joe when the fifth sailor had approached him within a time of less than two hours.

"Sir, I don't mean to interrupt, but since you're quite fond of female forms, I think, with all your girlfriends and stuff, we might honor the fair sex with a permanent name for our dear *Isadora*, wouldn't that be something, sir..."

Joe was already having an irritable day and yelled back at the poor deckhand so loudly that even the watch below, used to sleeping through the loud commands of a ship's running, almost tumbled out of their hammocks. After that, everyone knew that Joe Nelson would have the 'Lady' renamed in the ship's registry immediately after returning to Scotland. Unless he changed his mind and write 'Box of Horny Fornicators' on the registration form instead of *Isadora*.

"That is amazing, sir, thank you! But who exactly do you mean by that, sir?" the deckman had merely asked innocently, and had gone his way, satisfied.

The Templar ship let the galleon and her crew go their way after the Knights had made sure they were mostly true Scots and not carrying holds full of Spanish spies. When they had seen the djinns and fairies walking freely on deck, the elegantly uniformed Templar captain had saluted reverently and wished the 'Exalted Ones' a good time in Rhodes. They would surely be welcome in the palace of the Grand Master.

Ariane generously waved down to him from the maintop shroud.

"Well, one can have a good time in the Mediterranean," the fairy murmured softly to herself. "Everybody's so respectful, those bed sheet wearers and uniform sardines. Unless they want to put a collar on you and make you a slave. Well, let's see what the Templar head honcho has to offer. Maybe I should show him my breasts.", she mused. "They are all monks, after all, that could have some interesting effects. Celibacy and all that! He's probably never seen anything the like before."

She giggled and swang herself up through the shrouds towards the crosstrees like a circus acrobat.

Barely three hours later, the four-master entered the fortified harbor of Rhodes and was skillfully maneuvered alongside the spacious quay. Helping hands received the ropes and nimbly tied them to the large metal bollards, while the crew placed the swap slings over the bulwark that would prevent damage to the hull from the hard stone.

At the entrance to the city, a small delegation was already waiting for the arrivals.

A man of about forty, wrapped in a wide silk coat embroidered with gold, stepped forward and saluted smartly.

"I am Xavier de Vauldemolai, representative of the Grand Master.

Welcome to our island! We have learned by messenger pigeon from the ship you met that you have Gifted passengers aboard. I am to welcome you and lead you up to the palace, at your leisure."

The knight pointed to an approaching older man in a simple white shirt and black linen trousers.

"This is Kyros Ilpitrakios, our shipyard master. If you need supplies or other equipment, turn to him. You will have a long journey behind you. Since almost all of the Mediterranean is enemy territory for you, we don't often get visits from Scottish ships anymore."

Sir Elias bowed slightly.

"Thank you very much, Master de Vauldemolai. My name is Elias McGregor, merchant captain to Her Majesty the Queen of Scots. My companions here will introduce themselves. We gladly accept your offer and thank you for your warm welcome."

* * *

Calle Pagés, Granada

At the same time, in the headquarters of the Spanish-Ottoman Inquisition, three dissimilar beings faced each other. One was bald, blue-skinned and dressed in the ruby-red robe of the High Inquisitors. It was Krmkr, the head of the group of Kai'ala charged with manipulating the imperial court in the interests of his masters.

Krmkr bared his pointed teeth, reminiscent of a shark, lifting his lipless mouth into an uncertain grin.

His visitors, a man and a woman, looked down at him from above.

The man had long white hair and a pale face like an albino. Only, his eyes were not red, but shone in deep light blue. His companion was as tall as he was, her skin had a pearly gleam and her hair was of a pure golden blonde.

She raised one of her perfectly manicured hands. Her voice was soft as silk but had a determined note to it. This woman was not to be trifled with.

"On your knees, worm! And don't you dare look at me again without being asked."

The Kai'ala swallowed nervously and hastily lowered himself to his knees.

"Forgive me, mistress, I did not know..."

"Silence, creature," the white-haired man reproached him. "We are here because our spies have reported that magical creatures are once again said to be roaming free in the Mediterranean. What do you have to say about that?"

The blue-skinned being wrung its hands.

"I have not received any reports in this regard. If it is true, it must have happened recently—over the last few weeks. The Spanish couriers cannot work magic and depend on ships and horses. If only we were allowed to set up some directional radios in the main cities, then..."

"You know very well that the Atlanteans must not learn who is turning the Spaniards against them," the white-haired man interrupted him. "If you use any real technology, they will locate it and become suspicious before we are ready."

"Yes, Great Master," muttered Krmkr. "With respect, then we must..."

In a calm voice, the woman interrupted him.

"We are not here to listen to suggestions. Detach a thousand more leashed ones, with orders to help in the conquest of Pyrrha and to capture free-ranging mages. We will *shift* them directly to Alexandria. Then we will be ready. The defensive shields of those damnable heretics are already weakened and will not withstand this additional contingent. The sultan's attack order to the Spanish-Ottoman forces in the region has already been issued, we have taken care of that. I will supervise the whole thing myself."

Krmkr nodded hesitantly.

"Yes, Great Mistress. As you command. But, if I may ask, will they not become suspicious? You look neither like Spaniards nor Ottomans."

The woman laughed as bright as a bell. The air around her began to shimmer, and within seconds she transformed into a black-haired Spanish noblewoman in a gold-embroidered brocade robe.

"Let us worry about that, creature. The slaves must be here in half an hour. They must not know where they will go. Go now, and get to work!"

The Kai'ala rose slowly, keeping his eyes lowered to the ground.

"I live to serve you," he murmured, disappearing through the richly decorated door of the elegantly appointed room.

With a sigh, the woman sank into one of the soft armchairs, reverting back to her previous appearance and motioning the Atlantean to sit beside her.

"Will it be over soon, Uriel?" she asked, not really expecting an answer. "Are our plans, matured for so many centuries, finally ripe? I am almost inclined to believe so. Those primitive barbarians here and their somewhat more advanced brethren on the great island are behaving just as we predicted."

The man laughed, a deep, humming baritone.

"Divide and conquer. Still works just fine. Pity about the Earth creatures, actually. A few thousand more years of evolution, and they'd be civilized enough to teach even us something. Willpower, lust for power and ruthlessness they have to spare, anyway. We didn't even really have to feed them the idea for the Inquisition—they were already happily strapping their own kind to the rack in the name of the Lord. We just steered them in the right direction a little more precisely."

He smiled pensively. "It's kind of crazy that on this little rocky sphere, the only one in all of Lei'Atuan, which they so poetically call the 'Milky Way' here, there exists this little biological discontinuity beings that has become so important to us."

"I wouldn't call spell magic a little discontinuity," the woman interrupted him. "An organically generated ability to influence one's environment energetically, that's something. And the secret to our immortality. Without those helpful little barbarians, you and I would have aged and died long ago. If it hadn't been for Bar'ukin discovering the secret of milking the elixir out of magical creatures twelve thousand years ago, when he noticed that the ability seemed to significantly prolong the life of the bearers, everything would be different today. Everything."

Uriel nodded.

"It's fortunate that the last harvest from the time of the Atlantean settlement has lasted us so long, long enough for us to find a way around the banishment spells they had put around the planet. So, by now we've been able to extract not only the ability of sorcerers to prolong their life, but the ability itself. Probably not a single one of those laughable natural mages is our equal at the moment, Triabola."

He grinned devilishly.

Triabola made an impatient hand gesture.

"Let's not get cocky, Uriel. Your apparent compatriots, the Atlanteans, can still be dangerous to us if they should see through our plans. Not to speak of the Lemurians."

The white-haired man in the yellow velvet robe laughed loudly.

"Them? They'd probably try to solve the problem with a group hug, even if they knew that each of them would end up with a knife in their backs. I still wonder how these jokers ever built such an immense star empire. Violence, cruelty and an indomitable will to exercise power, that's how you do it! But those idiots? They still think they're part of nature! Ridiculous!"

Triabola only cradled her head thoughtfully.

"Not all of that people have taken the philosophy of peace as far as their ancestors on this planet. If they can get the Aalids or even the warlike Mirkans to help, things may still get pretty warm around here."

Uriel snorted, laughing.

"Don't worry, my dear. Before anyone else off-planet realizes what's happening here, we'll already control Pyrrha, and with that comes the entire planet including its ancient Lemurian defence systems. Then it will be too late for any outside force to intervene. We'll simply blow them out of the sky."

* * *

In Rhodes

The group of mages followed the templar emissary through the narrow streets of downtown Rhodes. Built of gray stone on myriads of different levels, the narrow streets wound through rows of similar-looking stone houses.

Between most of the houses, clotheslines were stretched across the alleys on the second or third floor, producing not only a constant, softly fluttering soundscape above the heads of the travelers, but also providing a pleasant protection from the burning Aegean sun.

Kaura asked the knight about the density of people living inside the fortified town. He half turned to her and nodded. "Yes, the attacks of the Saracen pirates and more recently the Spaniards have made space inside the city walls scarce. Lately, however, we have had peace. From refugee reports, we understand that the Spanish are massing large contingents of troops in Alexandria, probably for another attack on Pyrrha."

The templar's face was troubled. "The Grand Master has seriously considered sending the Rhodes Fleet to relieve the Portal City. But unfortunately, given the ever-growing strength of the Sultanate, that would be almost certain defeat, endangering our own, precarious independence in the process."

It was obvious that he, himself, would have liked to jump into the fray swinging his sword, even with the odds being as they were.

"Have you heard anything about the Spaniards using enslaved mages, djinns and fairies in battle?", Kaura asked him. "In Algiers, they raided Mira'aleitha a few years ago and took many prisoners."

Xavier shrugged.

"We have some refugees here from that unfortunate incident, but we don't know anything about combat operations. If the sultan uses Gifted slaves himself for fighting, he does it quietly, and well he should, considering his official position on magic. We think the captives may not be alive anymore at all. The Inquisition is known to burn those they call heretics at the stake, after all, with only a sham for a trial."

"Trial, my ass," intervened Ariane, who was fluttering along with Diana beside him. "Those guys don't even know what a trial is! Or a real court of law! A fair court for the peat-heads is probably the patio where they sit and stuff seafood paella into themselves for dinner. Juice heads! Olive eaters! Long-eared chestnut cucumbers!"

Their guide cleared his throat, and his voice sounded somewhat offended.

"Well, we're quite fond of olives here too, Exalted One. Have you ever tasted these noble fruits?"

Ariane nodded and waved it off.

"It's okay, it's okay. I like olives, too. Healthy Mediterranean cuisine and all," she muttered. "But these inquisitors just drive me up the wall!"

Xavier nodded in understanding, leaving it at that, then led them further up the hill.

They paused in front of the Grand Master's palace. Kaura put her hood back to take a closer look at the imposing building. Behind her, Sen, Joe, Abigail, and the two Lockwood mages also stopped, impressed, while the three freed slaves from the pirate ship and Sir Elias caught up with them. Simon had stayed behind on the ship with five of the guard fairies so as not to leave the ship unguarded.

The gate in front of them opened with a creak, and two white-clad guards with the red Maltese cross on their chests and large, dangerous-looking halberds let them pass unhindered. Diana saluted one of them dashingly as she fluttered past the serious faces.

"Heyo, temple banger! A horny toothpick you have there! I'll get myself one like that too, I think. In fairy size, of course. Such a butt poke would be just right for me the next time I meet one of these inquisitors."

The guard's breathing deepened. He was obviously struggling to maintain his serious expression and not laugh.

"Welcome to the Grand Master's palace, Exalted One," he said solemnly.

The courtyard and then the interior of the building, though impressive in size, were only plainly furnished. The cool stone floor was covered with laid carpets, and on the walls hung scattered weapons and oil paintings depicting ancient Templar grand masters or battle scenes.

Xavier de Vauldemolai led them directly to a gate in front of which two guard fairies hovered, grinning at their kin.

"They have two fairies!" remarked Ariane. "What do they expect here, an invasion?"

One of the winged guards had heard her remark and laughed.

"Decoration, my dear. We're a sta-tus-sym-bol, honey. Cool, isn't it? Good pancakes here at the palace, by the way. We taught them. But no matter how decorative we are, if anyone tries to mess with our Grand Temple Boss, we'll flatten them, of course. Come on in."

As if moved by magic, the door opened on well-oiled hinges, and the group followed Xavier inside the hall.

Two men looked expectantly toward them. On a massive wooden chair sat the man who must be the Grand Master of the Templars. His long gray hair fell loosely over his shoulders, over which lay a red velvet sash decorated with Maltese crosses, and his lips under his already almost white beard were lifted into a friendly smile. Apart from the sash, he was elegantly but simply dressed in a black silk doublet.

With a warm look in his gray eyes, he eyed the visitors and rose.

"My name is Lance d'Armancourt. I am the current Grand Master of the Order of the Knights Templar," he greeted her in impeccable Scottish with a slight French accent.

He pointed to the dark-haired man to his right. "This here is my partner, Lex. I've been told that most of you are from Britain. So shall we speak Scottish?" he added with a sideways glance at the two djinn. "Or better, Atlantean?" The two Algerian beings replied that they could magically understand and speak all the languages of the world.

Meanwhile, unperturbed, Ariane fluttered toward the older man and pinched his nose.

"Heyo, Megaboss, great to see a real grandmaster for once! How's it going? You're a monk, right? Must be boring, what with vows of chastity and all. Do you want to touch my breasts? I'm Ariane, by the way."

The Templar smiled at her in an exceedingly friendly manner, and a mischievous glint entered his gray eyes.

"Thank you for the offer, Exalted One, uh, Ariane. But I can assure you, it's not that boring here. And the ones with the vow of chastity, those are the others over there in Granada. It's just that I personally prefer more, um, masculine attributes, if you know what I mean."

He cast a sideways glance over to Lex, who was also eyeing Ariane kindly. The fairy grinned and pinched the Grandmaster's cheek before flying back to the others.

"I can't help you with that, unfortunately, Your Grand Mufti. But I am glad to hear that you suffer no lack here in your meager walls! May the Ix bless your love!"

The green hue of the two djinns had deepened somewhat. Kaura suspected that it must be something similar to a shameful blush in these creatures and made an effort to steer the conversation in a different direction.

"My name is Kaura Alenu'ala. I come from Lemuria and am on my way to Pyrrha to open the Portal to Aalid there, to ask the Aalids for help in our fight against the Inquisition and their patrons, the Kai'ala and the 'gods'. We hope to receive information in Rhodes on how to get into Pyrrha safely."

The Grand Master had studied the dark-skinned woman intently while she spoke. He leaned forward a little.

"What is the name of the Lemurian capital?" he asked her.

Kaura answered without thinking.

"We live decentralized in scattered communities. While there are a few cities such as Ilkarion, Ar'ten, Pape'ete, and Waipio, none of them could be called a capital. The main temple of my organization, the Temple of Ferns, is located in Ilkarion."

She thought for a moment. "Do you perhaps mean Ixche'len? That's the meeting place of the united councils and priests, where big meetings are held twice a year. Not a city in the true sense, though, more a huge grassy plain with a few temples."

The Grand Master nodded with satisfaction.

"That would have been my second question. Where do the solstice celebrations and the council take place? These two sentences, and the answers to them, have been passed from grand master to grand master for centuries."

He smiled. "So, you really are from Lemuria. Are you vouching for your companions?"

When Kaura nodded, Lance stood up and beckoned them to follow him. The adjoining room seemed to be a kind of private library. In the middle of the huge red carpet was a large oval table, in the center of which a lion had been engraved and coated in pure gold.

"King Arthur's original table," the Grand Master remarked with a casual wave of his hand as the group made themselves comfortable on the heavy wooden chairs. "It was retrieved from Avalon by Merlin's people just before Cloudcastle fell a prey to flames and Merlin had to flee. A couple of deserted knights brought it here as a gift of hospitality. Not everybody accompanied him and Arthur to Atlantis and on to the Starlands, it seems. But all of this happened so long ago that it's difficult to separate fact from legend."

A servant in the already familiar livery with the Maltese cross brought fruit juices and pastries.

"Regarding vows of chastity, you might be interested to know that we actually don't think much of alcohol," the head of the Templars winked over at Ariane. "After all, an orgy is only half as much fun when you're drunk."

The fairy mustered him thoughtfully and seemed to be considering whether she should now change her basic philosophy of life.

"Hm, yes, maybe I should try that too," she mumbled absentmindedly, then leaned over to Diana and whispered something to the other fairy that no one else could hear.

Kaura turned back to Lance d'Armancourt. The Grand Master's words had made her curious.

"So, Lance, does this mean you've been to Lemuria yourself?"

He shook his head.

"Not personally, although some portals in Pyrrha were said to have been still active when I first came to the Middle East as a young knight. But we have a prophecy here that asks us to do something very specific for a Lemurian woman seeking help. A Lemurian woman who knows the name of Ixche'len. But we will get to that, my dears."

He propped his arms on the table and leaned forward. "The prophecy was made by a psychic nun about four hundred and fifty years ago. She stayed here as a guest in the palace chambers. Only the Grand Master at the time and two knights witnessed this event. She said that the survival of all mages on Gaia, and even the survival of magical talent itself, depended on this moment we are witnessing. Now I also finally believe I understand the meaning of the prophecy. Until a few years ago, it seemed completely pointless to open a back entrance to Pyrrha. You could just take a ship and sail up the Nile, and within a few days, you were there. Of course, this was of no use to us non-magicians, since we were not allowed in. But it wouldn't have been a problem for you guys back then."

His gaze clouded over. "But now the Spanish and Ottomans are pulling together more and more forces in Alexandria. Our own scouts have not been in the area for a long time, but according to reliable rumors, the Inquisitors have surrounded Pyrrha in several lines of siege and are not letting anyone through."

The Grand Master explained that the city was the best shielded area on all of Gaia, protected by magical fields created thousands of years ago by unimaginably powerful beings. The Inquisitors could do no more than besiege it and cut off the supply routes. It was assumed in Rhodes, however, that self-sufficiency should not be a problem in principle for a city full of mages. It was unclear, however, why they did not defend themselves and let the Spaniards have their way. Lance was silent for a moment.

Sen leaned forward, curious.

"What do you know about the portals in Pyrrha, Lance? In Merlin's time, most travel seems to have taken place through such portals—there were over twenty portal halls magically connected on the British Isles alone. Today we know of only two, that we operate at times with a huge expenditure of energy."

The old grandmaster rose, walked over to one of the floor-to-ceiling shelves crammed with books of all colors and formats, and pulled out a small volume bound in gray leather. He placed the book on the table and slid it over to Sen. HISTORIA PORTALIS was written in gold-stamped letters on the cover.

"The book is sealed with a protective spell, but any magically gifted person is supposed to be able to open it, or so it says on the backcover. The authors obviously wanted to avoid that non-magicians would get to read this work. You are welcome to look at it while you are guests in the palace."

With an almost greedy expression in his blue eyes, Sen stared at the book, gently stroking its rough cover.

Ariane leaned over to him a little.

"What I wouldn't give to have you look at me like that, super-boss," she whispered teasingly, nudging him with her elbow. The headmaster did not pay any attention to her. He listened attentively to the Templar, who was now continuing his tale.

"To make a long story short, Pyrrha was the central power supply and portal point for Gaia, this planet we are on here. Some also call it Earth, Terra, or Solaris Terza, the third planet of this star system. Anyway, Pyrrha was—or is, I don't know for sure—the only place on the planet with enough energy to feed portals to reach not only all places on the globe, but also planets of other suns and maybe even other galaxies. Other, locally powered portals seem to have been limited to a few hundred to perhaps a thousand nautical miles."

Joe and Abigail stared at the gray-bearded man as if he had just lost his mind.

"Are you saying other planets exist like ours?" the Scotsman asked, puzzled. "And there were *Portals* to reach them?"

The old Templar raised his shoulders.

"Why not? Even the ancient Hellenic philosophers told us that each of those little stars out there in the night sky is a sun, just like ours. I'm just telling you what's in my clever books here. I have not been there myself. But even Pyrrha is said to be a fascinating city. Fireless torches. Alchemical devices that control the weather. Floating buildings. Music playing from the air everywhere."

Lance's eyes became dreamy. "The landmark of Pyrrha, it is said, is the Central Lighthouse, a huge, dazzling pyramid of light, hovering point-down over an even more enormous pyramid clad in white marble, which is said to rise over six hundred feet into the sky above the roofs of the city. Lord in Heaven, if only I could get to see that sight one day!"

He turned to Kaura.

"But if I am not mistaken, you could tell us much more about it. After all, it was your people who built Pyrrha, wasn't it?"

Kaura was silent for a moment and breathed deeply. Her eyes were lost in the far distance. She seemed to be thinking about how to begin. Then she began to speak.

"Pyrrha had been planned as the neutral capital of all earthly mages and magical beings. That must have been many millennia ago, long before even I was born. My ancestors, the ancient Lemurians, came from the celestial region we now call the Pleiades. They had discovered space travel many thousands of years earlier, built great starships of magically hardened steel and other metals, and set out for the stars. They found that there were innumerable habitable planets in the Milky Way, on which life in all possible stages of development existed. On some, where intelligent beings lived, they were received in good faith, and trade relations developed. For example, with the fairy beings on Sirius Quinta," she nodded to Ariane, Diana and Delpha.

The fairies listened with big, colorful, shimmering eyes, saying nothing, so she continued.

"On other worlds they were not welcome, and they traveled on. At that time, it is said, there were no desires for colonies, great empires, and no lust for power to rule over other peoples and make profit at the expense of others. Only the honest interest to get to know the life of other cultures and to become friendly with them. Many of the discovered planets were also still uninhabited, untouched by intelligent life forms. There, too, Lemurians settled and lived in harmony with the alien nature of other worlds. When they first set foot on this planet here, Gaia, they realized that there was something here that they had not found anywhere in the universe before: magic, similar to that of the fairies, but also accessible to them."

Kaura fell silent for a moment.

"Is this even interesting to you guys?" she asked. When everyone in the room nodded, she continued. "The ancient Lemurians moved the center of their world-spanning realm here, to the continent between what is now called the New World and Cipangu in Asia, the continent which we still inhabit today. They called it Lemuria, in reference to the mythical capital of their Pleiadian founders. The rest of the world was probably regarded as a kind of nature preserve, in which the Lemurians, however, quite tolerated the settlement or new development of other intelligent living beings. Meanwhile, the cosmic expansion movement continued for millennia. With new kinds of starships and huge portals, similar to those in Pyrrha, only much larger and floating in space to allow ships to travel through, the explorers even reached other galaxies, millions of light years away."

"That's really, really far. Almost unimaginably far." she added, noticing the blank expressions on everyone's faces except the fairies'. "Anyway, over the millennia, almost all of the old Lemurians' descendants lived somewhere on planets far away from here, adapting to their environment. The ancient Lemurian culture, left behind on Earth, had always been focused on living in harmony with nature, with the exception of some periods of, let's say, cultural turmoil. The birth rate was kept low by magical means since the natural life expectancy of members of my people is already several hundred years even without the life-prolonging measures that we know today. The Lemurians, thanks to their magic and superior alchemical apparatus, had become unimaginably powerful, almost godlike. By the way, it has proven over the millennia that the very magical abilities gained on earth were slowly lost to the descendants of the emigrants who went to live on other planets. There seems to be an energy field here on Gaia that is unique in the universe known so far—we call it the terranean field. Of course, there are beings gifted with magic on other planets as well, such as the fairies. But we assume that they use a fundamentally different kind of field. Which is probably why our collar release technique works the way it does," she said with a glance at Sen and the others.

As the uniqueness of Terra's magic field had slowly become known in the Milky Way, the number of immigrants to Gaia had steadily increased. The Lemurians had been largely content on their continent, and although there had been famous Lemurian travelers, they had remained mainly among themselves. Djinns, fairies, and isolated, returned descendants of planets settled by the Lemurians had settled on various parts of the earth. However, when the Lemurians realized that many were not as careful with the treasures of Gaia and her nature as they would have liked, they, with the help of some off-planet civilizations, first placed a technomagic field around the Earth that prevented the use of damaging high technology.

The high priestess blinked wearily.

"Please understand, this was several tens of thousands of years ago. Even in our country, this is largely legend, where fact is hard to distinguish from fiction. The immigrants were first to learn to live in harmony with their environment before handling potentially destructive technology, often brought from their home planets. Earth was to remain a magical, not a technological planet. However, the Lemurians—this is quite a weakness of my people—did not apply the same standards to themselves in full. Nevertheless, for example, the use and landing of interstellar starships on the planet was forbidden for all, since it was considered damaging to the atmosphere. As a substitute, my ancestors created Pyrrha—a distribution and travel center through which one could reach any place on Earth and many points in the known universe without pollution- and noise-producing ships. Those planets that were not part of this portal system could be reached via far out star port hubs."

For a few more millennia this had gone well. Since Pyrrha had been the only place on Gaia except Lemuria where high technology was allowed to be used, and the Lemurians were not too particular about the kind of technology allowed, the desert city's population increased over time to several hundred thousand magical beings and Gifted humans from all planets.

"Meanwhile, my people in the Pacific, I can't say it any other way, continued to degenerate, if we just look at the technical development. It seemed simply that no one was particularly interested in those things anymore. In our magic, on the other hand, we became more refined, more light-filled, and the Lemurian culture of that time could probably be taken as a prime example of non-violent, transparent and loving community. This also brought with it a certain small-scale society. In any case, it could well be argued that we were progressing more and more spiritually despite our diminishing knowledge. If any technical solution was still needed, we enlisted the descendants of Lemurian emigrants from outside, who had retained their engineering skills due to the lack of possibility to achieve the same with magic, and even refined them more and more. Can you still listen?"

She looked questioningly at Lance.

The old knight nodded with a smile.

"Very interesting, High Priestess. Lemurian history in fast forward. I don't think anyone outside the Pacific Ocean has had the benefit of this information for a very long time. Please continue."

The Lemurian bowed her head in agreement.

"Anyway, that went well until about ten thousand years ago. Then came the Atlanteans. And then my personal history begins, too, but that seems less relevant to me at the moment."

Sen almost choked on his cup of grape juice, and Diana and Ariane immediately fluttered over to pat him on the back.

When the scene had calmed down again, Kaura continued.

"According to your chronology, that was about the year 8,000 before Buddha, around the time of my birth. The Atlanteans of today are descendants of returned Lemurian settlers who had maintained some connections with the Aztec and Celtic cultures that had since arisen on both sides of the great European Ocean, who considered them Gods. They had tried for millennia on their planet, Ata-Lan, to engineer magical abilities by biotechnical means. With some success, but as a cost, as we later learned. As you may know, today's Atlanteans still work with energetically charged objects such as crystals or copper amulets and machines, and very complicated rituals that are specified to the last detail. Anyway, one day they were suddenly here, occupying what is now the double isle of Atlantis, which stretches in a wide arc from the Irish peninsula to the Te'ide volcanic archipelago off the coast of North Africa. As far as I remember, the arrival of the Atlanteans didn't particularly worry anyone at the time. It was on the other side of the globe, the area they had chosen was scarcely populated, and people felt connected to them by kinship ties, albeit thousands of years old. While there had never been an immigration wave of this magnitude—the Atlanteans were estimated at several hundred thousand—it was assumed that there would simply be enough space for everyone."

Her gaze clouded over before she continued. "The Fern Temple even sent mages to establish new portal connections to Pyrrha and between the cities of their lands. They never came back, and the Temple sent investigating priestesses who returned without having found out what had happened to them. Later we found out that the mages had probably fallen victim to scientific experiments, abducted by Kai'ala spies already operating undetected in Atlantis at that time. At that time, however, no one suspected anything, nor did anyone connect the rapid, unexplained weakening of the Source with it—a very similar weakening to the one we can observe now. The reason this was not investigated as thoroughly as it could have been, was that, for the first time after millennia of harmony and cooperation, Lemuria found itself in a difficult situation domestically. There were conflicts and power plays between an increasingly repressive Settler Council—a kind of public government and the Fern Temple, so everyone was even more preoccupied with themselves than normal. It wasn't until a few years later, when it was discovered that the magic field over the Atlantean continent had been overridden by counter-crystal magic and a secret starport had been established, that the Temple felt compelled to intervene. Especially since, at that time, the harvesting expeditions of the Kai'ala and their then-unknown masters were also assuming greater and greater proportions, and more and more mages were simply disappearing without a trace, all over the world and also in Lemuria."

Kaura took a deep breath. "It turned out that the Atlanteans, though willing accomplices because of their technical affiliation, had no idea of the true plans of the Kai'ala and had themselves been manipulated. A fierce battle ensued, from which we emerged victorious only thanks to the support of Atlantean crystal priests who had changed sides. Afterwards, we strengthened the already extremely complex technomagic protective field around Gaia, limiting communications and travel to Earth purely to the portals controlled by the Pyrrhean Council. This made people feel safe again. The Atlanteans who had not been allied with the Kai'ala also agreed to this solution but were able to negotiate far-reaching concessions regarding the use of technology on their own lands, before the Treaty of Ilkarion was signed."

Thus, peace had reigned for some millennia more, and the human civilizations outside of the isolated island continents had developed more and more. The Lemurians and the Atlanteans had sometimes intervened to help or direct but had largely kept their hands out of the affairs of the other budding cultures on Gaia. Then, about seven hundred years ago, shortly after the conquest of Europe by Genghis Khan, the off-planet portals of Pyrrha had simply closed.

Kaura raised her shoulders.

"No one knew exactly why, and since Pyrrha's technomagic central energetics had been established long before our time, we couldn't find the fault. Neither could we shut down the technomagic shield and bring in support with the few starships remaining in Lemuria. In short, we had become prisoners of our own protective measures. And for some reason that I still don't fully understand even after I regained my memories, even then nobody did something decisive. I had gone into retirement some centuries earlier already and didn't even realize something was amiss until, much later, the Temple sought me out in my hermitage and asked me to return to the council."

The connections between the earthly portals had also shut down seemingly of their own, one by one over the years, she continued. This process had begun shortly after that time and had lasted for several centuries. In the end, only a few portals within Europe had been open, and even these had closed a few decades earlier, without anyone being able to do anything about it or find the cause.

Kaura lowered her eyes and remained silent, seeming to consider how to proceed. Then she continued to speak, quietly but firmly.

"Then ten years ago, the disappearance of magical beings began again. Because my people live in such seclusion, it took some time for us to even learn about it, and it was from an outside visitor. It turned out that all of Lemuria had been surrounded by a magical shield that immediately killed any Lemurian who tried to cross it. This shook up even the most inert among us. We immediately tried to bring the starships back into service. But their main power sources had dried up, and we had no more technomages. That's when I decided to take another look at the dead portals. There is a way for strong high mages to magically pass through a dead portal, as Sen can confirm, although the risk of trying that on an interplanetary one is exceedingly high. After observing the spell-field surrounding our continent for some months, we noticed an irregularly occurring weakness in the death spell. We used a weave to hide my Lemurian energy signature so that I could get through the trap surrounding our continent in one of those moments. Unfortunately, in order to do this, we had to make my gift and much of my memory inaccessible and hide it, even from myself. So, when I set out for Pyrrha, I initially refrained from reactivating my abilities, hoping that this would make it easier to get through the blockade of the Spaniards in front of the portal city. This turned out to be a mistake, because on the way my ship sank, and I also lost the rest of my memory, presumably due to an Atlantean mental ray. At least, there was an Atlantean hover-ship present at the time when the ship went down. The role of the Atlanteans in this event is still not entirely clear to me. In any case, I lost a lot of time during which the Kai'ala and their cronies could continue their mischief unchecked. That is all.

We Lemurians have unfortunately not been able to fulfill our role as protectors of Solaris Terza as well as I'd have wished, lately."

For a very long moment, no one said anything. Sen stared at the Lemurian about as if she had just told him that she was really a green-striped elephant and had only disguised herself.

"And you're, uh, ten-thousand-years-old?" he finally asked. "I know you said you were old, but I wasn't imagining anything on that scale."

Kaura raised her shoulders. "What's a few years more or less? I had a good time, generally."

"But didn't you say Lemurians only reached an age of a few hundred years?" interjected Joe.

Kaura shrugged again. "There are special rules for high priest-esses. And I personally had, shall we say, an interesting encounter with a very extraordinary being at one time. I'm not really immortal, at least not absolutely. Just well preserved."

She smiled faintly. "Due to violence or an accident, my body can still die. However, we all know that this would not signify an end to things for us, not on the soul level, anyway."

Everyone was silent for a long time and seemed to be processing what had been said. Joe Nelson broke the silence.

"For a ten-thousand-year-old, you have a really healthy libido, I say."

Ariane immediately stepped in.

"Ha, the older the crunchier, take it from me, blondie! Do you have any idea how old we fairies get? I knew one on Sirius Duo once, she was sixteen thousand one hundred and seven and still throwing sex parties! Great girl!"

Sen made placating hand motions.

"Guys, take it easy. I've got to integrate this first!"

"You're not getting old, are you, superboss?" the fairy purred.

"You're not more than, say, two hundred or so. Young whipper-snapper!"

The headmaster was now a bit miffed.

"Well, that one is ten thousand and looks like twenty-five! And I shrivel up at two hundred and six like an old fart."

"Don't worry about it, superboss," Ariane comforted him. "We like you anyway! You want a young-looking wish?"

Sen waved her offer off generously, though his eyes lit up with interest for a moment.

"Later, maybe, thanks," he said. In the meantime, the Grand Master of the Knights Templar had slid a little closer to Diana and was whispering to her.

"He probably wants a young-looking wish too," Kaura thought with amusement. "Or, he wants to increase his male attribute," Ariane whispered to her behind her hand. "That's what you were thinking, right?"

Kaura giggled. Despite the responsibility that weighed on her, at that moment she felt again the lightness of the young woman without memory in Inmarsund. Great mother, this time had really done wonders for her. She hadn't felt that human in centuries.

"Are you reading my mind now too, bad girl?" she asked. "I don't even need to," the fairy replied. "I always thought ten-thousand-year-old high priestesses were, ahem, mysterious, inscrutable, above it all. But I can tell from your face what's going on inside you right now."

"Probably the five years in Inmarsund did me good," Kaura replied.

The fairy grinned, and then became serious again.

"But honestly, your Lemurian colleagues are real snorebags. The things you put up with are unbelievable. As long as there's still a tree somewhere in the world that you can collectively hug, every-thing's fine, right? Meanwhile, these blue-noses are kidnapping half the world's population and doing who-knows-what with it, probably with the support of the crystal pranksters in Atlantis. And the most powerful mage guild in the known universe is practicing self-reflection. Snoozing slowpokes!"

Kaura lowered her eyes.

"You're right, Ariane, and I'm not excluding myself at all. I may not have been the snoozer-in-chief, but I could have done more. The only ray of hope is that my people are now beginning to wake up. I wouldn't be surprised if things will soon change again on Gaia. Admittedly, the situation wasn't much different ten thousand years ago. But I think this time we've been shaken up hard enough not to fall asleep again."

"Yoy, let's hope you haven't heard the holy waking jingle too late," grumbled the fairy. "Otherwise, we may all soon be asleep forever."

The Grand Master, who wore an extremely satisfied expression on his face after his discussion with Diana, spoke up.

"Maybe we can speed things up a bit. You have come to the right place, Kaura Alenu'ala. Follow me. Joe, Sen, and your fairy friend can also come along. It's better if there aren't too many of us. Lex and Xavier, meanwhile, will show the rest of you to their rooms."

He waved at them, and walked over to one of the book racks that stood over two yards wide against the north wall of the room. Nimbly, he put his hand in the space between two books on human anatomy and seemed to be doing some kind of manipulation.

Something clicked inside the shelf. The bookcase silently turned inward on a hinge, revealing the dark, yawning entrance to a hidden passageway of rough-hewn sandstone.

Lance took an oil lamp from its hook on the wall, beckoned Kaura to follow, and stepped into the dark opening with a determined stride.

3

The Gaia Amulet

Kaura made a yellowish ball of light appear in her hand and was the first to follow the grandmaster into the hidden opening in the bookshelf. Behind her, Sen, who had done the same, and the others followed. The shelf closed automatically behind them.

A winding staircase led them upward to a higher room. Once upstairs, the old grandmaster put the lamp on the floor, and looked for something on the wall.

"Ah, here it is," he grumbled. "I haven't been up here in a very, very long time."

A click sounded, and suddenly the room was bathed in warm, golden light. In all four corners of the chamber, small glass jars lit up, remotely resembling oil lamps, though gleaming without the flicker of a natural flame. Somewhere, something was humming piercingly. One wall of the room suddenly began to flicker, and an image of nocturnal Rhodes appeared, as if seen from a window high up in the palace. Kaura looked around as the others came out of the archway behind her, their eyes narrowed against the glare.

The room was almost as large as the reception hall where they had first met Lance but had nothing else in common with the rest of the palace. The walls were covered with plain vertical slats of light-colored wood, with some space between each. A whiff of fresh air flowed from the vertical gaps. The buzzing seemed to come from behind them.

In front of the window-like wall was a large table with nine oddly shaped seats that looked soft, rounded, and somehow almost alive. Otherwise, the room was dominated by a freestanding archway that looked like the scaled-down entrance gate of a Greek temple.

"A portal," Kaura breathed. Somewhat next to the arch stood a metallic cube, above which mysterious reflections of light and color shone up in mid-air.

As the Lemurian approached, she realized that it was characters and diagrams trailing across various surfaces of the cube as well as above it. In another corner, a dark metal sphere floated unsupported in the air.

Next to the sphere a dumbbell-shaped thing—two golden balls connected by a cylindrical handle—lay on a golden stand engraved with characters. The device was about five inches long and small enough to be carried in a pocket.

"Welcome to the secret sanctum of the Palace of Rhodes," said the master. "This room was probably created by the Ancients in anticipation of this very moment. The prophecy has come true. For generations the Grand Masters of the Templars have been waiting for the moment when 'the ageless traveler from Lemuria will reveal herself, call the name Ixche'len, and lead the peoples of Gaia back to their ancient greatness.' As I understand it, this is the control center for all the facilities on Gaia created by the ancient Lemurians at the time the portals were established. Unfortunately, I can't operate it. We don't even understand the glowing symbols above that metal thing over there."

Questioningly, he looked at Kaura.

She nodded.

"Yes, that should be fine. But I will need some time to understand what can be done with the machines in this room. This is a control cube," she said with a nod toward the metal thing.

"And that thing over there looks an awful lot like a portal to me," Sen added.

The Grand Master nodded.

"There is a second gate of this type in the public area of the palace, which supposedly gave direct access to Pyrrha long ago."

In the meantime, Kaura had stepped in front of the metal cube and looked at the characters flashing on it.

"Ancient Lemurian," she muttered, "Probably the control device is voice-activated."

She said a few words in a language unknown to the others, and the activity of the cube seemed to intensify. A croaking sound rang out, and a voice seemingly coming from nowhere answered. Then some new diagrams and pictures appeared in the air above the cube, shimmering reddish.

Kaura worked with the highest concentration. She was only surprised that apparently everyone who came here and spoke ancient Lemurian was allowed to operate the device. She asked the auroric intelligence of the operating device about it.

"Your authorization, determined via mental key, is: Lemurian, security level High Priestess, maximum access rights," the device replied.

She breathed a sigh of relief. So not everyone here could do whatever they wanted.

"What is the status of the portals to Aalid, Mirkan and Il'aia?" she asked.

"Outstations: Signal ready to receive. The available power on

Gaia is insufficient to hold a permanent connection, however, so the devices are dormant."

Well, she already knew that. But at least the counterparts still seemed to exist.

A thought came to her.

"Is this portal here functional? Can you switch it to Aalid?"

"Negative. Insufficient power to reach off-planet receiving sites without reconnecting to central supply in Pyrrha. By means of emergency switching in Pyrrha, the portal from there to Aalid can be opened for one minute thirteen seconds."

"Can the main power supply in Pyrrha be restored to reopen all the portals?" she continued.

"Negative. Transformer stations in earth's core not responding. Cause unknown. Technical support unreachable," the device replied in a monotone drone. "Gaia central brain currently running on minimum function and emergency power supply. All auxiliary functions disabled."

"Can you also open planetary portals from here when the counterparts are powerless?"

"Affirmative. The security circuit of the central brain can connect this portal even without a remote station to any place on the planet, for a maximum of thirty seconds, after which the energy storage must be regenerated. Regeneration at the present state of supply takes five to ten days, depending on the distance of the previous connection. No connections are possible to the continent of Lemuria and to the inner world, due to unexplained technomagic interference that cannot be overcome with the available energy resources."

"If I travel somewhere in this way, how do I get back here from there?"

"Contact by means of the control device is possible at any

time if the authorization and sufficient energy for the transfer are available."

A graphic image of the dumbbell-shaped something on the stand appeared above the metal cube.

"Can you send us from here to Pyrrha?"

"Disturbances in the field increase the risk for malfunctions. There appear to be heavy magical interference energies around the central portal courtyard. A risk analysis will take several hours as the fluctuations in the field must be monitored. Shall I start the analysis?"

Kaura answered in the affirmative and asked the brain some other questions. Then she turned back to her companions.

Sen and Joe, not understanding a word of Kaura's conversation with the central brain, had sat down and were now lounging on the soft armchairs that had organically conformed to their bodies and were visibly performing massage movements.

"Ah, that feels good!" exclaimed Sen. "I haven't had a real massage in weeks. Did you know we have one of those in Lockwood?"

The London merchant's son shook his head.

"Never heard of them. If they're even half as good as these, I'll be happy to buy one from you..."

They both looked up when Kaura sat down with them. The Templar, who had been gazing pensively down at the lights of his city, now joined them again, too.

The priestess leaned back in her chair with a comfortable sigh. The events of the last weeks united in her in a polyphonic tangle of thoughts, impressions and feelings. Suddenly she felt more exhausted than ever before in her long life.

"Our situation has indeed improved considerably with the discovery of this room," she opined. "As Lance correctly pointed out, this is a direct access to the planet's central brain created by the ancient Lemurians. Its capabilities, however, appear to be limited, as it too relied primarily on Pyrrha's power supply."

She shrugged. "Still, much, much better than nothing. We can reach any point on the planet from here. We'll see if the same is true for Pyrrha, since the Kai'ala's anti-magic field is obviously interfering with the connection. The brain is currently analyzing this."

She turned to Joe. "What still concerns me is your role. The Kai'ala were looking for a key from you, seemingly in some way connected to the Portals. I still feel like I'm missing something essential here."

She looked at the Grand Master. The latter returned the look seriously and considered for a moment, but said nothing. He looked like an old Greek statue of a bearded hero of legends.

Kaura screwed up her face.

"The Inquisitors simply seem to know something about Joe that we don't. Well, maybe we'll find out more in Pyrrha. By tomorrow morning, the brain should be able to tell us if we can travel there directly. Let's get some sleep until then."

"And send a message down to the ship to tell them that we'll be staying in the palace," added Sen. "Simon and the fairies will want to join us."

The next morning, Kaura went back to the control room on her own before breakfast. The field analysis was finished by now, and the brain had identified a location within Pyrrha where a portal could be opened with an acceptable risk for malfunctions.

She stood pondering in front of the large, artificial window and looked out at the city, behind which the sun was just rising. Was she the right person for this task? Was she perhaps leading her friends to certain death by taking them into a besieged city whose protections could collapse at any moment under the onslaught of the Inquisitors? And yet, who should be able to put this unfortunate matter in order if not she? She was, without any doubt, one of the most powerful mages currently on Gaia. And she was a representative of the guild which had made itself guilty by its disinterest in the problem while things hadn't gone so far yet.

Kaura shook herself angrily. "Guilt or no guilt, it doesn't matter!" she muttered softly to herself. "I should know by now that it doesn't matter. Everything unfolds in accordance with the Great Plan of the Almighty Mother. I have the means to do something I deem necessary, and I can take responsibility. So, I do it. And the others know what they are doing as well. I have not deceived anyone about what we are heading towards."

She stepped up to the stand holding up the golden device and took it in her hand. She felt the handle of the dumbbell nestle into her palm and begin to interact with her. She knew now it was set to her personal vibration and would not serve anyone else who was not explicitly authorized by her to do so.

With a little sigh, she put the thing in her bag and went downstairs, looking for a terrace where she could watch the sunrise in reality and be alone a little longer. She hadn't meditated in far too long.

When she met her companions again at breakfast, she immediately noticed the Templar Grand Master's depressed mood.

"Bad news?" she asked.

Lance nodded.

"Unfortunately. During the night a carrier pigeon reached us from our envoy in Alexandria. The Spanish have launched their biggest offensive yet on Pyrrha. Thousands of soldiers and magical slaves are moving east through the city, with no end in sight. I fear you are entering a witches' cauldron."

"Well then, it's a good thing most of us are witches," Simon tried to joke, having arrived at the palace later that night along with the rest of the fairies. "We'll muddle through somehow."

In contrast to the sparse interior of the Templars' residence, the breakfast that the palace kitchen had prepared for them was extremely opulent.

Four different kinds of olives, platters of feta and other cheeses, boiled eggs, all kinds of salads with tomatoes and finely sliced cucumbers, crispy grilled flatbreads, Greek yogurt with a variety of exotic fruits, and much more. After the rather monotonous meals on the *Pride*, this seemed like paradise to everyone.

When they were all satiated and only the smell of the sweet Turkish coffee reached their noses, Kaura informed them of the result of Gaias calculations and about her plan. "The information from Alexandria has not changed anything," she concluded.

"It seems all the more important that we get into Pyrrha as soon as possible and try to open the gate. If the Inquisitors capture the city, we will also lose our last chance to reach the outside world. I will use the portal this afternoon to get inside the perimeter. Those who wish to accompany me are welcome. You know the danger. With this device here,"—she pulled the dumbbell from her pocket—"we should be able to get back to Rhodes if something goes wrong. But we don't know what will happen if Pyrrha's magical defense fields fail. The same thing might happen as in Algiers. Maybe then we'll be stuck."

Ariane squealed in delight.

"No risk, no fun," she giggled. "Did I ever tell you that my middle names are Daring and Heroism? Ariane D.H. Tinkerbell. Sounds good, doesn't it? You might want to get yourself a middle name, too, Lemur Kitten." She pinched Kaura's cheek. "After ten thousand years, you deserve something like this. How about Super Witch? You could even have the initials stitched on your dress! Or World Savior?"

Sen ignored the fairy and leaned forward seriously.

"I'm with you, Kaura. For the same reasons as before."

He turned to the rest of the Lockwood magicians. "None of you need be ashamed to return to Scotland now or to wait for us here. I'd like a few of us to stay here anyway, so that in case of doubt we can intervene from the outside or bring in more help."

Simon and Eagle came forward almost simultaneously.

"I'm in, too, of course, Sen!" they said in chorus, while the fairies loudly bawled their approval and Irene, somewhat sheepishly, also announced her willingness to travel with the group to Pyrrha.

Joe grinned weakly. He seemed to hesitate, but then nodded as well.

Abigail, on the other hand, waved it off.

"War is not really my thing, honestly. I'd rather stay here and try to negotiate some new trade relations for the Nelson family. Maybe you can help me with that," she said, addressing the Templars.

A little later, everything was settled. Abigail would stay in Rhodes along with Irene and two of the guard fairies, as would the Nelson galleon. One of the fairies would fly all the way across the continent to give the British mages the disturbing news, especially the existence of the collars and the Inquisition's use of magical slaves.

Diana hoped that her fairy could make the trip in a little more than five days. Joe additionally gave a verbal message for his mother in London to finally fill her in on his release and what had happened since.

Around noon, the whole group met on the roof of the palace to accompany the departure of the messenger fairy—her name was Maria—with their good wishes.

Sen and Kaura put protective spells around the little creature to ensure unhindered flight and safe arrival.

With a "I'm off then, Superboss! Leave some of the inquisitors for me, saps!", Maria soared into the air and disappeared like a shimmering green butterfly over the brightly glistening Mediterranean Sea.

Fifteen minutes later, the remaining companions found themselves in the control room. All of them, even the mages, were armed to the teeth with muskets, blank weapons and multi-barreled pistols.

"If this barrier field should catch us, I want to at least blow the heads off a few inquisitors before they put a collar on me," Sen had remarked, and everyone had agreed.

Like an honor guard, the three Templars and the friends staying in Rhodes had lined up on either side of the Portal. Kaura was engrossed in conversation with the control module in the dark metal cube, trying to get some last information about the facilities in Pyrrha. The rest had gathered in front of the portal.

Then the familiar blue wafting flickered up inside the archway. Here, however, it was accompanied by an intensification of the buzzing from the hall walls. Involuntarily, the companions gripped their weapons a little tighter. No one knew what they would meet on the other side of the gate.

Then a yellow marble ball at the top of the archway suddenly changed color and turned purple.

Kaura joined the others and nodded.

"We can go. The field is stable." The fairies immediately shot into the blue field like flickering arrows and disappeared. A little slower, Sen and Kaura stepped through one after the other, and the others followed them. About ten seconds later, the blue waft disappeared, and the buzzing from the walls became quieter again.

The voice from the control cube said something that none of the people now still in the room understood.

"Let's hope that was something like 'trip successfully completed'," Abigail muttered. Then she turned and followed the Templars down to the dining room. It was time for a late lunch.

* * *

Only a few seconds later, in the Quarter of the Luminous Sphinx, Pyrrha

Kaura was close to unconsciousness. Around her, colored lightning bloomed like the fire flowers of Mongolian pyronics, and the world spun at the seams. She felt nauseous, and her stomach contents began to rise. She breathed deeply, and the impulse to vomit lessened. Then, the disorientation was over, too, and she looked around in the darkness, which at first seemed impenetrable.

Next to her, someone was retching. Sen must have landed on his knees and was vomiting uncontrollably at Kaura's feet. She quickly stepped aside, although she still couldn't see anything at all. Behind her, the others pressed on.

Then a small light blossomed, from the end of a small wand. Diana, the fairy, grinned at her and blinked down at Sen's softly jingling mop of blond hair.

"Portal sickness, huh. Didn't think I'd ever see the superboss like that. But well, that was truly intense."

Kaura nodded, still trying to control her own nausea.

"Probably an effect of the magic blocking field that the Inquisitors installed. I can't explain it any other way. Portal travel should be completely imperceptible to the traveler," she explained.

Beside her, Sen straightened up again and wiped his mouth. "Great mother, what was that all about?" he asked. "Where are we, anyway? This is darker than a pig's stomach!"

Diana just smiled in understanding.

"Everything's under control, superboss! Your irreplaceably clever helpers have already looked around while you were decorating the floor. I think you're going to need a cleaning wish soon. You stink."

She contorted her pretty face into a grimace and swung her staff. The penetrating smell of vomit disappeared immediately.

"We are in a small rock chamber below a large statue. Woman

with cat body. Pretty hot. The woman, I mean. The climate, too, though. It's afternoon. We don't seem to have made a time jump this time."

Diana laughed as bright as a bell and motioned ahead. "The exit is over there. Sifa and Milaria just snuck out to scout the situation. So far, no one seems to have noticed us. They're all running around like startled chickens."

As Kaura's eyes adjusted to the semi-darkness, she also saw the bright glimmer that cast a faint reflection on the finely grained white marble wall behind the glowing fairy staff. That had to be the entrance. Cautiously, she groped her way forward, glad that the nausea was slowly receding without also forcing her to 'decorate the floor.'

Meanwhile, Ariane sat on her shoulder and remained unusually silent. Perhaps she, too, was nauseous—unlike her fellow fairies, who darted happily about like little colorful birds. Once in the front part of the dark room, she found one of the guard fairies sitting on a makeshift-looking board shack that blocked the lower half of the opening. The boards were probably meant to keep trespassers from entering the chamber.

The winged creature leaning against the wall looked like she was on vacation. Like a noblewoman who has just arrived at her summer residence and enjoyed the sweet idleness, Kaura thought to herself. How did the fairies do that, remain so calm even in extreme danger?

The fairy casually waved a wingtip as if she had guessed Kaura's thoughts.

"Looks like we're just in time, dearest bossbitch!", she drawled. "The blue space-turtles and their Spanish pets seem to have found a way to get past the barriers. But, magic still works." To prove it, she gently lit up the tip of her wand and picked her nose with it.

Cautiously, Kaura peeked beyond the wooden barrier into the bright sunlight. Behind her, Sen and Eagle had appeared as well.

The square they looked out onto had been made in what appeared to be a single piece of dark pavement, broken in some places by white marble slabs in the shapes of esoteric symbols. Flowers and palms grew on small, carefully tended islands of grass, rustling their fronds in the sweltering desert wind. The edge of the square was surrounded by low buildings. Between their columns of orange sandstone gleamed large, unpartitioned expanses of dark, obsidian glass that seemed to function as outer walls or doors.

The glass-like surfaces reflected the large statue of a reclining cat-woman, from whose pedestal the companions looked out. This had to be the Sphinx. Although it was made of stone, the statue was said to come to life once a year at spring solstice and to walk the perimeter of the magical city to renew the protective spells.

There was little movement in the square. A few men in purple uniforms and carrying black, musket-like weapons hurried by. A few women wrapped in different colored cloths walked in the other direction, not much slower.

Kaura waved to her companions before swinging over the wooden barricade with an energetic movement.

"Come! We'll check out the situation at the town hall and then head for the Portal to Aalid as soon as possible. The town hall is on the way there."

Just as she was about to disappear into one of the side alleys, one of the fairies bolted around the corner of the statue's pedestal. Her red hair was disheveled, and she wore a harried expression on her face.

"Serious business, boss," she gasped, turning to Sen. "It appears that the Inquisitors have breached a hole in the shield. Over a hundred Inquisitors and magical slaves are channeling tremendous amounts of energy against the shield to keep the hole open. The Pyrrhean Guard and a few mages are fighting at the entrance, holding their ground so far. And elsewhere, large beams of light are hammering against the shield like battering rams on all sides of the city. Do you hear the thunder? That's them. But so far, only the one gap there has been created."

She pointed to the north with her small hand. "A stray hit got through to me."

She stroked her singed hair, which gave off a pervasive, nauseating odor. "I was able to wish a protective field around me just in time."

Sen grabbed Kaura by the sleeve.

"You can handle your thing together with Ariane and Joe, right? Then I'll take my people and see if we can help at the breach. At the very least, we can buy you more time. Call me telepathically and give me your coordinates when you're ready. Then we'll retreat to the portal and join you. Tell the people at City Hall that we're there and on their side."

When the Lemurian nodded, he spoke briefly to Diana, then the whole group stormed around the statue and away to the north.

Kaura, followed by Joe and Ariane, turned to the west. There, three huge, pyramid-shaped stone formations rose into the air. Above the middle pyramid, which appeared to be at least three hundred yards high, hovered a light structure, also pyramidal, with its tip pointing downward. An unsteady, golden arc of light flickered between the two tips, seeming to stop briefly every now and then.

When they reached the great avenue of splendor that seemed to stretch through the center of the city, Kaura suddenly shivered. The temperature of the air had dropped from the sweltering heat prevailing in the square in front of the Sphinx to no more than what would have been expected in Baltic Inmarsund on a balmy late summer day.

"So, part of the energy supply still works," she thought, and hurried on, past gardens seemingly suspended in mid-air and rushing waterfalls, across squares with larger-than-life statues of famous magicians and sorcerers of antiquity, of all species present on Earth. The avenue was lined with flowering hibiscus and jasmine bushes and huge, shady plane trees, the monumental buildings of marble, sandstone, steel and glass were decorated and ornamented in the most opulent way.

The brightness of the sun was dimmed down to a pleasant level everywhere. Birds chirped and sang, while in the background the thunder produced by the Spanish energy attacks boomed like something out of place, not at all fitting to this picture of peace. Almost no one was to be seen, only a few people hurried here and there and paid only fleeting attention to Kaura and her companions. Many were carrying large bags and bundles.

As they crossed a large square to get to the City Hall on the other side, they finally saw more people at the end of a wide cross street. Several thousand Pyrrheans of all life forms had gathered in a large, tree-lined square and seemed to be waiting for something. Women, men and children and their equivalents of other magical races stood, sat and lay together in groups talking. The murmuring could be heard even over the distant thunder on the energy screen. No one seemed panicked, but the mood was subdued.

Kaura and her companions hurried past. Despite their armaments and multicolored clothing—most of the inhabitants wore linen clothes in natural shades of white, sand and brown—they were not hailed, although some of the children looked up curiously and pointed their fingers at them. The people here understandably had other things to worry about right now than some foreigners who didn't seem to be a threat.

When they reached the town hall, a ten-story building in the shape of a flattened pyramid made fully of obsidian, Kaura immediately turned to one of the djinn guards in purple uniform standing at the gate. The being gazed at them vigilantly but not unfriendly. She had taken off the fishhook amulet and stowed it next to the dumbbell in her pocket, so that initiates would immediately recognize her as a Lemurian Superior by her aura.

"My name is Kaura Alenu'ala of the Council of Lemurian High Priestesses. It is urgent that I speak with the Mahdi. Some of my companions have already gone to the gap to assist your defenders."

The guard held out a shimmering metallic flat object towards her and seemed to be checking something. Then he nodded.

"Come, Exalted Ones. You must leave the weapons here. You can take them back with you when you leave the Council Hall."

After they had put down their pistols and swords, the djinn led them through a field of reddish shimmering doors into the interior of the building. Some purple liveried men were in the process of hoisting various metal cubes onto a floating platform. The guard nodded towards them.

"We are already in the process of initiating the evacuation. You have probably come too late, Exalted One. The shield field will not last much longer. A millenia-old story is ending." The djinn shook his head sadly.

He led them through three more guarded doors into a half-darkened, cool room dominated by a round metal table standing in the center. Above the table flickered a three-dimensional image of a collection of streets and buildings that had to represent Pyrrha and his surroundings. Red, green and blue dots moved across the map. At the back of the room, uniformed messengers hurried in and out.

Around the table there were six beings, four humans, one djinn, and a kind of elephant creature that walked upright and had four almost human-looking arms. The elephant had three eyes, all of which he squinted in impotent rage now.

"We're just supposed to let them have our city?" he trumpeted angrily. "Mahdi, I bow to your authority, but I protest!"

"I don't like it much either, Gan'olin," calmly replied one of the humans, a gray-haired woman with Mongolian features. She wore a simple gray robe with a gold trim over her right shoulder, made of many connected triangular plates shaped from the precious metal. The woman continued in a firm, commanding voice.

"We have had ample opportunity to discuss our final options in recent years. Over ninety-nine percent of the population has already been relocated to the inner world a year ago. Now we need to start the final phase. I know that survival will not be easy for the last three thousand of us, since the escape passages from the city have been blocked and the intended escape portal, which can be operated manually by mages, was destroyed by the last act of sabotage. At least, our situation is not completely hopeless. We will use magical spellwork to make a breach to the south and then put the emergency portal in Aswan into operation, going north. This will get us close to the inner world entrance, closer to the protection of the witches. And once we are safe, we will try again to make contact with the Lemurians."

She looked up, surprise entering her features.

"Sublime?" whispered the old mage. "Have you received our call for help? Are you bringing relief? Troops? Energy? We thought perhaps you were all dead!"

Kaura humbly bowed her head.

"I'm afraid not, Mahdi. We were surprised and closed in ourselves. I am alone, accompanied only by a few Scottish mages and fairies who have already joined your defenders and are doing what they can there. I am here with a mission to open a portal to Alaris on Aalid and bring support from there."

The Asian woman's face fell in on itself.

"Exalted One, we are almost out of power. We can no longer even properly maintain our protective shields or activate a portal within Gaia. All attempts to find the transformers of the energy taps set up by the ancients have failed. For too long, we relied on the fact that everything just worked. Now we are paying the price. We are lost, if

I am to be perfectly honest. Breaking through towards the south is our only hope. Not a great one, though, unfortunately."

The elephant next to her trumpeted angrily, but remained silent.

Kaura smiled bitterly.

"I'm afraid a breakthrough by magical means will prove difficult. Do you know that there is a magic block around the territory of Pyrrha, of the same type as was used in Algiers five years ago? Have you even heard of that? It is to be feared that the powers of your mages will simply fizzle out outside the protective shield and you will fall helplessly into the hands of the Inquisitors. However, I may be able to offer you a solution. The central intelligence of Gaia still has some energy reserves, accessible only by safety circuit. I think that should be enough to get your people somewhere safe and still let us get to Aalid. Are you ready for evacuation?"

One of the Mahdi's generals nodded.

"The residents are all gathered in the Square of Solidarity. They are just waiting for the signal to march."

"How long does it take the group to pass through a standard-sized Portal, have you calculated that?" asked Kaura.

The woman with the insignia of the Mahdi had the answer ready at once.

"Two and a quarter hours with a safety reserve," she replied.

The Lemurian nodded and pulled out the dumbbell-shaped control device.

"Gaia, if you open the portal to Rhodes for two hours fifteen minutes using all remaining energy from Pyrrha's protective spells, will there be time for ten seconds of opening the portal to Aalid?"

"Negative. The portal G-ALI 338-A to Aalid requires a lot of energy due to the distance of seven thousand five hundred light years. With all remaining reserves, the portal to Rhodes can remain open for a total of forty-three minutes. If, in addition, the portal to

Aalid is to be opened for ten seconds, twenty-two minutes of that remain."

The voice remained calm and ethereal, as always.

Kaura looked down in consternation.

"Ask your spirit-thing which portal can be held open for the required amount of time," Joe suggested. "After all, people just need to get away from here for the time being."

Kaura asked the question. But the response from the brain was not encouraging.

"Negative. Next portal is Aswan, Nile. Maximum opening time with remaining energy one hour thirty-seven minutes."

Kaura exchanged a glance with the Pyrrhean city leaders. Gan'olin, the creature with the elephant head, snorted thoughtfully.

"The newest portals are the ones to Atlantis. There is an extra-wide gate there that's unique in Pyrrha, one for transporting big machines. Our people could probably go through that in rows of four. That would cut the time more than in half."

Kaura also asked about this.

"Affirmative," replied the technical-magical intelligence. "Maximum opening time of portal S·ATL 735-B XL fifty-seven minutes thirteen seconds, deduction of ten seconds opening of extra-planetary portal G-ALI 338-A to Aalid already included."

The assembled leaders looked at each other in relief.

At that moment, a uniformed messenger burst into the room.

"General Uzmirkan reports that a breakthrough cannot be prevented much longer, despite the arrival of Scottish reinforcements," the uniformed man reported, panting with exertion. He seemed to have run all the way. "Maybe another hour if they don't break through the shield anywhere else. The Spanish seem to have almost unlimited reserves of fighters and keep changing their mages. Also, they have fairies. Regular ones, but also ones with black bat wings that none of us have seen before. Terrible fighting machines!"

The man was trembling as he saluted. He was clearly at the end of his strength.

The Mahdi thanked him for his message.

"Tell the general to hold the fort as long as he can, then retreat toward the upper city. We're planning to evacuate via Portal 735 to Atlantis. He must try to cover us for"—she calculated briefly—"a little over an hour. Then the city will be evacuated. Have his troops defend the portal and then be the last to withdraw."

The messenger repeated the message, waited for a confirming nod from the purple-clad woman, and ran out the door.

The Mahdi straightened up and stretched her arms.

"Well, then, that's settled. We should send someone from the council through the gate first to explain to those on the other side that we come in peace and need help. The role of the Atlanteans in the whole game is too obscure for me. Maybe they are not happy to see a few thousand Pyrrhean refugees suddenly standing in the middle of their home. Or they might even attack us, if they are in cooperating with the Kai'ala. But we don't have to think about that now. The main thing is to escape the Inquisitors and their collars for now."

She turned to Kaura. "And thank you for your timely assistance, Exalted One. It seems that once again, you are saving our lives at the last moment."

Together they went out and went to the Square of Solidarity, where the inhabitants of the city waited patiently for the evacuation, their conversations almost drowned out by the increasingly loud din of the attacks.

The Mahdi climbed onto a small platform in the center of the square and amplified her voice with a simple air spell. With a few words, she explained to her fellow citizens the situation and the opportunity that had arisen with Kaura's arrival. Excited murmurs were heard in the crowd, and relief and gratitude appeared on some faces.

With the help of purple-clad djinns, fairies, and humans, the beings formed into columns of four, shouldered their bundles, and trotted off toward the north, toward the sounds of battle. Quite a few of them cast regretful glances at the still rich-looking city surrounding them.

Although, Kaura reflected, there must have been a ghostly emptiness here in the last year anyway, since almost all the formerly three hundred thousand inhabitants had already left Pyrrha. Did she really have to let all this fall into the hands of the Spaniards and their alien allies? What alternatives were left to her? None, except to return as soon as possible with help. A wave of helpless frustration washed over her. Couldn't she stop the Kai'ala somehow? What if she ordered Gaia to direct all remaining residual energy into the protective shield?

But no, then they would all be stuck here even more. And in a few weeks or months they would face the same problem, only without an escape route.

Without looking back, she hurried after the city's leader, followed by Joe and Ariane, ahead of the throng of plodding townspeople. The fairy fluttered over her shoulder, muttering imprecations. Kaura suspected she would rather have been at the breach, fighting. Surely, the small being was imagining what she would do to the inquisitors if she caught them.

"I'm afraid you're going to see even more of our inquisitor friends than is good for you in time, Ariane. Don't worry about it. We'll probably all have to fight," she murmured to her. In front of them, the violent flickering of witch fire could now already be seen, and the thundering of magical blasting webs effortlessly drowned out any normal speech. Why, of all things, did the portal to Atlantis have to be in the part of town closest to where the Spaniards had broken through?

Before they even got to see any of the fighting, however, they had arrived. The Mahdi led them to a huge, round square covered with shimmering blue mosaic tiles. The tiles depicted various maritime scenes. Huge fountains in the center as well as in the four quadrants of the square shot gushing water in all directions.

The buildings bordering the open space had also been adapted to the curvature of the open space. Corinthian columns of white marble supported high shady arches, under which in better times revellers had strolled and elegantly dressed people had sipped peppermint tea in small boulevard cafes.

A moment of melancholy threatened to overwhelm Kaura as unasked-for memories of her long-ago visits to the magical city rose. For a moment, it almost seemed to her that she had even been there when this place was built. But Pyrrha was older than she was by many millennia. Kaura shook herself. She probably also still felt some of the emotions rising from the refugees into the field. She strengthened her shielding.

"What do you have planned for after the occupation?" she asked the Madhi.

The woman looked back at her uncomprehendingly for a moment, then understanding slid over her features.

"We don't know any self-destruct mechanism, if that's what you mean—even if we wanted to use it," said the white-haired Mongolian. "We have magically secured the main headquarters and vaults with several spell layers and set some traps. Also, the Sphinx is being activated and should make life pretty tough for any non-magicians in Pyrrha. We've done everything we could to make sure the Spanish get as little out of their conquest as possible. Still, we're not book burners. And with the amount of mages they have with them, it's to be feared that they will get behind the secrets of Pyrrha in not too long a time after all."

A small shiver of fear ran through Kaura's stomach. What could the Kai'ala do with Pyrrha's alchemical and magical devices? They seemed to know things that were unknown even to her, the collars proved that. And they could probably provide an alternative energy supply, since their starships could now land unimpeded. What could she do? She was tired of running away or lagging one step behind the blue mock inquisitors. She wanted to finally take the initiative again. Force her plan on the others.

Thoughtfully, she patted the Gaia device in her pocket. The central brain was independent of the local control modules, and seemed to be less limited than what most users could get out of the old technology. Perhaps she could trigger a self-destruct mechanism via Gaia. Or at least shut Pyrrha down somehow.

The city superior interrupted her train of thought.

"There it is," she said as she pointed ahead. "The Atlantis Court."

At the western end of the circus was a small courtyard, also circular, the wall of which was decorated with filigree, golden-blue ornaments. Somewhat away from the wall there were eighteen round archways, somewhat flattened at the bottom so that a person could comfortably pass through. And in the center, just at the western end of the courtyard, a substantially larger square opening, its enclosure of shimmering blue metal adorned with silver mermaids that seemed to float playfully about.

All the archways were empty, none had the strange shiny surface of a working portal. Kaura could see the blue-gold wall beyond. Behind the small group, the first of the refugees already began to trot into the portal courtyard.

The city superior talked briefly with the elephant-headed man, then turned to the Lemurian.

"Gan'olin here will form the vanguard with fifty of our guardsmen and prepare the Atlanteans as gently as possible for our arrival. Then we'll send people through without wasting time. As you told us, there may be some nausea. The guardsmen will make sure that the space behind the Portal remains clear and that there are no delays. Can you open it now? Then you can go and take care of your own portal. Just make sure that this one stays open for about forty minutes. This should leave you more than enough time for the transfer to Aalid."

Kaura thanked the old woman and hugged her warmly.

"I wish you all good luck, and I will see you soon. May the Great Mother be with you!"

"And with you," the Mahdi replied. "Bring us the help we all need, that this planet needs!"

The Lemurian high priestess now took the small golden dumb-bell-device from her pocket. A few words, and the portal began to flicker bluish. The yellow light turned purple. Here it was designed as a flickering line around the portal, which made the silver mermaids next to the opening glitter colorfully.

At a beckon from the city's leaders, one of the guardsmen strode through.

The djinn returned after a few seconds and nodded to those present.

"The space behind the gate is clear, Mahdi. Just some passers-by," he said and turned around again. Gan'olin and the other guardsmen followed him.

Kaura had seen enough. Followed by Joe, she fell into a light trot and moved quickly out of the yard. Ariane fluttered high above them and seemed to be trying to get an overview of the situation. Fortunately, the portals for the Inner Milky Way were not far away. Through sparkling clean, deserted streets, the three rushed toward the off-planet district.

Ariane swooshed down from above and swung in beside Kaura, who was already breathing heavily from exertion.

"It doesn't look good back there. The first Kai'ala have already broken through the line and are spreading through town, I think. We're going to have to hurry. Do you want to call Sen now?"

Kaura nodded and tuned inwardly to Sen's vibration.

"Hello Sen, can you hear me?" she thought as she fixed an image of the head magician in her mind's eye.

"Yep," came the answer immediately and very clearly. "How's it going over there?"

"We have opened the escape portal to the Pyrrheans and are now on our way to the Inner Portal Courtyard. Portal G-ALI 338, maybe you can convince someone to guide you?"

"Okay," Sen's voice rang in her head. "We're falling back here anyway. Wait for us. And be careful. Some units of the Spanish have already broken through."

A few minutes later, they turned a corner and saw the Milky Way Portal Court in front of them, wholly constructed of a material that looked like pure gold. Kaura did not stop to admire the splendor but walked purposefully toward the portal she sought. Behind each of the archways in this courtyard, the star constellation to which the planet in question belonged was shown with huge green sapphires in the golden outer wall of the courtyard.

She turned back to Joe.

"This is one of the three portal courts for off-planet travel. This one serves the inner Milky Way. Another contains portals for the outer arms, and the third, smallest, leads to other galaxies. Even when these courts were in operation, only a privileged few were allowed to use them. Mainly they were emigrants, explorers and diplomats. Let's hope..."

She broke off abruptly as a dull thud sounded. Joe staggered toward her. A red spot blossomed on the front of his shoulder that had not been there before.

"Damn," her friend groaned, his face contorted in pain. "I'm hit."

Now everything happened as if in a dream. Joe slumped to his knees. Kaura felt a metallic chill around her neck. She yanked up the dumbbell device.

"Gaia, open for ten seconds, now!" she cried breathlessly in ancient Lemurian. The portal in front of them flickered and turned purple. With a hard shove, Kaura pushed the collapsing Joe through. With her other hand, she ripped the fishhook amulet from her neck and threw it at him. At the same moment she saw Ariane flying towards her and raising her staff.

"Take care of Joe!" she groaned, batting the fairy into the billowing blue field like a pesky fly, even as from behind another inquisitor tried to throw his flashing lasso across her neck.

As soon as Ariane was through, the portal went out. A sharp pain jerked through Kaura's entire body. A whispering, childlike voice spoke through the red streaks that almost made her lose consciousness.

"From now on, you won't make any move that I don't allow you to make, dirty little witch. We will have to train you well. But it will be worth it to break you. I see you are strong. You will be a good addition to our army, slave."

4

Escape to Atlantis

Kaura sank to her knees with a groan. Once again, a lashing, searing pain flashed through her martyred nervous system without her being able to pinpoint it in her body. "I did not allow you to kneel," whispered the being behind her back in its piercing hissing voice.

Kaura could literally picture the Kai'ala's lipless mouth twisting into a humorless grin, and his saw-toothed dentures flashing in the sun.

"Get up!" her tormentor hissed. "Irkail, let's keep moving. Maybe we'll find more scattered ones. The other two are probably gone for good."

She felt herself being pulled upward by the leash and found that she could no longer exercise conscious control over her limbs. Her willpower gone completely, she stood up and turned to face her leash holder. She was a spectator in her own body.

Everything in her resisted, rebelled in despair.

The Kai'ala pointed to the Gaia device in her hand.

"What is that? And why was the portal open? How did you do that? Who were the other two? Are you deserters?"

Shocked, Kaura felt her mouth begin to open to tell the inquisitor everything. She tried to reach her magic power, to lock her brain, to relax her tongue—but nothing worked.

The blue-skinned man laughed and showed his pointed teeth.

"You'll find out you better play along willingly, little one. If you're good, you'll live a good life."

His dark, seal-like eyes seemed to take on an even harder expression. "If not, you won't. So, I'm listening."

Kaura felt her head lower obediently. Just as she heard her own voice speaking without her wanting to, out of the corner of her eye, she saw the second inquisitor silently topple to the side. A metallic click sounded in front of her, and a fine little voice hooted happily.

"Ha! Got you hooked, wayward insult to all honest sharks! So, how's that for a taste of your own medicine, sea cucumber?" A burning trail began to spread across Kaura's back, causing her to cry out in pain.

"Stop, Diana, don't," she gasped, "I think if he holds the leash, I'll feel everything that happens to him."

Immediately, the pain stopped.

"Ah, okay," murmured the fairy with the pink wings, sounding slightly contrite. She held Kaura's tormentor by one of the glittering leashes, which she must have taken from the second inquisitor just before. "I had wondered about that. Strange things happen there on the battlefield. The slaves usually die along with their keepers, which makes it really hard for us to free them. Well, you always learn... Sen and the others are coming up. I flew ahead to get the lay of the land. Where are Joe and Ariane?"

Kaura indicated the Portal with a movement of her head.

"Through there. Joe is injured, I sent Ariane after him. It all happened way too fast."

She groaned. "And now we don't have enough power to open the portal a second time."

Diana shrugged.

"Never mind. Joe and Ari are inside. They'll tell those techno-bags what's what. Don't worry about a thing. It's all good."

A few minutes after Kaura's rescue, the remaining Lockwood mages turned a corner at a run and hurried toward the small group around Kaura and the fairy.

Simon immediately knelt down and, together with one of the fairy guards, began to remove Kaura's collar.

"So, what do we do with those?" Diana pointed to the inquisitor still kneeling bent before her and his still unconscious crony.

Sen smiled grimly as he answered.

"We'll take these with us. And we won't let them implode on us like the last one we caught in London. We're going to be very careful this time. I think they'll tell us everything we want to know."

"First, we have to get out of here," Kaura reminded him. "We could go back to Rhodes, but I'm worried about what awaits our Pyrrhean friends in Atlantis. That's why I want to accompany them. Since there's not much we can do here anyway."

A violent bang from the east, as if from an immense bursting paper bag, made everyone cringe. The ground trembled. Almost like an earthquake, Kaura thought.

"They've probably broken through the shield in another place, too," Simon surmised. "We should hurry if we want to leave the same way as the Pyrrheans."

Together they hurried off, over to the Atlantean quarters, the unconscious Kai'ala between four of Sen's guard fairies who held him suspended with glowing staffs. A little later, they were back in the portal circle, where refugees were still streaming and disappearing in rows of four through the blue pane.

Sen and the mages again fell in with the combatants trying to hold the courtyard against the ever-advancing Inquisition forces, while Kaura joined the Mahdi, who urged her fellow citizens in a loud voice to make the greatest haste. The ground beneath their feet vibrated from the increasingly violent energetic ramming spells, so that the two women had to strain to keep their balance.

Kaura turned to the gold dumbbell.

"GAIA, if you keep the portal to Atlantis open for another ten minutes until the city is fully evacuated, what countermeasures against enemy occupation will you have enough power for?"

"Calculating..." the planet's central brain replied in its ethereal-sounding, androgynous voice. "Switching the city into occupation mode time loop is still possible. However, a restoration of the central power supply in the Earth core is necessary for deactivation of the measure."

"How does this time loop work?" asked Kaura. "The occupation emergency mode stops time inside the Pyrrha security perimeter. All beings then inside or later entering the perimeter are frozen in time until they are freed by lifting the mode. Shall the occupation mode be brought up, Exalted One?"

Kaura glanced at the courtyard in the middle of which she stood. The people of Pyrrha had lined up neatly and were moving as fast as they could, four at a time, through the portal. There were still a few hundred left, but the crowd was now rapidly dwindling.

She nodded, and immediately became aware that the gesture probably could not be interpreted by the central brain.

"Positive," she said, finally. "I will be the last to leave the city. As soon as I cross the portal, you activate the loop."

"Order received," replied the ethereal being from the dumbbell, repeating the consequences, the warning regarding irreversibility and asking for another confirmation from the high priestess, which Kaura gave , now without hesitation.

Meanwhile, the group around Sen and the remaining Pyrrhean

guardsmen fell farther and farther back toward their escape portal, hard pressed by the huge pack of blue-skinned, cruelly grinning Kai'ala and human inquisitors in ruby robes, most of whom held a slave or two on gleaming silver leashes.

Kaura concentrated and connected with the eternal expanse of the universal field shining within her. As the familiar peace and joy flowed through her, she deftly wove the threads of power into a giant protective bubble and placed it around the portal slightly outside the farthest of the allied combatants from her.

"There, that should buy us some more time," she whispered with satisfaction. When no more Kai'ala followed, they being held back by Kaura's weave, the guardsmen and mages quickly dealt with the attackers still remaining inside the bubble. This time, most of the slaves were saved alive. The freed joined the sad little cluster of bewildered beings, who were assigned to individual passersby alongside the fugitive line of guardsmen to hold their leash until they would finally be uncollared on the other side of the portal.

The Kai'ala, meanwhile, focused all their energies on penetrating the protective bubble.

A few minutes later, it was almost done. Behind the last civilians, the exhausted guardsmen and mage fighters moved through the portal.

"One minute thirty seconds until the activation of the emergency program," sounded from the barbell. The last guardsmen disappeared, followed by the fairies. Now Kaura, Sen and the Mahdi were left.

"Go!" ordered Kaura briskly, "I'll be right behind you." The other two disappeared into the blue field. Kaura also turned to go. As she did so, she saw something that made her stare for a moment. Amidst the billowing witch fire and the booming energetic hammer blows that would bring the field down, a dark-skinned hulk approached her, a bear of a man dressed in black leather. His face was serene, and his green eyes looked slightly bored. Then their eyes met. How did she know this man, Kaura wondered. The stranger raised his arm and his mouth formed a few sentences. Immediately her protective screen began to billow.

As if through a mist, Gaia's voice from the dumbbell amulet penetrated Kaura's consciousness. "...seven, six, five, four, ..."

With a jerk, she threw herself around and tumbled sideways through the portal. At the moment of her disappearance, she saw how the protective field collapsed and at the same time everything began to slow down.

The man's face showed a moment of shock. Then the view was gone, and she was crashing to the hard stone floor on the other side of the Portal.

"...Zero." said the disembodied voice. Behind her, the blue surface of the Portal winked out. A moment later, she saw Sen's worried face over her.

"Are you all right?" he asked. "You've got some nerve. A few more moments and you could have looked at that time loop mode from the inside."

With difficulty she sat up and felt her aching limbs.

"Nothing broken, it seems. There was a man I knew from somewhere. Maybe one of the 'Gods.' I think he must have been captured by the time field too, unless he reacted very quickly."

"Well then, we can ask him on Saint Nevermore Day how his vacation was," Diana grumbled, wishing away a few scrapes on Kaura's knee with her fairy wand. "If we ever get Pyrrha off that loop again."

Sen cleared his throat.

"I think our friends over there are in trouble. Maybe your presence could help, Kaura."

He gestured to the edge of the large plaza, where Gan'olin and the Mahdi were engaged in a heated discussion with two uniformed men wearing strange, cone-shaped helmets. The elephant creature had turned red and kept trumpeting into the air.

Followed by Diana, the two approached the group with measured steps.

"...this is a forbidden zone for all Gaia residents!" the one blue-clad officer just said. His long hair was white, and the eyes in his pale face sparkled light blue. "We have orders to arrest unauthorized intruders immediately and deport them to Eire. There you can apply for asylum with local authorities if, as you say, you are really persecuted. Atlantis is closed!"

Kaura made her way through the Pyrrhean crowd, who were eyeing the Atlanteans suspiciously.

"But we are not just anyone," she interposed politely. "My name is Kaura Alenu'ala, envoy of the Fern Temple of Lemuria, and I invoke the Treaty of Ilkarion, according to which the government of Atlantis must always provide us with aid and assistance in cases of acute threat. This case has occurred."

The uniformed man was silent for a moment and didn't seem to know exactly what to say.

"I don't know anything about this treaty. Can you substantiate your claims?" he finally asked.

"We demand to speak with a member of the government!" trumpeted Gan'olin, upset. "You have absolutely no idea who you are speaking to! We are..."

Kaura put her hand reassuringly on one of his four arms.

"I'm sure this is just a misunderstanding," she said.

Just then, a shrill, screeching howl approached from beyond the buildings surrounding the square. Everyone looked toward the entrance of the Portal court. Under the arcades, which were partly occupied by stores and coffeehouses and, as in Pyrrha, also housed various portal arches, though here, they were all boarded up, the spectators, dressed in flowing, colorful robes and standing around in small groups, also pointed in the direction from which the noise was approaching at high speed.

A relieved expression appeared on the officer's face.

"This must be High Councilor Ixkarel, the Minister of Police. I'm sure he'll answer any questions you have, uh, Exalted One."

Through the entrance gate, designed like a silver wave, shot several squat, angular vehicles that seemed to be made of some sort of opaque, bluish stone. Gleaming white lights flashed and flashed on all five sides of the twenty-odd yard long constructs. The things had no visible wheels and seemed to simply float in the air.

Five of the vessels swung off at the entrance to the square and surrounded the group of three thousand Pyrrheans in an even circle. Out poured a few hundred light blue uniformed figures with their heads hidden behind opaque helmets of billowing blue light. In their hands, the uniformed men carried long, black staffs that remotely resembled a cross between a halberd and a mace with an overlong handle. The tips of the staffs flickered faintly reddish.

Most of the soldiers formed an inward circle around the square, while a few more seemed to be trying to turn away the curious bystanders in the arcades.

The Mahdi turned to one of her advisors.

"Try to keep our people calm. We don't want to start a fight here. The Atlanteans probably don't even know that they're dealing with three thousand mages here who are quite capable of fighting back."

The man relayed the order, and some of the Mahdi's people moved into the crowd and talked reassuringly to the people.

Sen cradled his head uncertainly.

"The djinn and fairies are hard to mistake for anything other than what they are. It seems that even mages are no longer welcome everywhere outside the Spanish Ottoman Empire."

"Just let me do the talking, and don't speak unless you're asked," Kaura hissed to the others as a slightly smaller one of the blue floating stones approached them. Up close, the thing looked something like a cut crystal flattened at the top and bottom, its walls composed of perfectly flat triangular crystal elements whose connecting joints glittered metallically in the sunlight.

With a soft hiss, the vehicle came to a stop and lowered to about a foot's width above the ground. Three adjacent triangular surfaces began to billow and seemed to simply vanish into thin air, creating an opening from which two young women in green robes and holding short energy lances leapt. The two stood on either side of the opening and took posture.

Out of the crystal climbed a small, white-haired Atlantean in an emerald cloak, whom Kaura instantly disliked, without being able to say exactly why.

"What's all the commotion about? Who are these people?" the newcomer asked the blue-clad officer in a whiny voice. The officer had also assumed posture and placed the edge of his hand on his metal helmet in greeting.

"They have come through one of the Portals, sir. They say they are looking for protection. I pointed out to them that Atlantis is closed. That woman there," he waved his hand in Kaura's direction, "says she's from Lemuria and invokes some treaty."

"The Treaty of Ilkarion on the occasion of the Lemurian-Atlantean Peace," Kaura calmly interjected, doing her best to maintain her facade of calm politeness. "I am Kaura Alenu'ala, High Priestess of Lemuria, Crystal Princess of the Il'itic Empire, Knight of the Silver Wreath—a title, by the way, bestowed upon me personally by the Atlantean High Council many years ago. I expect that I and my companions will be given a reception befitting our rank. Unfortunately, we were unable to announce ourselves because we were acting in an emergency."

The Atlantean stared at her for a moment. The corners of his mouth pulled down even further.

"Very well. I am Ixkarel, speaking for the Atlantean government. Unfortunately, Atlantis is also in dire straits at the moment, and we cannot honor millennia-old treaties. Come again when our borders are open, Excellency, and we will be happy to welcome you."

He raised his wrist to his mouth and spoke into a slim, silver metal bracelet. "Run Protocol C."

A reddish glow flared up around him, as well as around his companions and the vehicle. Out of the corner of her eye, Kaura saw the uniformed men in the cordon point their lances into the circle. Beside her, the two Atlantean officers slid down to the ground, unconscious, along with many of the refugees gathered in the center of the square, who also lost consciousness and collapsed in great waves.

Kaura saw some of the more responsive fairies and djinn surround themselves with protective fields. Fireballs appeared between some hands, ready to be thrown. Kaura felt a psychic pressure on the outside of the magical shield she constantly maintained around her, and reinforced the weave without thinking about it for a moment.

Then followed something Kaura could best describe as a click in the magical field, and her ability, the source of energy inside her, was suddenly disconnected from her.

"Great mother, them too!" it flashed through her mind as she felt her protective shield disappear. She had to get inside the red bubble around Ixkarel. Surely the people inside were protected from the paralysis rays.

With a violent jerk, she threw herself towards the vehicle that had come to a stop only three yards away from her. Still falling, she felt her ability return and the feeling of sleepiness that had already begun to subside as she pushed through the red field around Ixkarel and his vehicle.

Within a fraction of a second, she oriented herself. Next to her was Simon, who had been standing even closer to the bubble at the time of the attack, and had obviously had the same idea. The two guards behind the Atlantean councillor raised their weapons and one of them shouted at them.

"Don't move! You are under arrest!"

Kaura swept the light spears from their hands with a hair-thin beam of energy and simultaneously bound them with streams of solidified air.

Simon, meanwhile, reached for Ixkarel, wrapped his forearm around his neck from behind, and squeezed.

"You stop that right now, traitor," he hissed. "And then let's see what's going on here. We're not your enemies. But are you ours?"

The Atlantean moaned and gurgled until Simon reduced the pressure a bit.

"You're not getting out of here alive," he gasped. "Better surrender now."

Meanwhile, the guards surrounding the square did not seem to know quite what to make of this sudden change and stood frozen.

"Well, we'll see about that," growled the Scottish psychomage, holding the Atlantean with an iron grip. "You might even hear the angels sing before we do. But probably that won't be necessary."

Kaura saw a spell begin to build up in the Scot's aura, with which he was probably planning to impose his will on the Atlantean.

Just then, with a piercing hiss, another of the crystal vehicles hurtled into the square and came to a stop at its edge. Out stepped three elderly white-haired Atlanteans in white toga-like garments with red sashes. They contemplated the scene for a moment. Then the middle one of the three, a dignified-looking albino with a long, slightly purple-tinted beard, raised his wrist to his mouth. His voice boomed, amplified all over the place.

"Stop this action immediately! Who is the commanding officer here? Report to us! This intervention is not approved by the Senate."

One of the light blue uniformed soldiers broke away from the line, walked up to the group of three and pressed a button on the front of the uniform. The shimmering helmet of light disappeared, and a hard, but not unsympathetic man's face with a prominent hooked nose appeared. He began to speak to one of the violet-bearded man's companions, the leader of the newcomers having already moved into the field of slumped figures, walking in the direction of the people around Kaura, who stood frozen in their positions, waiting.

"Welcome to Atlantis, friends," he intoned, casting a sidelong glance over at Simon, who still had the police minister in a headlock. "You can let him go now, friend. You have nothing to fear. We have followed the events remotely from the glider and know what has happened. You are under the protection of the Crystal Priest Guild. This technocrat"—he cast a contemptuous glance at Ixkarel—"has far exceeded his authority. He will have to answer to the Senate."

The cordon around the square had dissolved by now. The uniformed men went around in small groups and woke up the unconscious. Now and then, there was a small scuffle until the disoriented refugees realized that they were no longer in danger.

The magic barrier field had apparently been turned off as well, allowing many mages, djinns, and fairies to participate in reviving their companions.

"Go now and do not disturb us any longer," the old crystal priest turned to Ixkarel. "These people are allowed to move freely in Atlantis. Your people must respect that. Otherwise, you will have to face the consequences."

The minister just gave the priests a nasty look and, followed by his bodyguards, climbed up with a "You'll regret this, Eriniel!" into the glider, which immediately soared into the air, sweeping several of his Atlantean guardsmen off their feet as it roared away into the sky.

"A dangerous man," the bearded man muttered, then turned to Kaura. "I am pleased to see visitors from Lemuria, High Priestess.

As you've probably concluded from this unfortunate incident, not everyone sees it that way. But with the magical population of this beautiful continent, you are most welcome. Unfortunately, we are not the sole determinants of Atlantean politics. Nevertheless, we are powerful enough to offer you refuge and protection. No one will dare to harm you now. At least not as openly and with the use of public forces as they have just tried," he said with a troubled look on his face.

Then a smile flitted across his face. "But, where are my manners? I am Eriniel Exhai'kaimiel Ir'man'ariel, first crystal priest of Atlantia. My friends call me Erin. Those over there are my colleagues Ikal and Merin. I am extremely honored to see you again. I don't think you'll remember me, Exalted One. The last time you were here, I was a young boy and only saw you from afar."

Kaura introduced herself and her companions, who were slowly getting back on their feet and rubbing their limbs.

Gan'olin, meanwhile, was trumpeting loudly in an attempt to rid his trunk of road dust that had apparently been blown in by the wind during his unconsciousness.

"I'll flatten him, the fatso!" he snorted between individual trumpet blasts and with him, this seemed much more serious of a serious matter than with Ariane, who also habitually threatened someone with flattening them. After all, Gan's legs, though shorter, were otherwise quite elephant-like.

Kaura thought to herself with a sideways glance that she would not like to dance with this creature. One step on a dancing partner's toes could have a seriously crippling effect. Then she turned back to the crystal priest, who had meanwhile formally apologized to the Mahdi for the treatment her people had been subjected to.

"The urban militia and the Atlantean Guard are under the authority of the High Council, but they cannot be used without the permission of the Senate, certainly not against mages inside the country," he explained. "Unfortunately, we could not prevent the law that closed all the external borders of our territory. Finally, three years ago, a provision was added that prohibited us from continuing to come to the aid of allies, such as the Inca Empire or your city. And then, a few months ago, the free ports that were still open were closed. Many even of the otherwise moderate senators were afraid, fears that of course were stoked by people like Ixkarel. That we were weakening and isolating Atlantis in the long term with this withdrawal was not realized."

He beckoned the other crystal priests to join him. "We will organize transports to take your people to the Crystal Palace in the Turquoise Quarter. The palace's old guest wing has about one thousand two hundred comfortable chambers for pilgrims and a large public bath. People will have to share beds for the time being, I'm afraid. But there are three other pilgrim quarters where we can surely get chambers as well. Until two thousand years ago, many thousands of people from all over the world used to come to the crystal festivals every year to see the great master crystal and be illuminated. Now it's all much smaller, with all the restrictions on entry."

He shrugged. "Jesus, Buddha, Shiva, Mohammed... the pie hasn't gotten any bigger. Everybody wants to cut a piece. But of course, we're the only true religion."

The priest grinned wryly, suggesting he wasn't all that serious. "And how's your treehugger clan doing, sister?" he continued, turning to Kaura. "Have you been through hugging all plants in Lemuria and now need new territories to expand into?"

"We plant enough new ones to leave some for everyone," she retorted. "But we also hug rocks, bushes, each other and whatever else comes our way. Even crystals."

"Well, then maybe you should try our master crystal, Kaura," Erin said. "It's already pretty intense just kneeling in front of it. Honestly, I don't even know if anyone has ever tried hugging it.

Probably that would be sacrilege, too. Blasphemy or something. I could check the old scrolls. Well, never mind. After all, tradition is just peer pressure exercised by dead people."

The chief Atlantean priest scratched his beard thoughtfully. From behind, Diana fluttered up and slapped him hard on the shoulders, which looked quite comical due to the size difference.

"I like you, brother! Yes, let's philosophize together about the value of tradition! Peer pressure exercised by dead people!"

She giggled. "I'll have to remember that one. Is that in one of the ancient scrolls, too?"

Beyond the archway leading to the courtyard, a convoy of elongated, greenish-opaque flying vehicles could now be seen approaching. The Atlanteans in the square seemed to have returned to their daily business. Most, however, gave the gathering of magical beings and guardsmen a wide berth. Some kept glancing over curiously.

The hoverboats slid silently into place and lowered in a long line to just above the ground. As their sidewalls opened with a slight hiss, the Pyrrheans, supported by their purple liveried city guard, began to spread out and climb into the hovering boxes.

Erin beckoned to Kaura and her companions to follow him. Together they went to the small hovering vehicle in which the three Atlanteans had come, and got in. With a sigh, the Lemurian let herself sink back into one of the soft, swiveling upholstered chairs that formed a three-quarter circle within the completely transparent, floor-to-ceiling walls of the vehicle. For a moment, she half-felt she was sitting in one of the hover ships of her homeland, which, despite the similarity in comforts, were usually roundish and irregular in shape, mostly covered in age patina, and generally more reminiscent of flat river stones.

As soon as the three priests had boarded, the sidewall materialized again, and the floor outside the windows sank silently down several yards without even the slightest sensation of movement inside the vehicle. Then the environment seemed to shift along the boat as the flattened diamond picked up speed.

Erin walked across the carpeted floor and touched a couple of glowing panels in the starboard section of the passenger compartment, which was flying completely without a helmsman.

"You must be thirsty," he said. "What would you like to drink?"

"Water, please!" said Kaura in the same breath as Sen asked "Do you have any whiskey?".

The priest smiled in amusement as he touched on a few more patches of light seemingly hanging in mid-air.

"Sure thing. The on-board bar can do anything. Water with or without fizz?"

A short time later, everyone was holding a crystal cup with a liquid of their choice.

Diana dipped her own size-adjusted muck into Sen's whiskey glass and clicked her tongue appreciatively.

"That tastes like real Irish, boy! At least twelve years old! Goes down like machine oil in a robot! Well, I must say, you know how to live, Violetbeard!"

Erin thanked her for the compliment. Silently, they watched the city pass by with its towers of gold, silver and glass dozens of stories high.

"Once we get to the palace, we'll see what you have to report and how we can help you," the crystal priest said.

* * *

Palace of the Beacon of Knowledge, Alexandria

In Alexandria, more than three thousand miles to the east, the inquisitors were having a hard time.

"We have lost more than four hundred and fifty High Inquisitors, as well as over one thousand and three hundred magical slaves with their leash holders, Don Alonso!" reported a messenger, trembling with fear. He had ridden as fast as he could and now realized that he would have much rather gone the other way.

"Losers! I'll have these idiots executed!" raged the Spanish crown's plenipotentiary for magical affairs, who had arrived in Egypt only two days ago with one of the Ottoman's fastest men-of-war, and had immediately taken command.

"Maybe they are not dead, sir, and we can still free them. Only, all the scouts we sent through the hole in the shield after the event didn't return. Shortly after the successful breakthrough, the area behind the shield became completely foggy. No one can even see what is going on a yard or two behind the barrier. When approaching the shield, a voice sounds from the air, yelling something in a foreign language that no one understands. Not Atlantean, not Arabic either. It wasn't like that before. The high inquisitors remaining outside ask that a fairy slave be sent as a translator."

"What?" screeched the Spaniard. "They don't even have a single fairy there anymore? Miserable bunglers!"

"All the fairies were sent into the city with the vanguard as per orders to round up the foreign mages, sir. They were in there when it happened."

"And the key-bearer?"

"Not a trace, sir. The whole area around Pyrrha has been heavily guarded for weeks. It's almost impossible that someone could have entered the city undetected," the man replied. "He must be somewhere else."

Don Alonso leaned back with a heavy sigh and dismissed the sighing messenger with an ungracious wave.

"Get some rest, man, and don't step under my eyes again! We will take care of the matter."

When the messenger had left the room, High Inquisitor Kraikh stepped closer to the still excitedly panting nobleman. The Kai'ala had watched the scene without speaking and now put back his hood so that his bald, blue skull became visible.

"Lord, I'm afraid our enemies have used a spell in Pyrrha that is unknown to us and are powerless against at the moment. We cannot enter the city. But without the key bearer we cannot open the Portal to get at the weapon, anyway. We do not know where he and his accomplices are currently located."

The Spaniard stared wearily ahead.

"What do we actually know? Only this strange prophecy of the witch whom you burned at the stake all those years ago. What she told her guards just before she was led to her purification. The key-bearer will get through the portal before you and find the weapon. This is the beginning of the end of the Spanish Empire. You are all finished. Unless the Sultan falls in love with a witch! No one really knows what that's supposed to mean."

The blue-skinned High Inquisitor nodded somberly, not showing his knowledge that all of the talk about the key-bearer, though based on a real event, was in truth just a diversion to hide the objectives of his true masters.

"We are all blind men groping in the dark, Don Alonso. But we must do everything we can to secure the world domination of our Great Sultan and King, may he live forever! No matter what is going on in Pyrrha now, we will continue to try to get in. And the way to world domination is through the fall of Atlantis and her mysterious brethren, the Lemurians. Our galleons in the Pacific have noticed strange effects that make a huge area in the middle of this ocean unnavigable for our ships. Compass needles are going crazy, winds are suddenly shifting or storms are appearing. Navigators believe that the Lemurians may be hiding somewhere in this zone."

Of course, the Kai'ala knew exactly where the Lemurian continent was. But the apparent servants of the Spaniards had so far had little interest in letting their superiors know. They preferred that the Empire's forces concentrate first on the conquest of Atlantis while they advanced their higher plans.

The Spanish nobleman listened up, but then slumped down again.

"Too far away," he growled. "First it's the Atlanteans. Then the Aztecs, once they've lost their protective power. Then the witches in the north. Then the Mongols. Or maybe the Lemurians first? Do we know if they have gold? The royal treasury is insatiable. Besides, we need to finance expansion."

His face contorted into a greedy grin as he thought about the fact that a not inconsiderable portion of these riches would inconspicuously flow into his own pocket.

"I'm afraid not, sir," the High Inquisitor replied. "We don't know much more about them than that they probably exist and use magic."

Don Alonso waved it off.

"After all, that's what almost everyone did before they were put on the right track. One thing at a time, then."

He was panting heavily. "Let's first see if our people can conquer Pyrrha after all. That would simplify things! Otherwise, we'll have to attack Atlantis directly. Have our people in Atlantia step up their destabilization efforts!"

The High Inquisitor disappeared with a "Yes, Lord" to take care of it. And to write a report for his true masters, which, carried by one of the dark fairies, would reach its recipients within a few hours.

* * *

Alaris Central Spaceport, Aalid

Joe was dreaming. A violent jolt, then a sharp pain jerked through his left shoulder. Before he really knew what had happened, Kaura next to him already wheeled around.

"How can she always react so quickly," a thought flashed through his mind even as he groaned.

"I'm hit!" he croaked with difficulty, realizing that she had probably already noticed.

A figure in a ruby robe appeared behind Kaura, wielding some sort of silver lasso.

"An inquisitor," another thought wafted through the fog in Joe's consciousness. "I have to warn her!"

But even as he was about to open his mouth, the silver noose fell around the Lemurian's neck and began to tighten. He saw Kaura speak a few phrases into her golden dumbbell that he couldn't understand.

Joe felt himself falling, still driven by the impulse of the hit, which at least had not killed him instantly, or so it seemed. Ariane shot toward him and Kaura like a bullet and raised her fairy staff. She didn't seem to notice the second inquisitor behind her.

Then Kaura seemed to want to strike him a blow. Joe saw her hand coming toward him as if in slow motion. Why did she want to hit him? Had the inquisitor already taken control of her? Then he felt Kaura's hand touch his sternum with a heavy blow, and he toppled over backwards.

Blue lightning flashed around him, and a feeling of nausea overcame him, masking even the pulsing pain in his shoulder. He landed with a hard thud on his right side that drove all the air out of his lungs. He felt his right shoulder bend forward at an unnatural angle under the force of the impact.

"Oh great, the other side too!" it flashed through his mind. Then he heard himself cry out in pain as the shock reached his injured left side. Everything went black around him, and he slipped over into the relieving expanse of unconsciousness.

Again and again, the same scene replayed in Joe's mind, wavering, fading, until it slowly released him from her clutches. Was he asleep? Was he awake? Confused, he felt inside himself. There was no pain. So had it all been a dream after all, just a nightmare?

Then he realized that his eyes were still closed. He tried in vain to open them, but his body did not obey him. On the second attempt, a twitch ran through his body, and the Scotsman was relieved to find that his eyelids were fluttering. His body control returned.

When he opened his eyes after what seemed like an eternity, he saw a white-grey grained wall in front of him that seemed to extend into infinity to his right. Stuck to the wall were two small, human-looking feet, their toenails painted purple. Some hard, woody object tapped persistently against the root of his nose.

"Finally, snoozybag!" he heard Ariane's impatient voice next to his ear. "Welcome back to the world of the living! That was a free wish. You're welcome! You may thank me later. Shoulder repaired, bullet wound patched, puke cleaned up, lungs re-inflated, concussion cured… you can leave a little donation there, sonny boy!"

Next, Joe became aware that he was lying on his side on the floor, and the fairy was right in front of his face. She had probably woken him up with her staff. Dazed, the Scotsman struggled to sit up.

"You're welcome to a huge donation, Ariane. Unfortunately, I don't have my wallet with me," he croaked. "Could you also conjure me up something to drink?"

The whitish wall turned out to be made of a type of wood completely unknown to Joe.

"Sure thing," grinned the fairy. "Vodka Martini, shaken not stirred? You probably won't get that joke, blondie."

"Water would be better for me at the moment," replied the young man, whose vision was still spinning despite the fairy's healing wish. Immediately, a cup filled with a clear liquid appeared beside him.

Joe took it, smelled it suspiciously for a moment, remembering the fairy's fascination with spirits, and then tipped the water down his throat with a few hasty gulps.

"Thank you," he said with a still slightly strained smile. Only then did he look around. They were in a circular hall about a hundred yards in diameter. Not a human being was to be seen. There were a few dozen seating arrangements of shiny, metallic, rounded sofas in the hall. The air smelled clean, but somehow sterile and stale. There seemed to have been stores or taverns in the wall niches around them in the past. He saw empty shelves, counters, and clusters of tables.

Above the niches hung signs made of glass, on whose smooth surface multicolored words had been imprinted. Some of them he could read, others seemed only vaguely familiar. Burger Queen, he read half aloud. What did that mean? On another, pineapples, melons, and apricots were painted next to the word φρεσκοι χυμοι.

"Fruit juices," Ariane said, noticing his look. "You'll probably need a Babble, er, Babel wish sometime soon. Did you know it was a friend of mine who caused that skyscraper construction to go wrong in Babylon some time ago? She was employed as a translation fairy and was supposed to facilitate communication. But then the chief architect grabbed her butt without being asked. Dirty bastard, huh. Anyway, she got pissed off and turned all the wishes into the opposite. After that nobody understood each other. Probably not even themselves…"

Joe stared at her in confusion.

"Fruit juices? Some time ago? Babylon? Wasn't that in the Bible?" He shook his head helplessly. "Where are we, anyway?" he asked the fairy. "Did the inquisitors get us? Where is Kaura, and what happened to the others?"

The fairy grabbed his hand and led him over to one of the metallic seats.

"Lots of questions, blondie! But sit down first. Otherwise, you'll tip right out of your socks again and I'll have to wish away a second concussion."

Gently, the fairy pushed him down into the cushions, surprisingly soft despite their steely appearance. The little woman with the purple wings cast a satisfied look around the room.

"We'll probably have some time before we're meeting the local chief Iroquois. After seven hundred years of dead Portals, I'm sure they don't check in here every five minutes."

With an elegant sweep of her semi-transparent wings, she plopped down on a second of the sofas opposite Joe. For a moment, she looked like a delicately crafted doll that a rich child had left on the sofa, sitting on the huge, glittering upholstered furniture.

She grinned smugly.

"So. question number one. That sign over there says 'Welcome to the Central Star Port of Aalid' in Lemurian, Hellenic, and Atlantean."

The fairy pointed her finger at a larger one of the glass signs, which was fixed in a plain Gothic archway made of the same wood as the floor, through which at least ten people could have passed side by side.

Joe vaguely recalled seeing similar writing on the metal cube in Rhodes that Kaura had operated to bring the portal into service. He could even read the Atlantean greeting now that his attention had been drawn to the sign. Next to the lettering, three-dimensional images of palm trees, waterfalls, and smoking volcanoes seemed to have been engraved into the glass in filigree work.

"So, I guess we're on Aalid," Ariane continued. "Where Kaura was headed. Since there are no blue-noses to be seen, I assume they didn't catch us. Did they?"

She looked at the Scot with a supremely cute upturn of her bright fairy eyes. "Kaura was wearing one of those nice silver necklaces the last time I saw her, which suggests she was caught by the inquisitors.

Otherwise, she probably would have come with us. However, Sen, Diana and the others knew where we were going. So, I'm going to assume that they took out the holey blue slippers and freed Kaura. As to what happened to the others, I don't know right now, because unfortunately my clairvoyance wishes don't reach further than a million miles. Not even to the next planet of these surely extremely nice starlets here."

She waved over to the large panorama window, where two suns stood not far from each other in the sky. Then she leaned back, nuzzled her wings into the soft cushion and closed her eyes for a moment with relish.

Joe said nothing. He looked up, where a large, midnight-blue dome stretched over the hall, bathed in soft light. In front of a background of flashing golden stars floated an extremely realistic and three-dimensional sphere, painted in blue, yellow-brown and green. It slowly rotated around its own axis. In long streaks and spirals, disheveled bands of white shadows moved, only slightly faster, across the surface of the sphere.

The Scot narrowed his eyes. Something about the pattern of the sphere seemed familiar. Suddenly, the scales fell from his eyes.

"Is that—Gaia?" he asked? "That shape there looks like Europe and the Mediterranean on the maps. Some kind of globe, like the Queen's?"

Ariane, who had meanwhile opened her eyes again, followed his gaze.

"Yes, that's it. The blue planet," she breathed dreamily. "The center of the known universe, still. Maximum magical desire potential field. My adopted home. I wouldn't want to trade."

She pointed to a ribbon surrounding the bottom of the dome with a large band of lettering in gold, highlighted letters. "The Gaia Portal Hall. Probably formerly the center of this humble space port here, where the inhabitants came on weekends, ate exotic foods, drank juices made from hard-to-find earthly fruits, and dreamed of long journeys into the depths of the universe, to where their ancestors had once come from. And watching those who had the right passport and could live that dream."

Her gaze fell back to where Joe had been lying earlier. On the floor was drawn a large circle, ten yards in diameter, inlaid with silver metal in the wooden floor. In the center of the circle rose two low, cylindrical columns of the same shiny metal, a little more than a yard apart. Outside the circle, lines were embedded in the floor in front of some sort of small bar table, which had probably been intended for waiting Portal passengers.

"When the gate is in operation, the arch is probably made of pure light," the fairy remarked. Then she turned around.

"Ah, we have company coming. And I'm still owing you the Brabbelwish."

She drew her staff and touched Joe's ears and mouth lightly with its glowing tip.

"Since we don't know if Kaura can still join us or not, I guess we'll have to negotiate with the Aalids ourselves to get the help we need to Earth. But I'm sure you're good at that, you trading shotgun, aren't you?"

Joe grinned weakly.

"Let's see. Most of the time I know what I'm doing pretty well, even though I've never had to deal with aliens before. Just try not to mortally offend everyone in the first minute, okay? I don't know how they're going to react culturally to that kind of thing here."

Ariane twisted her lips into a pout, with which she probably wanted to express that she once again felt misunderstood.

"Offend? Not me. Never. I merely gently point out everyone's most salient qualities. With us, that's considered a sign of utmost deference. Veritas numquam perit, if you know what I mean." She chuckled.

Hasty footsteps could now be heard through the Gothic archway of white-gray wood, resounding far through the empty hall and echoing back from the walls. Turning the corner were three dark blond women who, with their even faces and full lips, looked almost like triplets. They wore skin-tight pantsuits made of a silky, shimmering emerald fabric, which emphasized their feminine forms to their advantage and left only a few details of their well-trained bodies to the imagination.

Joe rose and walked toward them. He put on his most winning smile and slowly raised his hand in greeting.

"Hello," he called out when they were a little closer. "We are here on behalf of the High Priestesses of Lemuria, and we come in peace." It couldn't hurt, he thought, to lay it on a little thick right from the start. You never knew if they'd start shooting right away here or something. "My name is Joe Nelson. From Gaia," he added.

"Welcome, stranger," the foremost of the three women addressed him in a melodic singsong. Only in a back part of his consciousness did Joe sense that she was actually using quite different words. Ariane's translation spell seemed to work just fine.

"Our sensors indicated the activation of the portal," the woman continued. "We've been waiting a long time. Are you announcing new immigrants for our offspring diversity program?"

Joe shrugged.

"I don't know anything about that, unfortunately, Venerable, although I'm sure it can be negotiated once the Portals are open again permanently. I come with a request for help from the Lemurians. Can we speak with your government?"

The foremost of the three was now standing so close to Joe that their noses were almost touching. Joe felt a moment of uncertainty. He knew nothing about the greeting customs of these people. Was she going to kiss him? What was expected of him? He decided to just wait and see.

Gently, the woman bent forward a bit and touched Joe's nostrils once on the left and once on the right with the tip of her nose. She gave off a gossamer scent of rosemary. In the end, she grabbed the back of his head with both hands and pulled him down to her until their foreheads touched. Her breasts pressed gently against him. Joe took a deep breath as she let go of him again, one of her companions moving up for the same ritual.

Ariane enjoyed the same greeting, although it was a bit more difficult there due to the size difference. Helpfully, the fairy fluttered in front of the Aalids' faces, and everyone giggled until it finally worked after a few tries.

"I am Ojai Arineshel, the commander of this space port," said the first woman, also introducing her companions. "We will immediately provide you with transportation into the city to speak to the Great Circle, where you can voice your request. Please come with us."

She leaned a little closer to Joe. "And should you decide to join our offspring program after all, please think of me. Too many machines here, not enough organics," she whispered.

Joe was confused. Offspring program? Organics? Machinery? Well, he would certainly be able to get to the bottom of it.

"Yeah, I think you're cute too," the Scot muttered, before he could stop himself. That seemed to have been the right answer. Ojai positively beamed as she turned and led the two travelers out. Beyond the archway was a wide tunnel that seemed to hover a few dozen yards above a vast plain discernible through rows of narrow windows.

Outside, the sun was shining—the suns were shining, Joe corrected himself, because, after all, there were two of the golden glowing ember balls to be seen. One seemed to be a little whiter, the other redder in color. Through the tinted glass of the windows, Joe could view the bright celestial bodies without being blinded.

The plain was full of round and oval, shiny metallic objects standing around on circular platforms made of some kind of green obsidian, moving through the air in all directions, one of them disappearing now and then into the steel-blue sky like a fired cannonball.

Images of landscapes and cities flitted across the bright wooden slats on the rounded side walls of the tunnel. Joe recognized the Pyramids of Pyrrha and the Rock of Gibraltar. Everything else told him nothing. Red, huge arches of rock. A valley that was a mile wide and at least as deep. People below trees that towered over them a hundredfold. Animals with long trunks that reminded him of Gan'olin. Other animals like horses with unnaturally long necks, huge cats resting in a pack under a tree. The image of a street filled with people, where most wore multi-colored turbans.

Then they arrived at the end of the tunnel. It was cordoned off with a wide red cord, from which hung a golden sign.

"Zone closed. No entry," he read half aloud, surprised that he could understand the strange, spiraling characters.

"Not bad, my Babblewish, is it?" whispered the fairy fluttering beside him.

"Very classy, Ariane, thank you," he murmured back. There were more passersby out here. Travelers with floating suitcases, following their owners like obedient dogs, scurried about. Humans and some other beings sat at tables and on benches lining the walls, reading, talking, eating, or gazing as if spellbound at small, metallic boxes they held in their hands. There was a variety of colors and shapes of clothing and headgear.

Only at second glance did Sen notice that at least ten percent of the women looked remarkably like his three companions. Then he realized that many of the other passersby also looked almost as much alike as twin brothers and sisters. All in all, he estimated, he saw perhaps twenty or thirty starkly different basic types of people in various body shapes and skin types, but with little distinction within the group.

He asked Ojai about it. The blonde woman blushed slightly and lowered her eyes.

"A few centuries ago, there was a trend toward genetic standardization. Ideals of beauty, you know? People wanted to make themselves more beautiful, and most of them somehow had similar ideas of what they wanted to look like. Meanwhile, those who still look different in some way are considered most beautiful. But please don't mention that again, it's considered a grave insult in our culture to compare people's physical appearance."

Joe nodded thoughtfully, thanked her for her openness, then wordlessly followed her, passing under a sign that said *Port Authority*, with an arrow pointing up. He looked up in the direction of the arrow but saw only the ceiling. Shaking his head, he walked on. Ojai led him through a side door, which she opened with a word, into an area where everyone wore overalls similar to those of the three women.

Unconcerned, his guide approached an opening behind which there seemed to be a steep drop. Joe expected her to stop where the floor ended, but she simply stepped out into the void. Desperately, he reached out to stop her fall, but in the process fell forward himself with a yelp. Suddenly, he floated belly-down in empty space and widened his eyes, expecting to see the distant ground beneath him rapidly approaching. But he only floated gently downward. Next to him he saw the brownish boots of his companions, which seemed to be made of some kind of soft leather.

He tried to turn around but got caught in a fast rotation around his body axis, which made nausea rise up in him again.

"Ah, don't you have gravity elevators?" Ojai's voice asked from above. "Sorry."

She grabbed Joe's collar with a practiced hand, stopped the rotation, and stood him upright.

"Thank you," he said, tugging his linen shirt into place, struggling to maintain his composure.

She pointed to the slowly passing entrances.

"To get out, just move a little more toward the opening you want to take. There, the tractor field slows down and puts you in front of the entrance all by itself. But we want to go all the way down anyway, to the glider station."

She tapped her earlobe. "Ilat, a comfort glider please in a minute at the A gate. Thank you."

When the soles of his boots gently touched the bottom of the shaft, Joe managed not to fall this time. He quickly left the somewhat eerie chamber, as Ojai's companions came floating down from above. They deftly dodged him so that he didn't get one of their boots on his head.

Outside, Ojai exchanged a few words with her subordinates. Then she turned to Joe and Ariane.

"I will accompany you. You'll get through the Great Circle faster and won't have to explain the same thing to everyone."

Meanwhile, with a low hum, a bright purple thing slid up next to her that looked like two sofas, each with two seats, pushed side by side and hovering about a foot's width above the floor.

Invitingly, Ojai pointed to the left of them and sat down next to Joe. He winced as the two sofas turned crosswise, so that he and Ojai were now on the front of two rows of seats floating one behind the other.

There was a small, carpeted platform in front of the sofa that seemed to be meant to put their feet, which automatically adjusted its position to the length of Joe's legs.

"To the Grand Circle, Ministry of Extraplanetary Affairs," the

Aalid spaceport master ordered. The air around them billowed, and suddenly they were sitting in a semi-transparent purple shell.

"We could also make them completely transparent, but then people are more likely to get nauseous. And you seem to be a bit sensitive," Ojai remarked apologetically, while Ariane made a satisfied noise.

"Purple. Like my wings. These people here have taste," she murmured appreciatively.

The hover ship—for it seemed to be something like that, even though neither sails, steam engine nor any other visible source of locomotion were recognizable—took off and accelerated out of the forecourt at such a high speed that Joe involuntarily raised his arm in front of his face, expecting to be hit by a violent headwind. But nothing happened. The inside of the bubble remained silent.

Carefully, he touched the purple shell, which seemed to be made of glass or something similar. In any case, it offered noticeable, hard resistance to his hands, which he gratefully acknowledged, since the streets and buildings below him had now already sunk several hundred yards into the depths below them.

He pointed to the two suns, one of which was still near the zenith, while the second was just about to set, becoming redder and redder as it approached the horizon. Now expansive fields, forests and lakes were visible below him.

"Do you guys ever actually get night, or do you have even more suns?"

"No, just Tritavia and Piralum," she replied. "Night is about a third shorter than day in most parts of Aalid. We also have an inclined planetary axis. That means we have seasons almost everywhere, as in the home of the ancients, and at the pole facing the suns it never gets dark in summer."

She leaned softly against his shoulder, brushing him with her breasts as if unintentionally. "What's it actually like there? You must be incredibly advanced, with the Lemurians and all. The primordial mothers of technology and magic. After you have talked to the ministers, you have to tell me everything. Fashion, what you do, if you have several languages, what kind of landscapes there are... I'll buy you a drink. I'm sure the Aalid state will pay for a nice hotel for you. Off-planet guests of the state! From Lemur! Or Gaia, as you call yourselves now. The groupies will be beating down your door! And probably all the newspaper people will want to talk to you! After all, no one has been able to enter Gaia for almost a thousand years. They say that our grandmothers feared that something had happened to you when the portal closed so abruptly, and all lines of communication were cut off. Our government supposedly even sent a large expedition with many spaceships to support you. But they did not get through the Solaris system's barrier field. After they had determined by remote telescopy that the planet still existed, they turned back again. But the events still offer a lot of material for conspiracy theorists, especially since it was never officially found out what happened and if the contact break-off was wanted by the Lemurians or caused from the outside. They were the only ones who could create these Portals. No one else has ever reached their technical maturity."

Ariane listened to the Aalid with interest and seemed to be pleased that finally someone else talked as much as she did. But now she hooked in.

"What, I thought the Aalids built the Portals for the Lemurians because they weren't as interested in technology anymore? Strange."

"Well, I think now that contact has been re-established, we'll be able to get more clarity on this soon," Joe interjected. "Actually, I'm not the original envoy. But there was an accident at the gate, and the High Priestess they sent could not come. It was kind of a state of war. Gaia has some major problems right now, unfortunately."

Ojai looked at him sympathetically. "War? That's bad. We read about things like that here sometimes. So unnecessary. There still seem to be civilizations that do such primitive things. But on Gaia? That's not even possible."

Joe shrugged.

"Unfortunately, it is. It all seems to go back to a plan that beings called Kai'ala have concocted together with some people who call themselves the 'gods'."

"Kai'ala, gods, I've never heard of that," replied the woman, who otherwise seemed to know a great deal. "Here we are already. Soon you will be able to bring your problem to the right people."

The glider swung in an elegant arc to the left, approaching a building that loomed like a giant 'O'-shape in the afternoon sky, which now had become much dimmer after the setting of one of the suns.

Thoughtfully, Joe looked ahead as they dipped into the shadow of the monster building. Up close, he now realized it must have at least a hundred floors. He knew so little. With only that much, would he be able to convince the Aalid government to come to the aid of Kaura and the magical beings of Gaia? He didn't know. And even if he could convince them, they still had to get back to Gaia. Something that obviously no one had been able to do for seven hundred years, not even these strange people here with all their technology that seemed like high magic. So many imponderables.

But at least it had started well, the Scotsman thought with a sideways glance at the elegant profile of the woman next to him, who was talking to Ariane in a murmur and was explaining some details of the government palace to her. There was a wish fairy accompanying him, and he had already found a friend on this strange planet.

5

Treason

With her robe billowing, Kaura paced back and forth in front of the floor-to-ceiling glass window like a caged tigress. She pondered. In between, she broke her stride to gaze out over the nocturnal sea of golden, silver, and rainbow-colored dots that she knew were signs of the vibrancy of the Atlantean capital stretching out far below her feet.

The Lemurian was still annoyed, but didn't let it show, even now when she was finally alone. The Atlanteans reminded her too much of her own people, who simply didn't care about anything that happened outside their own small, comfortable universe. The Pyrrheans might have been much the same, she mused. But a few years of siege by the Spanish had woken them up. They had understood that, despite their technological superiority, they could not ignore what was happening outside their little bubble.

Probably Pyrrha had always been a little more open than the two ancient cultures of Gaia, Lemuria and Atlantis, simply because of its role as a link between peoples and planets. The crystal priests had provided them with excellent accommodations.

Kaura had been given a huge suite of rooms on the thirtieth floor of a distant pyramidal wing of the Crystal Palace, from which she had a good view of the auroric lights of the capital. The Pyrrheans had been taken to the pilgrims' quarters in a more distant part of the building. Presumably the chambers there were somewhat simpler, but still more than adequate.

Kaura had just showered for the first time in six years with warm water flowing from the ceiling. To have running water over a hundred yards above the park whose treetops she was currently looking out on! Crazy. But of course, in Lemuria there were also cities with skyscrapers of dozens of stacked, tree-covered and ivy-covered stories, into which the water they needed was transported by magically powered pumps.

She thought of Joe. The enthusiastic Scot loved new inventions and would probably have been in seventh heaven here. But he would get a fair share of surprises on Aalid, too. Kaura's elegantly curved lips twisted into a fleeting grin. The Aalid girls probably hadn't changed much in the last few hundred years. They would love to host a man from Gaia. She giggled. Hopefully there would be no civil war over the young Scotsman!

Thoughtfully, she watched the fast-moving lights of the hover gliders whizzing along about ten yards above the ground far below her. Small groups of passersby, small as ants from here, sometimes couples, moved through the park, which was lit in spots with golden and blue lights. Joe. Did she love the young man? Or was it just physical attraction? After all, she was more than nine thousand years older than the London merchant. She wasn't worried about him. Ariane was unbeatable as a bodyguard. And her friend would be able to convince the Aalids to send help without much trouble.

He only had to promise them a few volunteers for their 'offspring program', and they would do anything for him.

The only question was whether they could help. But they probably could. The shield had become penetrable for the ships of the Kai'ala and the gods. So, the Aalid star galleons would be able to get through as well. She took a deep breath and exhaled.

Suddenly Sen came to her mind. Had they thought of letting him, Simon and Eagle in on the operation of what was probably an extremely unfamiliar environment for them? She decided to go and see if they needed any help. She didn't worry about the fairies. Knowing them, they had surely already figured out how to operate the automatic bartender machine and everything else they needed for a wild party.

When she placed her palm on the control panel of the entrance door, the mahogany wooden panel, richly decorated with triangular and square metal ornaments, slid noiselessly to the side into the wall.

Quietly, she walked across the thick carpet to the door behind which she had seen Sen disappear when she arrived. From a door next to her came loud screeching, jeering and singing. Something seemed to break with a loud shattering noise.

Kaura grinned. Fairies and parties of any kind rarely stayed apart for long. At least, with a wave of their wands, they could right the havoc they wreaked. If they felt like it at the time.

When she arrived at Sen's door, she ran her hands through her hair and felt a moment of uncertainty. Would she disturb him? After all, it was late. On a small wooden plaque next to the door was his name in glowing letters that seemed engraved in the grain of the wood, but were probably simply a projected auroric effect: Prof. Dr. Dr. Seneca R. Lumisworth, Head of Lockwood Magical Society.

She raised her hand to the green backlit button, which was probably supposed to mean that Sen would receive visitors. That is, if he had any idea how to set the doorbell. When her finger was only a few millimeters away from it, the door swung aside without transition and Sen ran right into her. A shrill jingling sounded from his hair as he was slowed so suddenly.

She held onto the door frame to keep from falling and steadied the older man with a firm grip around his upper arm.

"Where to, Headmaster?" she grinned. "I was just checking to see if you can understand the room setup."

The Scotsman grinned and shook his head, whereupon the bells spoke up again.

"Don't worry, Venerable High Priestess, we've already had a technical introduction given to us. I was merely on my way to see if you would like to join our cuddle session here. He gestured over his shoulder into the room. On a sofa sprawled out to the maximum, Eagle and Simon leaned against each other. The Algonquin woman waved invitingly.

"Well, I guess I don't have anything better planned for today. We can't go to the Crystal Priest Council until tomorrow anyway," she said and entered.

Sen closed the door behind her.

"I assume, as a Lemurian, you are well aware of the eminent importance of cuddling after life-threatening actions," the principal said behind her as she walked over to the sofa. "Shake first, then cuddle. That's what animals do. Cleanses the nervous system. Have you shaken yourself yet today?"

Kaura nodded, slid onto the couch and leaned against Simon, who put a hand around her.

"Yeah, it wouldn't be good to keep trauma in our bodies," she replied. "The collar thing was really intense. I've been around a few years now, but I don't think I've ever felt so helpless."

Sen grumbled in agreement as he too slid onto the cushion with an elegant movement and nestled between Simon and Eagle with a satisfied sigh.

"Really nasty things, those collars."

His face lit up when he thought of something else. "But these Atlanteans are incredible. Take a look at this couch. Voice controlled, retractable, adjustable on all sides! You can even adjust the softness! And all this without a single magic weave. The attendant who showed us all this said it was aurorically controlled! Aurorically! I heard the Mongols were experimenting with auroric light, a kind of controlled lightning strikes. But other than that, I've never seen any practical application of this theory."

Simon sighed pleasantly.

"Yes, who would have thought... horseless, floating carriages. Houses as high as mountains. Glass windows taller than a person, completely transparent. Auroric sofas. Magic without any magic at all. Well, I can't wait to see what other surprises are in store for us."

Relaxing, he closed his eyes and allowed his body to melt even further against Kaura's.

Eagle moved and rested her head on Sen's lap.

"Do you know, Kaura, why all these things are only allowed to exist here? Why did you, or your ancestors, forbid people to use all this technology? After all, not everyone can wield spells like we can. For us, this is all nice, but superfluous. But many people could live much nicer lives with something like this, couldn't they?"

Kaura shrugged and adjusted her own position. She fleetingly stroked Sen's thigh, which he acknowledged with a low, pleasurable growl. She spoke softly, thoughtfully.

"Auroric sofas. Hover boats, starships. I don't know if that makes it all that much better. They say that the power generation for all these amenities was extremely dirty a few tens of thousands of years ago, when the Lemurians originally made these laws. Sewage was dumped into the seas, clouds full of toxins got into the clouds and into the lungs of people and animals. Magic was considered 'clean' at that time. But of course, the magicians also made up the vast majority of the population back then. Today this is probably still the case in Lemuria, but probably not even in Atlantis. And in the peace treaty of Ilkarion so much nature compatibility was demanded from the Atlanteans, that Atlantia today probably pollutes the earth less than London. Despite all comfort. We should probably fundamentally question these rules."

Sen nodded.

"Imagine what that would be like if we could just provide clean water and public lavatories to all the people in London. Probably dysentery and plague would almost disappear. We believe that probably today in Britain at most one person in a thousand is born with magical abilities. And there are more and more of us wingless flat-footed buggers, as the fairies are so fond of calling us. Human society is expanding all the time, it's probably part of our nature."

Kaura stared up at the ceiling above her, decorated with intertwining angular patterns.

"I will propose to the Council of Ixchel'en to reopen Lemuria and share our knowledge with the rest of the world. If we had done this from the beginning, it probably wouldn't have come to this."

Eagle sighed and shook her head.

"You don't really know. You may be a little too withdrawn and introverted. Others are too power-hungry. Maybe now the Spanish would just have better means to subjugate the people of my lands and resist you, and otherwise we'd be in the same predicament."

Simon shrugged.

"Who knows. It is what it is. And from here, we have to see where we go from here."

Everyone was silent, each with their own thoughts, as the night grew darker and deeper outside the pointed side tower of the Crystal Palace.

The next day they were received by the Crystal Council. The Mahdi—her actual name was Elane—and Gan'olin were also present. The two of them had preferred to take up quarters in the area of their fellow citizens in order to be able to assist them with questions. Furthermore, the experience of their arrival had not necessarily increased the refugees' confidence in their hosts.

Despite the assurances of the crystal priests to guarantee the safety of their guests, many were afraid of being taken away by night and fog and delivered to the Spaniards. The surviving remnants of the Pyrrhean city guard had spent the night organizing patrols in the refugee quarters to keep people calm. The Cristal Palace's own security guards, meanwhile, had kept a low profile, merely setting up a few posts at the entrances to the pilgrims' wing.

Still, some of the more enterprising newcomers had already left their quarters in the evening and had seen parts of the city. Since they had reported only positive experiences with the Atlanteans, the two Pyrrhean leaders hoped that the fears would soon calm down.

The Crystal Council met in a room far up in the south tower of the temple. The tower was shaped like an obelisk with a very sharply pointed top. All four sides of the hall were slanted inward from the bottom to the top and were made entirely of transparent crystal. Kaura could see no supports, so it seemed that the ceiling of gleaming golden metal, decorated with polygonal geometric patterns, hung above them completely unsupported. This gave the impression that they were standing in free air far above the streets of Atlantia, a free-floating pyramid spire weighing many hundreds of tons above them.

Even the two Pyrrheans, familiar with magical construction methods, seemed to be somewhat thrown off by this, casting a cursory glance upward now and then.

The purple-bearded Supreme Crystal Councilor sat in the middle of his exclusively male colleagues. The priests' beard colors seemed to have significance beyond mere fashion, for Kaura saw all the colors of the rainbow among the nine men present, plus white—this man had silver threads woven into his beard—and black, which was achieved not by dyeing but by strings of obsidian beads.

The Atlanteans were enthroned on semi-transparent shimmering chair-like structures. Otherwise, the hall was empty, except for a huge crystal in the center of the room. The stone had to be at least two yards high at its greatest extent, was almost transparent, and cast rainbow-colored reflections all over the floor, which was covered with a thick-pile white carpet.

Eriniel rose and came to meet Kaura and the others as the purple-clad guardsman who had brought them in stood back at the door. He warmly embraced the Lemurian and then turned to her companions.

"Once again, welcome to the Crystal Temple of Atlantia! We are pleased and honored to receive such a distinguished delegation of foreign mages. Be assured that we will support you with all our resources. This also applies to those who have lost—hopefully only temporarily—their homes in Pyrrha," he added, addressing Elane and Gan'olin. "Please sit down!"

Noticing how everyone looked around the almost empty room, he laughed good-naturedly.

"Just sit down. The system will recognize your intent and provide a chair."

Carefully, Kaura let herself sink backwards and, to be on the safe side, reached out her hand underneath her. In fact, she soon encountered a resistance that steadily increased its firmness on contact with her buttocks. Only then did she dare to give her entire weight to the unusual seat and lean back. Diana, meanwhile, took a bit of a run-up, folded in her wings, and shot like a glittering cannonball, butt ahead, toward a vacant seat across from the crystal priests.

"Yippee!" she yelled gleefully as her free fall about a yard above the ground also slowed down and another of the glowing chair formations formed below her. Sen and the other mages sat down with a bit more dignity.

Then Erin introduced his council colleagues individually, with their role and function. Kaura did the same for her companions. She then gave a concise overview of what had happened so far and once again formally requested assistance in resolving the crisis that had currently left Lemuria in an incapacitated state.

The man with the yellow-colored beard—his name was Akuel and he was responsible for security issues among the priests—leaned forward.

"We are deeply disturbed by the information that the Spaniards have taken Pyrrha. We know that the Spanish Grand Sultan Philip II in Granada has invasion plans towards Atlantis as well. But the fact that they are collaborating with these Kai'ala and are also not afraid to use magical slaves for warlike purposes is news to me. I think with this news we should be able to convince the Council of Seven and the Parliament to take more initiative in this conflict."

Erin shook his head.

"I wouldn't be so sure about that. We have to try, by all means. But the isolationist forces are strong. Ministers Ixkarel and Uriel in particular are doing everything they can to tell people they're safe here and just need to close their eyes, so to speak, so they can't be found and harmed."

Kaura thought back to the hide-and-seek games of her childhood so long ago. Indeed, Gifted Lemurian children could hide by closing their eyes and wishing themselves away from the world. Of course, the hunters usually also had psychic abilities, which simply added extra dimensions to the game. She cleared her throat.

"At least we were able to activate Pyrrha's security circuit. This means that all Spanish troops who were in the area of the tech-nomagic field at the time are now trapped in a time loop. If we assume that the Spanish used most of their slaves and Kai'ala in this attack—which would be logical, in view of their adversaries—then they are now decisively weakened. And we might just be able to go to Granada and put an end to it."

Erin stared at her.

"A Lemurian as an advocate of offensive warfare! Things do seem to have changed there. Do you have a fever or something? Been too long without hugging a tree?"

The supreme crystal priest broke off, only now seeming to realize what he'd just said. His pale face flushed slightly.

"Sorry, didn't mean it that way. The fairies do rub off a bit. I was invited to a nice party last night."

Diana giggled.

"Yeah, you sure let it rip, honey! I didn't know it was possible to party so well with you Atlanteans. And you guys look as serious as a pint of beer. Build all that angular stuff."

She made a debauched hand gesture over to the main crystal-shaped wing of the temple, visible far below them.

Then she grinned smugly. "Thank goodness we were around to fix up the decor afterwards! Otherwise, you would have had to answer some uncomfortable questions from your housekeeping, flowerbeard!"

Now the yellow-bearded man beside Erin cleared his throat at length. He was obviously embarrassed by his superior's slip.

"An incursion into Granada would require a declaration of war by Parliament against the Spanish," he said. "After the entire High Council and our intelligence services have downplayed the situation for years, that won't be easy to achieve, especially without evidence."

Now Gan'olin intervened.

"We have nearly three thousand witnesses to the aggression of the Kai'ala and their Spanish accomplices with us!" he trumpeted angrily, pointing his trunk over to the pilgrim wing. "Isn't that enough? Besides, there's a Lemurian high priestess sitting right here who can give you the legal right to use technology outside of Atlantis. You can do that, can't you, Kaura?"

The small woman looked uncertain for a moment but then nodded.

"I will release you from the contract in the name of the Council of High Priestesses, for the defense of Atlantis. I am convinced that I will be able to represent this later to my colleagues and also in Ixche'len and that you will not suffer any disadvantages from it. If the Atlantian Parliament is willing to act against the Empire in the interest of Gaia and of Lemuria itself, the chances are good that we will later be able to lift the restrictions of the treaty altogether. That should be interesting to your politicians, shouldn't it?"

Erin cradled his head.

"Ten years ago, I would have said they would be eating out of your hand for even a hint of that offer. Now I'm not so sure of that— it's become so difficult to predict the swinging around of reactions." He expelled the air in annoyance. Erin didn't seem like a man who enjoyed dealing with the subtle intricacies of diplomacy.

"The next parliamentary session is in three days," he continued. "I will announce us there. Are you ready to speak to the senators and present your case, Kaura? And you?" he turned to Sen and Elane. "It would certainly be helpful to have direct testimony regarding what happened in Mira'aleitha and Pyrrha. They won't be able to close their hearts to that."

All three reiterated their willingness to address the Atlantis Senate. The chief crystal priest nodded in satisfaction.

Now the priest with the green-tinted beard lifted his white-haired head, speaking up. His deep blue eyes shimmered unfathomably.

"Since the Kai'ala have reappeared after millennia, you suspect that the barrier field surrounding our solar system no longer holds off starships. No one here has ships built for interstellar routes anymore, so we can't verify that. At least you managed to send someone through a portal to Aalid for technical and military support. But the Aalids can't come through a portal, they must fly all the way until Pyrrha's main power supply can be restored. And that will take weeks at best, or even months. Did I understand that correctly?"

Kaura nodded.

"Nicely summarized. I can only add that Joe Nelson, the man we sent to Aalid, is wanted by the Kai'ala as a kind of key with which the Inquisitors want to conquer Atlantis. However, no one knows exactly how this is supposed to work. I almost think that the Spanish got something wrong. Or could it have something to do with the fact that Joe has Atlantian blood in him? His great-grandmother came from Atlantis."

Erin reflected.

"There was an emergency circuit in one of the portals in Pyrrha that allowed any Atlantean to open it to return home in an emergency. The emergency circuit is powered by crystal magic and thus independent of Pyrrha's energy supply. It is possible that the Spaniards had learned of this and hoped for easy access into the heart of Atlantia. But from what you have told us, Pyrrha has become an inaccessible zone for an indefinite period of time. So I guess we don't have to worry about that anymore."

The Atlanteans talked with their guests for some time longer. They also revealed more information about their homeland without hesitation, which was of great interest to Sen. At least in this company there was no sign of the famous reserve and secrecy of the islanders.

The two great islands which formed the Realm of Atlantis had a combined extent of over two thousand miles in length and about three hundred at the widest point. Atlantis ranged climatically from the more temperate climate of the mountain range connecting it to the Irish Peninsula down into the subtropics. It separated the Gulf of Atlantis from the Atlantic Ocean proper, which stretched all the way up to Viking-ruled Snow Country and down to the perennial ice rivers of Tierra del Fuego. The Spanish sent most of their gold and silver convoys from New Spain through two narrow passages, the Azores Strait between the two main Atlantean islands, and the Canary Strait between Africa and the South Atlantic.

The Atlanteans could have easily disrupted both of these routes and had indeed done so once when they came to the aid of the Aztecs under King Monteczuma in the war against the Conquistadors. No wonder, then, that the sultan wanted to get this obstructive block between his overseas cash cow and the motherland in southern Europe under control at all costs.

Furthermore, it was also known in Granada that the Atlanteans were no friends of the trade in African slaves, which was mainly operated from the Cape Verde Islands, located somewhat further south. However, the sultan and his people needed this 'human material' to operate the Spanish-Ottoman mines and plantations in the New World as profitably as possible. The fact that often only half of the men, women and children crammed into the bellies of the galleons under inhumane conditions survived the long sea voyage obviously mattered little to the ruler and the nobles in Granada and Havana.

However, the ease with which the Atlanteans had forced them out of King Monteczuma's kingdom had made them realize how easily the islanders could put a stop to this lucrative trade, too, if only they wanted to. And ever since then, they had been planning the conquest of Atlantis, which was an extremely difficult matter due to its technological superiority. Erin even suspected that this was the reason why the government in Granada had been so willing to fall for the Kai'ala's scheme and let themselves be manipulated. The aliens must have made the right promises to the Sultan, who had thrown overboard not only all moral qualms, but also the resentment against magic that had been fostered throughout the Spanish Ottoman Empire for centuries and had effectively handed over the management of the most powerful authority in the state to the blue-skinned mages.

Kaura felt more and more uncomfortable the further this discussion progressed. She could only follow the arguments because of what she had learned during her time in Inmarsund. She was only too aware that most people in Lemuria had no idea what the so-called 'noble barbarians' were doing to each other here. Among the leading thinkers in Lemuria, a largely idealized image of romantic Stone Age people prevailed regarding the rest of Gaia's population. Half-naked, noble savages who lived in harmony with nature and its rhythms, went hunting, gathered berries, sat together at night in front of the campfire and told each other stories. The fact that development had also continued outside of the Pacific region simply did not fit into the picture in the culture of the Lemurians, which had moved back to a high level of closeness to nature.

The Atlanteans were simply seen as evil technocrats from whom the innocent people in Asia, Europe and America had to be protected. But especially the Europeans and Asians had developed relatively advanced societies in the meantime, which had to be supported rather than kept small. Otherwise, they would be the ones who, through war, power games and underdeveloped technology, again initiated the very processes from which the Lemurians had been trying to protect the planet for tens of thousands of years.

The Kai'ala and their masters had recognized this and had taken advantage of the Spanish-Ottoman rulers' greed for expansion and gold, while the formerly most advanced civilization of Gaia had wallowed in its introverted delusion of nature and had even hindered the second real power on the planet, the Atlanteans, from doing the right thing. Kaura shuddered.

Hopefully it was not too late. No, it must not be too late. The

Lemurians could still intervene. And once the Spaniards understood what was at stake, they, too, would not be able to deny themselves a more progressive, more humane culture. They would...

Suddenly, she looked up. Sen had asked her something, and everyone was looking at her.

"Sorry, I wasn't listening just now," she muttered.

"I was wondering if the Lemurians couldn't assist us significantly if we can eliminate this death field around your continent," he repeated his question. "After all, you are the oldest race of mages on Gaia and possibly ever."

Kaura nodded.

"Of course. I now have regular contact with the Fern Temple via the dream world. Our people have been working flat out on a solution for years but haven't had any real breakthroughs yet. The fluctuation that allowed me to penetrate the death shield with the help of the strongest protection spells ever obviously only happens every few years and is not deemed safe for the transfer of larger groups of people. If we can do something for them from the outside, it would certainly speed things up. Just how do we find the place where this field is set up?"

Sen grinned.

"You really weren't listening, my dear. Erin here has just told us that the Atlanteans possess long-range hover ships equipped with the most advanced tracking devices. With that, the energy signature of such a powerful field emissor should be easily detectable, assuming it is auroric in nature. Or, if the field is magical in nature, Eagle can find it with her location pentacles. All we have to do," he happily drew circles in the air with his index finger, "is fly around your little island and not let the Kai'ala catch us until we find the installation."

"And then BOOM!" screamed Diana so abruptly that everyone cringed.

The fairy laughed crazily and seemed to enjoy the effect of her exclamation.

A long moment of silence followed. Then Kaura nodded slowly. She spoke softly, almost to herself.

"Yes. And then boom. Yes, that's a good idea. If the Atlanteans can provide us with an armed and properly equipped ship."

Erin made a throwaway hand gesture.

"We can take care of that. The Crystal Temple has its own small fleet. For now, it is important that we obtain the Senate's willingness to end the isolation of Atlantis and to be allowed to actively intervene in the conflict. I would prefer not to have to act in illegality."

Kaura sat up straight.

"We'll convince your people, Erin, don't worry. And now I'm sure you have other things to do. With your permission, we'll retire and discuss what's next between us. We also wanted to look at the city sometime."

The crystal priest nodded.

"You can move freely everywhere. You all seem to speak Atlantean. Do you need a bodyguard? I don't think Ixkarel will dare to move openly against you while you're under our protection, but you never know."

Kaura thanked him but declined.

"We do have the fairies. None of us will leave the palace without at least one accompanying us. That should be enough to be prepared for all sorts of problems."

Two hours later, Sen, Kaura, and Diana strolled through the large city park that stretched across from the temple's main entrance for at least two miles toward the city center proper. Behind them, the crystal-clad apartment buildings and counting houses of the Atlantean companies, some over a thousand feet high, shone and glittered in the warm afternoon sun.

Atlantia was located in the west of the southern continent, so it had a very warm climate, though tempered by the fresh wind that reached the city from the ocean just a few miles beyond the center.

In Lemuria, a park like this one would probably have been full of naked walkers and sun worshippers on a warm day, Kaura thought. Here, everyone wore those wide, silky cloaks and robes that seemed typical of the Atlantean fashion.

The park was full of varieties of trees from all over the world, most of which had been planted in angular geometric lines. Kaura saw three huge, tropical fig trees that had let their aerial roots travel to an extent of over a hundred yards into their surroundings.

Children played in the branches and natural caves of these giants. Furthermore, there were oaks, beeches, birches, immense plane trees and, a little further away, a redwood tree certainly over a hundred yards high, shimmering reddish in the sun. In the center of the park rose a giant fountain, where gushing water painted constantly changing geometric figures in the blue sky above the city. Triangles, squares, rhombuses, even hexagons seemed to dominate this work of art of water alchemy.

Along the paths paved with cool, milky roughened crystal, street vendors offered goods, drinks and food. Everywhere, steam emanated from gleaming metallic pots, and enticing scents of cardamom, roasted corn, freshly baked bread, and waffles drifted across the vast meadows dotted with grass and flowers of various colors.

One of the stalls offered freshly baked, spirally tapered waffles filled with some kind of colored ice cream or pudding. Kaura approached curiously and pointed at random to a white, green and pink mass, which was filled into one of the cones smelling of fresh dough by a smiling white-haired boy.

The crystal priests had given them each a small, thin metal card that could be used to pay instead of coins, and Kaura now held it out to the boy as she accepted the cone. With other passers-by she had seen that the mass was licked with the tongue. Nevertheless, she expelled the air in surprise when she felt that the colored mixture was indeed cold. And sweet. So much concentrated sugar, it really was a powerful drug, she thought, feeling her head suddenly lighten a bit.

Then she held the thing out to Sen.

"Try. You'll like it, I think."

Amused, she smiled as the chief magician's face contorted in surprise at contact with the cold stuff, but then he seemed to enjoy the sweetness of this food with the utmost attentiveness.

Diana shaped the tip of her fairy wand into a spoon—giant by her standards—and scooped a generous portion of the sugar ice onto it, in which, in addition to the strong sweetness, other flavors were discernible upon closer inspection, probably strawberry, mint, and something else.

"Hmm," she muttered with her mouth full, "I like these crystal pranksters better and better! Almost as good as on Sirius Q!" Feeling cocky, she did a few loops above the other two's heads, lost the rest of the ice cream from her spoon, and caught it again with a daring dive, just before the dripping mass hit the ground.

The three walked for about three hours before they reached the coast and the harbor on the other side of the city center. The sun was already low on the horizon.

The port of Atlantia seemed to be visited only by smaller, private ships and otherwise served as a recreational area for the townspeople.

Dozens of taverns with airy terraces, market halls with all kinds of goods and services built on the former piers, and a small fun fair, obviously permanently housed here, vied for the favor and money of passers-by. Kaura noticed a tavern that advertised 'Genuine Lemurian Specialties' and went in with Sen and Diana.

They ordered a rice dish with vegetables and fresh fish, which, according to Kaura, had little to do with Lemurian food except for the basic ingredients, but tasted quite good. As they left the restaurant again, something caught Kaura's eye in the hustle and bustle of the masts of the small and larger sailing ships that made her hesitate.

She held Sen back by the sleeve.

"Wait a minute. Those masts over there. That's not one of those Atlantean ships. Might even be a cog, like those still used by the Baltic city-states. My aunt commands a ship like that."

With determination, she wove her way between the numerous passers-by in the direction of the basin where she had seen the masts. When the ship came into view behind a former warehouse, she gasped in surprise.

"Yes, that's her! The Stralsund, Aunt Resa's ship!"

Suddenly she began to run. The lone guard standing midships looked uncertainly toward her and didn't seem to know exactly what to make of the woman rushing toward him. When Kaura was a little closer, he opened his eyes wide and raised a hand in greeting.

"Kaura, is that you?" the young, black-haired man called out in amazement. "What are you doing here? Wait, I'll go get Irma."

Kaura stopped as she stood in front of the ship on the pier.

"Hello Stan! Yes, please. May I come aboard? But what about Resa? Isn't she here?"

The guard swallowed uncomfortably and didn't seem to know quite what to say.

"Wait a moment, please, Kaura. Irma will explain everything."

A short time later, all three sat opposite the ship's first officer, Irma Hangesind, in the captain's quarters of the Stralsund.

"You're guests of the crystal priests?" she exclaimed when Kaura had given her a brief overview of what had happened. "Then maybe you can get us out of here! We've been stuck here for four months now, and all our applications for permission to leave have not even been answered. Then Resa disappeared the week before last when she went to see the Minister of Police about this matter. She did not come back. We approached the Port Guard, but they just refused helping us to find her."

She thought for a moment. "No, actually that's not true. At first, I spoke to an extremely helpful man who assured us of all support. But half a day later, a new guardsman came and simply told us that she had probably escaped on her own, trying to leave the country illegally. They would have her put on the list of wanted persons. Since then, we haven't heard anything, and on all my visits to the city guard, they tell me that someone would come to see us soon. But it never happened." The frustration was easy to see in the officer's face.

"Have you not been able to make your own inquiries?" asked Kaura. Irma's face twisted into a snide grin. "Of course, we tried to do that. We even found someone who probably saw her go into the police headquarters. But what can we do? I even sought an audience with Chief Minister Uriel. But without evidence, it will be difficult."

Kaura straightened up a bit.

"I will arrange for the Crystal Guild people to take care of it. I'm sure that awful Ixkarel has detained her because she became a nuisance to him. There may also be more political prisoners that no one knows about."

She bid a fond farewell to Irma and the crew members and assured them that she would get back to them soon. Then, using Erin's metal card, they summoned one of the automatic hover gliders, which took them back to the temple in less than five minutes.

Back in her quarters, Sen winked at her confidentially as she was about to pull the door to her chamber closed behind her.

"I sent for some fresh whiskey," he said. "If you want to come by for one later? Or for some chamomile tea, of course. I like chamomile tea, too. More or less... And there's no cuddle party scheduled tonight. I think Eagle and Simon want to explore the nightlife of this lovely little town."

Kaura smiled.

"Let's see," she said, pulling the door closed behind her.

After a long, warm shower and a short meditation, she stood again in front of Sen's door.

When the mage opened the door this time, she didn't back away, and gently returned his welcoming embrace.

For quite a long time they just stood there and breathed.

"May I kiss you?" she then asked. He hummed in assent. Then their lips met, and her belly and heart blurred in a pleasant, buzzing vibration, like so many jumbled butterflies, that spread to her whole body as the door slid gently shut behind them.

Three hours later, they were rudely awakened by a loud blaring siren. People were running back and forth in the corridor in front of Sen's chamber. Screams and commands rang out. Somewhere an artificially amplified fairy voice called out something. Probably Diana.

Sen caught himself a little faster than the Lemurian, pushed her gently away from him and jumped out of bed, over to the chair where he had neatly folded his clothes.

Despite the ambiguity of the situation, Kaura admired the tattoos that traveled across his muscular back like living creatures as he walked. Then she collected herself and rushed out of bed herself.

Sen had already put on a pair of trousers and a loose shirt, and she hastily slipped on one of the wide Atlantean robes that seemed to be in every room here.

Then the Scotsman operated the door opener with a slap of his hand.

As the wooden panel slid silently to the side into the wall, it became clear that the chambers really were superbly insulated from the corridor. The noise was deafening. Purple-uniformed temple guards ran back and forth, brandishing their weapons.

An acrid smell was in the air, of burning and something else, something chemical.

All the commotion seemed to be concentrated around the door to Kaura's suite of chambers, on either side of which the corridor was separated by walls of bluish flickering light.

Between the walls of light, three uniformed men with large masks of glass and metal in front of their faces were in the process of breaking down the door. Next to them fluttered an excited Diana and two of the fairies, shouting instructions, but no one seemed to care.

Sen nodded to her.

"If I were you, I'd protect my lungs with a filtering spell. There's something in the air I don't like."

She followed the suggestion. Then they walked together over to the light wall by Kaura's door.

A guard stopped them several yards ahead.

"This area is closed. We have a situation here. Please use the elevator on the other side of the corridor," he said. Kaura didn't take no for an answer.

"I live there," she said, pointing to the door from which thick, black smoke was now pouring. "What happened?"

The temple guard's face lit up.

"You are the high priestess? Thank Crystal! We were fearing you were still in there. After all, it's two in the morning." He pulled her with him a little further away from the entrance.

"About five minutes ago, the air sensors in your rooms sent out an alarm. Poison gas, apparently. A patrol of the guard was immediately sent out from headquarters and the air exchange was reinforced. Shortly after that, there was an explosion. That's all we know so far."

Diana and the fairies had also become aware of the newcomers in the meantime. The head fairy fluttered over.

"You seem to have attentive friends here, Kaura!" she said seriously. "Unless I'm very much mistaken, someone there wants you out of the way personally."

The very fact that she called Kaura by name and refrained from casual insults proved that she was seriously concerned.

"Well, fortunately I'm not completely defenseless," the Lemurian replied. "They might still have surprised me with that"—she pointed grimly at the smoking doorway—"but now that I know I have to be careful, I'll protect myself."

The fairy nodded.

"And we will protect you! I won't let you out of my sight again!"

She widened her iridescent pink eyes. "Not even if you end up in bed with that one," she pointed her pinky finger at Sen. "You were probably so loud that the assassins could have blown up the whole tower around you without you noticing!"

Sen cleared his throat.

"We were asleep, Diana," he said with an innocent twinkle in his eye that could have rivaled even Ariane's.

"And as it seems, even in the right place," Kaura added. "Let's go to the lounge on the top floor. I can't fall asleep now anyway."

At that moment, Simon and Eagle were coming down the hallway, giggling loudly. When they saw the scene, they both fell silent and looked at the small group in confusion.

"Yes, let's do that," Sen said quickly. "Simon, we'll explain everything to you later."

He turned to the countermage.

"But, Eagle, first I want us to go in there together and take a quick look around. There's been an assassination attempt on Kaura. Maybe we can find some trace of magic that the temple guards might otherwise miss."

He made a head movement toward Kaura's door, from which black smoke was still billowing, held back by the light barriers stretched across the corridor and disappearing in long streaks into an exhaust shaft in the ceiling.

"We'll have to be careful though, apparently there's some gas. Do you feel fit enough for that?" he added with a questioning look to his somewhat buzzed colleague.

Eagle, abruptly sobered up, nodded and started to put a magic web around herself. Sen followed suit. About ten inches around the two wizards, the air flickered slightly, the only sign of the gas-tight protective field they had woven.

Prepared in this way, they walked over to the barrier, spoke a few words to the guard in front of it, and disappeared into the cloud of smoke. The guard spoke a few words into his small wristband. He was probably informing his colleagues in the room that they were about to have company.

Inside the room, Sen slowly felt his way forward. He wasn't worried about himself or Eagle—they both knew what they were doing. But the fact that such an assault could occur within the well-guarded temple of the Crystal Guild, arguably the most powerful single organization in Atlantis, made him wonder.

The dense smoke made it almost impossible to see with his eyes. However, his heightened senses allowed the headmaster of Lockwood to see everything almost as clearly as outside on a sunny morning. He walked through the hallway and was about to enter the living room where he saw the three Temple Guard specialists working.

Suddenly Eagle grabbed him by the arm and yanked him back with force. Frantically, she pointed to a spot above the bathroom door. Sen narrowed his eyes. In fact, a tiny little spell weave was glowing there. He hadn't even noticed it, and at first glance, he could not see what it was. But now Eagle was already projecting her voice into his air- and thus soundproof protective field.

"This is a trap weave, Sen. Great mother, you should be more careful! I've never seen such a dense spell wrap. Whoever made this was incredibly powerful!"

"Can you tell what it's supposed to do and how it's triggered?" he asked her, sending his voice into her field as well.

She nodded.

"It is triggered by a Gifted person passing through the search grid. Non-magicians don't seem to be detected, or the guards wouldn't have gotten in there alive. One step further, anyway, and you could have seen for yourself what it does. I'd have to get closer to find out exactly. But it looks dangerous."

Someone approached them from behind. Sen turned around with a jerk. But it was only Kaura.

"I thought I'd take a look myself," she said through the voice field she had obviously intuited. "What did you find?"

Eagle pointed to the magic trap.

Kaura narrowed her eyes behind her energy screen.

"Ah, I've seen something like that before. Some kind of witchfire bomb. If someone had walked into it, they probably could have gathered their bones somewhere a floor above us. Let me get at it." She moved past Eagle and approached the pinhead-sized flare with extreme caution.

Then she stretched out her hand. A small, poison-green bubble of light appeared in front of one of her fingers. With a practiced motion, the little Lemurian threw the bubble like a lasso or butterfly net over the dot hovering in the corner of the room.

At the same moment, a bright glow of fire glowed within the bubble, and it expanded a few inches, only to immediately shrink and disappear.

"There, that's it," Kaura said calmly. "Let's clear the air in here."

She drew a symbol in the space in front of her face, and the air in the room promptly cleared.

The pale glimmer of light around Kaura disappeared with a soft pop. Sen and Eagle followed suit, dissolving their protective webs. The Lemurian walked over to the three temple guards.

"The air is okay again. You can take off the gas masks now," she said.

Suspiciously, one of the two looked down at the small metallic plate in his hand. It had to be a measuring device. Then he nodded, and the three slid their masks up. Meanwhile, Kaura had summoned a small ball of witchlight in her hand and hung it under the ceiling, which illuminated the surroundings better than the guards' portable lamps.

"I'm Raxel, shift supervisor of security," the Atlantean introduced himself, the metal plate still in his hand. He took off his gloves and shook their hands. "That was a fast-acting nerve agent that someone pumped into the room here. It would have paralyzed you instantly and possibly even killed you even before you woke up," he turned to Kaura. "The firebomb came later, possibly to cover up the tracks."

He pointed to the still glowing area where the bed had stood before. Only scattered, charred pieces of wood and linen remained.

The temple guard seemed to listen for a moment to something only he could hear. Kaura saw that he had a small, shiny metallic button stuck in his left ear. Then he turned back to the mages.

"My people have just examined all access points to the air-conditioning system and the records of the visio controls. None of the vents have been opened in the last few hours, not even by authorized personnel. The windows are closing absolutely tight. I can't explain it at this point. It seems like the gas and the fire bomb just appeared out of thin air in the room."

Sen nodded grimly.

"It's not that impossible. Very powerful mages can move objects or even themselves over certain distances. For that, it would have been enough if the person in question knew exactly where Kaura's quarters were. And the unknown person or persons left us another little surprise."

He told the guard about the witchfire trap that Kaura had disarmed.

The man was dismayed.

"Unfortunately, we cannot protect you against such attacks, Exalted One. This is beyond our capabilities. We will inform the priests about the incident. Perhaps they can do something."

Eagle stepped in and calmed him down.

"Just let us worry about that, friend. Now that we know where we stand, we can protect ourselves. Just keep making sure there are no unauthorized people hanging around. Even a mage can be surprised by an assassin with a knife." Raxel assured that all the guards had already been reinforced and not even a mouse could enter the temple undetected unless some form of magic was involved.

Kaura thanked the guards for their quick response, then went out with the others to confer. The chambers for high-ranking guests were located in the same tower as the living quarters of the priests.

On the top floor, under a pyramid-shaped crystal dome that was completely transparent on all sides as well as upward, was the common room. An automated bar offered light food and drink at all hours of the day, and comfortable armchairs and small tables were spread out on the thick white carpet. The light was dim at this late hour, casting only a few small golden circles on the soft floor, bathing the room in an indirect, warm glow.

Through the completely reflectionless crystal glass, Kaura could see the Milky Way above them, whose whitish glow not even the lights of the big city were able to drown out. Sen and Eagle moved some of the chairs so that they formed a loose circle, and found the switch for the table lights, which made the roundish structure glow with a soft golden glow.

Now there were five of them: Kaura, Sen, Simon, Eagle, and Diana. Another fairy stood guard at the entrance.

"I am convinced that someone wants to prevent you from speaking before the Senate, Kaura," Sen opened the conversation. "And it's a powerful mage. We will have to be very careful until the day after tomorrow."

Diana leaned forward.

"It must have been one of those high council fuzzies! Ixkasomething! The guy who already wanted to finish us off at the Portal!"

"But that man was pretty clearly not a mage," Kaura interjected. "Assuming he can't hide his ability. Okay, he'd probably be able to do this if he's powerful enough to pull off something like what just happened," the Lemurian immediately corrected herself, pointing diagonally downward in the approximate direction of her burned-out rooms.

Eagle smiled smugly.

"Well, we have ways of determining that, if only you give me some time. I would have to get close enough to our friends from the Council of Seven. Then we'll soon know if it could have been one of them. Of course, they could simply have hired someone. A Kai'ala, for example."

Kaura shook her head decisively.

"The Kai'ala do not reach that level of potency. At least, I haven't seen any who could do that, not even ten thousand years ago, when they had a lot of fighting mages out there. Not even the crystal priests we've encountered so far seem to have the power to teleport things. And they are considered the strongest mages of their people. No, that was someone else. A strong Lemurian, or djinn, or a fairy."

"Or one of those 'gods,' couldn't that be?" interjected Diana. She laughed. "Well, they don't suffer from lack of self-confidence, these planet-conquering power doggies! Gods! My face! Maybe I should get my own religion, too, if it's that easy. Like, with everybody wearing white robes and tattooing their faces pink. Tone in tone with my wings! Every morning they would have to prostrate themselves in front of me for half an hour and sing 'Ave Diana'! That would be such a nice boost for my battered guard fairy ego!"

Kaura pictured this and had to grin involuntarily.

"And to greet each other, they would all have to swear vigorously, I suppose. Well, that would at least be a completely new form of religion. Much more varied than just meditating or praying."

The fairy nodded eagerly.

"They're all way too serious, the religion fuzzies, you know. They haven't understood at all what it's all about. Life! Freedom! It's a cool world, this one! Much too cool to run around and torture others with thumbscrews like these inquisi-diots! Or to blow people up... Well, probably they find it somehow arousing, too, I don't know. Sex, violence and so on, still attracts, I guess..." She fell silent.

Erin had just rushed in through the entrance to the lounge. The head priest still looked sleepy, and his hair was a complete mess. Obviously, he had come straight out of bed.

"Hey, Flutterbeard, over here, here we are!" the fairy crowed loudly, waving cheerfully, though it was hard to miss the group in the otherwise completely unoccupied common room.

The old crystal priest immediately came over to them. His relief was clearly visible on his face.

"Kaura, I'm so glad nothing happened to you," he gasped. "I was immediately awakened by the temple guards when it became clear that the guest wing had been affected. What a devious attack! And I just heard something about magic being involved."

The Lemurian nodded gravely and gave the Atlantean an overview of what was happening.

When she had finished, the man looked down at the floor in dismay.

"So, we are no longer safe from our enemies even in our inner sanctum. Wicked thing, that. And new. You must know, since time immemorial, the crystal community has been the only group that uses magic in Atlantis. We never had to protect ourselves from magical attacks, simply because there were no mages here except us. Of course, from time to time someone from the outside visited us, at least before the era of encapsulation began. But those were few and far between, and they were immediately recognized by our ambassadors in the port cities. And we haven't had internal divisions for over two thousand years."

Erin was breathing heavily. "But we are prepared. I will have the crystal barriers activated immediately. Then no magical weave in the temple will remain undetected, and outside influence will become completely impossible. The crystals create an exceedingly strong protective field."

Kaura bowed her head in thanks.

"However, we must not forget that we are dealing with a very powerful adversary. I will gladly make myself available to test the effectiveness of your protective field from the outside," she said.

The crystal priest accepted her offer gratefully.

"Also, I suggest that before the Senate meeting the day after tomorrow, you only leave the temple under the protection of Temple Guards and Defense Mages.

Kaura shook her head.

"I feel protected enough by the fairies and my own abilities. I'll be careful. Now more than ever. And we will have some work to do here as well. I want us to be able to leave as soon as possible after the Senate's decision. In the meantime, can your people brief us on the operation and functions of the hover ship? It seems important to me that we can make ourselves useful on board."

Erin agreed.

"You will start training tomorrow. We have equipment that can teach you the essential skills hypnotically. Then all you need is a short practice session on the ship."

He spoke briefly into his metal bracelet and listened for the response, which again could only be perceived by him.

"The crystal field is set up. I will escort you out myself for the test, Kaura. After that, we will find you a new chamber to sleep."

Sen also stood up and followed the two out the door.

"Well, then we can finally go to bed," Eagle sighed. "And use those nice washrooms. Are you coming? I smell like a Viking fireplace!"

She grabbed Simon by the hand and pulled him with her to the elevator, followed by the guard fairy at the entrance, who casually saluted Diana before fluttering around the corner.

Now the head fairy was alone in the lounge. With a sigh, she leaned back into what was for her a huge, velvety cushion and gazed at the starry sky far above her. Orion was emblazoned directly above her, with its wide, sweeping "X" and the three stars at its intersection. Habitually, her eyes slid a little further down, where Sirius shone brightly and unmistakably, the sun she had seen rising on the horizon every morning in her youth. Did she miss her home? Did she even know such a thing as homesickness? She didn't know.

She had been on Gaia for a little over seven hundred years now, arriving a few months before the Portals of Pyrrha had closed, a thing that had not been quite as unexpected by everyone as even Kaura now seemed to believe. And she had many centuries more to live, if she did not fall victim to an act of violence or an accident, perhaps even millennia. No, she was in no hurry. But when the Portals were finally open again, she'd probably treat herself to a long, extended vacation on Sirius Q. It would be good to finally get some real pancakes again. Here with the barbarians, there just weren't the right ingredients for them. The right consistency could only be achieved with five-day-aged Kurin eggs. In her mind's eye she saw huge swarms of green-blue spotted Kurini females passing by, as they still existed in the swamps of Ema-Lirel. Or at least, as they had existed when she had visited her planet for the last time.

What had changed in the meantime in her homeland? It had been such a long time. Diana heaved a deep sigh and closed her eyes.

6

Parliament

The next day, a middle-aged Atlantean with pleasant features visited the mages at breakfast. His hair was tawny white like that of all Atlanteans, which made his age difficult to estimate. He was dressed in purple like the palace guards, but wore a bright yellow cloak over it, as well as some silver rank insignia on his shoulders.

"My name is Ux'makia, commander with the Crystal Fleet. I will fly with you to Lemuria as soon as we receive our permit for leaving Atlantis," he introduced himself. "When you have finished breakfast, I will take you to the hypnoschooling rooms, where we will provide you with the appropriate expertise for the flight. Priest Eriniel has ordered that you be given complete information for steering and repairing the ship, as well as for operating the tracking devices and, of course, the ship's guns. This is a great honor that has never before been bestowed upon a non-Atlantean in living memory. And it will tax your brains to the limit of their capacity. However, since you are mages, you should survive the procedure without any problems."

He cleared his throat. "It's the same technology used to erase the memory of those who want to travel outside our borders or to move away from here. Tried and tested a thousand times, that is. Still, we'll do a health compatibility check before we activate the program. We don't want to take any chances."

Sen thanked the man and assured him that, of course, he wanted to get his brain back in as undamaged condition as possible.

Commander Ux'makia just looked at him with a puzzled expression on his face.

"We're not going to remove your brains, of course. You can just lie down on the hypnotic couch. The download process is contactless."

The Scottish mage returned the commander's look gravely and replied, "Ah, good. Well, I'm curious then."

Half an hour later, the ship's captain led them to another section of the temple. On the way, they passed through the Great Central Hall, in the middle of which the master crystal towered, accessible to the faithful. There was reverent silence under the dome, which was over four hundred feet high and made up of nothing but hexagonal crystal fragments in all the colors of the rainbow, through which soft morning light fell inside.

The giant crystal, colorless in itself, shone like a rainbow beacon in the sunlight. Around it lay, sat and knelt about fifty pilgrims, whose faces betrayed the highest rapture. As they approached the center of the hall, Kaura also noticed the pulsation in her forehead, which probably came from the vibrational field of the great stone. This aroused her curiosity.

She held the commander by the sleeve and asked him in a whisper to wait a moment. Then she slowly walked over to the crystal. Fleetingly, she thought that perhaps it would be better to wait for a visit together with one of the priests. During her previous stays in Atlantis, so many years ago, she had only had the chance to visit the crystal chamber while taking part in their complicated, pompous rituals. But now she felt irresistibly drawn to it, and nothing could stop her.

Quietly, she tapped on her soft leather soles toward the God crystal, succumbing more and more to the rapture in her Third Eye. When she had been in Atlantis on behalf of the Council of Priests, this hall had always been full of praying priests and believers. She had never even thought of getting as close to the crystal as she could now.

"Hello, you cute little rock!" she greeted the giant towering over her by at least ten times her height as she moved ever closer through the rows of meditators. "How are we doing today? Would you like to cuddle?"

In response, a tremendous vastness and spaciousness arose in her heart that made her forget everything around her. Spontaneously, she pulled her light linen robe over her head and gently folded it beside her on the carpet. Now she stood naked in front of the crystal. Her entire body was vibrating. With the exception of the Holy Falls in her home temple, she had never felt a vibration of comparable intensity infuse her aura.

Smiling gently, she stepped over the velvet cords surrounding the stone and pressed herself against the hard, cool surface of the crystal, which instantly warmed beneath her body.

Kaura's consciousness was literally sucked into the crystal, and she felt one. One with all life, one with this planet, one with the people and beings that surrounded her. All at once everything had meaning and purpose, the Kai'ala, she, the Lemurians, the Span-iards and the Atlanteans were all just actors in a play of cosmic proportions that unfolded the full grandeur of Divinity, moment by moment, always in perfection.

She recognized the vastness of all life, her connection to all being, and for a moment was all that. The gentle Lemurian, the torturing inquisitor, the battle-ready Scottish warrior, the inquisitive mage, even the power-hungry 'god'. Now her path lay clearly before her, she saw her task to open this world again to the universe and to restore the connection between all beings, magical and non-magical, with all clarity like a shining line in the infinite tangle of the web of life—a thread that extended thousands of years into the future. And at the same time, she also realized that she could not fail.

There was nothing she had to do, had to be or had to have, except what she was experiencing right now, at this moment. Everything was indifferent to the universe. It thirsted only for experience, for play, for feeling itself!

What did death matter if perpetrator and victim, speaker and listener, the ones left behind and the ones gone on were really and truly one, united in the big cosmic play of becoming and passing away? She beheld the illusion, reality in all its grandeur and giggled merrily.

Then she felt her conscious core slowly separating from the crystal matrix. With a deep sigh she detached herself from the now body-warm, transparent shimmering surface.

Thoughtfully, she climbed back over the velvet cord, smiled at the worshippers looking at her, some admiring, some distraught, and picked up her dress from the floor. Leisurely she pulled it over her head and felt the soft fabric fall along her skin. The area between her legs pulsed gently, and her entire body was deeply alive. Everything around her also seemed clearer, more plastic, more colorful, more alive. She felt richly endowed. Before turning around, she threw a kissing hand to the crystal. Then she walked back to her friends.

No one among the meditators addressed her. Many avoided her gaze, only a few older women met it with knowing, shining eyes.

When she reached the others, who stood with deadpan faces, Diana cleared her throat in admiration.

"Well, I had always knew that you Pacific pacifists were a bit gaga. But you're the real thing! Cuddling with foreign crystals just like that. Even more, with the crystal. The super divine, unapproachable, infallible glitter thingy deity! Okay, at least you're a dignitary. They'd probably try to lynch me or something if it was me who did that."

Sen smiled at Kaura as if she was an apparition of the Divine Mother and said nothing.

Commander Ux'makia, meanwhile, just blinked his eyes in confusion.

"Well, I'm not particularly religious myself and have no idea about such things. As a high priestess, you're probably allowed to do that anyway. Probably everyone would be allowed to and you wouldn't even be lynched," he said with a sideways glance at Diana. "I've heard that the velvet cords are only there to protect the faithful. Weaker natures seem to get nauseous if they get too close to the crystal energy. In fact, people have died from getting too close to the Great One. It is said that during a dark time thousands of years ago, evildoers were executed by binding them to the crystal. They could not withstand the energy and within a few hours they died—and became enlightened. However, I don't know if this is true or just a legend."

His face lit up. "Today, fortunately, the death penalty has been recognized as barbaric and flawed for a very long time and has been abolished. Can we go on now?"

He thought for a moment as he led them on, then spoke again. "But I wouldn't do the undressing thing out in the park if I were you, Exalted One. I think nudity in public is forbidden here, except on the beaches and bathing lakes. Anyway, you never see anyone walking around naked. Probably that would be arousing public displeasure."

He shrugged. "At least in here you can talk your way out of it with religious rapture. And the priests like you."

Diana giggled in response and happily flustered her rose-colored dragonfly wings.

"Ha!" she crowed, winking teasingly at Kaura. "Well, naked tree hugging isn't the thing here, my dear Lemurian slug! Not that I personally mind, of course. On Sirius Q, we're almost all naked all the time. Good climate, you know. Unless someone wants to be particularly obscene. Then we put on skirts and pants and stuff! I can tell you, that's a good way to get in the paper with us! But of course, even then you don't get arrested! After all, everyone can do the dirty things one wants, as long as one doesn't hurt anyone. Whereas skirts, that is really pushing it! Do you know that we were sent into a desensitization cure before making the trip to Gaia, in order to endure all these clothed figures here?"

Thoughtfully, she tugged at the little skirt that barely covered her hips. "Well, after seven hundred years, I've almost gotten used to it. If I ever get back home, I can really shock people! My gosh, I'm looking forward to that! Shocking fairies! It's not easy, I tell you!"

A few corridors further, they reached the alchemical laboratories of the temple. A servant in blue robes and with freckles on his pale face led them inside the facility. He wore one of the copper conical helmets on his head that they had already seen when they arrived at the portal.

"Nice tin bag you got there, my friend," Diana addressed him as she fluttered next to the man. "Can you get sugar ice cream filled in there when you walk in the park, so you don't need one of those waffles? Or what's that for?"

The assistant grinned. He seemed to have a sense of humor and to take the fairy's jest as a compliment.

"We are asked that here from time to time, venerable fairy. The helmet is a sophisticated techno-magical apparatus that constantly supplies us with new body energy and facilitates intuitive communication with the central office and with the individual alchemical apparatuses. It could be built much smaller today. But tradition... and I personally think the priests just find it aesthetically pleasing to be surrounded by lots of people wearing copper helmets. You might ask them about it if it interests you. After all, you are guests of the council. Ah, here we are."

He led them into a large hall with several reclining chairs, around which several more men in copper helmets were scurrying and busy with some preparations.

A massive man with a green and blue striped beard immediately approached them.

"Welcome to the alchemical laboratories, friends! I am Alton Irgai'el, chief alchemist of the Crystal Temple Order. This is our hypnoschooling hall. We will feed you all the knowledge you need for your mission within a few hours." He pointed to the padded chairs set up in a large circle around a central crystal.

"On these advanced devices, we will first confirm your suitability for psychoprogramming. Then we will put you into an artificial sleep and, so to speak, bypass your waking consciousness and feed directly into your subconscious all the knowledge you need. From there it will seep back into your consciously available experience in usable portions. And tomorrow you will be able to pilot an Atlantis hover ship as if you had never done anything else! Do you mind?"

He made an inviting hand gesture.

"Not a man of big words, eh?" muttered Sen, but was the first to lie down on one of the comfortably upholstered narrow bed-chairs. Behind each of the seats was a huge tangle of copper wires of various thicknesses, crystal balls, and pointy antenna-like things. Many of the dangerous-looking outgrowths pointed directly at Sen's head.

"Are you sure one of those things won't accidentally drill into my brain?" the chief magician asked, only half joking.

"Quite sure," Alton smiled. "As long as the machine doesn't tip over, of course. But it's riveted to the floor just fine. You don't have anything to worry about."

Without further ado, Kaura climbed onto a second bed, and Simon and Eagle followed her lead.

"I'll stay out here and keep watch," Diana muttered meekly. "Somebody's got to make sure nobody bends your brains to the left."

"The process is completely safe and tested many times over centuries," the chief alchemist said. "Even for fairy brains. But if you don't want to, no problem."

He leaned a little closer. "Ah, that reminds me, you might find this interesting. The training program includes a complete sailor's vocabulary. More of historical interest. But there are"—he made some swiping motions on the small metal plate he held in his hand—"seven hundred and sixty-four present and historical curse words, sailor insults, and dirty jokes from the Atlantis Naval Museum's trove."

Diana's face lit up immediately. "All right, bossbrain," she said, "where do I put my capitulum? Just pour it in, that stuff!"

Kaura leaned back, closed her eyes and tried to relax. The copper apparatus behind her gave off a faint smell of ozone. Something hummed very subtly, almost inaudibly. One of the green-robed aides appeared in front of her and touched her lightly on the wrist.

"The machine is now ready for running the test program, your Highness. If it is positive, we will immediately start the training download without waking you up first. The duration of the procedure is four to six hours, depending on your receptivity. After that you will probably feel very tired and should not do anything major tonight. In particular, don't drink alcohol or listen to scary stories—most people feel very sensitive and a bit jumpy after programming. Any questions?"

Kaura shook her head.

"I'm ready, you can start." The buzzing behind her intensified.

The Lemurian split off a tiny fraction of her consciousness to follow the process. Perhaps, she thought, there was a way to achieve this effect by magical means as well. Her people used similar techniques to look at records and factual knowledge from ancient times, but, so far, not for training purposes. The Library of Pape'ete was known for its storage tourmalines on which the history of Lemuria and all knowledge created by her people since the Great Age of Darkness were preserved for posterity.

However, a direct anchoring of physical and mental abilities through condensed knowledge transfer had never been tried on the island continent, as far as she knew. Her conscious thoughts quickly evaporated into a kind of dreamless deep sleep, and only the small, luminous dot in a distant corner of her inner space remained awake, waiting and watching. She saw luminous bluish rays of light scanning her energy body and brain. Her memories appeared in this vision like accumulations of millions of transparent, small soap bubbles in all colors and shapes.

Between the free-floating piles of memories was empty space, punctuated only by isolated lines and structures that, Kaura knew, were parts of her personality and character. Many of the lines and string-like connections disappeared into a kind of gray wall of fog—the subconscious, impenetrable, opaque, mysterious. So that's where the Atlanteans wanted to plant the programs that would transform her into a highly skilled technician and pilot within hours. The scanning beams disappeared, and she was alone with herself for a long moment—maybe it was only seconds, maybe minutes—or it could have been years.

Time lost all meaning, did not exist, was pure illusion—a practical idea to make life easier, no more. Then she felt a glistening bright white beam of light penetrate her inner space. The straight, blinding beam inched forward very slowly until its tip connected with the opaque, gray wall of mist, and its end disappeared into invisibility behind it, while the beginning of the beam continued to connect it with some place outside of her. Probably one of those spiral copper tips, she thought. Looking more closely at the gray wall, she could see that it was not a smooth surface, as she had at first thought.

She noticed some strange-looking bumps and outcroppings. Fleetingly, she wondered if maybe she had not recovered all of her memories after all, as she had assumed until now. Was there something else? Something hidden even more deeply? But then, small, round bubbles began to float down the beam of light, and she forgot about everything else. An infinite number of them crossed the wide expanse within her like little carriages on a road, to disappear behind the gray wall.

For a long time, she watched the action without anything else happening. Thousands, even millions of small, luminous spheres. Other's memories, abilities, possibilities, she thought. Kaura idly wondered how these memories had gotten into the machine. Some way must have been found to copy these globules from people who had probably refined their abilities over a long lifetime and then had agreed to make them available to others. She would have to ask Alton about it.

Then something else began to happen. Slowly, a few of the small spheres spread all over the gray wall began to reappear, rising to the surface of the water like bubbles from the bottom of a lake. In slow motion, the initially few, then increasingly numerous spheres rose into her inner space and formed new clusters in the void. Some connected with already existing clusters of memories, others seemed to know exactly which space in the great void they should fill. Satisfied, Kaura let her consciousness shard rest, sending out calming impulses to her entire energy field. In this way, she hoped to emerge from the whole process as refreshed as possible.

Indefinitely later, her body sensations slowly returned.

The same, blue-robed man who had spoken to her before she had fallen asleep stood beside her chair.

"Please lie still for some time, Exalted One. Your body and mind will take a while to recalibrate. That was an extremely fast charge, barely three hours. You seem unusually receptive. Your friends probably won't be ready for a few more hours. Kaura made an agreeing noise, not yet feeling up to talking. She felt a little dizzy and there was a slight, uncomfortable pressure in her head, but otherwise nothing seemed out of the ordinary.

Gingerly, she swung her legs over the edge of the couch and slowly straightened over the side.

"Very good. Take it slow," the alchemist encouraged her, as Alton came over to them as well.

"Welcome back," the chief alchemist said with a smile. "So, how was the trip?"

Kaura returned the smile.

"Interesting. And now I know more than I did before?"

He nodded.

"The process will continue for another ten to twelve hours until the whole program is consciously available. What is to be done when the four-dimensional hypertransmitter terminal displays the error message 'A1'?", he asked abruptly.

Surprised, Kaura realized that she knew the answer.

"Switching on the alternative transmitter on ultra-long wave. Send the error report to the control center. Restart the transmitter terminal using code X-LAT-137," she said mechanically.

The alchemist nodded with satisfaction.

"Tomorrow you will all be ready for a test flight with Commander Ux'makia in the simulation device."

He glanced at the wooden board on the wall, where the current time appeared. The clock showed 40:5. Kaura realized she now didn't even have to think to realize that this, in Atlantis, meant it was around 2 p.m., while Alton continued.

"I would suggest you go for lunch now and then go to sleep until your friends are ready. You can always get hot meals at the cafeteria. I'll see you tomorrow."

He turned back to the large auroric machine, on which the progress of the processes was shown by means of hundreds of colored lights and graphics. Kaura thanked him and left. Fascinated, she tried to visualize the interior of the Atlantean hover ship, which she had never seen before in her life. And yet she felt as if she had already spent countless hours aboard this type of ship and knew all its functions inside out.

She knew which switch to press to open the door to the control cabin, which lights to set to green so she could gently push the control lever forward and down, allowing the ship to lift off. She knew how the various energy signatures of the Atlantean ships and power devices differed on the locator screens, and how to activate the weapons systems.

Slightly amused, Kaura thought about how different the Atlantean ships were from the organically engineered, primarily mind- and voice-controlled Lemurian hover ships with halminite cores. There, you didn't really need any buttons and switches to operate the vehicles. And the ships themselves were intelligent enough to repair themselves if damaged, or at least to give the human helpers the right guidance for repairs to be carried out successfully. Of course, one was also at the mercy of the technomagic systems. Yeat, she thought, without energy, nothing could be repaired on an Atlantean ship, either. The Lemurian ships had no weapons, though. This was potentially impractical when dealing with violent beings like the Kai'ala but could probably be made up for by the Lemurians' magical superiority.

The Atlanteans, on the other hand, could shoot with quite

physical means. The Lemurian now knew the difference between a pulse shot, an energy bomb, and a firebomb, and what they were for. Hundreds of technical terms, radio call texts, equipment settings, and possible conversations with her co-pilots flowed through her head.

Now she finally started to feel tired. Dragging her feet, she crossed the temple's main hall toward the large cafe, where one could order more than two hundred different dishes from all over the world at the touch of a button. Suddenly she was very much looking forward to her bed. And it was still only the middle of the afternoon! However, no matter how tired she was, she would not forget to shield her dreams before lying down.

* * *

Less than two days later, Kaura stood in front of the mirror and prepared for her speech before the Atlantean Senate. She carefully adjusted her purple silk robe, which Erin had sent her the night before.

"Purple is the color of the superiors," the messenger had explained. "It is considered appropriate to your status. The High Priest thinks it wise for you to conform as much as possible to the dress customs of the Senate. Especially since you are a woman. Women are not usually allowed in the Senate. But since you and the Pyrrhean Mahdi are members of foreign governments, an exemption has of course been granted."

Kaura had only nodded understandingly. She had thanked the messenger and sent him on his way.

Earlier that day, she had spent an intense sequence of practice drills and a tour of the ship *Crystal Clarity IV* together with the Lockwood mages and Ux'makia, an experience that had challenged her to the utmost despite the knowledge she now had at her fingertips.

Sighing, she looked at her long hair, which had been carefully piled up into a huge spiral curl by a servant of the Crystal Palace. Well, this audience would be interesting. Trying to bully a parliament full of men into action... Men who, for the most part, wanted to play ostrich and would only take their heads out of the sand when the whole thing was over—or when someone pinched them hard in the butt.

Despite the general ban on women in the Senate, Eagle would also accompany her as her official bodyguard. Her real task, however, would be to test the presence of magical abilities of all the ministers and senators present during the speech. Simon would also be there, as Sen's 'honor guard,' as he had announced with an ironic grin. The fairies would stay in the background, together with the crystal priests' security guards.

With another sigh, she opened the door and went down to the entrance hall, where the others were already waiting for her. Outside the door hovered three of the Atlanteans' small, open-topped hover dinghies that would take them across to the government headquarters. Beside each dinghy stood a younger crystal priest with a highly luminous protective crystal in his hands that, when activated, would provide a shielding field around the craft.

Kaura greeted Sen, Erin and the others. Together they climbed inside the vessels. The trip was uneventful, and after less than a quarter-hour flight to the other side of Atlantia, the massive, diamond-shaped building of the Senate rose up before them. The polished diamond stood in an improbable manner on its tip, which did not measure more than a few yards at the base, so the colossus looked as if it could tip in any direction at any second.

Kaura wondered at the symbolism of constructing a building in this way. What did the Atlanteans try to show the world by such an improbable architectural feat? That they did not feel bound by physical constraints? The dinghies spiraled up in an elegant arc to the official landing for dignitaries, located about fifty yards above ground. They came to a gentle stop a foot's width above the thick, red carpet.

The entire platform was brightly lit by two huge golden crystals, one on each side. Black-clad guardsmen with metallic rank insignia formed a honor guard, which Kaura and her companions were obviously supposed to pass.

A venerable-looking old Atlantean with his hair braided into a long pigtail awaited them at the door of their vessel. Glimmering purple metal threads were woven into his braid.

Next to him stood a serious-looking officer in black uniform.

"Welcome, Your Highness," intoned the man in a singsong, high-pitched voice. "I am Ilhamaka, the current president of the Atlantean Senate. We are deeply honored to welcome a guest from Lemuria once again. It has been too long."

Erin, who had stepped out of the glider behind Kaura, greeted the president warmly.

"Illy, you old fart, it's good to see you again! We meet far too infrequently these days! Hopefully we'll soon be able to call a meeting to depose these lazy high councilors!"

The old senator grinned.

"Sacrilegious thoughts, my friend. As a democratic body, we obviously must support our government, as long as it does what we want. Many senators seem to find a little inertia a good thing. But of course, we like our parallel government, the Crystal Guild, very much too..."

Meanwhile, the others had also stepped out of their gliders, were greeted, and followed the Senate chief along the lines of motionless guardsmen to the giant square entrance gate inside the Diamond Building.

A short time later, they had reached the large Senate chamber. Curious, Kaura looked around. The seats of the hundred or so senators were arranged in two legs of a large triangle about thirty yards on a side, three rows deep. There Erin and two other crystal priests sat down in their seats. Obviously, they were also senators. The third area of the equilateral triangle was reserved for the President and his staff, the guests and the High Council, four members of which were already seated.

Kaura cast an inconspicuous sideways glance at Eagle, who stood diagonally behind her. The Algonquin shook her head almost imperceptibly. So, none of the people already present was a mage in disguise. She studied the nameplates of the government seats. The seats labeled Ixkarel and Uriel were still empty. These two councilors were the ones who, according to Erin, pushed the isolationist agenda with particular vigor. They had already made the chubby police minister's unpleasant acquaintance in the Portal courtyard. If Ixkarel was Gifted, his ability had been well disguised. One of the other two, then?

Now the last senators entered the room. Some of them cast frankly curious glances over to the mages who had taken their seats to the left of Ilhamaka. From the right, two more ministers entered the room and greeted some of the senators and the president before taking their seats. One of them, Kaura recognized. Ixkarel. The other, a gaunt, blue-robed man with a prominent red-veined nose, was unknown to her. Now only Uriel's seat was empty, that of the chief minister.

Again, Eagle shook her head slightly. She had assured the crystal priest and the other mages that the tracking pentacle she wore beneath her robe would indicate even highly skilled cloaking webs to her. Kaura considered. Now only Uriel remained, in case one of the gods acted as part of the government. However, she probably would have chosen a more inconspicuous position, if she had been the spy. Especially if he, being the high mage he had to be, could effortlessly influence the thoughts and decisions of others. A minister was probably too exposed, to conspicuous for the devious manipulation this would require.

But suddenly she felt Eagle stiffen beside her. The defense mage bent down to her and hastily whispered in her ear what she had seen.

"That's him. The man in the black robe, just coming in from the right. That must be Uriel. Great mother, he is strong! Almost twice as dense an energy signature as yours! But something is strange." She fell silent, because at that moment the president opened the meeting.

Long words of greeting followed, during which Kaura eyed the minister. He was slim and held himself extremely straight. His white hair had a slight golden sheen, which might have come from a tint or from colored threads woven into it. The eyes under the bushy white eyebrows were blue like those of almost all Atlanteans, but somehow had an even deeper tint, subtly different.

Uriel's pale face wore a commanding, slightly dismissive expression and, taken as a whole, looked somewhat bored. The very image of a man who was aware of his importance and also knew that he actually had better things to do at the moment than attend a Senate meeting yet had to suffer the attention of his inferiors. She could not see any sign of magical talent with the naked eye. His camouflage spell must be extremely sophisticated. Yes, she thought. Only one of the 'gods' could dare to usurp the office of chief minister in the second most powerful empire on earth. How did they have to go about unmasking this man?

At this moment the welcome speech of the senate's president ended. With a few words he introduced Kaura and the other guests and then gave her the floor without further ado.

Kaura rose and began to speak. In simple words she described her experiences and the threat of the alien forces that wanted to enslave the entire population of Gaia and would not spare the Atlanteans.

After her speech, she earned cautious applause from some quarters. Most senators, however, seemed anything but convinced by her request.

After her, the Mahdi and finally Sen spoke, both painting an exceedingly vivid picture of their experiences with the Kai'ala and the Spanish Inquisitors. Sen, moreover, repeatedly stressed that the Atlanteans also had a responsibility to the rest of the technically less advanced world, invoking ancient ties with Merlin's Avalon and highlighting the potential benefits of a grateful Lemuria. He was the first to receive somewhat more enthusiastic applause.

"Probably just because he's a man," Eagle whispered with a disapproving twist to her mouth.

Then the discussion began. The three crystal priests and several other senators came forward with impassioned votes calling for immediate intervention by the Atlantean fleet to put a halt to Spanish expansionist efforts, as well as an investigation into the role played by the Kai'ala who had come to the planet as an outside force. Most speakers, however, were critical or even opposed to Atlantean intervention in world politics.

"When have the Lemurians ever done anything for us?" one of the senators shouted angrily. "After all, they have effectively imprisoned us here for millennia, with their impositions! Let them now spoon out their own soup! We're doing fine here, after all. Maybe we can even come to an agreement with these inquisitors. We don't need mages here!" He glared at the crystal priests angrily.

Thereupon the discussion became more and more heated.

Then, in a calm and melodious voice, Chief Minister Uriel spoke up.

"Gentlemen, gentlemen. Calm down! Nobody denies the merits that crystal magic has done for our land. And no one wants to sell our mages."

He cleared his throat. "But, to use our fleet for anything, there would first have to be a problem. However, our intelligence service informs us that the Spanish are in no way violating our moral principles and have only been pushing their expansion plans gently and with the involvement of local governments since we stopped them from annexing Tenochtitlán. I consider the reports of this alleged extra-planetary invasion to be a malicious rumor, an evaluation that is based on the information available to the government."

"Are you accusing us of lying, Minister?" shouted Sen angrily. "Three of the highest-ranking mages outside Atlantis?"

Uriel smiled mockingly.

"Not at all, dear Professor. I only state that we have no evidence that your claims are correct. And as we all know, mages and machines can fool people into believing realities that have no basis in fact. Perhaps we should ask our crystal mages here what they know about this?"

Erin paled.

"Are you suggesting that we have implanted false memories in these people? That is outrageous!"

The prime minister laughed arrogantly.

"Unfortunately, our intelligence reports say otherwise, your honor. We have been monitoring your activities for months. By now, we have enough evidence that you have been planning to overthrow the government for a long time. Guards!"

Alongside the crystal priests and a few other senators, uniformed men dressed in white and armed with dangerous-looking short spears appeared.

Erin puffed indignantly, rose, and leaned over his desk.

"These accusations are groundless! Besides, we have diplomatic immunity! We cannot be arrested without the consent of the Senate," the priest shouted.

Uriel shook his head.

"The security of our homeland comes first. We must fear that you would have senators with dissenting opinions killed. In fact, there have already been several assassination attempts, which fortunately were foiled at the last second! We will present the relevant evidence to the Senate, with the testimonies directly linking the assassins to these so-called priests!"

He pointed accusingly at Erin. "But to comply with order, I hereby make a motion to the Senate to have these ten senators arrested on suspicion of revolution and sent to the dungeon until the clarifications have been completed!"

Eagle nudged Kaura and pointed forward.

At first, the Lemurian saw nothing. But then she understood what Eagle meant when she saw an almost imperceptible movement in the air in front of her. Nearly invisible even to the mages, over a hundred pale blue threads of energy were moving from Minister Uriel to the senators.

Kaura was amazed. It revealed almost incredible power to send out and control over a hundred psychic weaves at once. Senate President Ilhamaka was already firmly under the control of the 'god.'

"I call for a vote," he shouted. "All those voting for the immediate arrest of all members of the Crystal Order, raise your hands!"

By now, the glowing threads had already penetrated more than half of the white-haired heads of the Atlantean senators. Now Simon and Eagle acted. The psychomage uttered a few hasty words. The threads of energy emanating from Uriel suddenly became visible to all and lit up in the air.

Chaos was the immediate result. The senators who had not yet been touched nearly toppled out of their upholstered chairs in their haste to avoid the rapidly approaching filaments. Those already partially under Uriel's control stared, fearful and paralyzed, at the strange, serpentine formations that had entered their foreheads above their eyes.

Eagle took a small wooden stick from her pocket and drew an

intricate symbol in the air with it. The threads went limp and faded from one moment to the next.

Almost at the same time, Sen and Kaura had joined together to form an energy circle. The Lemurian woman uttered a spell of bondage that settled over the chief minister like a red-hot grid.

Everyone screamed and stumbled around like madmen.

Uriel fixed Kaura with a contemptuous look.

"You'll all regret this," he hissed, and Kaura, oddly enough, could hear his voice quite clearly despite the noise. "You in particular, Lemurian whore!"

Then, with a loud plopping noise, he disappeared from in between the bondage weaves contracting over him. The air shimmered pink for a moment, and some of the senators looked fearfully at the spot where Uriel had been until a few split seconds ago.

Sen stared as well.

"Hmm, I'd like to be able to do that sometime, too," the Scottish wizard grumbled, unruffled, as he broke away from the circle he had formed together with Kaura. "Well, let's put our colleagues at ease."

He amplified his voice three to four times with a simple energy weave. "Silence!" he thundered. "The danger is over for now. The alien mage has fled. You may sit down again!"

Slowly, some calm returned. In the meantime, the black-clad Senate guards had also stormed into the room and disarmed the government troops in the white robes.

The Senate President and the other members of the government were discussing loudly with each other and did not seem to know quite what to make of the matter.

"Was that real?" Ilhamaka turned to Sen. "The chief minister influencing the senators with those light snakes?"

Sen nodded grimly.

"Yes. And it probably didn't happen for the first time. This time you could just see it because Simon here can make magical weave visible to non-magicians."

He patted his friend on his shoulder."

And Eagle has rendered the actual hypnotic influence ineffective. Otherwise, he probably would have taken complete control of you and carried out his plan to discredit the Crystal Guild with full legitimacy, given by the Senate he manipulated."

Next, Ilhamaka turned to Ixkarel, the police minister.

"Were there really such investigations against the Crystal Guild? And where are the results, who authorized it, who carried it out?"

The minister was visibly uncomfortable.

"Since it allegedly involved a plot against the government, the investigation was kept top secret and was conducted by the ministerial guard itself. I was informed of the results only the day before yesterday, but I had no reason to doubt the accusations. I have not seen the documents yet, though. Chief Minister Uriel always seemed above suspicion. Indeed"—he seemed to slowly regain his composure—"who is to say that this is not all a plot by the priests and their foreign friends? They are mages, after all, and can play us all they want! Perhaps Chief Minister Uriel was murdered by these... these... subjects, and we now believe them to be on our side."

"Don't be ridiculous, Ixkarel!" the Senate President rebuked him. "Even the accusations against the Crystal Guild seem more than groundless to me. There has never been even the slightest indication that they would act against the interests of Atlantis. Besides, Kaura Alenu'ala here"—he pointed at the Lemurian—"is personally known to some senior members of the Senate from her last visit three hundred years ago, and is beyond reproach. We will, however, sift through this so-called evidence of revolution in detail and question those who have conducted these investigations."

He spoke briefly with one of his co-workers. Then he raised his voice again so that everyone in the room could hear him.

"I have given orders for a search warrant to be issued immediately for Chief Minister Uriel to clarify his role in these events. Furthermore, his official residence will be searched. With this, we may be able to bring more clarity to this matter. In addition, I have summoned the head of intelligence, Xi'mal Irshamen, to question him."

After a short wait, the discussion continued.

The chief of intelligence arrived shortly and confirmed, in broad strokes, the actions of the Spaniards up to the capture of Mira'aleitha and the abduction of the magical population there. For the time after that he could not make any more statements, because within a short period of time all Atlantean spies working in the Spanish-Ottoman empire had been unmasked and captured or killed. Attempts had been made to send new people, but this had also failed.

"In short," he concluded his report, "we haven't had a clue what the Spanish have been up to in their empire for several years. We wanted to send at least periodic hover ships for reconnaissance, which were to fly over the areas outside our borders. Minister Uriel and the State Department have forbidden this, citing the ban on using Atlantean technology outside the continent."

A rather younger senator with garish green dyed hair intervened.

"Our Lemurian friend here has already promised us to officially lift the ban. You will have a completely free hand as soon as the Senate officially decides to open up and declare war on Spain. Can we finally proceed to the vote?" he turned impatiently to his colleagues.

Many of the senators were still not fully convinced. A short time later, both motions were nevertheless approved by a narrow majority, with all actions of the Atlantean fleet remaining purely defensive until further notice. However, the expedition flight of an armed Crystal Guild ship to the Pacific with the goal of liberating Lemuria was approved by a large majority.

"They can't burn their own fingers on that one," Eagle whispered to Kaura. "If anything goes wrong, they'll just blame it on the priests."

A few hours later, Erin came to see Kaura. Her new quarters had been specially secured, and a guardsman had been assigned to each end of the hallway. As well, one of the fairies sat perched on a corridor lamp and saluted Kaura nonchalantly when she opened her door.

"I'm sorry to bother you so late, but I wanted to tell you myself right away," he said. "Your aunt has been found. I'll take you to her if you like. She's doing well, considering the circumstances."

Kaura immediately agreed, even though she was completely exhausted, and got dressed again.

A Crystal Guard glider quickly took them across the metropolis pulsating with nightlife to a rundown neighborhood near the harbor.

The glider stopped in front of a brick warehouse of considerable size, surrounded by police hovercraft.

Erin glanced at her from the side as he gallantly helped her out of the vehicle.

"Minister Ixkarel decided to cooperate with us in light of Uriel's apparent treason. The documents found in the chief minister's office, together with statements of his arrested associates, have led the guard to this warehouse, where the two made their opponents disappear to. Of course, Ixkarel denies having known who was held here and that the whole thing was not legal. The investigation will show what the facts really are, and what happened here."

They passed through several doors that revealed that the interior of the building had been excellently shielded from the environment, even acoustically. Further inside were long corridors with thick walls and heavy, iron-barred dungeon doors. Kaura shuddered.

A little further on, they entered a section with two large recreation rooms that had probably served the guards.

"Most of the former prisoners have already been taken away," Erin explained to her.

"Your aunt has expressed a desire to be taken directly to her ship, but to speak with you first. Tomorrow we should have the official permission for the *Stralsund* to cast off. I have spoken myself with Minister Ihaimel, who has taken over the affairs of the Chief Minister on an ad interim basis. As a concession to the detained and, so to speak, as a preliminary to the agreements made with you, we will for the first time waive the enforcement of the usual departure memory erasure procedure for the released."

As they entered the room, Kaura immediately recognized the stocky, straw-blond woman with the coarse features who had initiated her into all knowledge of seafaring during Kaura's two years on her ship. She seemed as resolute as ever, and hardly marked by captivity.

"Ah, little one, good to see you," she bellowed in her broad Inmarsund sailor dialect, rising to enclose Kaura in a bear hug that nearly cracked a few of her petite friend's ribs.

Kaura laughed in relief as the other woman released her with a satisfied hum and she could finally breathe again.

"Great Mother, Resa, we were so worried about you! Aalyjah will be so relieved when you're back!"

The captain grinned.

"Weeds don't die, my dear. Would you like a sip of rum? These nice people here got it for me specially. Imported straight from the Irish peninsula. Better than the pills everyone here uses instead of getting decently drunk."

She handed the bottle to Kaura, not without pouring a good swig down her own throat first and letting out a satisfied belch.

"I'm glad to hear that this mad boar of a chief minister had to flee. But then, I don't hold grudges. Still, I wonder what they did with all those people with silver collars who did time in here. All were taken away somewhere a few days ago. Sad characters, those."

She contorted her face into a sympathetic grimace.

Kaura listened up.

"Silver collars? Then they must have been mages."

She told Resa what had happened since she had left Inmarsund.

"High Priestess, so you are, huh?" the woman said when Kaura finished her report, eyeing the shorter woman doubtfully and stroking her tangled blonde hair. "

Always knew you were someone from up there." She waved her hands somewhere in the general direction of heaven. "Spiritual, I mean. Never mind, I like you anyway. And you know something about seafaring. Best student I ever had. Well, with ten thousand years of experience, you should know the best way to learn new things... Come visit us in Inmarsund sometime when you're on a break from praying!"

She grinned and raised an eyebrow. "Or whatever else you're doing out there in your Lemurian temples. Anyway, I'll tell Aalyjah you said hello. She'll be happy to hear you're still alive."

Kaura hugged her again.

"And I'm going to do everything I can to keep it that way," she said simply.

* * *

The next morning, shortly after ten o'clock, the mages, carrying their very minimal luggage, were standing in Hangar 13A of the Crystal Fleet. The hangars were located in the farthest part of the vast temple grounds and nearly two miles from the main entrance but could be easily reached from the priests' quarters by small hover pods that traveled underground. All nine members of the Crystal Council had gathered to bid farewell to the expedition members.

Besides Commander Ux'makia, only four other Atlanteans were aboard the roughly galleon-sized, wedge-shaped vessel, one of them a crystal mage of the Priests' Guild who introduced himself as Ixamel and made a friendly but very introverted impression. Two pilots, a navigation officer and a gunner were normally enough to operate a ship of this size, the commander had assured them.

"But considering your training, we now have a full backup crew on board for safety. That makes me feel a lot better, too. No Atlantean ship has been abroad in a state of war for decades, let alone over such distances. We must be prepared for anything!"

A few minutes later, the shimmering bluish metal wedge of the *Clarity* lifted almost silently into the hall's oil- and ozone-scented air. A hexagonal gate in the outer wall of the temple slid aside with a humming sound.

Horizontally, the ship slid out into the open at about ten yards above ground level, then accelerated into a nearly vertical climb until she reached her cruising altitude of about forty thousand feet.

In a wide arc, the *Clarity* crossed Atlantia and turned south over the Atlantic Ocean.

The areas controlled by the Spaniards were to be avoided around so as not to draw the attention of the Kai'ala to the enterprise at an early stage. The plan was to reach the Pacific roughly on the line of the equator across Africa and the Hindustani subcontinent. The hover ship reached top speeds of just over one thousand nautical miles per hour. It was hoped she would take not much more than half a day to reach the other side of the globe and start the search.

A few minutes after take-off, the captain made contact with the Atlantis Frontier Guard, whose smaller, crystal-shaped vessels could be seen hovering on the horizon a little over a mile away.

"This is Crystal Fleet ship *Crystal Clarity IV*, Commander Ux'makia. We are now leaving Atlantean airspace on a south-southeast course. Our Border Crossing Permit has been issued per Senate order. You are informed?"

"Affirmative, commander," a harsh voice sounded from the speaker in the pilot's cockpit. "We wish you a safe journey and good luck!"

Like a launched cannonball, the Crystal Priests' ship accelerated diagonally into the blue, cloudless sky above the Gulf of Atlantis.

7

Dangerous Gods

The seemingly endless, yellow, red and orange great desert of Africa stretched out far below the *Crystal Clarity IV*. From this altitude, Kaura, standing just behind the captain's seat in the command center, could clearly see the curvature of the earth and the thin bluish layer of the atmosphere in whose upper reaches they were moving silently through the air.

The small rocks and furrows far below, which she knew were in truth vast mountains and wide valleys, passed as if in slow motion beneath the armed expedition vessel that the Atlantean Crystal Priests had sent on the long journey to the Pacific Ocean to explore ways for liberating Lemuria.

"From up here, it looks like we're going really slow," Eagle remarked next to her.

Commander Ux'makia nodded and half turned to the two women, looking at them over his shoulder. The ship did not seem to need direct attention from him in normal flight.

"Yes, isn't it?" he said. "Yet we are flying over the desert at a speed of over a thousand nautical miles per hour. They say that long ago ships like this one betrayed their presence by producing a painfully loud bang that could even be heard down on the surface of the earth. It probably had something to do with the shape of the wings and flying above the speed of sound waves. With this generation of vessels, introduced about a thousand years ago, the compressed air is swept widely around us by auroric umbrella fields. This means we can move in almost complete silence."

The white-haired officer smiled proudly. "In about fourteen hours we will approach the Lemurian West Coast. The range of our internal power plant is about one hundred thousand nautical miles, so we could circle the Earth many times without running out of energy. So far, we have not been able to measure any major auroric concentrations in the lands below us. If the Kai'ala have major technical facilities anywhere in the Spanish-Ottoman heartland, or even starships, their presence must have been very well hidden."

Kaura growled in agreement and continued to look down, lost in thought, at the seemingly unbroken, uninhabited wasteland of sand and stone.

Fifteen minutes later, she went aft. The *Clarity*'s cabins were unusually luxurious for a research vessel. She wondered if, in normal times, this vessel might be serving as a private boat for the priests' travels around the islands of Atlantis.

Passing the officer's mess, she found Simon, Sen, and Diana bent over a pentagram-shaped layout of crystal balls. Beneath it, spread out and weighted down with a few tourmaline stones, lay an Atlantean navigation map showing the Mediterranean region.

Sen looked up as she entered the chamber.

"Ah, Kaura!" he exclaimed happily. "Look! It's amazing what can be done with a tracking pentacle from this altitude! On the planet's surface, you can only 'see' a few miles, even with their help. But from this flying thingy, we can locate the Inquisitors almost one by one, over all of Europe! Here, this glowing spot, that's Granada, the Imperial capital."

He pointed to the Iberian Peninsula.

"There must be at least thirty or forty mages there. And here, Pyrrha, a real campfire of light dots! Pretty much everywhere we have found single spots, probably magic inquisitors, or magic prisoners—or, hopefully, some of our kind that are still free and have managed to hide. But now, look at this: There's another large cluster up here. Right in the Constantinople area. Either, there are tons of Kai'ala hanging around. Or, more likely, that's where they are keeping their magical slaves!"

The Scottish high magician was exuberant. "These hover gliders are just great! And so fast! We definitely need to get some of these things in Lockwood!"

Kaura, on the other hand, was more interested in the map and just waved absentmindedly.

"Yes, that's really interesting. We should let the Atlanteans know about it at once. Maybe they can organize a rescue operation for the mage slaves held in Constantinople."

Satisfied, she walked over to her cabin to lie down for a while. In front of the floor-to-ceiling crystal window, she saw, slightly dimmed by the tinted pane, deep below her on the horizon the end of the Mediterranean and the long, shining ribbon of the Nile.

Somewhere down there was Pyrrha, and beyond that Rhodes, where the *Pride of Edinburgh* and Captain McGregor were still waiting for news. In the excitement of the last few days, they had forgotten to send a message to their companions who had stayed behind.

Later. One step at a time. That's how you began long journeys. And that's how you reached your destination.

She sighed and closed her eyes, drifting off into sleep almost instantly.

Kaura was jolted awake by a heavy thud that almost threw her out of bed. A bright, beeping sound shrilled through the ship.

"Not again," she groaned. Fortunately, she had not undressed. Quickly she jumped off the bed, which didn't look much different in this luxurious chamber than in her Atlantia suite, and rushed out the door.

In the pilot's cockpit, Sen was just strapping himself into one of the navigator's seats behind the captain. Their flight seemed to have stabilized again after that strong shaking.

"What's going on, commander?" she asked.

"We are under attack," Ux'makia replied. "Three alien gliders, shaped like teardrops. They came like out of nowhere and opened fire immediately. Fortunately, we had kept our protection fields activated." He laughed grimly. "Oxgarm is already powering up the guns. If they try again, we will show our teeth."

Kaura leaned forward a little. On one of the screens in front of the commander, she saw three dots approaching from the front left. She peered out of the window. Below them stretched a wide, azure sea, dotted with green islands large and small.

Suddenly, the commander pulled the ship off course and dove into a wide left turn. At the same time, red reflections blossomed around the ship, and it roared and shook again. Kaura idly wondered why she didn't feel any centrifugal forces at all, even though the ship must have just been subjected to tremendous accelerations. Only the humming of the devices in the background increased somewhat.

Now she could see one of the attackers. The drop-shaped flying vehicle, glistening metallically in the sun, seemed to cross their flight path at high speed from the lower right.

Commander Ux'makia sucked in a surprised breath.

"He's not going to..." he muttered, even as he jerked his control lever backward, and then there was a crash. Fire flowers and large, glowing pieces of metal flew past the cockpit in long, smoking tails and disappeared into the blue background of the sea in the distance.

The *Clarity* shook and crunched in all her structures. New shrill tones sounded throughout the control chamber, and several yellow and red lights flashed.

The captain exhaled grimly.

"At least our shields are better than theirs, it seems. But I think we're damaged! One of the engines is going!"

He flicked a lever backward with one finger, speaking into the communication field in front of his face. "Take a look at engine B, Om'xikal! I'd hate to have to make an emergency landing in this situation! Oxgarm, try to get the other two with the tail guns! I'll go low between the islands to avoid them knowing where to find us in case we do have to land. This will buy us some time, even in the worst case."

The green spots dotting the blue expanse of the ocean in front of the ship quickly grew larger. Some machine was howling deep inside the *Clarity*'s belly, like a wounded animal. It was the gravity compensators, Kaura realized, accessing her still new knowledge about Atlantean hover technology. If they had had to endure that nose-dive unprotected, they would all be stuck to the back wall by now, barely able to breathe. She thanked the Great Mother that most of the ship's systems still seemed to be functioning.

Now the hull shook again several times when the rear impulse guns were firing. Cheers emanated from one of the loudspeakers.

"I got him, one is down! Exploded in the air! Now only one left. Can you pull up to the left, commander?"

Ux'makia did so while the damaged engines droned on, highly strained. At the same time, they heard a metallic crash and explosion somewhere in the upper part of the ship.

Again, the boat shook heavily.

A bit more soberly than before, Oxgarm's voice spoke up.

"The last enemy is also hit. He's trailing smoke and turning off to the southwest. But I'm afraid he's given us another hit!"

"I can tell," the commander growled, struggling with the controls as the ship thundered along a few hundred yards above the surface of the sea. He seemed to make some arbitrary course changes and then, several agonizing minutes later, slowed the hovership down. They had already passed several dozen of the islands and, at this speed, now were probably over a hundred miles away from the point of the last attack.

"I'm afraid we'll have to land and look at the damage from the outside," Ux'makia muttered as he intently surveyed the islands ahead of them. "The second engine won't make it much longer, and the hit on the top of the hull seems to have done something to the oxygen supply."

"Well, it's high time for a vacation on the beach," Sen tried to joke, which didn't fool anyone who saw the high magician's pale face.

The commander went even lower until the hovership seemed almost to touch the crest of the waves and slowed down. The speed indicator showed a groundspeed of 54 knots. After the extremely high speeds they had moved with during the last few hours, this seemed like an extreme slowdown of reality, although it was still much faster than even the best sailing ship Kaura had ever traveled with, where ten knots would already have been considered an impressively fast run.

In a slight arc, they circled a small island that measured just under two nautical miles in diameter and was shaped roughly like a crescent moon. When they had reached the southern end of the crescent, a paradisiacal sight opened in front of the pulpit. A wide, white beach, lined with palm groves, behind it a jagged mountain covered all over with dense tropical vegetation. The scene looked as if no human being had ever set foot on it. There were no signs of habitation.

"That will do," Ux'makia said laconically, sliding his control lever downwards. The ship glided gently over the light blue water of the lagoon. Kaura could even see yellow and red shadows through the now transparent floor plates under her feet, which must have come from large quantities of small tropical fish. A few handbreadths above the white sand, the ship came to a standstill.

With a piercing hiss, its extending props dug deep into the sand, causing the craft to sink a little more as the captain turned off the auroric levitation generators.

He pushed a green button on the far right of the instrument panel in front of him. "Cloaking," he explained. "From the air, we are now invisible, at least from some distance. But if we assume the others have metal detectors aboard, it won't do us any good. We need to get out of here and into the air as soon as possible!"

Sen smiled smugly. He seemed to have recovered from his indisposition.

"We can handle the metal detectors, commander. My people will make sure we're as undetectable here as we would be if we were ten thousand feet below the surface of the ocean."

The Atlantean nodded gratefully.

"Well, go ahead then and do that, sir. I'll go have a look at the damage meanwhile."

Kaura rose to accompany him.

"Maybe I can make myself useful. After all, my hypnosis training was only two days ago. It could be that I remember something you've forgotten."

Ux'makia nodded with a smile and made an inviting hand gesture.

"Om'xikal, our onboard technician, is one of the best. He will assess the situation and make the necessary repairs. It was tropically warm outside, so Kaura immediately began to sweat in her purple Atlantean pantsuit. By magical means, she regulated the temperature immediately surrounding her body, so that after a few seconds she seemed as relaxed as ever. She could have worn a Baltic fur coat now and remained just as serene.

Together, they walked around the ship. The second engine at the right rear end of the triangle was charred black. The hit had only grazed it but had obviously hit a power feed line and caused a short circuit. On one side of the air outlet, sheet metal hung down, bent and half-melted, and various cables lay exposed. The chief engineer shook his head worriedly.

"That's going to take a while. We'll have to produce new sheets in the dimensional printer, and replace a few dozen cables. At least a day, I'd say. And we haven't even seen what's happened on top of the *Crystal* yet."

As the other two were already climbing back into the ship's hatch to reach its roof from the inside, Kaura's magical senses felt a brief wavering around her. That had probably been the installation of Sen's cloaking spell.

She quickly took a few steps away from the ship.

When she turned around, it had disappeared. She saw only empty beach against a background of coconut-covered palm trees.

Slowly, she walked back toward the spot where she knew the hovership was, after all, over seventy yards long. When she was within a few steps of the hull, it abruptly reappeared in front of her.

"Good work, Sen," she murmured with satisfaction, following the two Atlanteans. Black smoke was also rising from the upper part of the ship's hull.

The ship's engineer and Ux'makia were standing next to the damaged area, which they had already sprayed with a kind of white foam but still emanated waves of burning heat. They were engrossed in conversation. The commander pointed to the structure of bent metal as Kaura approached.

"That was the air changer. The protective shield must have been completely overloaded here for a moment; I can't explain it any other way. The energy beam almost penetrated the armor of the interior. Not much more, and we'd be dead now, exploded in mid-air."

Kaura sifted through her recently acquired knowledge of Atlantean hovercraft technology.

"Hardly repairable with on-board resources, is it?" she asked grimly, not really expecting an answer.

"No, this can't be fixed by us. And the emergency power pack is only good for about an hour of fast high flight," the engineer confirmed.

The captain was thinking hard.

"In Atlantis, we could easily reach a repair yard in this time, but it won't help us much, here. After that, we'll have to fly at a maximum of one to two miles altitude to keep enough air pressure in the ship. And much slower. In combat, that's a critical disadvantage. I wouldn't want to risk a second encounter with those Kai'ala ships until we're fully operational again."

Kaura nodded thoughtfully.

"I wonder why these hoverboats showed up seemingly out of nowhere. They must have a base around here."

"That would be the logical explanation," the captain opined. "They weren't cloaked. Our tracking devices should have detected them much earlier if they had approached us from farther away."

"That's right, my dears!" intervened Sen, who had just joined the group. "There was no time to say anything during the attack. But Eagle just told me that the tracking pentacle kicked out pretty hard just before we went down. There's quite a cluster of Gifted beings on one of these islets here. Probably Kai'ala if I'm reading those dropshape ships correctly... Anyway, Eagle noted the exact coordinates despite the somewhat, um, hectic atmosphere, and we should find the place. To within about five nautical miles, she thinks. There can't be too many islands in that quadrant. So, what do you guys think? Do we go for a ride?"

He put on an exceedingly smug know-it-all grin. "And I haven't even told you the best part yet. The tracking pentacle indicated an extremely strong techno-magic field emanating from the enemy base. It fans out by about three angular degrees and points almost due east."

Sen paused theatrically. "And what's to the east? Huh?"

Kaura did him the favor and spoke up.

"Lemuria, of course. And in a moment, you're going to tell us that the fanning of the energy beam corresponds exactly to the extent of my continent."

The headmaster grinned happily.

"Intelligent girl! That's it. That means we just have to sail over there, a few dozen miles, capture the base, leash the Kai'ala, and take out that death ray! Or blow it up right away! And boom, Lemuria is free, your dear fellow Amazons can get out, and soon all of Gaia will be free again to devote itself to hugging trees and baking pancakes!"

Diana appeared from behind his shoulder and joined the conversation. The fairy, too, seemed to be in an extremely good mood.

"We're blowing something up? Blowing something up is always a good idea! We haven't blown up anything in far too long! Except for that little airship just now. But there our dear chief cannonballer had all the fun."

The two Atlanteans just stared at the wizard and the fairy as if they were two exotic animals.

"Well, you mages really can't take anything seriously at all," the captain said, shaking his head, sounding half reproachful and half admiring.

"Is a consequence of our long lives and, uh, broadened perspective," Diana explained magnanimously. "A few sex parties now and then can't hurt either. You should try them in Atlantis. Where are your wives, anyway? At home in the kitchen? All just guys there in your little temple! But maybe you have fun together!"

She grinned insinuatingly. Commander Ux'makia looked confused at the turn of the conversation.

"Well, what exactly the priests do in the temple, of course, I don't know. I'm just a soldier. I think they must be praying or something. My dear wife is at home most of the time, that's true. But she not only cooks, she also cleans, and goes shopping. And takes care of the children. That's quite a lot of work. It's a good thing that I'm not at home too often because of my function. I'd probably just be a nuisance."

Diana nodded knowingly.

"Ah, yeah, I was expecting something like that. You guys definitely need more sex parties," she commented.

Sen smiled. The fairies had a very simple answer for most of life's problems. And it was always the same. Life on Sirius Quinta had to be very exhausting, with all the sensual parties everywhere. It occurred to him that he had hardly ever seen male fairies on Earth. The only fairy-man they had ever employed in Lockwood had moved to the countryside after just two decades of service to 'retire and grow roses,' as he said. Emon had always been of select politeness and considered choice of words and had apparently suffered greatly from the vulgar language of his female peers.

Sen decided to organize a regular circle for male-identified magical beings in Oxford when the opportunity arose. That would be interesting and certainly provide some opportunity for healing processes. If he ever returned home, that was.

"So, what do you guys think about our trip?" he asked, trying to bring the focus back to what was important.

"Yes, absolutely!" Kaura replied. "That's why we're here, after all. But we should plan carefully. The Kai'ala probably outnumber us many times over, have those collars, and will have other defenses against intruders in their base. Besides, we'll need at least a day to get the engine fixed. Otherwise, we'll have to carve ourselves a canoe."

Diana raised her small hand and pointed to something behind Kaura's shoulder.

"Or we can take one of those!" she said calmly. Everyone turned around. On the beach were indeed three outrigger boats equipped with small triangular sails. Probably fishing boats because they had nets and spears on board. And below their feet, just in front of the ship, stood six almost naked dark-skinned men performing strange movements.

At first glance, it seemed to be a kind of dance. They bent their upper bodies here and there, shaded faces with their hands, squinted their eyes, knelt down and moved left and right in front of the ship.

Sen grinned.

"I think the ship's cloaking spell is confusing them. They realize something is wrong on the beach, but they don't know what. I'll go down and talk to them."

He was already turning toward the skylight they had climbed up through when Kaura tugged him by the sleeve.

"Wait, I'll do it. I look more like them. Maybe I'll confuse them less than a fair-skinned, blond Scot with bells in his hair. But you're welcome to join me."

She put a comprehension spell around her that would allow her to understand the islanders no matter how they spoke. Then she climbed down, went through the ship to the main hatch and stepped out into the open.

She was aware that she and Sen would seemingly appear out of empty air when they stepped through the camouflage field. Possibly the inhabitants would mistake them for ghosts. She sighed. Well, that could not be avoided.

With a friendly smile, she stepped toward the six men, spreading her empty palms in a show of good faith.

Sen was following her with measured steps.

"Greetings! We are friends and come in peace," she said as the islanders recoiled from her in fear. Slowly she raised her empty hands, showing her palms, then placed them together in front of her chest and bowed slightly. The men seemed to understand that. They relaxed a bit but remained suspicious.

"Who's to say you're not the blue demons in a new disguise?" asked the group's leader, a tall, muscular fisherman with large, intricate tattoos on both upper arms.

"My name is Kaura, and this is Sen. The blue demons are our enemies," Kaura replied. "We are on our way to drive them away, but we lost a first battle. That's why we're here to try again. What have they done to you?"

The black-skinned man's eyes clouded over.

"For decades the white-nosed strangers have been robbing us and kidnapping slaves from our villages to cultivate their great spice fields. Then, two years ago, other white-noses, light-haired like him" —he pointed to Sen—"came and fought with the other strangers."

Sen nodded in understanding.

"The Dutch, who wanted to take the spice monopoly from the Portuguese. That was not long ago. About 1596 Portuguese time. We must be in the Moluccas, the famous Spice Islands," he whispered.

Kaura shushed him.

The islander continued. "We thought things would be better now that the strangers with their thunderbolt throwers were busy with each other. But then the blue-skinned devils came. They occupied the sacred island where a great temple of the ancestors stands. They claimed that the temple of the shimmering walls belonged to them and their gods. Our medicine men and women did not believe them and we attacked them. Many brave warriors fell or were captured.

After that, they haunted the fishing villages twice more, and always kidnapped some children. They took most of the tribal shamans the first time, led away by glittering leashes."

The fisherman patted his chest. "I, Akao of the Mawak tribe, wanted to attack the strangers again and drive them away for good. But our chief fears their revenge and has forbidden it."

Kaura studied the islanders' canoes.

"You are a brave man, Akao. How far is it from here to the sacred island where the demons dwell?"

The fishermen's spokesman thought for a moment.

"Not quite from highest sun to dusk, when the wind is as good as it is today." "

About five hours, then," Sen muttered. "We could be there just after dark tonight if we leave in two hours. I'm sure the Kai'ala won't expect us that soon after we went down in a burning ship. Ask him if he can take us there."

Kaura began to negotiate with Akao. It turned out that three men were willing to go. The men of the third boat preferred to return to their village and notify their chief. The two dugout canoes would provide enough space for all the mages and their weapons. The Atlantean fleet officers would repair the ship as quickly as possible and then pick them up on the 'sacred island' in case their plans worked out, or launch a rescue attempt if they had failed.

Barely two hours later, everything was ready. The Atlantean mage would stay behind with the ship's company so as not to leave it completely defenseless in the event of any attacks of a magical nature. Kaura, the Lockwood mages, and all three fairies would use the boats to reach the Kai'ala base unseen and disable either its power generators or the death ray itself with Atlantean microbombs.

Sen now carried two of the things with him. They were about the size of a cannonball and almost as heavy. Commander Ux'makia had assured them that one of the explosive devices alone would be enough to penetrate a two-foot-thick steel wall and wreak havoc.

Diana had been thrilled. Since then, the fairy had been happily singing something to herself that sounded suspiciously like "Boom, boom, boom, bomb's boomily booming around." Furthermore, the mages also had conventional impulse ray guns, an auroric jamming device, and emergency transmitters with which a secure connection to the hovership could be established.

Everything had been packed in bags of wax-coated fabric. Kaura and the Scots had donned light, black uniforms from the ship's racks. When they approached the island, they would hide themselves by means of inverted camouflage spells, hardly detectable even by other mages.

Since the locals, as Akao said, still fished below the back bluff of the sacred island from time to time, they hoped that the two outrigger boats would not attract further attention.

The fishermen, with the help of their passengers, pushed the boats into the water, where the surf waves had by now become slightly higher than when they had arrived. Everyone pitched in at the gunwales of the dugouts, pushing with all their might every time a wave reached its peak and there was some water under the keel.

At the third heave, both boats floated free and were propelled through the rising surf with powerful paddle strokes. When they were beyond the surf zone, the fishermen set sail.

Kaura raised her hand in greeting in the direction of Captain Ux'makia, who was standing on the beach in the shade of a palm tree with the other Atlanteans, watching the departure maneuver with interest.

"Wish us luck," she murmured so softly that no one around her could understand. At the same time, she patted the small, golden dumbbell amulet in her shoulder bag. According to the central brain, the energy supply had meanwhile been recharged just enough to open a portal back to Rhodes again, if things went wrong and they needed a quick escape route.

The sleek dugout canoe with its far-reaching boom cut like a projectile through the green-blue crests of the waves, in which the tropical afternoon sun broke like in a living mirror. In a few hours they would have reached what was probably the most important Kai'ala base on Gaia. If they could make it unusable for the alien invaders, much was already gained. But they were not there yet.

Sighing, Kaura shook her head and tried to simply enjoy the feeling of finally gliding through the waves of her beloved ocean once again.

* * *

At the same time, only a little more than a dozen nautical miles away, two of the beings who called themselves 'gods' met.

Uriel had taken off his mask as the Atlantean High Councilor. He did not look much different without the sensory illusion spells he had laid onto himself in order to pass as one of the islanders. His skin now was more pearly than white and shone more. His eyes were about the same shade of blue as before, only now the irises filled them completely and there was no white background visible. His hair was more golden than white. In fact, he now resembled his companion so much that he could have been her brother.

"I could not do differently, Triabola," he said. "After the first attack had failed, there was simply no low-risk opportunity for another attempt. The crystal priests had become too cautious. And I sadly underestimated those Scottish naïfs." The right corner of his mouth twitched erratically. "But maybe they were aboard that Atlantean ship our people shot down. If they survived the crash, we'll have them in hand soon."

"You allow yourself too many mistakes recently, Uriel," the goddess said in her velvety, smoky voice. "Not that I personally have a problem with that. But Ha'akaminiel isn't a patient man. We'll have to send a report to Rignar soon. Too much seems to be going wrong here lately. We should make sure that we can communicate some quick success to offset for the failure in Pyrrha."

"That little Pacific whore," Uriel cursed. "Before she got here, everything was working just fine."

The human-like being from the planet Rignar, stared gloomily ahead.

Triabola could see him getting angrier and angrier. In secret, she prepared a few weaves with which she could quickly remove herself from the danger zone. Uriel was unpredictable when he got angry. Once, on Rignar, he had killed half of the guests at a dinner party with witch fire and had the other half slowly tortured to death in a heat chamber just because a servant had spilled some champagne on his robe.

This had caused a sensation even in Olympus, and there, God knew, people were not squeamish. But crazy sadists and psychopaths like him were still dangerous because you never knew when they would bite the hand that fed them. Triabola believed that Ha'akaminiel allowed the 'Architect of the Great Plan' to live only because he truly had a brilliant idea from time to time.

Yes, the chief planner of the 'gods' had to be handled carefully. Especially when his plans went wrong. And now, things weren't looking very good for him in that regard.

The other Riganian sat up a little straighter.

"All right," he growled. "They wouldn't have it any other way. Instead of allowing them the pleasure of serving us as slaves, we just kill them all."

He laughed maliciously.

Triabola stared at him.

"The Lemurians? The magical beings? All the earthlings? Who do you mean?"

"Exactly! The Lemurians! The little whore will be in for a surprise when she gets home and finds nothing but a big pile of rotting corpses!"

Uriel grinned cockily as he imagined that satisfying scene in front of his inner eye.

Triabola grimaced in disgust.

"Uriel, the Olympic Council will not take kindly to this. After all, the Lemurians will be the best harvest ever. This could be the key to super-galactic power. Ha'akaminiel will not be pleased if you deprive him of a few hundred thousand super-strong magical creatures because of your personal desire for revenge."

The former Atlantean Supreme Minister made a contemptuous gesture with his hand.

"Bah. Olympus will have to take what I bring them. The terramagic field of Gaia is, as far as we know, almost infinitely powerful. When a Terranean magical being dies, the energy just flows back into the overall field. And my people down there"—he pointed to the ground below the palm-fringed courtyard where the two of them were perched on comfortable reclining chairs—"My people down there are just a finger's breadth away from tapping into the Gaia Source itself. Then we can just forget about these stupid harvests. We'll kill all the magical beings and then we'll be the only ones left in the universe with magical powers!"

He chuckled like a maniac.

Triabola was not yet convinced, though.

"You sell the bear's skin before you have it, Uriel. Besides, there are always some others. The Kai'ala. And the fairies in the Sirius system. Plus, other races in the surrounding galaxies that access similar fields."

"You still don't understand my point, my dear," Uriel said. Now he was serious commander and statesman again, and one could well imagine that with this appearance he had won entire nations and parliaments over to support his apparent or real goals. Gaia was not the first planet that the Riganian sect, who had been banished from Lemuria eons ago, wanted to convert for their purposes. But by far the most important. And the one that had offered them the most resistance so far.

"The Gaia field is the only one that allows the weaving of magical elements," he continued. That is, it is the only one that we have so far been able to harness with our extraction methods to the point where it is compatible with our system. Of course, that's because our forefathers came from this planet."

His gaze suddenly hardened and lost itself in the far distance.

Triabola suppressed a sigh. Now he was starting to start his rantings again.

"And then they cast us out," Uriel hissed. "Because someone made a little mistake and wanted a tiny little bit of power. And if a few recalcitrant planets were destroyed in the process, what does it matter? The Great Prophet Ei-Kal Ga'maial could have led Lemuria to unimagined greatness! But they did not understand him and his followers! They ostracized them! Abandoned on a distant planet without starships and weapons, their magical abilities removed. The ancient legends tell of it! And now those filthy bastards shall pay the price for the sins of their ancestors!"

He had shouted out the last words at the top of his lungs into the warm tropical afternoon.

The second goddess swallowed uncomfortably. Unforgiving hatred shone from the eyes of her accomplice.

Uriel stood up.

"I am the commanding officer of this operation. And I have decided that the Lemurian threat must end. For the safety of the entire planet. Now."

He half turned away and continued talking over his shoulder. "I will arrange for the boundary beam to be varied so that it sweeps the entire area of the continent. No one will survive that."

His smile took on an even more diabolical streak, and the hardened goddess, who had personally ordered the deaths of hundreds of beings during her long life, shuddered. Then Uriel turned away and went inside.

Triabola shrugged and rose. She needed to cool down. With an impatient movement, she slipped her light robe off her shoulders, took a few steps, and dove headfirst into the large pool of shimmering azure water in front of her.

* * *

A few hours later, Kaura and her companions came within sight of their destination. The outrigger boats had covered the distance in record time. They had sailed past a good dozen small, palm-studded islets with snow-white beaches and crystal-clear water. Sen had sighed and muttered to himself each time.

"And another little paradise... Great Mother, what have I been doing all these years on this damp, cold British island. Two hundred wasted years of life! How am I supposed to survive this!"

Now he did so again as they sailed around a small cliff of the miniature islet offshore from the 'holy island.' This time Kaura nudged him from behind with his elbow.

"Don't worry about it, love. Now that Lockwood's been doing without you for so long anyway, why don't you settle down on one of these islets afterward and play catch with the sharks every day?"

A dreamy drawl played around the corners of the tattooed man's mouth.

"Yeah, maybe I should," he muttered and stretched himself, looking back over his shoulder at the Lemurian. "Would you come and visit me from time to time, then, to ease the agony of my loneliness, fair island beauty?"

Kaura laughed brightly and pressed a kiss to his neck. "Let's survive the next few hours first, then we'll see!" she shouted against the wind, holding onto the bulwark of the canoe as it tipped its bow into a particularly deep trough of waves.

Somehow the world felt all right again, despite all the problems they had. She remembered how often she had paddled her canoe in the calm lagoon near the village she had grown up in. Here, even the water was just as warm and had a similar salinity. She murmured a love chant, and in response a few small drops of spray splashed up and wetted the spot between her eyebrows.

Their destination grew larger and larger on the horizon, and as the sun sank into the sea as a glowing red ball, they had already come close to the cliff. Dark and threatening, the steep volcanic cliffs towered in front of the two outrigger boats, tiny in comparison.

Akao pointed ahead to starboard.

"There is the cave I told you about. It is a back entrance to the temple. I don't think the blue devils use it. But maybe they know of it and have posted guards. We can't be sure. But it is our best option. If we approached from the other side of the island, we would surely be discovered."

The fishermen hoisted the sails and threw their nets. Kaura wanted it to look like they were merely trying to catch fish. Everyone hoped that the Kai'ala were not interested enough in the customs of the locals to know that the fishermen usually only went out during the day. Under cover of darkness, they would then try to penetrate the temple and destroy the energy transmitter.

As anywhere in the tropics, darkness fell quickly and almost without transition, like a velvet curtain covering the sea, which shortly before had still been gleaming in pink and silver. The first stars twinkled in the heavens. Kaura's eyes routinely searched for the North Star. At this time of year, she could easily see the constellation of the Great Dipper. Extending the back wall of the cart in her mind about five times, she unfailingly found Polaris, who seemed to blink lovingly at her. North lay exactly behind the steep wall toward which they were now heading with quiet paddle strokes.

"A good omen," murmured the Lemurian, once again checking the inverted camouflage weaves that the mages had placed over the two boats. They should make them undetectable to all technical and all but perhaps highest energy magical search spells. She forced her breathing to calm and anchored herself in the soothing sway of the waves running a little shorter and sharper here in the shadow of the island.

Within a few minutes, the fishermen found the huge mouth of the cave, which, even seen from close up, was hardly distinguishable from the black and looming cliff of volcanic rock. Only the sea was somewhat less white and foamy at this point than at the others, where the waves lapped against the jagged stones at the foot of the cliff.

It was unnaturally quiet and pitch black in the cave. The water had become almost completely calm in here. The fishermen seemed to be almost as comfortable in the dark as the magicians and fairies, who could amplify even the most minimal amounts of light with the help of simple weaves so that they could practically see as well in the dark as they could during the day.

From the boat next to theirs, Kaura saw three soap bubble-like weaves rise and float purposefully toward three spots in the darkness ahead of them.

"Motion detectors and cameras," Eagle whispered over from the other canoe. "The time loops will fool them into thinking there's still nothing going on here."

"Meanwhile, we can have a dance party, cant we?" Diana added beside her. Her eyes and those of her two companions glowed fluorescently in the darkness. Then she began her peculiar chanting again. "Boom, boom, ...," Kaura heard her sing softly to herself.

"So, we can light up the place now?" she asked Eagle. In response, a small witch light flared up above the other woman and slowly floated upward to the ceiling of the grotto. Kaura reassured Akao, who at first was not sure if they had been discovered. Then the side wall of the canoe scraped against solid stone. In the back of the grotto, a proper dock had been created out of hewn lava stones, which easily accommodated several of the local canoes, one behind the other.

The mages pulled themselves out of the only slightly swaying boats, which immediately cast off again. They would try to reach the next island and then their home village under the protection of the cloaks of invisibility that would keep their effect for some time.

Sen had rigorously refused to allow the islanders to participate in the attack, although Akao was eager to prove his qualities as a fighter.

"The demons fight with weapons of the demons," was all the mage had said. "We can't take care of you, too, when we're probably going to have to fight for our lives ourselves."

Akao had reluctantly agreed. On either side of the ancient-looking jetty loomed great statues of stone, their huge, fearsome eyes and jaws lined with mother-of-pearl and obsidian, gleaming softly in the glow of the witch's light.

"Guardians," Kaura remarked. Cautiously, they continued toward the back of the stone platform built into the cave, where Akao said the entrance to the 'Temple of Shining Walls' should be. There, after a long row of human-sized wooden statues on both sides, they found a shimmering wall on which the greenish light refracted in irregular, billowing waves. In the center of the gate was a highlighted, spiral-shaped emblem. Kaura drew in her breath in surprise.

"This is a Lemurian symbol," she said. "The fern spiral has been used by my people since the beginning of time to mark the entrances to temples and other important facilities! Most likely, this 'temple' is a Lemurian site that has been abandoned thousands of years ago!"

Suddenly she remembered something. She pulled the small, golden dumbbell amulet out of her pocket.

"Gaia, can you check something for me?"

"Gladly, Exalted One," came the disembodied voice's immediate reply.

"Are you familiar with the facility we are currently in?"

"Affirmative. It is Fleet Base Rai'atea II of the Lemurian Starfleet. Status: out of commission."

"Can you shut down the station's power?" she continued.

"Positive. But the power supply is running at minimum. Only lighting and ventilation are operating."

Sen cursed.

"That means, the Kai'ala brought their own equipment and power supply."

Kaura nodded and turned to Gaia again.

"Are there any larger rooms in the station that would be suitable for the installation of large generators and magic beams?"

"The base's starship hangars are the only very large spaces not occupied by fixed equipment. There are six hangars for Vulcan-class starships and two hangars for smaller ships, atmospheric fighters and planetary hover transporters. All were vacated twenty-four thousand six hundred and three years ago when the remnants of the Lemurian fleet were withdrawn to bases at Ilkarion and on Aalid."

The dumbbell fell silent. Kaura stared at the gate thoughtfully.

"If we open it, they'll know we're there right away. I will take us through by shifting. At this distance, it should work, even here. Let's form a circle."

At her instruction, they all joined hands. Kaura concentrated until the whole group began to shimmer and disappeared. A heart-beat later, they were standing in an artificially lit room.

Sen looked around. Behind them was a gate similar in color to the one she had just been standing in front of. So probably they had only jumped a few yards.

"You're always good for a surprise," he muttered in Kaura's direction. "So, what now?"

In response, the Lemurian had Gaia display a three-dimensional map of the base.

She pointed to a series of large, box-shaped rooms.

"Those are the hangars. That's where we're going."

She turned and walked briskly down the hallway. The others hurried after her.

Suddenly Simon jumped up next to her and yanked her back.

"Someone's coming," he hissed. "Let me take care of that!" He ducked and cautiously approached the passage into the next corridor, which was perpendicular to the one they were in. A grayish magical bubble appeared before his fingertips. Then he jumped out and disappeared behind the bend. The others followed him cautiously.

Kaura glanced around the corner, then gave the all-clear.

"He's got them. Come on!"

A few yards away, Simon was talking silently to two figures kneeling in front of him.

"A Kai'ala," whispered Sen. "And he has a witch on his leash. Probably one of the native shamans."

Simon nodded.

"I took them both over," he said. "No time to be squeamish. Can you and Eagle free the shaman from this thing?"

He waved over to Diana and the two fairies, who came over immediately.

Simon bent down to the Kai'ala.

"I'll try to read his mind," he growled grimly. "Then we shall know exactly where to go."

His eyes went blank as he concentrated. Then his face turned pale.

"We're just in time," breathed the young Oxford mage. "They are in the process of adjusting the death ray aimed at the borders of Lemuria so that they can brush the entire continent with it. They intend to kill all Lemurians. In half an hour they will be ready, it seems."

Kaura stared at him uncomprehendingly at first. Then the full implications of what the psychomage had said dawned on her. For a moment everyone was silent, trying to grasp the enormity of this.

Sen collected himself.

"So, what are we waiting for then? Have you found out where this thing is, Simon?"

Simon nodded.

"Spread out in hangars two and three. Hangars one and seven hold the ships they came in, and small fighters like the ones that attacked us."

Diana tugged at his sleeve.

"We have removed the collar. Can you release the shaman from her compulsion spell, please?"

The mage nodded, and the islander startled out of her stupor with a frightened whimper. Eagle and the fairies immediately attended to her and explained that she was in the company of friends and in relative safety.

Kaura had been standing there stiffly for several minutes without saying a word. Now she turned to Diana.

"I can jump into the two rooms with you and plant the bombs. That's the only way there's little enough time for anyone to find and disarm them. I need you to empty the hangars with a panic wish, and as quickly as possible. I don't like the Kai'ala, but blowing people up from ambush is not my style."

The fairy nodded seriously.

"That honors you, my dear. I don't know if I would worry so

much if someone was about to wipe out my home planet. So, shall we go? I'm looking forward to the big bang!"

Kaura smiled sarcastically.

"Two big bangs, Diana, if you please." And, turning to the others. "Wait for us here. We'll blow their thing up, shut down the power to the Kai'ala base, and jump back here. Then we'll take it from there. I should be able to open a portal to Rhodes, and from there Gaia can take us directly back to the *Crystal Clarity* later, if there's enough energy left for that, or at the latest after some time of recharging. There, hopefully, they will be done with the repairs by then, so we can attack the base from the outside and destroy the alien starships. Unfortunately, we only have two of the bombs with us, otherwise I would do it right away. Agreed?"

All nodded.

Kaura took one of the bombs in her hand. She quickly checked how the mechanism worked and prepared everything so that she only had to push two buttons, and the inconspicuous but so dangerous thing would ignite within ten seconds. Then she grabbed Diana by her little hand.

"Ready?" she asked.

The fairy pressed her hand.

"Yes. Let's get some steam up those gods asses," she said seriously. Kaura concentrated and vanished into thin air along with Diana just as Simon shouted, "Kaura! ..."

But the two didn't hear any more. The woman and the fairy materialized in a corner of a huge room crammed with humming devices, one side of which was open toward the tropical night.

Suddenly the air was warm and humid again, and only now did Kaura realize that the interior passages of the base must have been artificially cooled. Kai'ala in their typical ruby robes walked back and forth between the machines, paying particular attention to a copper device protruding from the opening, distantly resembling a cannon. This had to be the device, the death ray, with which they were planning to wipe out an entire people, Kaura thought dazedly.

None of the technicians, who were busy with themselves, seemed to have noticed her yet. Diana, on the other hand, immediately went to work. She brandished her fairy staff, and, at once, the first of the Kai'ala began to scream in sheer panic. Without knowing what they were actually afraid of, the scrawny, bald creatures nearly fell over each other as they fled the room.

Kaura nodded to the fairy.

"Good job! Now it all comes down to speed."

With the bomb in hand, she ran down to the death ray projection device, activated the magnetic connector, and simply pinned the little metal thing to the bottom of the gun. She activated the timer. Then she took the fairy by the hand and *shifted* again.

When they reappeared in another room, Kaura knew immediately that something had gone wrong. There were no devices here, just some of the small, teardrop-shaped combat hoverboats standing around. She cursed. Two Kai'ala technicians standing next to one of the ships pointed at her and excitedly shouted something she didn't understand. Immediately, she *shifted*.

At the moment of their disappearance, she could hear the distant thunder of a tremendous explosion, which grew louder at the same moment they re-materialized in another hangar. This room had to be closer to the first one. And yes, there were machines here. This simply had to be the right hangar. They didn't have time to check it out any closer. The first technicians, still puzzled wondering what the explosion meant, had already taken notice.

"Diana," she hissed, and the fairy waved her wand like a star conductor. The Kai'ala immediately forgot everything around them in their panic. Kaura had no more time to check the function of the individual machines. She simply stuck the bomb to the largest of the devices near her and trusted that the explosive power would be sufficient to destroy the entire hangar. Then she took Diana by the hand again, activated the detonator, and shifted back to where their companions were.

They arrived in a witch's cauldron. Diagonally beside her, she saw Sen, Eagle and the fairies kneeling on the ground. They were all wearing silver collars, and the two humans were bombarding Simon and the freed shaman with witch fire.

Behind the captives stood a tall woman with golden hair and a triumphant smile on her face. Something clicked next to her, and she saw Diana being pulled away from her out of the corner of her eye. Reflexively, she threw herself around and jerked her arms up. She felt something metallic bounce painfully off her wrists. Behind her back stood a softly smiling man who reminded her of Uriel, although the Atlantean minister had been paler and most definitely did not have such huge blue eyes.

In a dreamlike slowing down of reality, she saw Simon's resistance weaken when a separating field, coming from the captured fairies, surrounded him and cut him off from the source, the Gaia magic field. She understood that they had lost. At least someone had to escape and bring help. But if she used the dumbbell now, she might not have enough energy to return immediately. No, she had to do it herself! She tried to shift, somewhere, not far away, just away from the immediate danger, losing precious fractions of a second.

But nothing happened. She felt herself being cut off from the source. The male mage had cast another separation field. At that moment, a second, deafening detonation boomed through the hallway. The light flickered and went out. This distracted the man, who was just picking up the metal collar again, just for a moment.

This moment was enough for Kaura to activate the dumbbell amulet.

"Gaia, portal to headquarters," she whispered hurriedly, and immediately the blue billowing wall of energy flared up beside her.

She simply dropped through, for at the same time the stranger had recovered from his surprise and raised his hand.

A glowing beam of magical fire shot toward her heart, but since she was already darting sideways through the portal, she was only hit in the side. However, she would only learn that much later.

Searing pain immediately took away her consciousness, and she didn't even feel the shocking, bone-breaking impact on the cool stone floor on the other side of the portal, which winked shut behind her at once.

8

Help Is Coming

When Kaura's consciousness returned, she still felt as if she were dreaming. Around her, she heard voices. The space she was in seemed infinitely wide. She sluggishly tried to open her eyes, but soon gave up the attempt when she realized that her body was not yet responding to her effort of will.

A woman's voice was talking to someone.

"The healing weave has worked. She's going to pull through. She'll be awake in a few hours."

A man's voice answered.

"That was a close one. It's a good thing we've always had a guard in the portal room for days now. I'm very worried about the rest of our friends. They…"

Then Kaura's senses faded again, and comforting, velvety darkness enveloped her. When she surfaced again, her eyelids fluttered, now letting some light through. When she fully lifted her eyelids, she looked directly into the bearded face of Lance, the Grand Master of the Knights Templar of Rhodes.

"Welcome back," he said. Kaura made a feeble attempt to struggle to her feet, but he gently pushed her back onto her bed. "Try not to move just yet. Irene over there thinks that all your organs and bones are like new because of the fairies' healing spell, but I still want her to look at your condition first."

Kaura turned her head with difficulty and saw the Scottish defensive mage stepping toward her. Behind her hovered one of the fairies left behind on Rhodes. Her name was Amina, Kaura remembered darkly. Both looked worried.

Irene nodded to her, stepped without further ado to the large wooden bed on which she lay, and held her hand to Kaura's forehead. The cool, searching sensation of a tactile spell flowed through her. Satisfied, the woman nodded.

"You're going to be fine. Probably a little tired for another day or two. Your organism is almost incredibly resilient. If you want, you can sit up now."

Kaura did, and slowly swung her legs over the edge of the bed. Then she had to rest for a moment.

"A little tired, you say? Then I don't want to know how a less resistant organism would feel now."

In response, Irene pointed her thumb diagonally down to the left.

"A less resistant organism wouldn't feel anything now, but would be down there waiting for a burial in the palace graveyard. You had almost half of your organs and ribcage burned away by a massive beam of witchfire. If it hadn't been for Amina standing guard here and starting the healing just seconds after you came through the portal so suddenly, it wouldn't have been fast enough for you either. Like this, we were able to restore you with some effort."

Kaura swallowed and contorted her face painfully.

"Thank you. When... how long...?"

Amina's big green eyes lit up. "You came through only about five hours ago. But maybe that is still too long. Now, more than anything, we want to know from you where the superboss and the others are. We've been trying to get back to where you were with this dumbbell thing, but it's not responding to any of us. Are they still in Pyrrha? What's going on there?"

She raised the amulet in the air with a twist of her wand and sent it over to Kaura as she held out her hand.

"It's set to me," she said quietly. "While I can probably get us back to where the fight was, since the portal was only open for a second or two, first we need to plan. Is there somewhere we can sit down? And I'm thirsty."

Irene and the Grand Master helped her over to a sitting area with heavy wooden chairs.

Lance adjusted some seat cushions for her while Amina brought up some water with a twist of her fairy wand.

"First of all, Sen and the others are likely not dead, but in the captivity of two of the beings who call themselves 'gods,' Kaura began. Then she told her friends everything that had happened since their trip to Pyrrha a little over a week ago.

"Whoever or whatever these 'gods' are, they are exceedingly strong in their magic," she concluded. "I think we should send someone to Atlantis to call for reinforcements. And then try to free Sen and the others as quickly as possible."

The Grand Master leaned forward.

"So, if I understand you correctly, you can use this thing to open portals from here to anywhere on Gaia. And if you have it with you, you can get back here from anywhere, too, at least as long as the control center still has enough power."

Kaura nodded, and he continued.

"So, let's send one of the fairies to Atlantis with a message reporting on your ship's accident and the Kai'ala base in the Pacific, and requesting more support. Then you'll open a portal for us and some of my people directly into the base, and we'll try to free your

Scottish friends, preferably without meeting up with those god-beings. What do you think of that?"

Irene screwed up her face.

"Risky. But right now, I don't see a better option. The problem is that we obviously don't have much to counter two gods, and as I understand Kaura, we will almost certainly have no energy left for an escape after opening the second portal. It's also possible that we'll just be jumping into captivity. We won't help anyone with that. Maybe we should think the whole thing over once more. Or even bring in the Lemurians. After all, according to Kaura's report, the Kai'ala's death field is probably now turned off and they can leave their continent again."

Kaura nodded and drank the rest of her cup of water, already feeling much better.

She rose.

"Let's go to the control room. Maybe we can learn more there. After all, the enemy is in an old Lemurian base that is still connected to the Gaia central brain."

Together they went up the spiral staircase. In the room, Doraline, the second guard fairy who had stayed behind in Rhodes, welcomed them.

"Nothing special happening, guys," she reported succinctly. "Unless the appearance of some new dots over there should be interesting."

She pointed her finger over to the metal cube next to the portal. Above it hovered a few reddish spheres of light, which Kaura could not make anything of at first. Between the outer of the spheres glowed five bright green dots that seemed to move very slowly toward the center.

Slowly, she walked over. Then she understood.

"This is an image of our solar system and its planets!" she explained to the others. "And the five green dots are obviously alien starships approaching. Here, they're even labeled. They're probably sending some kind of identification."

She leaned closer and squinted her eyes. "AAL-KBJ-1756," she muttered, "And the others also start with AAL. Probably Aalid ships." She thought feverishly. Should Joe and Ariane have made it? And so quickly? Or could this be another trick of the gods? She shrugged and gave Gaia the order to establish contact with the alien ships.

* * *

Sen stared somberly into empty space. He and the other Lockwood prisoners had been chained to a long metal bench next to the Moluccan shaman and several other slaves who were obviously coming from the same region. Strictly speaking, their captors had simply hung the leashes attached to their collars on hooks above the bench, and that was enough for them to barely be able to move or even touch each other.

The Kai'ala had taken them aboard one of the larger, teardrop-shaped hover ships shortly after their capture. Now they were on their way somewhere. They had not been told the ship's destination. Simon's injuries worried them all, but there was nothing they could do for him. He was the only one of them who had suffered some deep cuts and burns in the battle, which would not have been a problem if he had been given proper care. But the inquisitors refused to supply any medical assistance, and he himself shrugged it all off as minor.

"We have bigger problems than my few scrapes now. I still feel pretty good," he had said, although his burns looked pretty severe.

Sen hoped that at least Kaura's mission to destroy the death ray had been successful. The two explosions they had heard, as well as the surprised reaction of their captors, offered reason for optimism. As well, Kaura seemed to have escaped, which gave reason for some optimism. But out of the corner of his eye, the principal had thought he saw that she had been almost fully hit by the beam of witchfire summoned by the strange mage. Sen felt his breathing quicken fearfully at the thought.

Diana, who was sitting next to him, winked at him encouragingly from below.

"We'll get out of here all right, superboss. The Atlanteans know where we've been. And Kaura is probably already getting help, too. I'm sure she's made it."

A Kai'ala guard hissed from his place at the end of the cabin that they should be quiet.

Sen turned to him.

"What is happening here? Where are you taking us, and what are you planning to do with us?"

The blue-skinned creature, dressed in the ruby robe of the Spanish Grand Inquisitors, spat at the mage's feet. "You'll find out soon enough. Be quiet now."

A few hours later, the boat landed. The prisoners were rudely pushed out of the hatch and gathered on an uneven, dusty place somewhere out in the countryside. Some mounted soldiers in the uniform of the Inquisition were waiting for them. While behind them the teardrop-shaped hoverboat immediately took off again, the inquisitors mounted horses as well and held the prisoners' leashes on a kind of extension chain in their hands, four slaves to each of them. The prisoners had to walk, or, in the case of the fairies, fly themselves behind the horses.

It was less hot than on the island where they had been taken, but much drier. The sun was still almost at its zenith; it was obviously early afternoon here. The path was lined with gnarled olive trees and thorny bushes.

"Mediterranean," Diana whispered, and Sen nodded.

After about an hour of hard walking, they reached the shore of a body of water where a boat was waiting for them. Sen saw the fairy next to him nod in satisfaction as they saw beyond the water's surface a giant cluster of buildings, domes, and minarets that the magician immediately recognized from various copperplate engravings and book illustrations.

Indeed, this had to be Constantinople. Eagle had guessed correctly.

Roughly, they were pushed onto the benches of the big rowboat, which was moved by soldiers. The inquisitors sat on the front bight, keeping an eye on the prisoners, and doing nothing else. Here they also had their hoods pulled far over their faces again, so that no one would see at first glance that they were not human.

Another hour later, they docked at a pier in the middle of town. It seemed to have rained here recently because the stones of the docks were damp. Steam rose in the heat, enveloping the whole scene in a mystical, fine haze. If their situation had not been so serious, he could have enjoyed it more, Sen thought bitterly.

Behind a large expanse of cobblestones and a few warehouses, the hill of the old town rose into the air. Huge domes, palaces, towers, monuments and gates of all kinds were stacked all the way up like a man-made mountain.

One of the soldiers gave Sen a crude jab with the blunt end of his halberd.

"Come on, get a move on. Soon you'll be where you belong, dirty witches!" Some passersby dressed in loose robes and turbans stared curiously at the group. Many others quickly turned away and hurried on. In the faces of some, Sen thought he could see compassion.

The soldiers and inquisitors drove them forward through the bustle of the city. Two of the men went ahead and by shoving and shouting created an alley for the others to follow. A little later, one of their guards knocked on the wooden gate, set inside a nondescript wall.

The gate opened and the prisoners were herded through. Behind the wall was a fairytale-like garden with fragrant flowers of all varieties and artfully arranged fountains and gazebos. They did not see much of this, however, for immediately they were led through another gate and descended into a dark vault lit only by torches.

All together they were locked in a dungeon, and the heavy, iron-barred wooden plank door closed behind them with a massive crash. Simon, despite his weakness, immediately set about looking for ways to loosen the collars from the inside, but soon gave up.

"I'm afraid all we can do at the moment is wait," he said. "Either for a favorable opportunity, or for outside help."

Sen nodded.

"This must be the location of the cluster of magical creatures that Eagle has located. The Atlanteans know about it. We can just hope that someone gets us out of here before they kill us all."

Eagle thoughtfully fingered the lock of the heavy door. Obviously, here they were able to move quite freely within the room despite wearing the collars.

"I don't think they would have brought us here in the first place if they wanted to kill us. We're probably meant to end up as slaves to the Inquisition, I suppose. And as long as we're alive, we have hope."

* * *

The two gods, meanwhile, sat on the bridge of the larger of their two interstellar-class starships at the Rai'atea base, ignoring the frantic activity of the Kai'ala crew around them with long-practiced arrogance.

"You see, Triabola, I had the right idea, just a bit too late, unfortunately. We should have been a little faster, and the Lemurians would be no problem by now," said Uriel. "Now we'll have to finish them off by other means. Fortunately, our ships are sufficiently equipped. We launch, go into space above Lemuria, and BOOM!"

He clapped his hands, unaware that he had just used one of the fairies' favorite expressions.

Triabola nodded, agreeing for once.

"We have indeed been put on the defensive by the Lemurian initiative. But none of the terrestrial civilizations have functional starships anymore. Our agents have long since seen to that. And by the time they have made the ships usable again, our plans will have long been completed. So, we have unrestricted air power over Gaia."

A Kai'ala approached them and bowed humbly.

"We're ready to lift off, master," he intoned.

Uriel waved his hand graciously.

"Launch immediately. Put the ship into stationary orbit over Lemuria. After leaving atmosphere, clear for action and make all weapons of mass destruction ready to fire."

The officer nodded and walked back over to the control console, where the ship's commander and navigator were busy with final preparations for take-off.

* * *

Ishe'melen was commander of the star battleship *Uma* and the Aalid fleet unit assigned to her. Wearing a stony expression on her face, the forty-odd year-old woman stood in front of the panoramic window on the command bridge of her three hundred yard long, distantly zeppelin-shaped giant ship and looked down at the minuscule sphere in front of her, glowing blue in front of the starry sky. It was about the size of a pinhead.

Without turning to the *Uma*'s first officer standing next to her, she gave the orders that would in a short time take her into orbit around the third planet of the system known since time immemorial as 'Solaris'—the parent star for the inhabitants of hundreds of other solar systems.

"No one has been able to view this planet from the outside of a starship for many thousands of years," she mused. "And now we've passed through without our readings indicating the slightest resistance. The information from Alaris is indeed correct. The staggered protective shield around the outermost planetary orbits of Solaris has been shut down."

"Or it was destroyed," interjected her first officer. His name was Ike'rion, and he was a recent graduate of the Fleet Academy. Black-skinned, muscular, with soft brown eyes and an easy laugh, he was one of the most highly decorated graduates of his class, a fact that had earned him this post on the flagship. He belonged to the generation in which genetic diversification had resumed after Aalid society had striven for centuries toward standardization in the sense of common ideals of beauty. It was easy to see on the young officer's face how much he enjoyed the opportunity to be one of the first Aalids in centuries to see the planet of the Ancients, and not even to reach it via a portal, but to actually witness the approach in a starship.

His commander nodded.

"Have the radio center keep trying to contact Ilkarion or Pyrrha. Perhaps someone in Atlantia could respond as well. And have Im'kaniel see to it that the ship is cleared for action. According to the message we received from the headquarters in Alaris, Gaia is under attack by Kai'ala and another unknown power. We must assume that they also have armed starships."

Her even, slightly freckled face was grim.

A three-dimensional hologram flickered up in front of her.

"Stevenson from Communications, my lady," an older woman with spiraling tattoos on her lightly purple-tinted face spoke up. "We are receiving a request from Gaia Central Brain on behalf of Kaura Alenu'ala of the Lemurian leadership. Shall I put it through?"

Ishe'melen answered in the affirmative.

A brown-skinned face with a gently curved nose and full lips appeared in front of her, smiling at her kindly but with a commanding expression on her face. Involuntarily, the commander drew in her breath in admiration. Despite all the efforts of recent years to reverse the visual uniformity of the Aalid population, such a unique, characterful face was still a rarity back home and would betray either extreme luck in genetic reorganization or extreme wealth.

Behind the woman, an older, gray-bearded man and a fairy could be seen. The Aalid admiral had to control herself not to stare. Fairies were rarely encountered outside the Sirius system and even more rarely engaged in interstellar shipping, although they undoubtedly had the technical means to do so.

"My name is Kaura Alenu'ala," said the dark-skinned woman. "On behalf of the people of Gaia, I thank you for coming so quickly. Am I correct in assuming that you have been notified by Joe Nelson and Ariane Tinkerbell? Are they with you?"

Ishe'melen introduced himself and said that no, the two were not on her ship.

"We were on a routine flight to the Betelgeuse system and were detached here from headquarters to assist you. That's why we were able to get here so quickly, although a direct hyperspeed flight from Aalid to Gaia takes about four weeks. Our information is minimal."

Kaura told her about their situation.

The commander listened with growing concern. She asked Kaura to wait a moment and immediately issued some orders. Then she turned back to the hologram platform in the right corner of the command bridge, where the image of the Lemurian was waiting patiently for her to finish.

"We are immediately launching fifty battle boats that will form a spherical cordon around Gaia and monitor the space," she explained to her.

"Our four escort caravels will circle the Earth further out. Is there a place where we can land the flagship?"

Kaura thought for a moment.

"Atlantia," she finally said. "The city has appropriate space port facilities, and you shouldn't attract as much attention there as you would elsewhere. We'll meet you there. How long will it take you to get there?"

It turned out that the Aalid ship could be in Atlantis in less than fifteen minutes. Kaura had Gaia calculate the coordinates of the hover port of the Crystal Guild and gave them to the Aalids. Then she said goodbye, and the hologram disappeared without a transition.

Ishe'melen turned to her first officer. Ike'rion was still looking with a dreamy expression at the place where until a moment ago the slender silhouette of the Lemurian had been. A simultaneously admiring and regretful smile played around the corners of his mouth.

"What a woman," he murmured so softly that the commander could barely hear. Smiling, she nudged him in the side. "If you're done idolizing alien heads of state, please initiate your approach to the coordinates you just received, sir!" She winked at him mockingly. The young man's face immediately lost its absent-minded expression.

"Of course, Admiral, right away."

He turned and walked over to the course control area, where the navigator was already busy with the appropriate circuits. The admiral herself went to the communications console and spoke to the radio officer. With the frequency information she received from Kaura, she was able to contact Atlantia's control center and the Crystal Fleet headquarters to announce her arrival.

Their interlocutors were surprised, but agreed to a landing after Kaura's name was mentioned. Smiling contentedly, the Aalid woman sat back down in her command chair and watched the blue sphere in front of her grow larger and larger. Like small glistening dots, the battle boats strove away from the mother ship to take up their positions outside Gaia's atmosphere. No alien ship would be able to break through this ring undetected.

A shrill howl broke her train of thought. A message came from a speaker.

"Navigation department here. We have detected the launch of an unknown starship Western Pacific. They seem to aim for an orbit above Lemuria. It's energy signature suggests that the ship is heavily armed and cleared for action."

Deciding quickly, Ishe'melen changed her mind.

"Set a course for the orbit above Lemuria," she ordered, pressing the button that connected her to the communications center. "Make contact with the alien vessel and request that it disarm its weapons and move alongside!"

Then she walked over to the central control panel where the ship's gunner sat. She put her hand on the bearded man's shoulders.

"Put a warning shot across his bow, Im'kaniel. See how he responds. Fire at discretion."

The man nodded.

"Aye, aye, my lady."

His fingers played over the control area of the weapons control panel. A projected firing line of the depth bomb appeared on the panoramic window, which the weapons control officer now fired with a keystroke.

Nothing could be seen of it in the empty space, except for the explosion that blossomed on the starboard side of the ship slowly coming into view a few seconds later, illuminated by the glow of Earth.

* * *

Aboard the Kai'ala ship, Uriel suffered a fit of rage. "Exterminate!" he shouted in a voice that tipped over. "Exterminate everybody!

Have all weapons ready at once! Blow up the whole planet! And that ship over there first!"

The Kai'ala commander in front of him literally shrunk.

"But sir," he whispered in the hissing, whispering tone typical of these creatures. "These are Aalid ships. They are technically far superior to us. We can't even penetrate their shields with our impulse cannons! With respect, we should withdraw in order to avoid capture."

All at once, the Kai'ala's eyes went blank. He grabbed his throat for a moment and gasped. Triabola, who was standing next to him, was amazed. Whatever one might think of her companion, in psychomagic control no one could beat him. He had the commander completely under control, the man's will had been broken in the space of no more than a blink of an eye.

Uriel smiled and suddenly seemed completely calm again.

"Well, if you don't want to just do as I say, then so be it. Set a collision course, and fire from all guns. He won't dare destroy us, because if he does, we'll all come crashing down on Lemuria below, burying their precious 'Ancients' underneath us!"

Stiff as a puppet, the commander moved across the bridge, shouting orders to his subordinates.

Triabola weighed her head indecisively.

"You think so? After all, we're aboard this ship, too. Don't you want to use another one for your suicide mission?"

Uriel turned to her. His eyes sparkled dangerously. They were the eyes of a fanatic, a dangerous demagogue.

"Are you thinking of mutiny?" he asked quietly, in almost a conversational tone.

Triabola swallowed. Now she had to choose her words carefully. "Nothing would be further from my mind, my friend. I'm just worried about our safety. After all, something can always go wrong. I think I'll go down and have one of the lifeboats made ready, just to be on the safe side. With an impatient movement of his head, Uriel gave her permission and turned back to what was happening on the bridge.

In this pose, he reminded the goddess again of a general. A profoundly mad commander. She felt no regret for the Kai'ala he was likely to sacrifice in his insane attack on Lemuria and the Aalids. But she was beginning to worry seriously about her own life.

* * *

With a deadpan expression, Grand Admiral Ishe'melen watched the enemy ship change course.

"They're attacking us head-on," she muttered, "That's not exactly textbook tactics. Are they crazy?"

The projectors on the transparent outer wall of the battleship bridge displayed the firing lines of the Kai'ala's light potential cannons. Nothing could be seen in the empty space. However, when the energy discharges broke in the form of fiery flowers on the *Uma*'s defensive shield, the space around the Aalid warship shimmered in all the colors of the rainbow.

The gunner laughed dryly.

"Do they seriously have nothing more to offer than that? May I return fire, Commander?"

Ishe'melen answered in the affirmative.

"But try not to destroy them, just take out the weapons and their propulsion systems. However, if it does blow them up completely, so be it."

The black-haired Aalid nodded. Again, his fingers flitted over the control panel and through the holograms of the fire control system projected in front of him. The only sign that large energy units deep in the *Uma*'s belly were activating and building up huge amounts of destructive power within them was a slight amplification of the hum of the engines in the background.

Straight lines appeared on the hologram projector, this time directed concentrically at the large, teardrop-shaped starship in front of the *Uma*, which in turn continued to fire its laser cannons at the Aalids in rapid succession.

Im'kaniel pressed two buttons this time. By now, the distance was so close that even the debris could be seen flying in all directions when the rays hit the enemy ship, some of it moving out into open space and some of it burning up in bright sparks of light in Gaia's atmosphere.

"That should do it for them," the gunner stated with no particular satisfaction.

The enemy ship, driven by the momentum of the hits, veered slightly off course to starboard. It seemed as if the commander of the disabled vessel was still trying to set a ramming course with the part of the drives that remained intact, but that could only elicit a weary smile from Ishe'melen. If the Kai'ala even got that far, the *Uma* would easily be able to avoid them.

"Notify the *Kina*. Have her take the enemy ship over and hold her in a tractor beam in lunar orbit until we decide what to do with her," she called over to the communications console. "And we'll be on our way to Atlantis in the meantime."

The tracking officer signaled her.

"Milady, an escape pod has just been ejected from the enemy ship. Set a course for Gaia. Your orders?"

"Leave it to the combat boats. Have them intercept the capsule, board it, and confine the occupants for questioning," she replied.

Then the admiral turned back to the brown, green, blue, and white structures passing rapidly beneath her.

With its throttled speed of only about one hundred thousand knots per hour, the *Uma* would be starting its descent into the airspace above Atlantis in a few minutes.

* * *

Boatswain's Mate Era'kael was the commander of the armed tender *Irma*, which formed part of the flagship's combat fleet.

When he received the order over the radio to bring up the Kai'ala lifeboat heading for Earth, he turned with a cocky grin to his crew, which consisted of three other men from the Aalid combat forces.

"There's work for us, folks," he flapped in his broad dialect, which told insiders that he had grown up in Aalid's polar region, where winter, it was said, usually ended on a Thursday and began again the following Saturday.

He looked strikingly alike to the *Uma*'s weapons officer in appearance and with his black beard, but in character, he belonged to a completely different breed of people. Impulsive and quick-tempered, he was nevertheless an experienced combat boat commander who rarely made major mistakes and always treated his people well.

The pill-shaped space-boat shot diagonally through the outermost layers of the Earth's atmosphere, on a course toward the speeding escape pod. Serenely, Era'kael put his finger on the tractor beam's activation button. He was not unduly concerned. Their target appeared to be a small escape pod, probably with minimal controls and almost certainly no guns. Whoever was trying to reach Gaia could probably not be very dangerous to them.

The capsule slowly moved into the central field of the tractor beam detection projected onto the command cockpit window. It clicked as the commander activated the machine. Immediately, the pod slowed down. Era'kael was about to order two of his companions to put on their spacesuits and prepare to board the small ship, when he felt his field of vision blur for a moment.

He felt his consciousness being pushed to the very edge of his being by something. Almost impassively, he noticed how his hand slipped into the holster of his uniform and drew his service weapon—a class three light laser gun. His other hand turned the tractor beam off while he pointed the weapon at his copilot. With a pang of panic, he felt his index finger slowly pull the trigger. A shot in the middle of the pilot's cockpit would kill not only the copilot but all of them instantly, effortlessly perforating the hull of the boat and allowing its inside atmosphere to escape.

A violent blow from behind made him topple sideways out of the pilot's seat. Another's hand held his pistol with an iron grip, forcing his index finger slowly but steadily away from its trigger.

Suddenly, the pressure vanished from his mind. He stared into the horrified face of Ike, the boat navigator. Behind him, equally surprised, were the other two.

"What was that just now, sir?" the man asked him tonelessly. "You turned off the tractor beam and let the lifeboat escape. And you tried to kill us all with that gun. I've known you for years, Era'kael, but I'm afraid I'm going to have to put you under arrest."

The boatswain nodded.

"I can't blame you. I was no longer in control of myself. I don't understand what happened. I think I was taken over by something. Now it seems to be gone."

The navigator nodded grimly.

"So are our friends down there. They seem to have landed somewhere in the Western Pacific. We won't catch them anymore. If they can do something like that to you, at that distance, I think they're really dangerous. We have to report this immediately."

He turned to the radio, where the flagship was already calling, wanting to know why the boat had let the enemy escape.

* * *

Uriel stormed out of the hatch of the lifeboat that had just landed and into the Rai'atea hangar, followed by Triabola, who was looking as composed as always, though her thoughts were not calm at all.

The chief planner of the gods was showing more and more weaknesses, reflected the Riganian woman, who, together with Uriel, belonged to the innermost circle of the power-hungry sect of the A'kaala, which had named its capital 'Olympus' after an old Lemurian legend.

Admittedly, he had just saved them both from capture, using his superior psychomagic powers. Nevertheless, all in all, he was performing rather weakly. How could she use this fact and her knowledge of it to further her personal goals? There would be ways. After all, her desires were not complicated: she wanted absolute power over Olympus.

Ha'kaminiel was growing old, despite the constant injections of immortality serum extracted from the cultivated mages. Complete cell renewal was not possible even in this way, after all. But she had been much younger than him when she had become a member of the Olympian Order, which was engaged in taking power over the galaxy. This meant she had much more time because the age of the cells when they were first injected determined the magnitude of the inaccuracy factor, which caused aging that was greatly slowed but still noticeable over the millennia.

Ahead, Uriel rudely pushed aside the Kai'ala guard standing at the gangway to the second starship they had available here before the blue-skinned alien could even begin the customary bow. The last starship they had available on Gaia, Triabola corrected herself. It stood to reason that the Aalids would take their flagship and capture the crew. The Kai'ala would not activate the self-destruct circuit of their own accord. They were too cowardly for that.

The goddess made a mental note. Back on Rignar, she would suggest that the ships of the Olympian fleet be equipped with self-destruct mechanisms that could be remotely controlled by the members of the Order. At the same time, a shiver ran down her spine. If she would still be in a position to suggest something, then Ha'kaminiel would indeed not be satisfied. She had not been exaggerating when she told Uriel. And it seemed more and more unlikely that they would be able to save the situation without major military support from Rignar. Well, she would make sure that the name of the responsible person would be known everywhere: Uriel.

The chief planner now slammed his palm with brute force on the opening mechanism of the door to the starship's bridge. Unimpressed, the door slid aside with a slight hiss. The crew of the command bridge looked up. Uriel must have been a frightening sight, Triabola, coming up behind his back, thought to herself as she saw the shocked expressions of the beings, who were not exactly squeamish themselves.

"Launch!" screeched her companion. "We'll pick up the last of the harvest in Constantinople and then retreat to Rignar! We need reinforcements. This is all no good like this!"

Triabola retained her outward calm, which the Kai'ala commander acknowledged with a grateful look.

"Have the crew manning the base boarded first, commander," she said. "Tell them to leave everything behind except the essentials. Launch as soon as possible. And have the combat hoverboats ready. We must expect to be attacked from the air. If that happens, they'll have to cover our departure."

* * *

The *Uma* landed on the outer field of Atlantia Hoverport, with its landing supports extended. Kaura, along with Lance, Irene, and the fairy Amina, had arrived at the Crystal Temple via portal a few minutes ago, been greeted by Eriniel, and taken directly to the landing field by one of the temple's gliders.

As the ramp of the spaceship lowered with a hydraulic whoosh and the commander and a few people stepped onto the floor of hardened cast stone, the crystal priest took a step forward.

"Welcome to Atlantis and to Gaia, friends!" he intoned in his strange singsong. "Thank you for the support you bring us!"

Businesslike, but with a smile, Ishe'melen shook his hand. Then she turned to Kaura.

"The Kai'ala have attempted to destroy Lemuria by means of an attack from space. We took on the ship and prevented it from doing so. However, it seems at least one being with very great magical powers escaped back to Earth by means of a lifeboat."

Kaura nodded seriously.

"Thank you, commander."

The other woman smiled.

"Ishi, please. We are not usually so formal on Aalid."

Kaura grinned.

"Very nice, Ishi. I am Kaura. Do you have fast and armed hover-boats on board? I think the gods are getting nervous and unpredictable in their actions. They hold many magical beings in a prison in the Eastern Mediterranean. I fear that they might try to hurt them. Also, some of our companions have been captured on a Moluccan island in the Pacific."

The commander had listened attentively.

"We can give you about three dozen atmosphere fighters, in addition to those securing the orbit above us. However, we are ill-prepared for attacks of a magical nature, as has been shown," she said. "Can you provide us with some Gifted for each of our boats? I'd also like to send some people to our patrol ships in space to protect their crews."

Questioningly, Kaura looked over at the representative of the crystal temple.

"Do you have that many people with strong enough powers, Erin?"

The head priest nodded.

"Equipped with big enough crystals, almost a hundred of our priests can create magical protection fields. For offensive combat, slightly fewer are strong enough, but a few dozen should be able to help. All our people are at your disposal."

The Aalid commander noted this with a grateful nod of her head.

"Then we will take twenty priests, who can mainly create protective fields, to the four caravels and some of our boats in orbit. Please have your people ready as soon as possible. We will leave a few dinghies to bring them up."

She pointed with her hand to a large hatch in the belly of the star cruiser, which was just swinging open.

Behind it, several smaller vessels could be seen.

"We will send the rest of your people with the remaining four boats to Constantinople to free the mages captured there. And how many people do you need for the Moluccas, Kaura?"

Kaura thought for a moment.

"I think a circle of myself, Irene, and five of the stronger priests should be enough to deal with the two mages we encountered at the base. We can use the portal in Rhodes and be there practically immediately. There won't be enough energy for a return, though, so we'll need a boat to pick us up as soon as possible."

Ishe'melen nodded with satisfaction.

"All right, then. Have the mages brief our people along the way on exactly what to expect from these Kai'ala and gods. The *Uma* will stay behind here for now as an operational reserve to intervene where necessary."

9

The Battle of Constantinople

Simon coughed. One of the cuts on his lower left leg had become infected, and the pain from the burns by the witch fire that Sen and the others had been forced to shoot at him was worsening by the hour. As before, no one had come to attend to his injuries, and his friends' increasingly frantic banging on their dungeon door had gone unanswered all night.

Eagle gritted her teeth in exasperation. Normally, a small healing spell would have brought relief to her friend within seconds, but this terrible collar prevented her from even conjuring a small light to see better in their damp and dark vault.

"I'm really very sorry, Simon," the headmaster meanwhile said for about the hundredth time. "I can tell you; it doesn't feel good to use one's magical abilities against friends. And to be able to do absolutely nothing about it."

He stared gloomily into the darkness. It smelled of mold and moss, and brackish water dripped from the walls, collecting in puddles on the uneven clay floor.

"I don't blame you, Sen, will you finally believe me?" Simon replied between two fits of coughing, looking at his superior out of feverish eyes. "Stop chastising yourself! After all, none of us have found a counter-spell for those devilish things yet. I'm just wondering why they put us in this filthy hole. As mages, we should at least be treated something like first-class prisoners, shouldn't we? Like officers in war."

Eagle's features were indistinct in the dim light entering through a small grille set far up the wall as she answered.

"I think they just want to break us first," she commented. "Hungry, exhausted slaves are easier to train. After a few days in here, we'll probably be grateful to see a normal, dry cell and some food, and may thus be more malleable for the leash holders to work with."

Sen laughed dryly.

"At least we're still together now. Who knows how long it will stay that way. But I just have no idea how to get out of this mess!"

He made it sound like he seriously expected to be able to just walk out of their dungeon and into freedom if only the right idea would rise in his mind. The irony of this did not escape him at all.

"We've gotten too used to the idea that we can just flick away all difficulties with the help of our Gift," he said. "But, for the love of all that's good, I just hate having to sit here and wait for someone to find us and get us out of here!"

Eagle shrugged.

"Kaura knows what she's doing. And so do the Atlanteans. They'll think of something. After all, they know from our message that the captured mages are being held here in Constantinople. It was sent over the Mediterranean while we were still within range of Atlantean radio receivers. Sooner or later, someone will come to check on the situation here."

Heavy footsteps sounded from the corridor, and the iron fittings of the door clanged loudly as the lock was removed and the bolt pushed back. Outside stood three of the figures dressed in ruby robes. The mages had already learnt that it usually meant some new torment when the High Inquisitors came to see them.

Nevertheless, they just stared at the newcomers blankly, blinking in the glare of the witch lights hovering over their captor's heads.

"You, there!" The foremost figure pointed at Sen, waving a leash. "Come here!"

The mage straightened up and took a step towards the door. At the second step, a sharp pain flashed through him.

"Go on!" the figure commanded in its ghostly, whispering tone. Sen took another step because he himself was curious about what the inquisitors intended to demonstrate with this. Suddenly he cried out and sank to his knees, bent over with a searing agony that seemed to come from nowhere and everywhere, all at the same time.

"Sen!" Eagle wanted to rush over to him, but immediately began to scream in pain as well, frozen where she stood.

The inquisitor laughed maliciously. He waved one of the shiny silver lengths of chain. Leisurely, he walked over to Sen, who was crouched on all fours on the ground, panting like a trapped animal.

With a practiced movement, the creature hooked the leash into the small protruding ring on Sen's collar and jerked his head back.

"This was to show you that you cannot approach me or move away from me without my permission. From now on, you will move only if I allow you to. But when I give you an order, follow it quickly and precisely as I want you to. When I say 'Sit,' you will kneel and lower your eyes. When I say 'Down,' you will bow and put your forehead on the ground."

The inquisitor continued. "When you see one of the inquisitors, you will also bow unless you are with me. You will address all who do not wear a collar as master or mistress, and you will not look them in the eye unless you are asked to do so. If you speak without being asked, we will cut out your tongue. Do you understand, creature?"

With his face still contorted in equal amounts of pain and rage, Sen nodded. It would do no good to provoke the Kai'ala now.

"Speak, dog!" whispered the creature.

"I understand. And I protest against this treatment," whispered the tattooed man.

Once again, that lurid, seemingly inescapable pain, which was everywhere and nowhere at once in his body, flashed through him.

"I understand, Lord, that is! And for daring to protest you will be punished later. But now the mistress wants to talk to you. Come on, dog. Heel! For every time I need to pull on your leash, you will be punished until you learn proper behavior."

With a helpless glance back to his companions, Sen followed the Kai'ala out into the corridor. Behind him, the heavy door slammed shut and he heard his tormentor's colleagues slide the massive latch shut again.

Two corridors away, there seemed to be considerable activity. Sen heard shouts and footsteps echoing on the stone floor, indicating many people or beings being on the move. At one point he caught a glimpse of a side corridor where djinns were being chained together in rows of four.

Concern rose in the old mage. Did they know that the location of their prison was known? Were they moving them elsewhere? Well, there was nothing he could do about it, even if that was the case. They walked back into the garden and soon entered the grounds of the palace itself. No one there seemed surprised by the presence of the collared man, which told Sen that the inquisitors probably walked their slaves here often.

He decided to learn as much as he could about his surroundings and use any opportunity to escape that might present itself. After all, he was being led to someone who seemed to be high up in the hierarchy of these people. But he had to be careful. The Kai'ala's offhanded mentioning of having Sen's tongue cut out didn't feel like an idle threat. And if the stories he had heard about Constantinople were true, they were possibly cutting off all sorts of other body parts from the people here if they didn't follow their rules. Involuntarily, Sen's gaze wandered down to the area of his loins. He shuddered and immediately looked straight ahead again.

Just then they passed through a long, airy corridor whose Gothic-looking side arches were decorated all over with white filigree stone carvings in the tradition of the Ottomans, without faces or statues, but consisting only of flowers, geometries, and Arabic script motifs. To their right stretched a flowering garden with elegantly shaped fountains, lined with date palms. To their left, the intricate arches framed a wide panoramic view over the stone roofs of the city, even allowing him to see all the way down to the great harbor of the Bosporus. Hundreds of ships and boats of all sizes moved back and forth on this strait between the European and Asian continents, the deep blue sea glistening in the morning sun. Even in his desperate situation, the Scot was not completely unmoved by the magic of this sight. He resisted the impulse to stop and look, though.

They ascended to the top floor of the palace through two staircases with wide curved staircases and artfully finished marble railings. 'His' inquisitor approached two guards dressed in the ruby livery of Inquisition soldiers.

One of the Spaniards saluted. "Doña Triabola is expecting you, sir."

Without a reply, the inquisitor led his prisoner through the door, which was held open by the other guard.

In the hall, a woman sat on a throne-like chair by the window, positioned so that she could take in the panorama outside as well as the room with one glance. He had already seen her briefly at the time of his capture—she had to be one of the masterminds of this unfortunate project. A 'goddess.' During the battle, however, he had not had the opportunity to study her more closely.

The aura of the woman immediately fascinated the magician. She radiated an amount of magical power that seemed beyond anything Sen had ever seen. And yet, something was not quite right. Every gifted person, and also every other magical being, as far as he knew, had a very personal signature in their magical aura.

Particularly skilled witches and wizards could even find this signature in each individual magical weave, and so know who had created it. But this woman's aura was somehow different. It seemed as if her power was nothing personal, but something lifeless, soulless.

Again, the Scottish master magician shuddered. The woman's eyes did not help to reassure him. They were deep blue with their irises filling them out completely, which gave them a piercing expression. Her mouth had a hard, possibly even cruel twist. For sure, this was a woman who expected to be obeyed without argument.

The inquisitor gave him a hard push between the shoulder blades.

"Get on your knees and bow, dog! Don't you dare look at the mistress again if you want to keep your eyes!"

Sen did as he'd been instructed.

"Thank you, servant," the woman said somewhere above him. Her voice was dark and velvety soft. "You can leave us now. I will let you know when I've finished with him."

With a muttered acknowledgment, the inquisitor withdrew, and Sen heard the door close.

Then, the sounds of softly padded moccasins gliding across the polished marble floor beside him. He felt ridiculous. In Lockwood, at any rate, it was not the custom to receive guests in this strange manner.

He cleared his throat.

Suddenly, he didn't care about anything, even though he knew that probably wasn't very rational thinking. If they wanted to cut out his tongue, then they should. But he wouldn't lick the floor here in front of this alien! With difficulty, he pushed himself up on his knees.

"My name is Seneca Lumisworth. Wouldn't you like to introduce yourself instead of just walking around me?" he said, regretting his carelessness almost immediately. But the woman only laughed.

"The Kai'ala would probably do some nasty things to you if they knew how forward you were. But don't worry, they won't find out from me, child."

She pointed to a chair diagonally across from her richly decorated wooden throne. "Sit down over there. Don't worry, the collar won't do anything painful to you here. I have wireless control, you might say."

Another low laugh.

Sen did as he was told and heaved himself up onto the chair, while the 'goddess' was sitting down herself.

Triabola leaned her elbow on the back of her throne so that the fabric of her white silk dress stretched slightly over her breasts, and her nipples were clearly visible. Against his will, the Scot admired the soft curves of the human-like being.

"So, you are one of those who call themselves gods," he stated, half questioningly. "And you want to enslave us all."

Triabola nodded and smiled at him with a gentle expression on her face.

"It can be quite pleasant to become my slave. Fortunately for you, I like tattoos," the woman said. "You won't want for anything. You know, my friend Uriel is quite upset with you. He thinks you've messed up his plans. He'll probably have you flambéed alive if no one stops him. Over a low flame."

She sighed theatrically.

"But I think we can come to an agreement, you and me. Of

course, I would insist on certain, services, on your part. In return, I'll protect you. And first, you must give me some answers."

He laughed.

"You know, I don't really have anything to hide from you. So, what do you want to know?"

Feverishly, he considered how to hide the only truly critical piece of information from the goddess, namely that the Atlanteans knew where the mages were being held.

Amused, Triabola laughed out loud.

"You still think you can keep something a secret from me, boy? You should know that I can read your mind like an open book. All shields and protective fields that you have put around your mind have, of course, been rendered ineffective by the collar. We know that the Atlanteans will probably want to come visit us soon. But we'll be long gone by then if all goes well. And the Atlantean hoverboats are no match for ours."

She leaned closer, lowering her voice to a whisper. "Of course, you can't hide from me that you find me attractive either. You've always been attracted to the dark side, haven't you, sweetie? And you'd give anything to get into bed with me, wouldn't you?"

Sen swallowed dryly, and had to admit to himself that, despite all the evil that he could see in this woman, there was a part of him that desired her.

* * *

Surrounded by a glowing aura of power and ready to immediately counter any attack with the most massive fighting spells they could wield, Kaura and her comrades-in-arms poured out of the portal Gaia had opened for them. They entered the sixth hangar of Rai'atea at a run. But there was no opposition, no one to meet their advance.

The Atlantean priests, clad in dark blue uniforms and armed

with heavy laser beamers, immediately spread out around the room, making sure there was no immediate danger.

The leader of the Atlanteans approached Kaura, holding a small device in his hands, and pointing to its screen.

"I'm afraid most of the birds have flown the coop," he said quietly. "This base is almost completely deserted. But there are still some signatures of living beings, probably in the station headquarters and in the hangar next to us. We must be very careful. This could be a trap."

Kaura thought for a moment and then decided to wait for Irene. The witch was hastily installing her tracking pentacle on the steel floor of the hangar. As she slid the last crystal ball into place, a few glowing dots immediately showed.

"Quite a few mages here," she remarked, "at least fifteen. Most of them in the control center. And all nearly as strong as you, Kaura. That doesn't look good. Although the two 'gods' should probably more powerful still. So, they're probably already gone. Maybe some unusually powerful Kai'ala."

Kaura shook her head impatiently, her black hair flying around her head.

"Whatever. We'll link up, and then I'll jump into the room with you guys. We'll try to separate them all at once from the Gaia field. And if that doesn't work, we start shooting. But make sure who you're aiming at. Maybe our friends are still with them."

She had already explained to the others that her powers became greater the closer she was to her mother continent. Here, she could already teleport over short distances and even take others with her. The seven people joined hands, facing outward, so they could survey the room as soon as they arrived.

Kaura focused on the place in the hologram map where the headquarters had to be and shifted. They materialized in the middle of a room filled with people who jumped aside in surprise as the group suddenly appeared out of nowhere.

Kaura tried to force the pale blue bubble she had prepared around them when she realized her mistake. "

Stop, stop, don't shoot!" she shouted. "They're friends!"

In front of her stood a group of women and men dressed in semi-transparent white robes, who all had a similar dark skin color as herself and, after their initial surprise, now eyed her with calm curiosity. Between them, Kaura recognized the Atlantean captain Ux'makia with them, waving pleasantly over to her.

A gray-haired woman stepped up, wearing a sash decorated with hibiscus flowers over her netted dress that only slightly veiled her nudity. Her gray eyes seemed impenetrable.

"We're happy to see you, too, sister," she said, "but you wouldn't have to aim those crude weaves at us as a greeting, would you?"

Then a happy smile appeared on her face. She ran the last few steps up to Kaura and hugged her.

"I'm so glad nothing happened to you, Highest!" she gasped, moved almost to tears.

Kaura herself now felt the tears welling up inside her that she had held in for so long. These people, this language, these clothes meant home. She had forgotten them, repressed them, thought she didn't need them, and yet now she felt this tremendous relief, this familiar feeling, this deep joy! She hugged her sister's body tightly and greedily absorbed the familiar scent of jasmine and plumeria that her sash exuded.

Selena, for it was she, gently disengaged from the embrace again and looked deep into Kaura's eyes. "That Atlantean captain there told us that we probably have you to thank for the dissolution of the death zone around our continent. Our people will never forget this."

She smiled. "As soon as our instruments indicated that the field had gone, we took some of our boats and flew to where we suspected the originators had been for some time by now. We thought that you might need help. But all we found here was Commander Ux'makia and his ship. At first, we thought that maybe the Atlanteans could be behind the whole thing and were suspicious. But it quickly turned out that he knows you."

Ux'makia now also approached her and formally shook her hand.

"I am glad to see you back unharmed. We had already been most worried not to hear from you for so long. Our people have out-done themselves with the speed of the repairs. A few times we were passed by enemy ships, but the cloaking spell held."

He paused. "Where are your companions? Are they well?"

Kaura's face clouded over.

"They were captured. I myself just barely escaped. We had hoped to find them here."

The captain shook his head.

"We didn't miss them by much, I believe. But of course, with their starships, the Kai'ala could be who knows where now. That's troubling news."

Irene tugged Kaura's sleeve.

"What would you do if you were the Kai'ala or their masters?" she asked.

Kaura thought.

"I think I would retreat or hide for now. They can't fight the Aalids on even terms. Our friends have superior technology, or at least that's what Admiral Ishe'melen says. The Kai'ala should have realized that by now. I would probably try to break through the barrier and get the hell out of here. If they stay, they'll be found out sooner or later."

The other woman nodded.

"And what would you do with the captured mages in Constantinople?"

"Probably try to take them with me," Kaura mused. "After all, they seem important to them. Depends, of course, on how many they've already brought to their planet and whether that's enough already."

Her face hardened. "Either way, our best bet is Constantinople. We'll probably find the gods there, and our friends, too."

She turned to Selena.

"What kind of ships have you come here with?"

"Planetary expedition boats," she said. "The best we have, since the sun ships still haven't been repaired."

Kaura nodded with satisfaction.

"With this, we can be at the Bosporus in ten minutes."

She waved at Captain Ux'makia, who looked at her in slight consternation at this announcement. He was probably calculating how much slower his own boat was.

"Come, captain. We'll try to help your people in Constantinople free the hostages."

Accompanied by some of the Lemurian priestesses, they walked down to the hangar. Selena and the rest of her people, meanwhile, would secure the place. For sure, Lemuria would need some airbases outside the continent again soon.

In Hangar Five stood the three expedition boats that the Lemurians had brought. They were completely different in shape from the Atlantean hover ships with their clean, hard lines. About forty yards long and remotely reminiscent of flattened, mossy eggs or river stones, the Lemurian craft would hardly have stood out in a natural setting.

Here, in this cavern formed of steel and molten lava rock, they did not appear as if their builders could have been descendants to those who had constructed and used this base eons ago. Briskly, but without haste, Kaura went ahead, together with the Lemurian commander of the ship.

She could not resist asking for news from the Old Continent.

"You will hardly recognize Lemuria, High Priestess," was the reply. "Once the realization was widely publicized and we learned of your mission, everyone wanted to get involved."

The pilot, a slim, black-haired woman, smiled confidently. "The archives were opened and many old tourmalines containing combat and technical training data were found. By now, we already have thousands of skilled pilots, battle mages and scientists, and production of new hover ships is in full swing. Our best tech experts are working on restoring the starships' hyperspeed drives. Now things are likely to move even faster, as the Death Zone Breach Team can be deployed elsewhere. These are our most capable minds. You will probably know most of them."

The woman, she had introduced herself as Zik'adela, was visibly proud of the developments that had been achieved. Kaura showed herself duly impressed, and asked some pertinent questions. When they arrived at the ship's boarding hatch, Zik'adela placed her slender hand on a dark red plate on the hull of the ship and gently stroked it, almost as if she were caressing the vehicle.

"Welcome, dear Zik'adela," the ship said in an almost motherly voice. "How may I serve you?"

The pilot turned to her companions.

"This is Mirafin, my ship. We are psycho-organically connected to each other. Of course, any other authorized person can pilot her. But it was felt beneficial to have a personal relationship between each pilot and her ship. It makes the cooperation smoother."

Amina, the fairy, fluttered up.

"Is it jealous, too, when you're making out with other people and stuff?" she asked.

Smiling, Zik'adela shook her head. "Jealousy is almost non-existent in Lemuria due to our advanced social development. And it would probably make little sense to endow our techno-organic intelligences with such base emotions. But they do, of course, have a fairly extensive degree of emotional autonomy."

The fairy nodded with a somewhat doubtful expression on her face.

"Emotional autonomy. Ah...," she murmured, and a little more quietly so that only Irene, walking right next to her, could hear, "I knew it. The treehuggers even cuddle with their hover ships! If I tell that to Ariane..."

Meanwhile, the commander turned back to the ship.

"I and my companions here are heading for Constantinople, dear Mirafin. Fighting is to be expected. A larger number of hostages must be freed, who can probably be used against us by their slave masters. Aalid and Atlantean ships are also already on their way."

The boarding hatch floated to the ground, whirring softly. "Come aboard first, friends," the ship said. "Meanwhile, I'll calculate the course and work out some possible strategies."

At the front of the ship, they appeared to be standing on a platform floating freely in space in the middle of the hangar. Some comfortable looking furniture, but still equipped with sturdy seat belts and headrests stood around in a haphazard fashion, looking quite like a cozy lounge.

Kaura explained to Irene that depending on the function of its user, different instruments and controls could be projected in front of the respective chair. However, the ship did most of the work herself anyway. She already knew these vehicles well, and yet after her long absence she was once again fascinated by how easy this technology made it for its users.

Again, the voice of the ship spoke.

"Predicted flight time to Constantinople ten minutes forty-three seconds. Please confirm correctness of position. I suggest we move to a holding position fifteen thousand feet above target to analyze the situation on the ground. We do not have satellite data for this area at this time."

The commander glanced at Kaura.

"The launch of geostationary satellites is planned soon. As we found out, Lemuria had about thirty such observation stations in orbit until about fifteen thousand years ago, so our ancestors always knew what was happening on Gaia," she explained.

Kaura nodded her thanks. Meanwhile, in front of Zik'adela's seat, a globe had appeared with a flashing red dot on it. Kaura wanted to get out of her seat to look at the projection, but the commander simply sent the globe over to her with a snap of her fingers.

"Mirafin, please record Kaura Alenu'ala as the leader of this operation," she said. "I acknowledge," the ship replied. "Do I have launch clearance, Kaura?"

Kaura moved the globe in front of her with her fingers and pulled the area with the red flashing dot closer to her. Clearly, she could see the area of the Eastern Mediterranean, the Black Sea, and the Bosporus in between. The luminous dot blinked exactly where Constantinople was located, to her knowledge.

"Launch clearance granted," she said. "Shields at maximum power. We may be attacked on the way or upon arrival." Then something occurred to her, and she hesitated. "Hold on for a moment, Mirafin. First establish a connection with the Aalid ships orbiting around the Earth."

She gave the frequency, and after a short time Admiral Ishe'me-len's face appeared on the screen."

Kaura informed her that there were now Lemurian ships in Gaia's airspace, and the Aalid woman confirmed that she would inform her people immediately. She asked them to wait another two minutes before take-off, until the information had passed.

Shortly thereafter, clearance arrived from the Aalid battle head-quarters. Mirafin slid out of the hangar into the tropical night with virtually no sound. Under the occupants' feet, the small white whitecaps of the waves rippled in the light of the setting moon.

Then they suddenly shrank at an almost inconceivable speed. A split second later they could see the whole island, many islands, then only darkness below them and barely more than two seconds later they saw the sun rising behind the globe, which was strongly curved from up here. Immediately Mirafin, now hovering at an altitude of about a thousand miles above the surface, shot westward back into the darkness.

Kaura observed the ground far below while they were moving across the Arabian Peninsula, behind which a white-crowned, sweeping mountain range reflected the faint moonlight. Some larger settlements spread faint light, but overall, the whole planet looked virgin, untouched from this altitude. The high priestess gazed thoughtfully out into the darkness. In the transparent dome above her, the stars shone with a clarity and density that did not even appear on the highest mountains of her home island. She had her family back. Friends accompanied her. And some of her best friends were waiting for her to assist them.

She breathed deeply. These gods were unpredictable, and more dangerous than any threat she had ever faced in her long life. How could they have become such powerful magicians without living on Earth? Had they discovered a new way to use magic, or perhaps an entirely new field? Could she defeat them? Or perhaps negotiate with them?

But no, they had tried twice to wipe out all the Lemurians, without even having contacted them or having tried to set any conditions. That didn't exactly feel like a willingness to negotiate. She sighed again and turned to her sisters and the other mages to use the few minutes until their arrival over Constantinople for a brief strategy meeting.

* * *

Sen was fascinated. With one leg over the back of his upholstered chair, he talked to Triabola like to an old friend, trying not to forget the danger he was in. This goddess told him much more than he had revealed to her about himself. The woman seemed lonely, despite or perhaps because of her immense power. He wondered how this A'kaala order, to which she apparently belonged, really functioned. How many of these people were there out of conviction, and how many were simply afraid of this Ha'akaminiel, the chief god, or madmen like Uriel?

If one managed to neutralize some of these key people, perhaps the whole system would collapse in on itself. Or would it?

How much initiative did the Kai'ala have? Were they just servants, controlled by the gods? Or did they have their own agenda? Disciplined, he forced himself to turn his full attention back to the conversation. After all, she didn't seem to be constantly monitoring his thoughts. Otherwise, she probably would not have left his train of thought uncommented.

"...I can get you an injection once we get to Rignar," she just said. "Then you'll become immortal."

Sen listened up.

"As mages, aren't we almost anyway?" he asked. "What's better about this injection? And what does it consist of?"

Triabola shook her head.

"Naturally, earthly mages just get very old. Rarely more than a thousand years or so, you should know that! With the serum, we're talking tens of thousands, hundreds of thousands of years! Completely different orders of magnitude. And not only can we extend your life with it, but we can also potentiate your magical powers. Do you think I was born that powerful?"

He forced himself to look innocent.

"You don't? I thought there might be a different magic field operating on Rignar that would make you stronger."

She laughed. "Oh no. Gaia still has the strongest field, by far. The only one, even, at least for those of us descended from humans! And soon we will be able to tap into the field ourselves, without having to go through the extraction of magical beings. That will multiply our power again. No one in this galaxy—or in any other—will then be able to resist us!"

She leaned in closer to him again. "And you can be a part of it, child."

Sen forced herself to think seriously about the offer. She would immediately expose any form of insincerity. Could he go over to her for appearances, and then desert later? He suppressed even the approach of this thought and tried to weigh the pros and cons of defecting to the gods seriously. There were attractive sides to it, he thought. Enough to take some time to think it over. One never knew what might happen.

"And what will happen to my friends?" he asked. "I won't defect without them. They are too important to me."

Triabola sighed.

"You earthlings are so emotional. Gross. But well, if you prove yourself loyal on Rignar, you can have them as slaves later."

She considered for a moment. "Of course, we will subject you to the oath process first. The rituals of admission to the Order of the A'kaala are strict, but doable. You will probably have to ritually mutilate and kill one or two of your friends to prove your loyalty. But you can have the rest."

Sen swallowed.

"That does sound quite tempting," he croaked. "But I still really need to think this through. Can I let you know my decision in a few days?"

Her gaze became hard.

"You can have a few hours. Your tattoos are sexy, and you're entertaining. Besides, as the head of an earthly mage guild, you're a nice trophy. That's why I'm still patient with you. But we will cut off your horrible bell hair. That mane will not do at all on one of my pets."

Sen jerked violently with shocked outrage.

"What?!" he shouted. "My bells are signs of my high magical rank and instill fear and terror in any enemy! Over my dead body!"

Amused, the alien looked at him.

"You don't really mean that, do you? I..."

At the same moment, she wheeled around as a deafening detonation sounded just outside the palace. People screamed in panic and surprise.

Sen glanced out at the harbor. Just then, a light blue, triangular shape whizzed through the air above the Bosporus. The people on the ships looked up, scrambling like startled chickens, and pointed to the sky.

"Atlanteans!" it flashed through his mind.

Triabola took his leash.

"Well, we will continue this discussion later. It seems like we have less time left than we thought." She led him out of the room into the corridor. "Go and help load the prisoners," she said to the two guards outside the door.

Then she went down with him to another wing of the palace. On the way, they met Uriel, who fell in beside them. The god's face was furiously pinched. He glanced darkly at Sen, who was trotting behind Triabola on his leash, but he said nothing.

Outside, more and more detonations sounded. In the meantime, the palace guard seemed to have recovered from the initial shock. Musket shots barked, and sporadically the thunder of a heavier gun sounded. 'Have fun trying to penetrate an Atlantean shield with that, amigos,' Sen thought to himself. The two gods didn't seem to need to talk about which was their destination. Wordlessly and with determined strides they went ahead.

But then Triabola did ask a question.

"Is the mechanism ready?"

Uriel nodded.

"It's already charging up. I've surrounded the Blue Room with a shield that should hold off the Atlanteans long enough, even if they find the machine. We have fifteen minutes. Then the death field will spread and render all the mages on Gaia unusable. By then, we ourselves and the portion of the harvest we can save must be in the ships."

The old mage felt hot and cold shivers running down his spine. He was close to stumbling and simply lying down, so discouraged was he. How many more instruments of murder did these beasts have up their sleeves? And no one even knew about it. He had to do something! And soon! Increasingly confused and close to panic, he stumbled after Triabola and Uriel, who were now approaching one of the lower, more harbor-like areas of the palace. Suddenly, a wall in their immediate vicinity exploded inward with a ghastly force. Sen and the two gods were caught off guard by the blast and swept off their feet. Triabola lost the leash from her hand in the process. Even as the gods struggled back to their feet, shadowy figures appeared in the thick smoke behind the cracked wall.

"There they are!" someone shouted. "The gods! A circle, quickly!" Sen perceived somewhere in the smoke the formation of a tremendous magical cluster. The Atlantean mages must have joined together to form the largest possible circle, which transferred the powers of the individual mages into the control of a master spellweaver.

Massive beams of witchfire hit the spot where he and the other two had landed. In the thick smoke, however, he could not see them anymore. A psychocontrol field wafted in from some distance, but it bounced off the Atlanteans' shield. So, the others had already gone on without him? Hopefully it wouldn't occur to Triabola to come back for him after all!

"I have to get out of here and warn the others," a thought flashed through his mind. He struggled to get up and slowly moved diagonally across the room toward the Atlanteans. Sen only hoped they wouldn't shoot him on sight before he could make himself known. But there was the collar. From the first step, a sharp pain jolted through him. He gritted his teeth and went on. The pain increased and he walked hunched over at first, then fell to his knees and crawled forward on all fours. He breathed intermittently and was close to losing consciousness.

Sen coughed in agony, his strength draining fast.

"Hello, here I am! I'm on your side. Don't shoot! Please help!" he croaked, as loud as he could. As the smoke slowly began to clear, he realized that he was alone in the room. The Atlantean mages seemed to have already gone on. The Scot cursed. And the clock was running! He had to warn someone as quickly as possible.

"Blue Room. Fifteen minutes. Death field," he muttered, close to unconsciousness. He continued to crawl toward the hole in the wall from which daylight was entering. The sounds of battle had moved a little farther away from him again but were still all around.

"If only it weren't for this damn collar," he moaned in his pain. He could have just gone out and looked for the next Atlantean team. But this way, every single step was agony. Slowly, he crawled out into the open. His pants tore as he pulled himself over the sharp edges of the cracked wall into the open. Damp grass touched his hands, but he barely felt it through the pulsing of pain released by the collar.

The slave spells were trying to prevent him from leaving his assigned location, clearly. He had to find someone to accompany him and hold the leash. But there was no one there. He crawled on, ignoring the pain, the increasingly intense nausea and the racing of his heart. Then he collapsed without transition on the meadow and lost consciousness.

As soon as he regained consciousness, he forced himself to open his eyes again and lift his head. How long had he been unconscious? How many precious seconds or minutes had his weakness cost him? He didn't know. He only knew that he had to keep trying. In front of him he saw a kind of terrace and a railing. Maybe he could give a signal to someone from there, a call for help?

Almost out of his mind from pain, he put one hand in front of the other and crawled on, toward the railing. When he reached the railing, he raised his head with an almost superhuman effort. White, flashing stars and dark streaks rippled before his eyes.

He blinked. Before him, the image of the lower palace gardens and the harbor beyond suddenly disappeared, replaced by a moss-green, roundish wall that seemed to float freely in the air.

A dark opening appeared in the wall and a fairy fluttered out of it. Sen was barely able to form a clear thought when he recognized a familiar face.

"Amina, is that you?" he moaned, struggling to keep his head up and not collapse completely.

"You don't look so prime, Superboss," the winged creature's small voice sounded above him. "But wait, we're about to do something about that. Kaura! Get your cute ass over here and help me get this thing off Sen!"

Two boots appeared beside him, and then Kaura's worried face, leaning down to him.

"Great heavens Sen, what have they done to you? Wait. Amina, can you give me the release impulse?"

With a click, the metallic feeling of tightness around his neck dissolved. The pain surged on for a moment, and then simply gave way to numbness.

His muscles failed, and the stone floor seemed to move toward him. But even before he hit it with his nose, something held him back. Out of the corner of his eye, he saw the glowing tip of Amina's fairy staff beside him.

"You need a healing wish, my dear, and rapidissimo. You're already holding your spoon in your hand to deliver it at the gates of heaven," said the fairy. "But I'm afraid your system can't take much right now. We'll get you to the ship first. Good thing Irene has located the gods, and on the way, we found you here in prayer posture. Don't worry, we'll straighten you out. Besides, we've got a whole bunch of treehuggers with us. Nothing can go wrong now."

Sen was still fighting another loss of consciousness. He had to tell the others something, but it kept slipping away.

Suddenly it hit him like a hammer blow. The field of death! When they tried to lift him with magical powers and push him toward the ship, he squirmed and struggled with all his weak strength. But at first only inarticulate, animalistic sounds left his mouth. Desperately he tried to form the words.

Concerned, Kaura leaned down to him.

"Are you in pain, Sen? We'll examine you more closely in a moment. But it's too dangerous out here."

Sen could only whisper.

"Mage death field," he groaned. "Activated. In a matter of minutes. Worldwide. Control is in the blue hall. Protective field. Trap. Quick!"

Then his senses faded, and he knew nothing more.

Kaura left her unconscious friend to Amina and immediately ran to the radio.

"Kaura here. All units!" she yelled in. "There's some kind of time bomb in the Blue Room. We need to know where that is immediately! Does anyone have any prisoners from the palace staff?"

There was a crackle on the line.

"This is group leader Aix'melen, Aalid fleet. We have some servants here who surrendered. Please hold a moment."

A pause followed.

"The blue room is in the middle wing, first floor," the man reported again. "Has a balcony facing west and columns with leaping dolphins on the railing. Should be easy to find, says the woman we interviewed."

Kaura thanked him and disconnected.

"Well, here we go," she murmured, then raised her voice. "Mirafin, take us to the middle wing. Sisters, we're going to take a look at this thing. And it's probably a matter of minutes. If we fail, we probably won't even have a chance to regret it."

It crackled again in the communication device.

"Ux'ikal, Atlantis task force seven. We seized one of those devices that the Inquisitors use to block magical powers and weaves. Our mages were disabled, but we got through with conventional weapons."

Kaura thanked the man and considered for a moment whether they could use the device. Probably there was no time. But one never knew.

"Ux'ikal, have the device brought to the Blue Room as soon as possible. Can you do it in three minutes?"

The man on the other end drew in his breath in surprise.

"We will try, exalted one. We will run at once. But the palace is not yet completely in our hands. Over."

Outside the Lemurian boat appeared the facade of the central wing of the Ottoman palace. Zik'adela pointed to larboard.

"See, there are the pillars with the dolphins. Mirafin, take us forward of the balcony. Leave shields at medium power."

"Gladly, love," the ship confirmed, gliding gently closer.

Irene touched Kaura on the arm.

"There is a massive black magic field up ahead. This is probably the trap Sen was talking about."

Kaura nodded.

"Yes, I feel it, too. It's a good thing we have some Lemurians with us here. Sisters, may I ask you for a weaving circle."

The six Lemurian women on board grouped behind Kaura, clasped hands, and closed their eyes. Immediately, a blissful smile blossomed on the dark-skinned faces of the Pacific witches.

From her place next to Sen in the back of the pulpit, Amina whispered over to Irene.

"Bet they're all thinking about treehugging now, and then this black magic thingy crumbles just like that!"

Irene smiled at her.

"Maybe you're right. Anyway, it works. Look!"

She pointed through the transparent outer wall over to the balcony. To the Lockwood witch's magical senses, it looked as if a huge, cloud of something she could have best described as love-joy-peace, glittering in a sort of white-gold-pearl-color was expanding from the Lemurians.

Within seconds, the cloud grew beyond the confines of the ship, moving toward the balcony.

Wherever it touched the dark, sharp, and poisonous weaves of black magic energies, golden sparks flew in all directions—and the weaves simply dissolved, as if they had never been there. Within a few more seconds, it was all over.

Kaura opened her eyes.

"Well, let's go over there and finish the work. Commander Ux'makia, can you accompany us? I have a suspicion that these machines the gods use have a lot to do with Atlantean technology. Perhaps you can help us to understand what we're dealing with."

The Atlantean nodded and joined the women as they were stepping across the pale green energy gangway that the ship had projected across to the balcony. The Pacific priestesses were still surrounded by that unearthly, white-golden glow. Behind them fluttered Amina, who had left her place at Sen's side to Irene.

The door leading from the balcony to the inside of the Blue Salon stood slightly ajar. Kaura hoped that this was only a sign for a hasty escape of the people who had installed this machine, and not an indication of another trap. Inside the room, they found a large, copper installation built of dozens of tubes, wires and insulators.

On four diagonally opposite sides of the apparatus, large, spiraling antennas protruded from the tangle, filling the space almost to the upper corners. Kaura drew in her breath sharply.

"Damn it," she cursed, ignoring the surprised looks the other Lemurians were giving her. "I can't even see where the controls are on this infernal contraption.

Captain Ux'makia walked past her and pointed to a copper cube slightly off to the side.

"That should be it. But there are no holographic displays. Strange."

He walked over and fiddled with the device, on which only a few small, unlabeled buttons were visible.

"And we don't even know how much time we have left," Kaura muttered. "Do any of you have any idea how we go forward? Can't we just destroy the device? Cut off the power supply? Put a shield around it?"

The captain at the cube threw up his hands helplessly.

"I can't even get to the controls. It seems to have some kind of fingerprint sensor."

Kaura composed herself.

"So we'll try to destroy it. Preferably with witchfire." She raised her hand and shot a concentrated beam of energy directly into the center of the machine.

The beam simply disappeared a few inches before reaching the contraption. Nothing happened. Kaura swallowed. She reconnected with her sisters and did the same with a hundred times stronger energy. But the result remained the same. Perplexed, the mages stood around the apparatus.

Then Amina spoke up.

"I think the energy feed is there in the middle, and it's a magical source. They've attached it directly to the Gaia field. And because you're also applying power from that field, you can't touch this thing."

Kaura's eyes lit up with understanding.

"But fairy magic works differently, as we know. Can you stop it, Amina?"

The fairy nodded.

"I believe..."

She broke off abruptly as the alien object in front of her activated. Lamps lit up all around the machine. A deep, auroric buzzing sounded that grew louder and louder.

For a moment, everyone stood frozen in shock.

The fairy was the first to recover. Without further comment and wildly waving her fairy wand, she dove headfirst into the melee of copper and crystals.

Kaura yanked the Atlantean captain by the arm back into the protective love field still maintained by her priestesses. Starting from the four antennas of the apparatus, a spiraling dark cloud expanded from something that Kaura later could only try to describe with the term anti-magic.

A few billowing extensions of the dark weave touched the love field that still surrounded the group. Immediately, Kaura felt her heart weaken, beating only with the greatest effort. She gave a tortured cry.

Then the world went down in a bright flash. As if in slow motion and completely without sound, Kaura saw her surroundings collapse. Stones flew past her, pieces of copper wiring, shards of razor-sharp crystal, flaming fireballs.

"The protective field has retained its power," a thought flowed sluggishly through her consciousness like honey. A blink of an eye later, they were all floating in open space, and the grass of the palace garden could be seen below her. With a lightning-fast sweep and irresistible force, the small group was moved up high in the air across gray stone roofs and domes and out over the glittering waters of the Bosporus.

A dark hole opened in front of Kaura. This had to be Mirafin's cargo hatch. Then they were gently set down on the rough, marble-like flooring of the Lemurian ship's cargo hold.

"The ship saved us with a tractor beam," was Kaura's first conscious thought. Then she realized what had happened.

"Amina," she muttered. The fairy was not there. "Mirafin, can you hear me? What do you know about the whereabouts of the fairy who was with us? We must save her."

The ship replied in a tone that betrayed sincere regret.

"I am sorry, Kaura. I cannot locate any signature of living beings in the vicinity of the room you were in. We must assume that there are no other survivors."

10

High Priestesses

When the first muffled explosions had sounded around the palace, the prisoners in its dungeon had raised their heads with renewed hope. Now they were listening intently for changes in the soundscape. Eagle glanced up hopefully at the small, barred light well.

"Someone is attacking. It must be the Atlanteans."

Diana nodded.

"Yep. For sure. Now all we have to do is make sure the Kai'ala don't kill us off or carry us somewhere else before some nice crystal pranksters pick us up here, wrap us in warm blankets and give us hot chocolate to drink." The fairy sounded almost cheerful, given the circumstances.

As if in response to the expression of all their hopes, someone was already shaking the door. Eagle's hope that Sen in would be returned to the cell after his hours-long absence was dashed.

Two inquisitors, each with three leashes in his hand, entered the room. As usual, their faces were not visible under their wide hoods, but their hectic movements suggested that they were feeling anything but comfortable.

"Come on, get up. Come on! Or shall we force you?" whispered the first of the cowl wearers.

Diana couldn't resist provoking the inquisitors.

"Why, are we getting a little nervous? Are you about to wet your diapers, sharky-dorky?"

The Kai'ala, however, had other worries and paid no attention to the fairy at all. They clicked the leashes into the corresponding rings of the collars and dragged the prisoners out into the corridor without further words. The babble of voices and pitter-patter everywhere revealed that they were not the only ones who had been rudely taken from their cells. Djinns, desert dragons, human mages, fairies, and some members of other magical races were herded through the corridors with blows, lashes, and kicks.

After a few minutes in the catacombs of the Ottoman palace, during which Simon, weak and feverish, kept slipping and had to be supported by his companions, they were driven into a large cavern, the height of which was at least two hundred feet, where they were forced to form a long line of six together with the other slaves who had already been gathered there.

The cavern appeared to be a natural cave that had been expanded by artificial means. Water dripped from the walls. The light came from blazing torches that emitted a pervasive smell of smoke and burning pitch. One side of the hall was open, but it did not seem to lead directly to the outside. In any case, there was only darkness in the opening.

Like an anachronism, one of the teardrop-shaped Kai'ala boats stood in the center of the cave. It measured about twenty yards in diameter and was close to sixty long. The prisoners were taken inside the boat through two boarding hatches in the stern. Inquisitors dressed in ruby red robes were everywhere, supervising the loading process.

Mercilessly, Eagle and her companions were whipped through the hatch. The shaman from the Moluccas had become more and more silent and apathetically let everything happen to her. Diana, meanwhile, cursed incessantly and uttered foul-mouthed threats, but was still ignored by the redcoats.

The hold of the Kai'ala boat was packed to bursting. Magical beings and humans were crowded everywhere. There was already no more room to sit down. Some children were screaming and crying. More and more beings were pushing into the room from behind.

Finally, the loading process seemed to be completed. With a screeching sound, the hatch closed and slammed shut thunderously. The air quality was rapidly deteriorating. Probably the ship's ventilation had not been built for so many passengers, Eagle thought. The hum of the engines increased, and the ship began to sway. The hold had no windows, so no one could see what was happening.

The floor seemed to be moving. Suddenly the engines howled abruptly, and the boat accelerated upwards at an angle. The prisoners were thrown against each other, and some fell to the ground, while others were already trying to help them up again, making sure that no one was crushed. The ground shook and swayed while the engines had found their way to a continuous roar.

But the relative quiet lasted for a minute at most. Then loud detonations could be heard from outside. The ship accelerated erratically, swerving left and right, diving and pulling up again as if the crew were flying desperate evasive maneuvers. Then there was a loud crash and the engines howled again. This time, however, there was no more acceleration. The ship shook and vibrated violently but didn't seem to budge.

Two Kai'ala inquisitors appeared on a small platform above the hold, in the company of a figure in a green uniform, also blue-skinned. Probably an officer, Eagle thought. The inquisitors were armed and seemed to be engaged in a heated discussion with the officer. "...instructions!", Eagle heard from the green-clad man's words.

"We're not going to kill these people," one of the inquisitors hissed in a high-pitched voice, close to panic. "The Aalids already have us in their tractor beam. What do you think they'll do to us if we follow these instructions now and render the cargo useless?"

He pointed his gun at the officer. The other Kai'ala shrugged in resignation.

"I was just saying," he muttered and walked away with his head down.

A short time later, there was another crash and crunch. Hope was slowly reviving among the prisoners. After a few minutes, the boarding hatch lowered, and cool artificial light penetrated the interior of the boat. Outside stood a large number of armed people in tight-fitting clothes who had surrounded the ship.

A woman touched her earlobe and spoke in a thunderous voice that was probably magically or technically amplified. She spoke Atlantean with a strong, strange accent.

"Hello, good day. You are aboard a ship of the Aalid Starfleet. You have nothing to fear from us and will be returned safely to your home planet. Our people will supervise the disembarkation process to ensure that everything proceeds safely. No one moves from their place until they are told to do so."

Eagle breathed a sigh of relief and waved frantically.

"We have an injured man here who needs immediate medical assistance!" she shouted, pointing at Simon, who had his eyes closed and seemed to be going through some kind of feverish hallucination.

v

Somewhere almost five thousand yards below the surface of the Mediterranean Sea, an airlock opened with a hiss. Gurgling, some seawater entered from the outside until complete pressure equalization was achieved. In floated one of the teardrop-shaped Kai'ala ships, and settled on the floor of the hangar.

The pressure chamber hatch closed again. It could handle water just as well as the empty space between the stars. The water surface inside the chamber slowly lowered until the last remnants of the salty liquid had drained into the scuppers at the bottom of the hangar. Everything dripped and smelled penetratingly of algae and fish.

Slowly, a gangway extended from the boarding hatch of the teardrop. Uriel and Triabola stepped out, followed by several Kai'ala in red robes. Uriel turned to the first of the inquisitors.

"Have the part of the harvest we were able to save taken to the cells immediately. We will remain at the bottom of the Hellenic Trench for some time, until the blockade ships over Gaia have become less alert. And then we will break through to Rignar. Without the mages, the takeover of Earth will go smoothly after that, if only we muster enough military resources and divert the Aalids' attention away from Gaia again before then. Now that their allies are gone, maybe they'll just leave, anyway."

The Kai'ala in green uniform who had stepped toward them from the hangar bulkhead cleared his throat.

"Sir, our instruments indicate that the antimagic field has probably failed. We can't be sure from this depth, but we continue to locate magical life forms."

The chief planner of the gods immediately began to hyperventilate.

His blue-skinned counterpart realized his mistake and went deadly pale.

"Sorry, Lord, I didn't mean to upset you," he said in a feeble attempt to salvage the situation.

Uriel turned away without a word and walked to the exit of the hangar. The Kai'ala breathed a sigh of relief.

Triabola eyed him not unkindly before following her colleague.

"You're lucky to be alive, comrade," she muttered and disappeared.

* * *

Sen opened his eyes and found himself lying inside some kind of half-transparent silvery bell.

"Like being inside a drop of water," was his first thought.

The second thought was less pleasant. "Did Triabola come and get me? Is this a Kai'ala ship?" he wondered with a touch of panic, before his senses finally awoke fully and he spotted Kaura's smiling face beyond the bubble wall, slightly distorted by the soap bubble-like reflection. His lover's lips moved silently. She said something he couldn't hear, and the bubble burst with a soft pop.

"Welcome back, dear," she said, "You've been asleep for a long time."

Sen felt into his body and was surprised that nothing hurt anymore. He did not even feel weak. But suddenly the memories flooded him.

"What about the death field?" he asked.

"Destroyed, literally at the last moment," Kaura replied. "And mostly thanks to you. Otherwise, we never would have gotten there fast enough."

Her gaze clouded over. "Amina died in the machine. None of us knew how to shut that thing down. When it activated, she just dived into it."

Sen took a deep breath and lowered his gaze. "She came here because of me, you know," he said softly. "She was taken in as a guard fairy by Lockwood. I hired her, almost ninety years ago. And I asked her to come here with me."

He fell dazedly silent.

Kaura gently grabbed his arm.

"And if you hadn't asked her, we'd probably all be dead now. I already felt this devilish field reaching for my heart to bring it to a halt. I wish it could have gone differently. But she saved us all with her courage and decisiveness. All of Lockwood included."

Sen nodded.

"I know. I don't blame myself either. She was older than me and knew as well as any of us what she was getting into. We'll remember her fondly. And hold a dignified celebration of her onward journey as soon as we can."

Just then Diana fluttered in and had obviously heard his last words.

"Heyo Superboss, sure thing. I'm sure Amina has collected so much good karma that she'll be reborn as a sex party guru on Sirius Q."

She chuckled and winked at Kaura, probably assuming that, as a high priestess, she had a similarly deep insight into the reality of things as the fairies and knew that life and death were just an interesting game of the One Consciousness anyway.

"Anyway, glad to see you are well, boyo. Simon and the others are fine, too. An Aalid courier boat just dropped us off here."

She thought for a moment. "Now you can get a new tattoo. "World Savior' or something. But please with some fairies on it! Do you even have a fairy tattoo yet?"

Sen grinned faintly.

"Sure I do, Diana. But not in a place you usually get to see."

The fairy grinned insinuatingly and cast a sideways glance over at Kaura.

"So right on the money. Glad to hear it, Superboss. I'll go see where the others have gone. They're probably having a good time with Mirafin. Great jokers, those Lemurian ships." She fluttered away.

Sen sighed.

"I'm glad to hear that at least the others are doing well," he said. "But other than that, I don't understand anything anymore, Kaura. Aalid and Lemurian ships? Mirafin? Where are we? Is there still fighting going on? Where are the gods, did you get them?"

Kaura walked over to the door and pressed two buttons. With a soft hiss, the organically shaped door slid shut, and a yellow light flared up next to it.

With a deep exhale, she sat down next to the mage, who was dressed only in a light pair of white pants from Mirafin's trove. The rest of his clothes had been so torn and bloodied from his time in the dungeon and the explosion in the Ottoman palace that they had been discarded.

"I'll tell you all about that in more detail later. For now, just this: we are in a Lemurian airship named Mirafin, standing on the private hoverport of the Crystal Temple at Atlantia, it is late in the evening, and tomorrow morning there will be a round of consultations with the crystal priests and emissaries of the Atlantian Senate. The gods have unfortunately escaped for the time being, but don't seem to have gone into any new activity recently. It looks like we've won, at least for now."

Constantinople was fully under their control, Sen further learned, because the Atlanteans had come to an agreement with the Ottoman authorities and had assured them that they were not planning a long-term annexation.

At that moment, the Aalids, together with the Atlanteans, were in the process of taking the main bastions of the Inquisition in covert actions and freeing scattered magical slaves.

Kaura smiled.

"We have plenty of time before tomorrow morning." The Lemurian leaned over, gently stroked the Scottish mage's cheek, and kissed him squarely on the mouth.

Sen sensed from the tingling in his body that the Lemurian healing had indeed fully restored him, leaving not even a trace of fatigue. With a blissful sigh, he returned the kiss and reached for her soft, vibrating body that pressed impatiently against him.

* * *

Barely two weeks later, Mirafin was gliding across the dancing reflections of the Pacific Ocean at a speed of little more than two hundred miles per hour. Kaura had asked the ship to travel this slowly because she did not want to approach her home at triple the speed of sound and in a vertical drop from the outer atmosphere.

Even less did she want to simply step through a portal from Rhodes into the Temple of Ferns, which would have been just as easy. It all just felt too fast, too disrespectful for the whole process she had gone through. Irregularly shaped cliffs covered with dense, tropical forest now rose up in front of the ship.

In the distance, the huge volcanic cones of the Sima'ren Mountains stretched more than ten thousand feet into the sky, some with dead-straight, smoking columns rising above them, telling of their activity.

Shortly after, Mirafin swung in parallel to the coast and set course for Ilkarion. Kaura almost wept with joy when the waterfall of Karapo appeared, shaped like a ponytail, and a few drops merrily jumping out of one of its many arms burst on the transparent outer wall of her flying ship. Golden beaches gleamed against the green backdrop of swaying palm groves, alternated with jagged rocky zones and smooth, finely polished lava plateaus, at the foot of which the waves broke and shot up in the form of fountains of spray dozens of yards high.

Sen sat next to her, held her hand, and again had that dreamy expression in his eyes that Kaura had already noticed during their canoe trip through the Moluccas. The Scottish headmaster and Diana had decided to accompany the Lemurian to visit her home continent, while the other mages and fairies had returned to Oxford for the time being.

"I guess you really like the tropics, Sen," she murmured.

He nodded.

"Yes. Maybe I should really turn my back on Oxford and move here with you."

The high priestess smiled.

"We'll see. Once the portals are active again, Oxford will be just a step away from Ilkarion anyway. You could set up your office in the Fern Temple and run your society's fortunes from there."

He looked at her and raised his eyebrows questioningly.

"You really want to reactivate the portals? I thought no one remembered exactly how they were built."

She hummed in a way that made him unsure if it was meant to be an affirmation or a denial.

"The Lemurian libraries before the Great Age of Darkness are said to have been very extensive," she replied. "This knowledge must have been preserved somewhere for posterity, although the exact location is no longer passed down even to the members of the Priests' Council. We will find it, and we will reopen those energy stations and Pyrrha. If only because there are thousands of magical slaves trapped in the time loop in there. We owe it to them. And later we'll build new portals again, too."

He laughed.

"You've got some work cut out for you there, sweetheart."

With half lowered eyelids she looked at him.

"Have I? Does that mean you don't want to be involved?" He made a dismissive hand gesture.

"I didn't say that. I just thought that after all these problems, we should take a rest. And the gods are still at large."

Kaura shrugged.

"It's not pretty, but it can't be helped. Maybe they were able to sneak past the Aalid blockade ships in some way. In any case, those criminals won't catch us as unprepared as last time. After all, in the last conversation with the newly formed technomagic council, they promised us to deliver a techno-magic neutralization field for this death ray that the gods wanted to use against us very shortly. Then we will be safe from new surprises for the time being."

A wide, tranquil bay now opened up in front of them. Mirafin rose a little higher above the turquoise, calm surface of the water inside the outer reefs and swung in an elegant arc toward the interior.

"Ilkarion," Kaura breathed. The rocks and hills surrounding Ilkarion were irregularly shaped. Soft, flowing forms dominated the landscape. Dense vegetation lay like a mossy, soft covering over everything. The valley floor was primarily green and sprinkled by huge, roundish treetops whose leaves shimmered in all possible shades of green and silver.

Houses were indistinctly visible in between the giant trees, distantly resembling termite dwellings, but more harmonious and flowing with the branches. Extending along the ground were sprawling gardens, organic round stone buildings that seemed to be predominantly overgrown with something like moss, and the brightly shimmering palm frond roofs of larger stone and wooden structures.

Sporadically, large, rounded spires of red and black volcanic rock rose from the plain, with irregular paths winding up and leading to terraces scattered throughout, houses built close to the rock, and pavilions jutting freely into the air. Openings carved into the rock revealed that people lived here as well.

Everywhere, waterfalls bubbled and sprayed out, seeming to

gather in the shelter of the dense canopy of leaves in the center of Ilkarion and flow into the sea in the form of two elegantly winding rivers. In the farthest part of the valley, a large freestanding rock ensemble stretched upward, probably originally resembling a spiral arrangement of giant organ pipes. Now the huge knobs of rock had been decorated all over with stone carvings and with niches containing trees and creepers. In between, there were natural openings in the rock, terraces with columns, entire gardens with fountains and small waterfalls, and large, golden statues.

Mirafin was heading straight for it.

"I am now completing the approach to Hangar Spira 3 at the Temple of Ferns, my dears," the ship said. "We have already been given permission to dock."

Diana, contrary to her usual habit, had said nothing the entire time. With a look almost as dreamy as Sen's, she looked out at the scene, which resembled a huge, inhabited forest rather than a city. "That I live to see this again!" she muttered, directed to no one in particular. "The home of the treehuggers! Well, the trees here really do look cuddlier. At least from the air. Maybe I should hug one sometime, too..."

Kaura gave her an affectionate smile as the ship floated into the dark maw of a fern-covered cave opening about halfway up the south spire.

"Yes, maybe you really should. Just be sure to ask the tree first. Consent is very important here. I don't think any will say no, though. Fairies don't come by here every day either. I'm sure they'll love it."

The ship sighed comfortably as it gently touched down on the irregular stone floor of the hangar.

"So, here we are. Don't forget anything on board. Transportation of your luggage to your rooms will be taken care of. I hope you enjoyed the flight with me, and I'll see you again soon. Do I get a hug for goodbyes?"

After many more hugs from Zik'adela, and Mirafin's Lemurian crew, Kaura, Sen, and Diana stepped—or flew, in Diana's case—out through the boarding hatch and into the open. A breeze of balmy air, distantly scented with jasmine and tropical blossoms, welcomed them.

Their reception committee, men and women wrapped in gauzy, semi-transparent clothing, waited near the hangar entrance, which was also covered in ferns. Selena was one of them, and the others were familiar to Kaura as well. Sen observed with fascination how his lover was greeted on the one hand with the respect due to the highest Lemurian and on the other hand also with that care-free cordiality which seemed to characterize this egalitarian society through all classes.

Selena warmly welcomed all three of them and, after introducing everyone, invited them inside. Despite its outwardly massive appearance, the temple was full of plants, shafts of light, and bright earth-colored walls painted in ocher, beige, and white. They crossed several bridges that connected the widely spaced rock pillars at dizzying heights. At last, they arrived in a hall that at first almost took Sen's breath away, so beautiful was it. One side of the irregularly shaped vault was open to the outside through a completely transparent wall and allowed a wide view over the valley from what must have been almost six hundred feet above the ground.

On the far left, the shiny surface of the sea could be discerned in the far distance. To the right, only a few hundred yards away, a huge foaming waterfall fell over a fern- and moss-covered precipice into the depths. A transparent wall of energy muffled the roar of the falling water down to a comfortable level. Outside, it had to be deafening.

Part of the floor was carpeted, and Sen felt immediately reminded of the meeting room in Mira'aleitha where they had first heard of the Inquisition's collars. But this hall was at least a hundred times larger than the interior of the djinn's small mud-brick house. In one corner of the hall, a giant tree grew into the sky through a hole in the ceiling.

Kaura had taken control with natural authority.

Sen, however, did not have the impression that this was a necessity because of her rank. Rather it seemed to him that in a flowing way always the one determined what happened who just felt an authentic impulse or was most suitable for it. The others followed that one's lead then as a matter of course. On the large carpets in the center of the hall sat and lay about two dozen people who had divided into small groups and were engaged in animated discussion. Some were dressed in wide skirts, shawls and capes of all colors of the rainbow, others were simply naked and had spread cloths below them. Under the tree, two men were sitting in lotus position and seemed to be meditating.

When Kaura, Selena and the others entered the room, the conversations fell silent. Those present stood up, talked wildly, formed a circle around Kaura, and all seemed to want to hug her at the same time. A quarter of an hour of group hugs of all possible compositions followed, in which Sen and—as far as possible because of her size—Diana were also included. Sen was pleased with the warm welcome. However, it was still difficult for him to understand how this loosely buzzing, colorful crowd of completely relaxed and uninhibited people of all ages could be the leading class of Gaia's richest and most powerful continent. For there was no doubt that they were here at the supreme council of the Lemurian temple priests.

"They're even crazier than we are at Lockwood," a thought flashed through his mind. Then, two attractive, half-naked priestesses embraced him and he decided to just stop thinking about it.

At some point, everyone began to sing, and naturally a circle formed in the center of the room, with everyone holding hands. It seemed to be some kind of ancient hymn of blessing and welcome. Sen thought for a moment about using a translation spell, but then decided against it so as not to disturb the ceremony. Energy like he had never felt pulsed through his hands and heart. This had to be pure love energy, he thought.

Then he felt a light tug on his hand. Gently, he, Diana and Kaura were pushed into the center. The feeling and vibration in the center of the circle of over three dozen Lemurians was beyond description. Waves of rapture, gratitude and joy flowed through the Scottish mage and through the other two companions. It was suddenly inconceivable that anything in the world could not be perfect, just as it was.

Sen literally felt all the inner tension, which he had for the most part no longer been consciously aware of, fall away from him. He knew that he was at home. And that these people recognized him as one of their own, not only because he was one of their own, but especially because they knew that everyone in this room was merely a slightly different-looking expression of the one life force. He closed his eyes and let himself be lifted away by the ecstasy of oneness.

As the ritual came to its natural conclusion, everything around him seemed to vibrate, to glow with a vibrancy that had never before been revealed to him, even with all his magical powers and all his knowledge. He knew at that moment that he and all these beings around him were one. They appeared to him like luminous, pulsating hearts floating amid a matrix of only superficially solid and impenetrable bodies and matter. He could see, feel the life force of the tree next to him as a deep, confidence-inspiring pulsation. Even the stones had personalities of their own, each one of them. And they were parts of his personality, just as he was part of theirs.

He sat down on the sitting cushion offered to him, composed of colorful patches of fabric, which seemed to groan comfortably under his weight when he relaxed onto it. A wave of compassion for all being washed over him, and at that moment he thought he understood the meaning of everything that had happened in the last few months. The divine played its eternal, colorful play, and he was an actor in this immense show. The same soul, the same power manifested through the gods, through the Kai'ala and the Inquisitors as through him and these high priests and high priestesses. She played with herself. He was playing with himself. Why? He didn't know, and at that moment it was completely meaningless to him.

Suddenly he became aware that Kaura was speaking, probably had been for some time already. Her words seemed to him at first only vibrations, sounds of joy and celebration of all aliveness, without meaning beyond that, without context, without words. Only sounds, infinitely beautiful sounds. He very slowly brought part of himself back out of the rapture, into some kind of focus so that he could understand what was being said.

"...We don't know where the two A'kaala have gone. Either they have hidden somewhere on Gaia, or they have already escaped into space in ways unknown to us," she said just then. "We should focus our magical efforts on finding them. Until we finish building the protective field against the death ray, we are vulnerable."

A naked, bearded man took the floor. Sen vaguely remembered that he had introduced himself as the head of the technomagic council of scientists.

"In three days, we will be ready. The machines are already in place and the energy supply from the Gaia field has also been tested. We will be able to cover the surface of all of Gaia with the technically reinforced protective spell. For a year or two, at least. Always assuming that the drying up of the magic source doesn't accelerate significantly."

Kaura nodded with satisfaction.

"Another point," she continued. "I propose that we abolish the old isolation policy of Lemuria within Gaia and of the whole planet itself. It has been shown that we are stronger when we work together. The Aalids have, without hesitation, brought us help when we needed it. Among ourselves, we have long agreed to find our decisions together. We should include the other peoples of the earth in the future. I therefore propose that we make efforts to form a World Council for Gaia, in which the Spanish-Ottoman Empire should also be represented. And that we again maintain our own starfleet, at least until the portal problem is solved."

Kaura's proposals were approved by a large majority, although many of those present were concerned about the means of ensuring the protection of Gaia and its inhabitants from any misguided decisions of this world body, especially since many of the noble governments ruling the nations of their world had not proven to be particularly philanthropic. Some sort of citizens' council would have to be formed, and guidelines would have to be drafted for the council to follow. But until the next assembly of Ixche'len, they agreed on preparing a good proposal to present the Lemurian people.

A few volunteers were immediately found among the priestesses and scientists to take up the project.

A short time later, contact was established with the Aalid government via infradimensional waves. The Lemurians themselves currently no longer had this technology, although according to Selena, the newly trained specialists were already in the process of rebuilding their own facilities. For now, one of the Aalid ships, which was stationary above Lemuria to protect the continent from attacks from space, served as a relay.

Above an elongated pool several yards long, into which two rippling rivulets of water flowed, the hologram of an all-white hall flickeringly appeared, in the background of which, through a huge oval window, the panorama of an alien-looking city with huge, strangely intertwined skyscrapers could be seen. Five people dressed in skin-tight, snakeskin-like suits sat in a semicircle around an oval conference table. There were three women and two men.

From a comfortable chair next to the conference table, Joe Nelson faced them. Behind and beside him sat three more women, each of whom had placed one of their hands casually, yet undoubtedly with a possessive note, on his thighs. Ariane sat on a corner of the board, dangling her feet, and forming a hand sign with her thumb and pinky finger splayed, which was unfamiliar to Sen but seemed to be some sort of greeting. The mage cast a sidelong glance over at Kaura. He knew by now that she—like most Lemurians—had little understanding for any monogamous impulses or possessiveness of lovers. Still, he couldn't help but feel a tinge of jealousy. After all, she had known his fellow Scot for years. And Joe was at least one hundred and seventy years younger than Sen.

Laughing inwardly for a moment, the magician marveled at how quickly his almost otherworldly mood had given way to mundane ego reactions and turned back to the vastness and vibration still prevailing in his heart. After all, he would have no trouble being intimate with Eagle or any of his other girlfriends, past or present, if they met again. But Kaura... she touched him in a way that no other person had ever been able to. What did that mean for him? The only thing that was certain was that he wanted to spend more time with her, wanted to become a part of her life—a shared life—in some way. And he believed that she saw it that way, too. And that, even though he might age and die in a period that was of little con-sequence to her. Ten thousand years! He could still hardly imagine what kind of perspective such an age opened for a person.

Kaura had been very reluctant to talk about her life so far. He almost had the impression that she was clinging to the illusion of her five years in Inmarsund in a way—a time when she herself had believed she was still a young woman.

Now the woman sitting in the middle of the group gathered

behind the conference table took the floor, green-haired, elderly and of exceedingly dignified appearance. She had had her neck tattooed with elegant floral patterns. It was Imarion, the president of the planetary government of Aalid, which presided over all the inhabited planets of the two-sun system.

She immediately introduced herself and those present. The Lemurians did the same, limiting themselves to Kaura, Selena, Sen and the most important members of the priests' council. Polite phrases and words of thanks were exchanged. The

Aalids were thrilled that the Priests' Council granted them an immediate permission to establish passenger service on the roughly month-long starship passage between Aalid and Gaia, and pledged further technical assistance in restoring ancient Lemurian knowledge and reopening the portals. It turned out that on Aalid and other systems of the Milky Way lived large populations of exiled Lemurians who had been cut off from their home planet during the last seven centuries and who should be allowed to return to their home planet if they so chose.

The Priests' Council also assured the Aalids of support in finding volunteers on Gaia to participate in the planet's so-called 'offspring program,' which aimed to restore genetic diversity.

"Your envoy Joe Nelson has already decided to participate in the program and grace us with his valued presence for several more months," the president said. "I'm sure he can confirm that participation is extremely enjoyable for the volunteers."

The Scot actually blushed slightly and did not respond to the remark at all.

"Hello everyone, good to see you safe and sound! I'm glad my mission seems to have brought the desired results."

He held something in his hand and now lifted it up for all to see. Sen saw that it was the fishhook amulet that Kaura had brought from Inmarsund. "This pendant immediately convinced the government in Alaris that my request was genuine, and I was really sent by the Lemurians. Kaura seems to have thrown it through the portal behind me, and Ariane found it and gave it to me. After an analysis confirmed the authenticity of its origin, the space patrol closest to Gaia was notified immediately. You know the rest."

Kaura smiled.

"I apologize again for my somewhat rough treatment of you, and I'm glad everything went well. Then I expect we will be able to welcome you back to Gaia in a few months, my friend. By the way, the questioning of captured Kai'ala revealed that your reputation as a key bearer was probably due to a misunderstanding by the inquisitors. It was about the prophecy of a Spanish mage. Possibly it meant your role in soliciting help from Aalid—if it was really about you. But to be honest, it simply spoke of a blond man with Atlantean blood. That could be you, or not. According to the inquisitor who spoke, you would also still need to find some kind of weapon to fulfill the prophecy. Unless they meant the Aalid flotilla by that."

She shrugged, and Joe grinned.

"It may yet come, perhaps. From what I've heard, the A'kaala 'gods' are still at large. And nobody knows exactly where to find this planet Rignar, where they have pitched their tents. So, there should still be plenty of work to do. If the Aalids send an expedition to find them, I'll probably go along. I've never been able to resist an adventure."

The grip of the woman to his left on his thigh seemed to have tightened, for his face contorted slightly. But then he smiled lovingly at her. "Until then, of course, I will continue to participate in this wonderful program they have developed here for people coming from out of planet. Highly recommended."

Next to him, Ariane laughed happily.

"Yeah, I guess it's paradise for that one. Almost half as good as on Sirius Q. I'll come back over to you on the next passenger ship and help with the collective treehugging. I think you need me more than these overcivilized bores. Too much love, joy and not nearly enough pancakes. Hunting gods and opening portals sounds more like my thing!"

It also turned out that the Aalids had even thought of connecting the Scotsman with his family by means of a remote hologram projector brought to London by a one of the flagship's dinghies, and that he had already spoken to his mother at Nelson House. Apparently Mercurio Nelson, Joe's grandfather and patriarch of the Nelson shipping company, was already busy in preparations for establishing an interplanetary Scottish Chamber of Commerce.

Both Lemurians and Aalids still had various questions about the historical development on both planets in the last seven hundred years, during which the communication links had been cut off, and they talked for some more hours before they said goodbye to each other on the best of terms.

A short time after the remote hologram conversation ended, the gathering of the Lemurian priests' council had already largely dispersed and turned into an informal group huddle.

Then a messenger dressed in a flowing skirt and colored scarf walked into the room and tugged Kaura by the sleeve. The high priestess had just made herself comfortable between Sen, Lorenia, and Selena, with whom she was leaning against the trunk of the great oak tree in the back quarter of the room. Diana lay across her belly, purring contentedly.

"Urgent message from Ishe'melen, the Aalid fleet commander," the woman said. "A large starship, probably of Kai'ala origin, broke through the blockade an hour ago and vanished into hyperspace! They waited for the moment when the Atlantean priests maintaining the magical shields changed shifts. The entire crew of the guard boat and the mages for that sector simply fell asleep. The other boats located the alien ship but arrived on the scene too late. According to the tracing of the launch trajectory, they came from a particularly deep area of the Mediterranean Sea. Probably they hid below the surface from the Aalid tracking devices."

Kaura thanked her for her message.

"Well, at least I guess we're rid of these characters for the time being," she sighed, "although I'm sure they won't just give up."

Diana nodded.

"I'm sure those divine morons are already concocting another atrocity. Unless their mufti-in-chief is flattening them because they had to pinch their tails here. But at least now we have time to prepare for them."

She closed her eyes and snuggled closer to Kaura's belly.

Epilogue

On a sunny day in June of the year 1869 after Buddha, a luminous apparition opened up on the beach just outside Inmarsund. So dazzlingly bright that even the sun paled against it for a moment, two shimmering golden pillars grew vertically from the ground, curved inward toward each other at a height of about two yards and met in a final flash of cosmic forces beyond the imagination of most earthlings.

A blue wisp arose between the columns, growing more and more dense, until a figure emerged from it, blinking.

Another human figure followed, then another, very small one with glittering wings, and finally a four-legged creature hopped through the blue light plane with an elegant leap and a joyful bark.

Kaura looked around. It had been less than half a year since she had last seen this beach, and yet even to her, a near immortal, it seemed like an eternity. The waves of the Baltic Sea broke on the beach with a gentle rush that seemed almost like the ripple of a duck pond now that she had felt the wild shores of her homeland again for a few weeks. And yet she loved that duck pond as much as she loved the immense waves of her Pacific Ocean. In any case, Atam, her dog whom she had left in London when leaving to rescue Joe from the Inquisition, was visibly happy to see his home again and was barking like mad, rolling playfully over the sand.

The Lemurian thought for a moment. She was sincerely looking forward to meeting Aalyjah and telling her about the events of the past months. Probably Resa was also back by now—unless her adoptive aunt had already left on another great journey. Kaura smiled. Right now, it felt like a period of her life was coming to an end, one that had become one of the most important to her. Here she had never been a high priestess, never an immortal who was appreciated by everyone, but always somehow took on a special role. Here she had simply been Kaura, one young woman among many.

Her thoughts traveled back over the week that had passed since they had left Ilkarion. To the moving farewell ritual for Amina in the great temple hall of Lockwood in Oxford. To her meeting with her young Scottish friend Loren, who in the meantime had passed her exams in Magobiology with flying colors. To Afternoon Tea with the Nelson family in London and her reunion with Jane and Atam, who was now just behind her happily sniffing and yipping and digging a hole in the sand. To her dinner with Lance, Abigail and Captain McGregor in Rhodes.

Abigail, as soon as she learned of Joe's plans to remain on Aalid, had immediately contacted Commander Ishe'melen and asked for a place on the next courier boat to the far away planet. Kaura had told her what she knew of the Aalids and hoped that she would not experience a disappointment. Captain McGregor had left for London with a cargo of the finest Hellenic fabrics, olive oil, and wines, as well as the trade agreements negotiated by Abigail with the Knights Templar and their local allies. He had received a communicator and letters of protection from the Atlantis Mediterranean Protectorate that would guarantee him safe passage.

The Spanish-Ottoman Empire had been forced to acknowledge the superiority of the Atlantean military power, and peace negotiations were already well advanced. Philip II, the Spanish Great Sultan, had already agreed to dissolve the Inquisition and legalize magical powers on the territory of the Empire. Negotiations were still ongoing as to the rights of the natives in the Spanish-occupied territories of the New World.

Kaura looked out at the horizon of the Baltic Sea and drew the salty smell of the sea deep into her lungs. She would spend some time here before returning to Lemuria with Sen to start planning the liberation of Pyrrha. That would do her good. From behind, her lover put his hand on her shoulders, and she let herself sink back a little so that her back was nestled against him. Yes, there was still much to do. But for now, everything was fine the way it was. She could just relax.

THE END

Andreas Farmann was born in the Alpine part of Switzerland and now lives on the subtropical island of Tenerife, Spain. After many years of teaching and writing about Yoga and Meditation, as a result of a profound spiritual transformation, he rediscovered his vocation to write stories, which he's been pursuing ever since. Andreas already completed the manuscripts for all "Priestesses of Lemuria" novels and is currently working on a prequel series set in the time around Kaura's birth.